A PATIENT FURY

by the same author

IN BITTER CHILL
A DEADLY THAW

A Patient Fury

SARAH WARD

FABER & FABER

First published in 2017
by Faber & Faber Ltd
Bloomsbury House
74–77 Great Russell Street
London WC1B 3DA

Typeset by Faber & Faber Ltd
Printed and bound by CPI Group (UK) Ltd, Croydon CR0 4YY

A CIP record for this book
is available from the British Library

ISBN 978-0-571-33232-8

FSC
www.fsc.org
MIX
Paper from
responsible sources
FSC® C020471

2 4 6 8 10 9 7 5 3 1

For my brothers, Adrian and Ed

PART ONE

The Wrong

I

In Derbyshire there's a tale that if you want to conjure up the devil then you need to take a trip to an ancient village sheltered in the brow of one of the dark peaks. There, in the church-yard, lies an empty stone coffin. A classic example of an early medieval sarcophagus, say the history books, but generations of children have been reared on a bedtime story that remains in their souls until their own turn to occupy a place amongst the dead. You take a walk around the bare tomb three times, then climb inside and lie still with your eyes closed. Your reward, if you've been very bad, will be the sound of the rattling chains of Old Nick.

But children also instinctively know that the devil comes in many forms and pretences. It arrived this evening, in disguise, out of the shadows where they'd been waiting with a patient fury. The still night belied a wind that was making its way across the rough Irish Sea towards that middle England town. There would be no Shakespearean weather backdrop to this night's tragedy, though. The tempest would come in its own time.

The figure looked down on the sleeping form of the small child. Charlie had spent a fractious evening crying because of a lost Spiderman figure that he'd buried in a forgotten location in the garden. The genuine sobs had become crocodile tears and, in desperation, he'd been given a small cup of sweet hot chocolate and carried to bed still dry-heaving at the perceived injustice of the world.

Charlie's father was the first to die. He'd been fearful of recent heart flutters and had made several trips to see his cardiologist that spring. He had the heart of an ox, the specialist informed him, a metaphor that had made the evening glass of cognac all the more enjoyable. The cardiologist had failed to appreciate that even the heart of a beast of burden cannot outlive the ministration of a claw hammer. It continued to beat for a few seconds after the first blow but then stilled, now unconscious of the sustained ferocity of the continuing attack.

The noise in the adjacent bedroom failed to waken the exhausted Charlie, who slept on, his breath whistling softly as he slumbered. The figure also felt the pull of exhaustion but there was the second part of the three-act tragedy to complete. Padding across the thick-pile carpet in the hallway, the figure reached the sleeping child, paused for a moment and then raised the hammer.

Detective Inspector Francis Sadler woke with a start as the phone on his bedside table shrilled across the night silence. His first instinct was to check he wasn't dreaming. Twice in the last week he'd woken abruptly, positive his landline was carrying an urgent summons. The dreams had been so vivid, his subconscious had replicated exactly the pitch of his home phone's ring. Both times there had in reality been no call, just a reminder of the primeval fear that news of a matter of life or death could be delivered by that worst of instruments, the telephone. It left him unnerved, the sound so clear in his head, but this third time it was no dream. His phone was ringing in the night. Sadler switched on the bedside lamp and scrabbled for the handset.

'Sorry to disturb you, sir.' The voice of the duty CID officer was subdued. 'There's a fire out at one of the detached houses on Cross Farm Lane. The response car has called in to inform us of the likelihood of fatalities.' The voice hesitated.

Sadler raised himself up to check the time on his alarm clock. Four thirty in the morning. 'Is there something else?'

'The fire officer in charge has indicated the blaze is of doubtful origin. Those were his words, sir. But our guys on the scene say he's also, well . . .'

'What?' Sadler was now out of bed and pulling on a pair of trousers, the phone cradled in his neck.

'He's saying CID needs to come down as soon as possible. I

was going to go. They're still putting out the fire but, given that there are fatalities, I'm calling you. There needs to be a senior investigating officer present.'

'You've no other information?'

'According to the constable I spoke to, the Chief is pretty agitated. That's all I can tell you.'

'Right.' Sadler headed towards the bathroom. The glass of wine he'd drunk with his evening meal had long ago left his bloodstream but his mouth still had a sour, metallic taste. 'I'm on my way. What's the address?'

'The house is called Whitegates. It's number 42 Cross Farm Lane. Do you want me to call anyone else?'

'Don't worry, I'll telephone Connie, DC Childs, myself. Leave it with me.'

Sadler clicked off the call and, after brushing his teeth, rang his colleague who answered immediately, her greeting hoarse. 'Hello?'

'It's Sadler. I'm sorry for waking you.'

Connie gave a deep cough down the line. 'You haven't . . . I couldn't sleep. I mean I must I have slept for a bit and then woken up. Can you hold on a sec?' In the background, Sadler could hear more coughing and then the sound of a tap being turned on. When she came back on the line, her voice was clearer. 'Are you still there? Has something happened?'

'There's a suspicious fire with fatalities and I want to get there as soon as possible. Are you okay to come with me?'

Connie's reply was tinged with irritation. 'Of course I am. I just need to get dressed.'

'Is ten minutes enough?'

'Umm, sure. I'll be on the street waiting for you.'

Sadler wondered if he should have called a different DC to assist him. After six months' sick leave, Connie had only recently returned to the team, subdued and refusing to attend any social occasions, not even the one to celebrate the birth of DS Palmer's son. Sadler had opted for a wait-and-see approach but, as he contemplated her insomnia, he wondered if they needed to have a more substantial discussion about her health.

The night was mild. They'd had a week of blazing weather, shocking the tourists who'd arrived for their holidays with raincoats and a list of attractions suitable for inclement days. The cloudless sky revealed a panoply of stars and the waxing moon meant Sadler could reach his car parked by the canal without resorting to the torch he kept by his front door. He turned back towards the row of terraces where he lived and saw a light leaking from one of the upstairs windows of his neighbour, Clive. Clearly wakefulness was rife this night.

Connie, as promised, was waiting by the entrance to her apartment block, a converted warehouse further along the same stretch of canal where Sadler lived. Despite the mild night, she was wearing a black trench coat belted over her thin frame. She was smoking a cigarette, the vaporiser she'd been using last year consigned to the bin. She threw the half-finished stub down the drain and climbed into his car.

'Are you all right?'

'I'm not particularly looking forward to this,' she said, her voice subdued. 'I don't like house fires.'

'I don't think anyone does.'

'You know what I mean. The ferocity is unbelievable and we have to just watch and wait until everything is made safe. It's frustrating.'

7

Sadler caught a glimpse of her tired face. 'Are you sure you're okay?'

She kept her face turned away from him. 'Of course. Why?'

'It's nearly five in the morning—'

'I told you, I was already awake. Is it far?'

'About ten minutes' drive, but brace yourself for a lot of hanging about as they're calling us in early. The watch commander apparently isn't very happy.'

'When are they? Do you have any more info? Arson?'

'I don't know.'

She gave a deep sigh.

'Doubtful origin, that's the message I got,' said Sadler, 'which probably means arson.'

'And fatalities, you said?'

'Yes. Although there seems to be something else.'

Connie turned to him now. 'Like what?'

Sadler put his foot hard on the accelerator. 'I don't know. We'll find out when we get there.'

Cross Farm Lane was an arterial road leading out of the west of Bampton towards the hills of Manchester in the far distance. It was a long single carriageway lined with large detached houses that showed the expansion of the town over the twentieth century. Nearest to the centre were twenties and thirties properties with white rendered exteriors and rounded windows decorated with small panes of glass. Next came commuter houses from the fifties, their red bricks out of place in the Derbyshire countryside. Finally, as the town petered out, a hotchpotch of sixties and seventies executive homes, closed off and secretive behind tall hedges. After that, nothing, the town planners finally cottoning on that unless they called a halt to development, Bampton would merge into nearby Buxton. Sadler's architect father had designed one of the houses; a huge modern building, all angles and glass, that he'd been inordinately proud of. Sadler mentally clocked the building as they passed, decelerating quickly as they approached a police car with flashing lights parked behind traffic cones blocking the road. One of the constables came over to speak to them but, recognising Sadler, moved a cone to one side.

'You can only go as far as the fire engines, sir. It looks like it's going to be a while. The house is a furnace.'

'Do you know what's happened?'

The constable inclined his head. 'I think the watch commander wants to speak to you.'

Sadler drove slowly towards the yellow lights of the pumps. Despite the closed windows a smell of burning now permeated the car. Not the soothing wood smoke of countless winter fires but something much darker. A wretched, astringent smell.

Connie pointed towards an orange glow, only just visible in the middle of the thick smoke. 'It looks bad.' They sat in silence for a moment watching one of the firefighters, impossibly high in the air on extended ladders and holding a pump from which a large arc of foam poured onto the glowing blaze.

'The rest of them must be inside tackling the flames,' said Sadler. 'It's the quickest way to extinguish a house fire, apparently. Get inside the building.' It wasn't a job he'd fancy himself and glancing across at Connie it looked like she concurred.

'Shall we?'

Connie nodded and, as she opened the car door, made a face. The smell was far worse in the still night air, a cocktail of sickening aromas assailing them. They approached the nearest firefighter, who nodded when she saw their ID. 'It's Alan you want,' she said and spoke softly into a walkie-talkie.

The wait was short. A large man with a white helmet, identifying him as in charge, hurried towards them, his face grim. 'I'm glad you're here.'

'Have you been here long?' asked Sadler.

'The call was received about an hour ago from one of the neighbours. According to her, there's a family of three who lives there. Mother, father and a small child. I'm getting varying accounts of his age. Around four or five years old, according to the neighbours. I've got personnel inside the house now working on the blaze. There are definitely bodies inside.'

'You think it's arson?' asked Connie.

The man wiped his face. 'The guys inside are saying the fire's unusually resilient. That usually means an accelerant of some sort, probably petrol. We'll confirm it when the specialist team comes in. But for the moment I can definitely tell you the fire is suspicious.'

'So you think no one's managed to leave the building.' Sadler looked up again at the arc of foam. 'How long do you think before we can get a fuller assessment?'

'At least mid-morning. I'll issue the stop message as soon as I can.' He saw the confusion on Connie's face. 'When I confirm we don't need any more help and we can pull out.'

'But you think that the occupants, the family I mean, are likely to have perished in the fire?' asked Connie.

The man hesitated. 'Perished, certainly.'

'But not in the fire?' Connie's face was puzzled.

'I think you need to look at this yourselves. This is a new one on me. None of the crew like it either.'

Connie frowned. 'What's the matter?'

'You can see better from over here. We had to evacuate the neighbouring houses as a precautionary measure anyway, but I extended the cordon so the people opposite had to go somewhere else for the night. I didn't want them to see what we could. Come this way.'

Sadler resisted the temptation to put his arm over his nose and followed Connie and the fire officer, keeping his head down. They weaved between the engines towards one of the houses opposite the burning building and the uniformed man led them onto the front lawn.

The stink of the smoke was stronger now but clearly this man hadn't been spooked by the strong acrid smell. Something else was evident. Connie was the first to spot what it was.

'Jesus.' Her thin face was shocked as she looked towards the house. Sadler turned around and followed her gaze. It was a large brick house with four oblong windows at the front, the sort of home a child might have drawn. From the upstairs right windows, orange fire was pouring out in pumping gusts towards the roof where black smoke gathered. In the middle of the house was an arched latticed window, tall and narrow, illuminating what must have been the landing. The individual panes had shattered and smoke rose in the background. But Sadler was no longer taking any notice of the fire. For dangling behind the ruined glass was the outline of a body slowly revolving in a sickening dance. As they watched, the face turned towards them.

Sadler felt the bile rise in his throat and, out of the corner of his eye, he saw Connie vomit on the grass.

3

Julia Winson lay in the darkness enjoying the weight of the night on her. Outside, the milk van, a remnant of a bygone age but still stubbornly held on to by Bampton residents, whirred down the street. From the basket underneath her bed, Julia could hear Bosco snoring slightly, another reassuring sound in the lightening day. Her natural body clock always woke her at this time but she allowed herself the luxury of another hour to get used to the new morning. She resisted the temptation to reach for her tablet and check the day's news online. Instead she focused her thoughts on the wall opposite and prepared herself for the day coming.

Bosco stopped snoring and lifted his head, alert. He whined at Julia, who leant over the edge of the bed to pat his head. Bosco twisted away and began to growl.

'What is it, boy?'

She watched as her barrel-bodied dog sprang from his basket with surprising agility and rushed towards the window. He jumped onto a chair, put his two front paws on the sill and poked his head through the curtains.

'Bosco?'

Julia got up and went to the window, peering out into the night. Dawn was breaking; it must be around five-ish but gloom still cloaked the street and the lamps had not yet been extinguished. She craned her neck until her forehead touched the glass, straining to see what had disturbed her dog. The street appeared asleep.

A fox, she thought and padded back to bed, but Bosco wouldn't follow her, remaining at his window vigil.

'Leave it, boy. Come over here.' In vain, Julia patted her bedspread as her dog raised his head and let out a howl of displeasure.

Bloody hell. The elderly couple to her right would still be fast asleep. She had trouble making herself understood when she was chatting to them in the street so they would hardly hear Bosco's baying through the thick terrace walls. It was the new neighbour she was less sure of. Recalling his closed face when she'd introduced herself, Julia got out of bed and yanked the dog by his collar away from the window.

'Do you want some food?'

She opened her bedroom door and Bosco shot past her, feet clattering as he made his way down the wooden stairs. He pawed angrily at the front door and Julia stopped midway down the flight, frowning. Bosco was used to going out the back door to stretch his legs and do his business. The front door was used only when they went for a walk in the early evenings. She moved into the living room and looked out of the front window. From the corner of her eye she saw a shadow move.

Shit. Heart thumping, she considered opening the front door and letting Bosco have a pop at whoever he or she was but doing so would put herself at risk too. Instead she switched on her hall light and that of her dining room, hoping it would illuminate whoever was hiding in the dark outside. She went back into the lounge and peered out of the window of the still dark room but could see no one.

'Bosco,' she whispered. 'Stay with me.'

Her dog brushed against her legs, breathing hard. Slowly Julia turned each of the lights off and peered once more into the darkness but could see nothing. She could swear someone was still outside. *The absence of absence*, she thought. She stayed still for a moment then moved to the front door and checked the lock. She retreated to the kitchen, switched on the kettle and settled down to wait for dawn.

4

'Murder-suicide then.'

Connie was subdued and looked embarrassed at being sick. Sadler wondered if it was too early to call DS Damian Palmer or whether his young baby meant he was already awake. He looked at his watch. Ten past six. Surely his sergeant would be up by now. 'The fire crew can't yet say how many bodies there are inside. There's the person we saw hanging from the window and they've found another adult in the back bedroom. Neighbours have told the crew they think the child slept at the front of the property. There was a child's aeroplane dangling in the window.'

'At the front of the house? That's an odd place to put a child. In a room looking out onto a busy main road.'

He turned to her. 'Is that important? Perhaps it's the smallest bedroom and if they've got good glazing he might not hear the road anyway.'

He expected her to look sulky. Connie never liked anyone to disagree with her but clearly nausea was battling for ascendency. She put a tissue to her nose and blew. 'If the fire crew can't see the child, he might not be inside.'

Sadler shrank from the note of hope in her voice. 'It looks like the front bedroom floor has collapsed into the room below. I think he said it was the dining room underneath. Assuming the child was in his bedroom, it might be a while before he's discovered.'

'What about the possibility of an external presence in the house?'

Sadler felt the weary nights of disturbed sleep catching up with him. 'The front and rear doors were locked. The rear one had deadbolts fastened. The patio doors in the kitchen were locked. The front door was also locked and chained.'

'Well, that's that then.'

'I really don't think it will be, do you?'

'What I mean is, we're not immediately looking for someone else to account for the fire.'

'Not immediately,' he agreed.

'Where do you want me to start?'

Sadler looked at his watch. 'It's a bit early for door-to-doors, although I'm sure all the neighbours are awake and on the street. We need to start with whoever first reported the fire. Do we have that information?'

Connie shook her head.

Sadler looked in his rear view mirror. In the pale light he could see a woman in a lemon dressing gown with its hood pulled up over her head. She was watching the proceedings intently.

'Stay here for a second.'

'No. I'll come with you.' Connie opened the car door, gagged again and clutched her stomach.

'Get back in the car. I'm just going to have a chat with the neighbour. You don't need to be there.'

Connie opened her mouth to protest and then paled. She clapped her hand over her mouth as she hurriedly slid back into her seat.

The woman in the dressing gown made to move away as he

went up to her but stopped when he held out his ID.

'Do you know the family in the house?' *Thank God*, he thought, *from this position you can't see what we've just had to endure.*

The woman nodded. 'There's a couple with a little boy.'

'You know them well?'

The woman pulled her dressing gown tighter around her, more for comfort than warmth. 'Not very well. I mean, that's the trouble with living on a main road. You don't get to know your neighbours at all, really. Are they okay?'

'We're not sure yet. We're waiting for the fire to be extinguished.'

She looked at him with large eyes. 'I don't see them on the street.'

'You know them well enough to recognise them?'

'Yes, just not to talk to. Peter and Francesca are the parents. He's much older than her. When I first moved in, I saw him wheeling the pushchair along the pavement and I thought he was the child's granddad. I stopped to talk to the little boy and nearly said something along the lines of "out with your grandpa?". It's just as well I didn't because I later found out he was the child's father.'

'So his wife was much younger than him?' The question sounded prurient, like a gossipy remark about a newly arrived family. It must have been the sight of the body that had made him so squeamish. The woman answered readily.

'A lot younger. At least thirty years, I'd say. She was young enough to be his daughter.'

'Did you ever speak to her?'

'Only the once. She came around about a year ago when

17

there'd been a burglary five houses down. She was thinking of getting a neighbourhood watch or something like that together. She was really agitated that someone might get inside her home. I mean, none of us like to be burgled but you can't live in fear of it, can you?'

'You think she was worried about a specific threat?'

'I don't think so. Why? Do you think the fire was started deliberately?'

'I don't know.' *At least*, thought Sadler, *I can tell her that much*. 'What was Francesca like?'

'All right. Her English wasn't brilliant. I think she was Italian. She sounded a bit panicked and I told her Bampton was pretty safe. I invited her in but she preferred to stay on the doorstep. She was friendly enough but didn't want to stop and chat.'

'A burglary?'

'They'd left the front windows open and the robber just shinned up the drainpipe. The police said it was an opportunistic act. I don't think anyone was interested in a neighbourhood watch scheme. We've all got burglar alarms and most of us put them on at night even when we're home for extra security.'

'You live next door?'

'Next door but one. Barbara and Ian are between us but they're away. I'm wondering if I should call them. You don't think the fire will spread to their house, do you?'

'It looks pretty contained to me. I'd wait.'

The woman nodded. 'That's what I thought.'

'So, if you're next door but one, you'll have heard the family in the garden.'

'Sometimes. They weren't out that much, to be honest.'

'They were a quiet family, even with a young child?'

The woman tugged at her sleeves. 'More or less.'

'More or less?' Sadler asked.

The woman shrugged. 'There'd be loud shouting sometimes. It was the father who was the excitable one. He would shout something along the lines of "this place is a mess" and "I'm sick of all this noise" and there'd be this deafening silence. I'd listen out for the little boy, in case there was any funny business, but I never heard him crying. It was more silence than anything. When he did shout, I'd just shut my ears. It can't be easy bringing up a young child, especially at his age. He probably needed to let off steam.'

'He'd shout at his wife? How often?'

The woman looked at the pavement. 'A lot.'

5

The scare of the early morning made Julia feel heavy and sluggish and she was late leaving her house. Her New Year's resolution to make more of an effort with her appearance had long been abandoned and she contented herself with hiding her hair, still damp from the shower, under a cotton beret and dabbing on some foundation in front of the hall mirror. Bosco was whining at her not to leave even though he knew the routine and could look forward to Jean from over the road letting him out around mid-morning. She threw his ball from the front door into the kitchen and, as he bounced towards it, she made her escape.

The wide street lined with terraces was waking up. Doors opened and its residents spilled out onto the pavement heading towards school and work. She looked back at her house and made a mental note to close all the curtains that evening once dusk fell. When she saw her bus rounding the corner she put on a spurt and made it just as the doors were about to close. The regulars were there: the man who'd once tried to chat her up, the woman who always smelled of alcohol early in the morning and, at the back, the teenage boy who, come rain or shine, always sat with his anorak hood pulled up. True to form, she too took her usual seat and pulled out a paperback.

After half an hour she realised she needn't have rushed. They came to a grinding halt along with the rest of the traffic on the outskirts of Bampton and didn't move. Her book forgotten, she used the time to check her phone, with anxiety gnawing away at her stomach. Her first group would be assembling and waiting for instructions. Here she was, their leader, stuck with nowhere to go. She put the phone in her handbag and made her way down to the front.

'Is there a hold-up?'

The driver pointed at the line of traffic in front of them. 'According to the radio we're being diverted away from Cross Farm Lane. I think there's been an accident.'

'Where? Where along the road is the problem? My family live down there.'

The driver shook his head and Julia went back to her seat and pulled out her phone. Finding her father's home number, she listened as the phone rang unanswered. Half past eight. Francesca would be out with the other mothers transporting Charlie to school but her father should be at home. She tried his mobile and then Francesca's. Both were turned off.

It took another hour before she reached Anchor Cavern, the double decker bus lurching down narrow side streets before picking up its normal route again. Maureen was standing at the entrance looking at her watch and gave a wave of relief when she saw Julia.

'I heard about the diversion. I've put your first group in the coffee shop and given them free drinks.'

'Are they okay?'

'It's a bunch of Scouts so all they want is something fizzy and sickly. They're probably drunk on sugary Coke as we speak.'

'Do you know what's happened? The driver said something about an accident.' Julia walked into the boot room and pulled on her overalls. Maureen followed, chewing on her lip.

'I don't know. The group leader thought it might be a fire. He heard lots of engines passing the campsite early in the morning. Apparently he can tell the difference between the sirens.' She rolled her eyes at Julia who was thinking of the ringing phone. Surely if there had been a fire, her father would have picked up or, in the worst case, one of the fire crew.

'I tried to ring Dad to see if he was okay but there was no answer.'

'If they've cut off the road, they might have evacuated some of the houses. I'm sure it's fine. Do you want to give him another ring before you start?'

Julia's father would be irritable if he was being made to stand outside, however mild the morning might be. 'I think I'll leave it. Lead on to the depths.'

6

DS Palmer arrived at Cross Farm Lane and noted a dried patch of baby milk on his trousers. It wasn't the real stuff, thank God. Joanne had stopped feeding after a month, complaining of sore breasts and feeling depressed. The health visitor had been disapproving but Joanne had never taken to it and their son, Max, had refused to latch on properly. The first night Palmer had prepared the formula, they had both given a sigh of relief and later Joanne had confided this was the first time since pregnancy that she felt normal again.

The call came while he was in the shower and he'd rushed his morning dressing in the hurry to get to the scene. The milk from the bottle must have landed on him when he'd kissed Joanne goodbye. He picked at it now, wondering if he could cadge a bottle of water to sponge it off. He looked around for Connie. Once upon a time, he would have resented their boss's decision to call her before he had been contacted. These last few months, however, he had made a decision. Transfer plans had been put into motion, which meant it mattered less who came where in the pecking order at Bampton, although it was hard to quell completely those old jealousies.

It was difficult to make out anything amongst the steam rising from the carcass of a once grand house. As the wind changed, a waft of putrid stink overwhelmed him and he realised a splash of baby milk would be the least of his problems today. The fire was extinguished although steam rose like a scene from an apocalyptic film. Forensic officers were walking into the wreckage, their white suits blending in with the foam and the billowing white tents that had been erected. Palmer counted them. Three in total.

Sadler, spotting him, walked over to where he stood.

'Good, you're here. Was the traffic bad?'

'It's chaos. I'm in my own car so I couldn't put on the lights. They're diverting everyone and now I'm here I can see why.'

'I've sent Connie home. It was a grisly sight earlier in the morning and she needs to have a shower and clean up.'

'Is she okay?' It slipped out before he could stop himself.

Sadler's eyes were cold. 'She's fine. As I said, she needs to freshen up.'

Palmer looked over to the house. 'Three tents?'

Sadler didn't follow his gaze. 'Two definite bodies and one is what we think is the remains of the young son.'

Palmer winced. 'God.'

'The pathologist is in there now. Once he's confirmed three bodies then, pending official identification, this would tally with the missing family members.'

'We're looking at suspicious death then?'

'One body was hanging suspended from a fitting on the landing ceiling, so, yes, I would say so.'

'A murder-suicide. Do we have any background on the family?'

Sadler turned away. 'Not much. I need to get home first to change before I go into the station and update Superintendent Llewellyn. We also need to check about next of kin; I've got

DS Matthews on that. Can I leave you here to coordinate the door-to-door questioning?'

'Of course.' Palmer looked over to the ruined house. 'How old was the child?'

'I'm not sure. Young, I presume. A neighbour thought around four or five.' Palmer found himself being scrutinised by his boss. 'Are you going to be okay?'

'Of course. Why are you asking me that?'

'Those fire crew will have young kids too, not to mention the forensic officers.'

Palmer felt the prickle of irritation. 'I'm not Connie. I can do my job without involving my personal feelings.'

It was the wrong thing to say. Sadler stepped back and looked at him with cool eyes. 'Can you?'

7

'On the count of three I want you all to switch off your torches and enjoy the darkness.'

An expectant hush fell over the group. Part excitement with a large dollop of fear. A bunch of Scouts who'd fallen out of their camp beds ready for a bit of subterranean adventure. They were 150 metres below the surface in a cave hollowed out by lead miners centuries earlier. The group had made whooping noises on the barge taking them along the underground canal, competing with each other as to who could make the most sinister echo, but now, standing deep inside the bowels of the earth, they were quiet. To make matters worse, Julia was asking them to take a step into their most primeval fear, the heart of darkness.

'There's no need to be scared. When I tell you to, switch off your torches and stay completely still. You can keep your hands on the buttons if you're scared. But I want you all to switch them off. Ready? One, two, three.'

The light was extinguished with a snap and they were plunged into total darkness. The group fell silent and listened to the absence of sound that roared in their eardrums. But Julia, used to this drill, could hear other noises far in the distance: the drip of condensation down the stone walls, the slap of water against the barge boat.

In her head, Julia counted slowly to thirty. Rarely in modern life were people exposed to silence like this. She reckoned around half a minute was the maximum she could get away with.

'Okay, everyone. Switch your torches back on.'

Relieved laughter and a few elbow shoves as the lights flickered on. One child, a small curly-haired boy, came towards her.

'What was that noise I could hear?'

She peered down at him, careful not to shine the light from her helmet into his face.

'What noise?'

'Like whispers. I could hear someone whispering.'

She patted his arm. 'It was probably the wind. It comes down the old ventilation shafts. That'll be what you heard.'

She shepherded them back onto the barge and pointed out geological features as they left behind the chilly depths of the cave and headed towards the entrance.

Climbing the iron staircase to the surface, Julia stayed at the back of the group, helping a young boy who'd insisted on taking the tour despite a broken arm. She peered at her watch in the gloom. If she was quick, there was time for a brew and a croissant before she had to take charge of the second group. She'd also try her father again. Reaching the top she puffed slightly, her experience in climbing the stairs no match for the youthfulness of the children. As they handed back their helmets and torches at the desk, Julia could see Maureen from the office squeezing past the group to get to her.

'Julia! Your brother's been trying to get hold of you on your mobile. He's called a couple of times here too. I said I'd let you know as soon as you came up.' Maureen's face was pale. 'You don't think it's about the fire up on Cross Farm Lane, do you?'

'How did he sound?'

Maureen looked stricken. 'It was difficult to say but he said it was urgent. I tried to get him to tell me what the matter was but he wouldn't.'

'Really? God, where's my phone?'

'I could see on the CCTV you were on the boat so there wasn't much I could do except wait. I didn't want to use the walkie-talkie in case I panicked you and the children.'

Julia hurried to the staff lockers and retrieved her phone. She'd missed eight calls from her brother. A thud of fear in her heart, she dialled his number.

He answered on the first ring, his voice icy. 'I've been trying to get hold of you. It's Dad.'

'What's happened? Is it the fire?'

She heard her brother take a deep breath. 'Not just Dad. Francesca and Charlie too. There's been a fire. The police are here with me now. The house is a mess. Can you come? Come here to my place, I mean. Don't go to the house.'

'Why not? Are they okay?'

'No.' George was speaking very slowly. 'No one's okay.'

8

Connie wasn't a frequenter of church services. A couple of weddings and a murder victim's interment. That was about the sum of it. Her own mother's funeral hadn't even been held in a place of worship. Her family had used the chapel of a local crematorium where a locum vicar had intoned meaningless words about a woman he'd clearly never known. She did, however, visit the silence and the coolness of Peak District churches. She liked the sense of a Derbyshire that her family had inhabited for generations but which was disappearing. The marble statues she occasionally found inside the recessed walls also fascinated her. Women primly clasping their prayer books and rosary beads lying next to men with ruffs and pointed slippers. It was the faces of these statues that came to Connie's mind now. Sadler was alabaster pale with his eyes registering shock as Nigel Rooth, the specialist fire investigator, laid out the morning's horrors.

'So we have, with the help of the pathologist, identified three human remains at the property. One adult in the back bedroom, one adult hanging on the landing near the top of the stairs. In the downstairs dining room, one child lying on what we think was his mattress, which had fallen through the ceiling from the room above. Two of the three bodies were too badly burnt to make immediate visual identification possible, especially the child. One of the adults was in better shape so we could tell gender, approximate age and so on, but that's it.'

Sadler reached for his coffee and then, thinking better of it, put it down undrunk. 'I'll talk to the pathologist in due course. Can we go back through the timeline again? I want to get the sequence of events straight. The first emergency callout was received from one of the neighbouring houses at 3.24 a.m., is that correct?'

Nigel checked his notes. 'A Mrs Misra in number 41, directly opposite the affected property. She's just had a baby and was breastfeeding the child in an upstairs bedroom. She was alerted by a flickering she could see behind the drawn curtains. When she opened them she could see flames coming from the upstairs right window of the house opposite.'

'She didn't notice the body in the window?' Connie couldn't stop herself blurting out the interruption. Nigel looked at her in sympathy.

'She says not. She woke her husband, who called emergency services, and the Misras immediately took the child and drove to a relative. Their newborn baby was their primary concern. She says they didn't see a body and it might not have been visible when the fire was just in the front bedroom.'

He looked at Sadler. 'This initial testimony is important. The flames, in the first instance, were coming from the bedroom where the young son was sleeping.'

Connie wanted to jump in with questions and demand he get to the point. Articulate the horrific thoughts that were crowding out her mind. Sadler appeared to appreciate her agitation. He shot her a warning glance and Connie took a deep breath.

'So the fire probably started in that bedroom. Where the flames were first seen?' prompted Sadler.

Nigel nodded. 'It should be fairly easy once we undertake a close inspection to identify the exact point of ignition.'

'Neighbours indicate the house was occupied by three members of the same family?' said Sadler. 'Francesca and Peter Winson and their son, Charlie, aged five. We've begun with the assumption that these three family members are our victims.'

Nigel nodded. 'I think we're fairly confident about the identity of the victims. There is every indication the Winson family were inside the house during the night and none emerged. Have you contacted the relatives?'

'We have specially trained officers with Peter's adult son from an earlier marriage. There's a big age gap between his children,' said Connie. 'They're trying to contact his daughter.'

Nigel began to doodle on the notepad in front of him. He was picking his words with care. 'You both saw the body suspended from the landing. Of course, you'll need to wait for the post mortems so I'm not going to speculate on the cause of deaths. Fire is my speciality and we'll soon enough be able to come up with a sequence of events in relation to that.'

'But we need to proceed on the basis of something,' said Sadler. 'Can you at least give me a likely scenario?'

Nigel Rooth leant forward. 'Based on initial observations, I believe the fire began in the child's bedroom and then, following a trail of accelerant, almost certainly petrol, it made its way across to the back of the house to the parents' room. From this, a blaze of considerable intensity developed that caused most of the west side of the building to ignite.'

'So the trail of accelerant, in your opinion, stops in the back bedroom?' asked Connie.

'Based on the unusual resilience of the fire in this area as identified by the firefighters, that would be my conclusion.'

'So a likely scenario is that the adult hanging from the

landing set a trail of petrol from Charlie's bedroom to the master bedroom, and then hanged themselves on the landing.'

Nigel Rooth looked wary but nodded. 'Yes, I think you can proceed on that scenario.'

'What about evidence of external presence within the building?'

Nigel looked grim. 'Neither I nor my men saw any evidence of a break-in. As I mentioned to you this morning, all the locks were intact. We're giving the building a forensic search now to look at all exit points. All I can say to you is it doesn't immediately look like anyone had forced an entry point into the house.'

'And it will be up to Bill to confirm whether the victims in the bedrooms died from the fire or were already dead,' said Sadler.

At the thought of the rotund pathologist, Bill Shields, Connie felt her frayed nerves relax a fraction. Bill would be the first step in bringing the start of sense, of a sort, to this madness.

Sadler was still pale. 'Whether the cause of death was due to the fire or other methods, if the final act was suicide and the other members of the family were already dead then we have a major murder investigation.'

'A family murder?' Connie exhaled heavily. 'They're often foreshadowed by a history of domestic violence. We're going to be looking at another case where a man thought it was okay to obliterate a family because of his skewed thinking.'

Nigel Rooth shook his head. 'The bodies may have been badly burnt but I can assure you the person hanging on the landing wasn't an adult male.'

Sadler froze. 'You mean . . .'

'If it is a murder-suicide that you're looking at, and I think it is, it's the mother of the family who is the murderer.'

9

Julia sat on her brother's sofa and for the first time in her life felt an absence of any feeling. Well, this wasn't completely true. There was something trying to infiltrate the vacuum that had robbed her of any emotion. With a shock, Julia recognised it as the instinct to survive. However devastating the words were that were continuing to emit from the kind woman's mouth, there was another current pulsating under the surface of her emotions. Some primitive force telling her that she would survive this. She looked over to George who was sitting immobile. He looked as shocked as her but also, she thought, very angry.

She tried to catch his eye but he was ignoring her, instead firing rapid questions at the composed family-liaison officer, Pat. Dry-eyed, Julia forced herself to concentrate on what the woman was telling them. Police were on their way. For it seemed that although Pat *was* police she wasn't, as far as Julia could see, important. Her news was the worst anyone could receive but she couldn't supply them with any more information. There had been a fire at Cross Farm Lane. The house was burnt, badly burnt, and the firefighters had found fatalities. Her family, all her family except George and that person she couldn't think about now, were presumed perished in the inferno. That's all Pat could tell them. Just the same information over and over again. But others were apparently on their way and they were to just sit there until these *important* police officers arrived.

The bus to George's apartment from Anchor Cavern had been mercifully short although she'd been aware of a little boy trying to talk to her as she hurried towards the stop. She'd brushed him away and had been conscious of a small figure standing disconsolately at the visitor entrance as she'd run for the bus. She'd been desperate to get here, receive any comfort even if it was the little that George could offer her, but he had been distant, his face a frozen mask. She was now waiting for information, and deep down in her secret self was the knowledge she'd done all this before. That was what she'd wanted to say to George if she could get him on his own for two minutes. *We've survived this before and we'll do so again.* Perhaps that was why he was refusing to look at her. Perhaps there was a limit as to how much pain and loss people could accept. Julia disagreed. She knew if you acted fine, eventually you were fine. She wished again the family-liaison officer would leave them be. Pat, however, looked like she was going nowhere. Perhaps that, too, was part of the procedure.

Julia got up and walked into George's kitchen. Like the rest of the apartment it was immaculate, granite surfaces and chrome fittings. There was no evidence George ever did any cooking although he had none of the middle-aged paunch she associated with those who live on a diet of takeaways and sandwiches. Lobster and champagne would be more his thing. She took a glass from the open shelves and filled it with lukewarm tap water. George was still sitting stock still on the sofa and Julia could feel irritation beginning to prick at her scalp.

From the kitchen window, she peered three storeys below

and watched a car pull up alongside the kerb. Out of the dark blue Mercedes came a tall man with fair hair parted at one side. Wearing a blue linen suit, he gave off an air of both youth and authority. From the passenger side a small woman emerged, frowning as she searched in her handbag for something she had clearly forgotten. They crossed over towards the flat and, as they reached the building, Julia heard the buzzer go in the living room. The important police had arrived.

10

'I've forgotten my fags.'

The sun was beating down on Connie's head and she could feel a tear of sweat slide down her back. She rubbed at the spot with her fist.

Sadler smiled at her. 'You'll have to do without then. Where did you leave them?'

Connie thought for a moment. 'On the window ledge outside the station. Do you think they'll still be there when I get back?'

Sadler continued to smile and raised his eyebrows as he pressed the buzzer. Connie swore under her breath. It was a packet of Richmond Menthols, full bar the one she'd smoked; that was ten quid down the drain. To take her mind off the ache for nicotine, she studied the façade of the building. The name, St Alkmund, was engraved into the stone arch above where they stood and a date she couldn't quite decipher.

'What was this place originally used for?' Sadler would know. He was a Bampton boy and liked to point out the history of buildings in his home town. And she was right. Without looking at her he pushed the door open at the sound of the responding click. 'It used to be a workhouse.'

Inside was a spacious hallway with the original stone flagstones buffed to a shine that couldn't have been a feature two hundred years earlier. A small lift with gold doors stood in the corner. Connie saw Sadler frowning. 'What's the matter?'

'It's hardly in keeping with the building's original use, is it?'

Connie rolled her eyes, walked over to the lift and jabbed at the button. 'What do you want? The smell of cabbage soup and a recording of women sobbing?'

'Of course not but conversions should respect the origins of a building. Why put gold doors in a former institution for the destitute?'

'I can't make out the date over the front door. Perhaps it was a rich philanthropist's house who gave it over to the parish.'

He looked down at her in amusement. 'A Victorian heiress with a penchant for gold door furniture. I think, Connie, we've lost some subtlety over the subsequent years.'

The third floor consisted of a small corridor with two doors facing each other. The right-hand one opened and Pat, whom Connie had worked with on previous cases, came out to meet them, pulling the door slightly behind her.

'I've got them both in there. The son, George, is taking it okay. Too well, I think. He's just sitting there, frozen and not saying anything. He looks really angry and keeps asking me questions that I obviously can't answer. The daughter, Julia, is trying to communicate with him but he's ignoring her. She's on autopilot. They're both trying to digest what's happened, which is to be expected.'

'Have either of them expressed anything other than shock? Anything out of the ordinary?' asked Sadler.

Pat thought for a moment and then shook her head. 'I don't think so. They're just aware of there having been a house fire and that we believe the family has perished. I didn't know any more to tell them anyway. There is one thing, though.'

'What?'

'They're a bit more fatalistic than I'd expect. Don't get me wrong. They're both really shocked. It's just they seem, well, a bit resigned too. I don't normally get that.'

'Resigned?'

'I don't know. It's just my first impressions; something I can't put my finger on.'

'Right,' said Sadler. 'Let's go in.'

The front door opened on to the living room with a high ceiling from which hung a large crystal chandelier. Two paintings graced the pale walls, rural oil colours in fox red and mud brown. Connie's eyes, however, were drawn to a small statue of a female nude in the corner of the room. Sculpted in bronze, the torso was twisted so the woman was looking over her shoulder and staring directly at her and Sadler. Connie shifted her gaze to the sofa. There sat a man in his late forties, his greying curly hair slightly too long, which gave him a Byronic air. He was bulky without being fat. A solid man wearing a white shirt and dark blue checked tweed trousers. A sort of county look that Connie had seen before. Posh Derbyshire, she mentally clocked, and shifted her attention to his sister standing in the doorway holding a glass of water. Julia was fine-boned with the muddy blonde hair you can't get from a bottle. Her pale skin was covered with a smattering of freckles. To Connie, she looked more ordinary probably because of the olive cargo pants and a striped Breton sweater that had a smear of dirt down it.

George took the initiative, his anger barely controlled. 'You've taken your time coming to us; are you going to tell us what happened? We've been sitting here all morning and we've been told nothing.'

Pat, face impassive, sat down on a chair behind him at the back of the room out of his sightline. Julia's eyes followed her. 'George. Take it easy. They're here now, aren't they?'

Neither had invited them to sit so Connie took the initiative and sank into the depths of the opulent sofa opposite the man.

Sadler, after a moment's hesitation, joined Connie. 'I know Pat has given you some preliminary information about what's happened. We're here to tell you what we know but the facts are, at the moment, only sketchy.'

Julia crossed over and sat next to her brother but didn't touch him. 'There was a fire?' she asked.

Sadler nodded. 'There was a significant blaze at the house of your father and stepmother. It destroyed most of the house and, I'm sorry to have to tell you this, we have discovered three bodies at the property.'

'All of them?' *She looks upset*, thought Connie. *What had Pat meant by them being too composed?*

'It was an inferno and the occupants of the house, your family, would have had little opportunity to escape. I'm sorry but the bodies, as far as we can ascertain, match the description of your father, stepmother and brother.'

'Half-brother.' The comment came involuntarily and George appeared to regret it. Pat looked shocked.

Julia remained composed but a red hue bloomed under her skin. 'I don't understand it.'

'What don't you understand?' asked Connie.

'Dad was very safety conscious. There are smoke detectors all over the place. The same when we were growing up. I wasn't allowed even a candle in my room in case it started a fire. I would have said that house was fireproof.'

'You grew up in the house on Cross Farm Lane?' asked Connie.

Julia looked to her brother. 'Since we were teenagers.'

Sadler hesitated, picking his words with care. 'When did both of you last see your family?'

'I saw them just under two weeks ago for Sunday lunch,' said Julia. 'Why?'

'And you?' Sadler asked George.

He reflected for a moment. 'About four months ago.'

A long time considering they live fifteen minutes' drive from each other, thought Connie. Neither George nor his sister were inclined to add anything else.

'And how was everything, Julia, when you saw the family?'

The meaning of Sadler's words began to sink in. 'What do you mean, how were they? They were fine. What are you saying?'

Connie was aware of George's stillness and Julia's agitation as they waited for Sadler to speak.

'We're, at the moment, trying to establish the cause of the fire: how it came to start and why it spread so quickly. All I can tell you right now is that both the point of ignition and its ferocity are suspicious.'

'They were murdered.' George's voice was flat. Pat again looked shocked.

'I can only tell you it was suspicious and I need to know how things were last time you saw the family.' Sadler looked at George. 'It was about four months ago for you. How were they then?'

George looked at them blankly, his eyes giving nothing away. 'It was Charlie's birthday. I went round and brought something from the shop. I have an antiques business in town. I gave him some tin soldiers from the 1950s. Francesca was there when I arrived and we had a coffee together. Then Dad came in from the garden and made some disparaging comment about my gift. About tin being poisonous or something.'

'It upset you,' said Connie.

George stared at her, angry. 'It was typical of him. Why say something nice when you can be cruel.' As if recognising this wasn't the time to air old grievances, he made a visible effort to pull himself together. 'They seemed fine.'

'And you, Julia?'

'I went around for Sunday lunch every other week, which fitted around my shifts. I'm a tour guide at Anchor Cavern. It gave me an opportunity to see Charlie. The last time was like any other Sunday except it was really nice weather so we ate in the garden.'

'And everything was okay?' asked Connie.

'Things were a bit formal in the house and mealtimes could be torture. It was the same even when we were eating in the garden. It would depend on Dad's mood. Things were okay from what I remember. Certainly not different from normal.'

'Your dad had a short temper?' asked Connie. 'Was he ever violent?'

Julia again looked to her brother. 'Of course not. He was just, well, bad-tempered. He's always been like that since we were kids. We managed him and so did Francesca.'

'Had he fallen out with anyone recently? Perhaps in relation to his job?' asked Sadler. 'Someone who might have wished him harm?'

'He was retired,' George said in a flat voice. 'I took over part of the business from him. I bought him out of the shop he had and combined it with mine.'

'You were both in the antiques business?'

'Yes, although he also owned an auction house. He'd stepped back from that too but he was still a shareholder and would occasionally visit the place. It's a small business I know well. I can't imagine anyone there who might have had a grudge against him.'

'And Francesca? Was she working then, if your father was at home?'

'There was no need for either of them to work.' His voice shook with anger and Julia gave her brother a warning glance that he ignored. 'My father was a successful businessman. They had plenty of money and he was, in effect, retired.'

'And Francesca?'

'Francesca was a full-time mother. She didn't have many friends to fall out with. In fact, I'm not sure she had any at all,' said Julia.

'Why's that?' Connie, who had few friends herself, blamed her anti-social working hours. If Francesca didn't work, it couldn't have been her job.

Julia just shrugged. 'It was the way she was.'

'What did you both think of her? It must have been a surprise when your father got married to someone much younger than him. What about your own mother, was she divorced from your father or was he widowed?' It was now Connie noticed it. Julia trying to catch George's attention. Communicate something to him. Pat had been right about that and about the unnatural composure of these two.

'Francesca was reserved but a great mother to Charlie as far as I could see. Our own mother is no longer around.'

It was an odd turn of phrase. Sadler had noticed too. 'She's no longer alive?'

'That's right. Is it relevant?' George crossed his legs and reached for a cigarette.

Connie felt her lungs contract, desperate for nicotine. 'Can I ask you both, where you were last night?'

George made them wait while he lit his cigarette with deliberate slowness. 'I went out with my partner about seven and we came back here afterwards. She stayed here overnight and I drove her home this morning.'

'She was with you all night?'

'That's correct.'

'Julia?'

Julia looked like she was trying to make sense of something. 'I was on my own but, you know, I thought I saw someone hanging around outside my place this morning.'

'What time was this?'

'I think it was around five.'

'Do you think someone was trying to break in?' asked Connie.

'I'm not sure. It was just a shadow. I have a little dog so I'm not usually scared of potential intruders.'

Connie made a note of it in her pad, aware that at around five that morning she and Sadler had been together watching Francesca suspended in front of the window.

'Is there anything else you want to tell us?'

One final time, Julia looked at her brother. *She takes her cues from him*, thought Connie.

George, however, shook his head. 'I'd like you all to leave.'

Chilled to the bone despite the heat, Julia rang her work and told them there had been a family emergency and she wouldn't be in for the rest of the week. A summer seasonal worker took the call and wasn't interested enough to ask for any more information. Julia wouldn't have got away with revealing so little to Maureen. Her voice felt strange, as if she were speaking from a long way off, and she marvelled she could get through something as innocuous as a phone call when everything else around her was disintegrating. Pat hadn't wanted to leave but she could hardly force herself on them. She'd departed after handing out small cards with her contact number in case they needed her. Now they were on their own, George had lapsed into silence.

'I can't believe anyone would want to harm Peter or Francesca, let alone Charlie. I felt awful having to explain my whereabouts. At least you have an alibi. It was just me and Bosco and he's not talking, is he? Who's this girlfriend, anyway?'

George's eyes flickered in irritation. 'For someone so bright, you can be incredibly dense sometimes.'

'What do you mean? Do you know something I don't? Dad never said he felt threatened.'

'They weren't that interested in your answer, were they? They asked the question, they wanted to know our alibis that's for sure, but the little detective never even looked up when you said you thought someone was hanging around outside your house. It was the first question they were more interested in.'

'Which one?' Julia moved in front of George.

'They wanted to know how Dad and Francesca got on with each other. Was Dad violent? That's when the lady detective went still. She was listening for both our answers.'

Julia felt her legs weaken and sat on the arm of the sofa. 'Good God. You don't think Dad's going to be held responsible for this?'

'That's what they seemed to be implying.'

'Haven't we been through this before? You know what he was like. A miserable sod but he was never violent.'

George set his features into the familiar blankness. 'Shout at me all you like, but those detectives were only interested when we described the relationship between Dad and Francesca. You wait and see what happens next.'

'Wait and see? We know what happens next, don't we?'

*

She left him in his sterile flat still sitting on the comfortable sofa. As she shut the door behind her, she saw him retrieve a mobile phone from his trouser pocket. Outside, the policeman's car had gone but she spotted the female detective coming out of the newsagent's and unwrapping the cellophane from a packet of cigarettes. The detective clocked her at the same time and crossed the road towards her.

'Are you okay? I saw Pat leave.'

'What can she do? We're fine by ourselves.'

45

'I can understand you not wanting anyone with you but you're not going to the house, are you? You really don't want to see that at the moment. We can take you at a later date.'

Julia looked at the card Pat had given her. 'She's nice but she doesn't seem to know much. You're the one with answers.'

Connie's eyes were appraising and she held out her hand. Julia handed over the card and, with her cigarette dangling from her mouth, Connie scribbled a mobile number on the back.

'You can call me instead if it makes you feel better.'

'The questions you asked us in there. About Dad and Francesca. What did you mean?'

Connie, turning her head to one side, blew out a long puff. 'It's the first thing we do. Find out about the family history and so on. It's a suspicious death and that's what we're treating it as until the post mortem and fire investigation results come through. Look, why don't you go home? We can contact you and George again when we have more news.'

Julia stepped away. 'I don't want you to get the wrong impression about George. I've just got this horrible feeling he came across a bit odd in there.'

'He didn't get on with your dad and his new family?'

'It's not that, it's just that it was a big shock when Dad decided to get married again. After Mum left, he brought us up by himself and any girlfriends were kept in the background.'

'Then he met Francesca? Where did they meet?'

'Through work.'

'In his antiques shop?'

'She worked at the auctioneer's in Bampton. They met there.'

'You liked her? You spoke well of her just now in the flat.'

'I did actually, although she was a very private person.'

'And George?'

Julia hesitated. 'He liked her too.'

'Come on. That's not the impression I got.' The detective inhaled deeply on her cigarette.

'It took George longer to get used to things, I think.'

'He said it'd been a few months since he last visited.'

Julia, feeling the threat of tears, took a step backwards. 'I'm surprised it's that recent.'

'Fathers and sons. It can be a difficult relationship.'

The detective was fishing. Julia could see that. In the flat, she had longed to be free of its confines but now, in the street, the questions were as oppressive as George's pristine cell.

'It was nothing special. No falling out or anything. Dad was a difficult person, that's all.'

'Difficult?'

'You know what I mean. Irritable. Like George, maybe.' Julia tried a smile but her face wobbled with the effort.

'He didn't mellow with his remarriage?'

'You've got to be kidding.'

'You went around there every other week, you say?'

'To see Charlie, mainly.'

Connie took another deep drag of nicotine. 'Did George get on with Charlie?'

Julia knew she should go. Leave the detective and her questions, but she needed one answer herself.

'George got on fine with everyone.'

Connie looked unconvinced and squashed the stub of her cigarette on the top of a nearby bin. Julia took a steadying breath. 'Why all the questions and the same inside? Why were you asking about the relationship between Dad and Francesca? We both noticed it.'

'Did you?' Connie fiddled with the packet of cigarettes still in her hand as if debating whether to light another one. 'These are suspicious deaths. The questions are going to feel intrusive.'

Julia hesitated. 'It *is* really hard for us, you know. Going through it all again.'

'Again?' Connie had gone still.

'You know, raking over old coals.'

'Old coals? The past, you mean?'

'Exactly. It's why George is so angry. Can't you see?'

Connie hadn't moved. They stared at each other for a moment. It was Julia who broke the silence.

'I was waiting for you to talk about Mum. I thought you'd ask about her but you never mentioned what happened to Mum at all.'

1 2

Wednesday, 4 June 1980

Joan Pondson had miscalculated her cardigan by two skeins. She hadn't told anyone, so scared was she that the dementia that had taken her mother into her twilight world was now making its claim on her. She particularly hadn't mentioned it to Jack. He would have scoffed something along the lines of 'you could never add up', but when it came to calculating the measurements of her knitting projects, she reckoned she could do it off the top of her head. But she was wrong. She'd just started the first sleeve and there was no way that ball of wool would cover what was left to do. The only consolation in the sorry mess was Elizabeth who ran the shop wasn't the type to make a fuss. She'd be in and out within minutes and she'd have to pray the balls of wool left in the shop were of the same batch she'd already bought.

Joan arrived at Knit and Purl on Horncastle high street at five past one. She was to remember the time perfectly because when she read the note on the door she looked at her watch in dismay. *Back in two minutes.* Joan knew the post office shut at one o'clock on a Wednesday afternoon so maybe Elizabeth had popped out to post a parcel to a customer. Joan waited outside the door for five minutes. No one else came to get their wool or material. At quarter past,

Joan nipped into Lipton's supermarket across the way and bought three slices of haslet for Jack's sandwiches the next day. This errand completed, she left the shop and could see across the road the note still pinned to the door. At a loss where to go next, she made her way to the library and looked ineffectually around the shelves. But her sense of order had been disturbed. Monday was library day and not every week either. She shouldn't be here on a Wednesday. She dawdled amongst the Mills & Boon section for a few minutes.

It was quarter to two by the time she got back to the shop. The note was still pinned to the door and the lights were on. In a temper, Joan went home, taking satisfaction in the fact she clearly wasn't the only one losing her marbles.

13

'Had you heard of the case before?' Connie was sitting opposite Sadler picking shards of leather off her boots.

He rubbed his eyes with the tips of his fingers. 'It rings a very distant bell. If only for the note on the shop door. It gives an ordinary missing person's case an added twist. It's a long way from here, though. Lincolnshire isn't a county I know well at all.'

'Like Derbyshire, only flat as a pancake.' Connie smirked, a proud Peak District girl.

'Then it's going to be nothing like here then, is it? Can you imagine this county without the hills?'

Connie shrugged. 'Should I get Palmer in? He'll want to hear about this as it could be important.'

Sadler found he couldn't quite look his detective constable in the eye. 'DS Palmer will be taking a wider strategic role in this investigation. There's no need for him to come into our meetings.'

Connie looked at him in astonishment.

'I've had a think about it this morning. I'm not sure if you know but he's put in for a transfer to another station. There's a possibility it might come through sooner rather than later and I don't know how long this case is going to last.'

'He's leaving? He never told me.'

'I've put him in charge of the door-to-doors so he can play

an important role in the early part of the investigation until he departs. I want someone else who'll last the course, though, so I've asked DS Matthews to work with us on this one.'

Sadler could see a range of emotions move across Connie's face. Palmer's transfer news was a surprise to her. She would also have to get used to working closely alongside a female colleague. Carole Matthews was a seasoned detective sergeant who, in Sadler's opinion, should have made inspector by now. She'd passed the exams but never the interview when vacancies had arisen. She was possibly too forthright, which, pitched alongside Connie, might make for an interesting dynamic.

Connie was struggling to hide her disquiet. 'Matthews is okay. She sent me a card and some flowers when I was in hospital.'

'Good. I'll call her in so she can hear what you have to say.' Sadler opened his office door and motioned across the open-plan CID room. Matthews entered, a tall ginger-haired woman with a lean body that comes from regular intensive exercise. She nodded at Connie and sat in the seat next to her.

'I've got you in here because Connie has discovered an old case that might be relevant to the suspicious fire and I'm not sure where it takes us. We'll talk about it further at the team meeting but I'd like your initial thoughts now.'

'The family was involved in an earlier criminal inquiry?'

'It seems so. In June 1980, a woman called Elizabeth Winson who ran a knitting shop in Horncastle, Lincolnshire, left her premises with a notice saying she would be back in two minutes. No one saw her leaving the shop but subsequent police inquiries identified a customer who had been served by Mrs Winson at around quarter to twelve. Another customer tried to enter the shop at five minutes past one, she was very definite on the time, and the note was there.' Sadler stopped for a moment and looked at Matthews. 'Do you know the case?'

Matthews shook her head. 'No, not at all.' She turned to Connie. 'You?'

'Only what I've found out today.'

'Did the woman never return?' asked Matthews.

'Never.' Connie picked up her notebook. 'The note stayed on the door and that's how it remained until Elizabeth's husband, Peter, came to look for her after getting a call from his daughter's school. As normal, after classes ended, her two kids, Julia and George, walked to the shop. George was in the first year of high school, Julia the last year of juniors. They both usually went to the shop when their respective schools finished and they'd hang around in the back room until it was time to close. But, of course, the note was on the door and George found his sister waiting on the doorstep.'

'What did they do?' asked Matthews.

'Julia clearly had her head screwed on. After waiting ten minutes or so, she took herself and her brother back to the junior school where the head teacher was still in her office. Although George wasn't strictly her problem, she remembered him as a former pupil and was happy to help them both.'

'She called the police?' asked Matthews.

'Apparently not. She rang the kids' dad. He came to pick them up and they went on to his wife's shop, which was still closed. I think he then waited a few hours back at the family home and called the police himself in the early evening.'

'And she was never found?' Matthews frowned. 'I don't like cases like this. Unsolved mysteries. They muddy waters, especially when current investigations are involved.'

'Agreed,' said Sadler.

'It is a weird one, I agree.' Connie was skimming over her notes. 'Nothing was discovered about the woman. I mean nothing. No one saw her leave the shop after that last customer and no one saw her in Horncastle. Of course, the press loved it; the case got a fair bit of attention because of the note on the door. It was literally as if she'd popped out for two minutes.'

'There were no sightings at all?' asked Matthews.

'Someone in Aberdeen claimed to have seen her. Another reported sighting in Germany. Later still in Australia. Only the one in Aberdeen seemed remotely credible and that never came to anything. She was eventually declared dead by a court in August 1991 after an application by Mr Winson.'

Sadler sat in silence for a moment, thinking. 'Was the husband ever implicated in the disappearance?'

'I've only been able to look at press reports so far. Quite a few of them were insinuating he *might* have had something to do with it. My guess is he would have been investigated as a matter of course. He doesn't appear to have been arrested at any point.'

'You think it might have something to do with what happened last night?' asked Matthews. 'I thought the preliminary conclusion was the woman, Francesca, was responsible for the murders.'

Sadler's eyes were still stinging from the smoke. He'd gone home to shower away the smell and detritus before coming into work but his broken sleep had made his eyes gritty. Now, by mid-afternoon, his lids felt heavy and he was resisting the urge to lay his head on the desk.

'Francesca is the prime suspect in last night's fire. It's early days, though, and we're not going to be able to close this case until we've at least got a narrative of events that led Francesca to this point.'

'If she did it.' Connie's face was impassive.

'I'm sorry?' asked Sadler.

'I'm just saying it all sounds a bit odd. First off, the fact Francesca is supposed to have murdered all her family. It's usually the other way round. It's men who are the aggressors.'

Sadler could feel his temper beginning to rise.

'And secondly, we now find out Peter Winson had an earlier wife who one day just disappeared. So I think it's a bit soon for us to be automatically assuming it's all Francesca's doing.'

Sadler made an effort to calm himself. 'We're not proceeding on any assumptions, just the likelihood of what may have happened based on initial findings of the fire investigator. You were there when he went over the likely sequence of events, Connie.'

'It just all sounds very odd.'

'What's that got to do with anything? Murder cases frequently have unusual elements to them. Anyway, I don't want our views overriding any facts. Nigel Rooth is a very competent fire investigator and I intend to use his suggested narrative of events as the basis of this case. All possible scenarios will be investigated.'

This appeared to appease Connie. 'You want me to look into this old case?' She was affecting a nonchalant pose that masked her interest. Sadler prevaricated, not wanting her sidetracked by the past.

'I want you to dig beyond the press reports and see if

you can speak to someone who was around on the original investigation. They're almost certainly retired now. But see if you can get a lead investigator's name and find out Peter's history. We have two crimes connected to him. It's a lead we need to follow.'

'And me, sir?' Carole was looking at him expectantly.

'Can you start with Charlie's nursery or school? According to the neighbour I spoke to, the family kept themselves to themselves. I'd like you to talk to those who knew Francesca and her son. Also, I want you to look at the subtext of what both his adult children said, about Winson being easily irrit-ated. We'll have a full team meeting later but remember . . .'

Sadler could feel two pairs of eyes on him.

'This is a tragedy and we're going to treat it as such. But underneath that it's also a mass murder. I don't want anything missed.'

14

Bosco was Julia's saving grace that afternoon. As she let herself in through her front door, he came hurtling towards her, the first tap on the latch alerting him to her arrival. Jean was in the kitchen, her hands in a sink full of soapsuds.

'Jean, please don't wash up for me. All you need to do is let Bosco out. I feel guilty when I come home to a sparkling kitchen.'

Jean was a gigantic woman, unsteady on her feet, who loved dogs and doing errands for her neighbours. She came in every day to let out Bosco but couldn't resist unwashed dishes or clothes sitting in a washing machine.

'No need for you to feel guilty. What are you doing home so early?'

Julia leant against the kitchen counter. 'I'm not feeling very well. Can I talk to you about it later?'

A shadow crossed Jean's face. 'You're looking a bit peaky. There's been a lot of negative energy since Morell moved in. He's not said anything to you, has he?'

'Morell? Who's Morell?'

'Your new neighbour. Didn't you recognise him?'

'I'd never seen him before. He wasn't much interested when I introduced myself.'

'He's the guy whose brother was lost in that caving accident when they were kids. A bunch of them were larking around on a hot day and his brother was separated from the rest.'

'Oh God. I've heard about that.'

'He was never found, the little boy.'

Julia felt the pressure behind her nose begin to mount. She rested her face in the palm of her hand for a moment. 'This was years ago. Why would I recognise his adult brother?'

'He's campaigned for cave safety ever since. I thought you might have seen him as you work in the caves. It doesn't matter. Why don't you take a couple of aspirin and go to bed?'

Jean wiped her hands on the tea towel and then draped it over the sink. After she'd gone, the house felt hot and airless. Bosco was scratching at the back door so she let him out, bringing in a welcome draught. Julia rested against the doorpost and watched as he galloped around the lawn. Even the act of watching him raised her spirits enough to realise if she didn't eat something, she wouldn't get through the rest of the day. Food seemed like an abomination but her clenched stomach warned her she had eaten nothing since supper the previous evening. She got an apple from the bowl and cut it into quarters, forcing the acid pulp down her throat. She then leant back against the counter, the heaviness once more threatening to overwhelm her.

I will survive this, she thought. *The darkness won't overcome me. This is not the first bad thing to have happened to me.*

For a moment she allowed herself to think of Charlie, a little imp who, like the boy in the cave, would never now become an adult. George had shocked that nice policewoman by referring to him as her half-brother but there had been a kind of truth there. He hadn't felt like her brother in the way George did. There was no shared history. No quiet acceptance of loss.

Her only interaction with little Charlie had been under the watchful eye of Francesca.

A rattle on the front door made Julia jump and she thought back to the early hours of the morning and the unwelcome shadow. She ignored it and then came a louder bang. Christ. She opened the door and saw a tearful Maureen.

'I've heard.'

Julia pulled Maureen into the narrow hallway. A shadow passed in the doorway, causing her heart to lurch, but the shape settled into the form of her new neighbour.

'Your dog's been howling all day.'

Julia opened the door fully and took a good look at him. He was in his mid-sixties with sparse, shoulder-length hair that was stuck to his scalp in the heat.

'He can't have been barking all day. He's not a noisy dog.'

Morell refused to look her in the eye. 'All morning he's been barking. He needs more exercise.'

Ignoring him, Julia slammed the door shut and turned to Maureen. 'How have you heard?'

'It's on the news. About the fire I mean, and they've released the names of the dead. I recognised the family name straight away. I'm so sorry.'

Maureen was crying the tears locked deep down in Julia. She felt the tweak of irritation and a foreboding of the weeks to come. A tragedy everyone would feel part of and grieve for their own dead and for themselves. 'Look. I'm not feeling brilliant.'

This seemed to rally Maureen who visibly pulled herself together. 'God, I'm so sorry. I came around to ask if there was anything I could do. I could spend the night here if you need company, or I could take Bosco for a long walk if you want to be by yourself.'

Touched, Julia bent down and picked up her dog, holding his warmth to her. 'I'm okay here with Bosco and I really don't need anyone to stay the night. Does everyone in work know?'

'I'm not sure. I heard it on the way home. Maybe they all know. You've got an unusual surname.'

'Oh God.'

'How's George taking it? Is he being a help?'

'George? George is doing what he's always done. He's all ice and reserve.' It was the right thing to say to Maureen.

'Men find it more difficult to show their feelings. I've got a brother who lost a child to leukaemia. The little thing was only three. Jane, my sister-in-law, was devastated but it was normal. She got through it, within a year of the funeral was pregnant and had a lovely little girl. The baby's now twenty, would you believe. My brother, he was at work the next day. Wouldn't talk about it and has never, according to Jane, spoken of it again. Men. How do they cope when something awful happens?'

Julia thought of George and his pinched face when their mother had first gone. 'I have no idea at all.'

15

Julia woke and from the thickness of her blankets struggled for air. In her uneasy dreams the bedclothes had become tangled around her head and she pushed at them hard to free herself. As she lay gasping on her bed she could see the lights of her alarm clock at ten past midnight. She'd only been asleep for a couple of hours and it was still too early for her father to be back.

Julia pushed back the covers and walked out onto the landing. From over the banisters, she could see the light of the porch confirming only she and George were in the house. It was the dark that was proof of the reassuring presence of their father's return from his evening work visits. Down the hall, light seeped from underneath her brother's door. She made towards it, feeling her way along the landing by trailing her fingers along the embossed wallpaper.

She pushed her brother's door slightly, allowing the light to spread over her bare feet. George was kneeling in front of her long-discarded dolls' house. The wooden doors were swung fully open and his curly head was peering inside. One chubby hand was thrust into the living room as he rearranged the small dolls on the sofa.

Perhaps aware he was no longer alone, George turned

around. His guilty face flushed at her. She tried to reassure him.

'I don't mind. I've finished playing with it. You can have it if you want.' As she said the words, she glanced down. One of the small figures was out of kilter with the rest. A woman with black wool hair and a little red painted mouth was hanging suspended from the living-room lampshade. The rest of the group stood around observing the figure, a still, watchful group. Julia leant in for another look but George had turned back to the house and was carefully shutting the two doors and checking the fastening was secure. Only then did he turn around fully to face her.

'Don't tell anyone.'

16

It had been a long day and Sadler felt the urge to stretch his legs. He left his airless terraced cottage, built for one of the waterway workers before rail was deemed to be an improvement on sluggish travel by boat, and walked along the canal. He quickly grew irritated. Tourists were walking four abreast, eating ice-creams bought from a van that should have only been occupying the roadside spot on a temporary basis. When he was nearly run over by a mountain bike, Sadler crossed over the first bridge he came to, leaving the laughter and shouting behind him.

A wooden gate gave way onto a path that climbed steeply up the hill overlooking Bampton. Sadler walked it slowly, allowing the muscles in his legs, unfamiliar with the exercise, to stretch out and enjoy the pressure of the incline. The ripe air of the lower banks of the town yielded to a purer fragrance and a slight chill that made Sadler pull the sleeves of his jumper down over his hands.

He thought about the events of the day. Connie's astonishment that a woman could have murdered her family he was willing to accept but not her assertion that it made no sense. There would be some logic to this case, he was sure. It would be up to him and the team to find it. And he suspected it would be the forensic evidence that would conclude the matter, which meant Connie needed to remember not to let her heart lead her into unnecessary speculation.

Julia and George were an unusual sibling pair but, given their shared past, it perhaps wasn't surprising. What was interesting was that neither had felt inclined to tell them the story about their mother when they were sitting in George's flat. It was the younger of the two, Julia, who had made the revelation to Connie on the street. A reflection, perhaps, of how the story of their mother's disappearance must have been suppressed over the years.

As he reached the brow of the hill, a lone figure was walking towards him wearing a loose, blue T-shirt that billowed out like a parachute behind her. She was checking her mobile. Sadler wondered if she was using the phone's GPS instead of a map. It wouldn't matter here so near the town but it had been the downfall of a number of walkers already this summer, rescued after getting lost in the hills with no signal. As he drew nearer, he could see she was typing a message. She looked up at him briefly as they passed and then did a double take.

'Francis?'

He turned and squinted at her. 'It is.'

The woman had long fair hair with silver threads that glinted in the evening sun. She was small, tinier even than Connie, and like his detective constable wore her diminutive height with an air of confidence. 'You don't remember me? It was a long time ago. I was Miles's girlfriend.'

'Karen?'

She smiled at him now. Pleased he'd remembered. 'That's it. Have I changed that much?'

'Not really.' And it was true. She hadn't substantially altered although it was years since he had thought of Miles, his friend from university in Sheffield. Miles, fuelled by his love of these hills, had often visited Sadler's family to stay in the holidays, occasionally accompanied by Karen.

'Do you hear much of Miles?' She looked embarrassed to be asking. It was like that with former partners. You were interested to know about their welfare but worried that curiosity might be construed as something else. Again Sadler could answer truthfully. 'We lost touch. I heard he was in Canada. I have his address somewhere.'

She made a face. 'He's definitely in Canada. We have mutual friends and he's certainly there. Married now with three kids.'

Sadler wondered if the betrayal still hurt. Karen had been treated badly, and surely, even after all these years, that must rankle.

'What about you? Are you married now?' he asked.

'I was. I got married on the rebound really. It was three years after I broke up with Miles. So not quick or anything, but still, it was on the rebound. It lasted five years so I gave it a decent crack.'

'Do you know what, I haven't thought about Miles for ages.'

This time she did laugh. 'Wish I could say the same. Do you still drink bitter by the halves?'

'If anything, I'm worse now. It's a glass of wine and that's it for me.'

'Well, how about a glass now? Only one as I have to drive back to Sheffield. We could have a catch up and you can tell me what you've been up to in the last two decades. You always were a secretive bugger.' She moved to his side and linked her arm through his. 'And I promise not to talk about Miles.'

17

Before leaving work, Connie logged into her profile to check the details once more of the man she was meeting. Oliver wasn't, at first glance, the most promising of candidates. For a start, his name didn't really belong with the type of man she was looking for. It sounded posh and her experience of privately educated men wasn't a good one. Of course, everyone was naming their sons Oliver now. Back in the early eighties, however, Oliver signified wealth and class. She nearly passed him over when he'd sent her an 'interested' notification but a closer look at his profile proclaimed him as a 'proud Derbyshire lad' so she'd replied in a cheery but cautious way.

He was a teacher in Whaley Bridge High School. It was near enough to make their meeting possible but a decent distance so Connie wouldn't know any of the pupils in the course of her work, as it were. From his photo, Oliver had fair hair cropped in a way that reminded her of Palmer. He looked fit. He was a PE teacher, which might make him okay or he could be a dick. Either way, it was the first date she'd had in a year and she was going to go for it.

She decided to drive so she could make a quick getaway if needed. She spotted him as soon as she entered The Lime Tree. He was sitting at a table, fiddling with the cardboard menu and looking down at his mobile. As she approached, he jumped up and put the phone in his pocket. He seemed unsure what to do and shook her hand.

'Sorry. That wasn't how I intended to greet you. I don't know why I just did that.'

She relaxed into his discomfiture. 'Don't worry. Do you want a drink?' She saw he had a full pint in front of him, probably bought so as not to look out of place.

'Let me get this. What would you like?'

'Just a diet Coke. I'm driving.'

As he headed off to the bar, she took a look around her. She'd last been in here with Scott, Bill's laconic assistant. They'd had a bit of a laugh and he'd warned her off Palmer. Well, he'd been right about that, at least. *Don't think of Palmer*, she cautioned herself. *Don't go there. Stop beating yourself up and give yourself another chance.*

Oliver returned carrying her Coke and seemed to have regained some of his composure.

'So you're a copper? You didn't put it on your profile.'

She'd only revealed this as they were making final arrangements to meet. A last chance for him to back off. 'Would you have clicked on me if I had?'

He shrugged. 'I might have done. My brother's in the Force.'

'Oh no.' She couldn't prevent the words slipping out.

'He's down south. He went to uni in London and it was Oxfordshire who were recruiting. We call him Inspector Morse, which he quite likes.'

Connie relaxed. 'Then I won't know him. Does he like crosswords?'

Oliver grinned. 'He's in uniform but an inspector and a clever so-and-so. He's the ambitious one in our family. He wants to become chief constable.'

67

Again her thoughts turned to Palmer.

'What are you working on?' he asked. His manner was casual. 'Or would you rather not talk about it?'

'I don't suppose it's any big secret. We're looking at the fire out on Cross Farm Lane this morning.'

Oliver grimaced. 'Horrible. It's been all over the news. The thought that you go to bed and then never wake up. I have a colleague who knew Francesca. She taught her for a while. I think she's pretty cut up about it all.'

'From school? Francesca wasn't local, she was from Italy.'

'I think she does a bit of adult teaching during the summer holidays. You see foreign students knocking about that time; they're starting to arrive now. Anyway, she had Francesca staying with her for a bit and I think they kept in touch, of sorts.'

'You mean she saw her recently?'

He looked at her now. Inhibitions gone, talking as one professional to another. 'Fairly recently, I'm sure. She mentioned to me she'd seen the little boy. I think she said she was going to leave flowers outside the house. People have started to leave them as a memorial to the family and she was going to go down too. Why? Do you want to speak to her?'

'Almost certainly.' She looked back at him. 'I'm sorry, this isn't much of a date, is it?'

'Oh, I don't know. I was worried that we wouldn't find anything to talk about. Your eyes lit up when I mentioned Jenny, that's my colleague. Do you want me to call her now?'

She looked at her watch. 'I don't think so. I've suddenly had an urge for a drink, though. How about I buy a shot of vodka to go in my Coke and I'll call Jenny tomorrow morning?'

He grinned again. 'Sounds like a plan.'

Connie went over to the bar and ordered her drink. As she took the shot back to her seat, she looked in surprise as Sadler walked in, more casually dressed than usual. In front of him was a petite woman, no taller than her. She too looked like she was dressed for walking, with a fleece wrapped around her waist. Her eyes flickered over Connie and dismissed her.

Connie, who'd made an effort with her clothes for the first time in months, fumed. 'Hi.'

Sadler looked taken aback. His companion stood next to him frowning. 'Connie,' he acknowledged.

He stared at her, taking in her make-up and knee-length skirt and wedge heels. 'This is Karen,' he said finally. 'A friend from long ago I've unexpectedly met.'

Something in the description irritated the woman, and Connie, good at reading people's faces, wondered what it was. Perhaps she was an ex-girlfriend.

'Nice. I'm meeting a friend too.' She nodded over to Oliver who was now getting stuck into his pint.

Sadler looked across at him. 'We won't disturb you.'

She returned to her seat and tipped the shot of vodka into her Coke. 'I've just seen my boss.'

'Really? Do you want to go somewhere else? I wouldn't fancy bumping into my head of department on a night out.'

'No, don't worry. It'll be fine.'

She glanced across at Sadler and his friend. Karen was standing next to him, her arms folded. She looked bad-tempered and Connie thought of Peter Winson. Why would you choose to be with someone miserable? Sadler was ordering drinks from the bar, not looking over at them. When he had finished paying, he led his friend to the other side of the pub, out of her sightline. Connie picked up her glass and turned her attention back to Oliver.

'Tell me again what your colleague Jenny said about Francesca.'

18

Before going to bed, Julia bolted the front door and gave it a sharp tug to check it held. She walked away but then returned to the door and repeated the action. She could hear Bosco moving about upstairs making himself comfortable for the night. Three times around the bed. She had initiated her own routine, walking around her downstairs rooms, checking the window fastenings. Finally, if not satisfied but aware there was little else she could do, she went upstairs and ran a bath. As the water splashed into the tub, she stared into the swirling eddy for a moment then went to the spare room where her laptop sat.

She found the forum in her bookmarks and her eyes skimmed over the new, heart-breaking, pleas for help. She clicked to add a new post and in the subject line she carefully typed in *Looking for Elizabeth Winson. Now urgent.* In the main body of the post she struggled to find the right words. She didn't want the oddbods and losers who lurked in the shadows to come out but she did want to get her message across.

Mum. If you're reading this, we need you more than ever. Wherever you are, we still miss you. Please get in touch. Love, Julia.

Before she could regret it, she pressed send and then shut down her laptop. It would take half an hour or so until the post was approved by the moderator. Then the comments would start. The salacious, the kind, the concerned, the investigative. She would see them all when she next logged in. Behind them all, though, someone who knew what had happened to her mother might also read it. For the times Julia had posted a request for information, she could see by the hits on the post there were plenty of people who read her appeal but hadn't commented. Casual observers perhaps but behind this, just maybe, someone watching, observing and holding their breath.

She heard her phone ring and dashed to the bedroom to answer it. She expected George, but instead it was Maureen breathlessly apologising for disturbing her.

'There's something I forgot to mention when I saw you earlier. It completely slipped my mind with everything we had to discuss. That group of Scouts you took down into the cave this morning?'

'What about them?'

'Did you have any trouble with one of the young lads?'

Julia thought back. 'I remember one had a broken arm and I had to steady him a few times on the stairs. Why? Is he okay?'

'I don't think it's him. They all went home today from the campsite and one of the boys' fathers has called. He didn't mention anything about a broken arm, though.'

Julia moved to the bathroom and turned off the taps. 'What's the problem?'

'He says his son's distressed. Something about hearing noises in the cave. Whispers he thought it was. You weren't adding a bit of the supernatural to your talk to the kids, were you? I know you like that sort of thing.'

'You mean ghost stories.' Julia was confused. 'What do you

72

take me for? Of course I'm not going to try to frighten the kids while I'm down there. What's the guy's problem?'

'I'm really sorry about this, Julia. I never thought in a million years you'd do that. It's just with your other job . . .'

'I don't combine the two.'

Maureen sounded near to tears again. 'I'm so sorry. I feel awful now what with everything's that happened. It's just the dad was really angry and he sort of made me promise I'd talk to you.'

I've just lost nearly all my family, thought Julia. She wanted to get off the phone. 'I never said anything, although I think I do remember a boy saying he'd heard some noises. It was probably the wind echoing around the cave.'

Maureen sighed. 'I'll call his dad back in the morning. You know what some parents are like. It's all about nothing, isn't it?' She hesitated. 'Will you be able to sleep?'

Julia looked at the bath full of soapy water and thought of the diazepam in her washbag, the remnant from a trip to Spain when she'd been fearful of the flight.

'I doubt it but I'm going to try.'

19

Matthews was stuck in her car on the M56 just outside the entrance to Manchester airport. Rush hour, combined with holiday travellers, meant a snake of traffic that choked out fumes into the summer air. She usually enjoyed visiting the place; it had a satisfyingly provincial feel to it that made her proud. She'd once had the misfortune to fly from London's Heathrow. Never again. She'd felt like a lost infant and had been awed at the prices in the shops. Here she could pick up a sarong from Monsoon, a bottle of perfume and a new set of headphones and still get change from fifty quid. The delights of Terminal 2 weren't going to be hers today, though.

Half an hour later she was inside and waiting for the flight from Rome. Mr and Mrs Marchesi had travelled from their house in the small town of Collodi the night before, staying with a relative who had dropped them off at the airport at 3 a.m. Worried about his aunt and uncle, he had texted Matthews to say they were safely deposited his side and would she let him know they had arrived in Manchester?

They were initially hard to spot. Matthews had a vision of a little old Italian couple, the man perhaps supporting his wife. It was a testament to how foolish it was to make assumptions because Mr and Mrs Marchesi walked straight past her. She was tall and thin with iron-grey hair pulled back into a bun. Her cream silk shirt was tucked into her pale yellow jeans. Her husband was wearing a light grey suit, double-breasted and immaculately cut. They spotted her first, pointing at their names written on the sign she held. 'You're Inspector Matthews.'

She blushed. 'Sergeant.'

He held out his hand, controlled, in charge. She shook it, still feeling foolish, and sent up a silent prayer of thanks to her partner, Ruth, who had hoovered out the car recently.

The drive towards Bampton was slow and undertaken in silence. Even the majesty of the Peak District failed to draw any comment from the couple. Stefano Marchesi was a retired lawyer and, while Matthews had steeled herself for questions and heartache, the silence was more disturbing. She couldn't understand why they weren't asking her anything. She could feel sweat beginning to trickle down her back from the stress of it all. She took them straight to the hotel and checked them in, then called Sadler to say they had arrived.

'I'll come to the hotel. Where are they?'

'The Wilton.'

There was a short silence as he digested this. 'Not my favourite place. Last time I was there, I was seeing a dead body.'

'Do you want me to take them somewhere else?'

'No, don't worry. I'll be there in fifteen minutes.'

The couple left the luggage untouched in their room and went into the lounge for coffee. In the ornate and over-styled room they were more at ease and Mr Marchesi excused himself to go out for a cigarette.

Maria Marchesi, by far the worse English speaker, leant forward. 'He stopped and now started again. Very stressed.'

'I understand.' Stressed was an odd word, thought Matthews. Why not devastated or grieving? Or numb. Perhaps these words weren't in Maria's vocabulary, but she had hit the nail on the head. The pair of them appeared to be stressed.

Sadler came in, following Stefano Marchesi, introductions already made. They sat down in front of the pot of coffee and Sadler was keen to get down to business. 'I'm sorry for what has happened. I can't even begin to imagine how you feel. I have two nephews, older than Charlie, but I remember them at that age. I can only guess at your sense of loss.'

'I only see him once.'

Stefano waved at his wife not to talk and she lapsed into silence. Sadler was picking his words with care.

'I believe one of my colleagues in the Collodi police visited you to talk about what has happened. Is that correct?'

Stefano nodded. 'I'm acquainted with the older generation of police well through my former occupation. An officer from our *questura*, the local station, who knows all the family, visited us and told us the news.'

'You know Francesca and the rest of the family died in a fire.'

'Yes. It was an accident?' He sounded hopeful, an odd note, and Matthews looked across to Sadler to see if he had spotted it. The flicker in his eyes suggested he had.

'I'm afraid to say we believe the fire to have been suspicious.'

Neither Stefano nor Maria touched each other but the man looked like he wanted to comfort his wife. A couple of the old-fashioned kind, not inclined to show each other affection in public. Matthews again looked at Sadler.

'Did they seem happy? Francesca and her husband.'

'I only see them one time,' repeated Maria.

'And they were happy?'

'I fly over after Charlie born. She didn't want me here. So

76

from then I just send presents. I have other grandchildren in Collodi who need me.'

'You didn't think Francesca wanted you here? Why was that?'

Maria drew herself up. 'Francesca a girl of many secrets, wanted to get away from Italy, from us. So I stay three days and go.'

Sadler and Matthews both looked to Stefano for confirmation. 'I never saw my grandson and now I never will.'

'Did you go to the wedding?' asked Matthews. They both shook their head.

'So you can't tell us if they were happy?' she asked, desperate for a drip of information.

Maria looked at them with sad dark eyes. 'Francesca never happy.'

Sadler took a breath. 'Based on current evidence, we think it's possible Francesca may have been responsible for the killings.' He slowed down his words, to make sure both knew the import of what he was saying. 'We think Francesca may have killed her family.'

He stopped and looked at the pair, gauging their reactions. Matthews found she was holding her breath. The couple looked stunned and yet resigned. What was going on here?

'Can you think of a reason why?' she asked.

Now Stefano reached out and grabbed his wife's arm as silent tears fell down her cheeks. 'With Francesca, there was never a reason.'

They left them there, mourning over cooling coffee. Walking to the car, Matthews remarked, 'They have no trouble believing their daughter is responsible for the slaughter, do they?'

Sadler slid into the car seat. 'No, they don't.'

20

Julia went to Waitrose and picked the items she knew Holly
liked. Brown mackerel pâté and slivers of anchovies from the
deli counter. From the organics aisle she selected small seaweed
crackers and a bottle of elderflower pressé. None of the items
she would have chosen herself, let alone eaten. Holly, however,
relied on these delicacies to make her day more bearable, tiny
morsels to ease the monotony of her existence. Julia paid for
the groceries on her card, shocked at how much four items
could total. She put them in her rucksack, praying the crackers
wouldn't get crushed, and hopped onto her bicycle.

The ride to Holly's house was short. She lived in one of
the bungalows that ringed a cul-de-sac behind the town's small
swimming pool. The street was comfortable, well maintained
and with an air of affluence. It was still a jarring choice for the
elegant Holly. She deserved to be in a glossy apartment like the
one George lived in; indeed the flat had once belonged to them
both. When the break had come, however, Holly had been relieved at the move from a residence that even the presence of a
lift failed to mask was no longer suitable for her needs.

Julia rapped on the glass door and waited for the whirring
in the distance to get nearer. The electric chair was the newest
model, thin and lightweight, that never managed to over-
shadow the stylish woman sitting in it. Holly was wearing
a summer dress that fell below the knees of her thin legs.

When she had been well, she had been a solid woman who had dressed artfully to hide her large hips. She had lost a vast amount of weight and some of her spirit. Holly reached up to give her former sister-in-law a hug and Julia had to stifle the urge to weep into her bony shoulders. She gently took the package from Julia's hands and inspected the contents.

'Perfect. Never underestimate the benefit of decent food when you're feeling terrible. That and a restorative hot-water bottle. Just a shame we can't have gin to go with the meal. Well, I can't at least as it gives me terrible indigestion. It'll have to be elderflower instead. Do you want anything?'

'I daren't.'

Holly, familiar with tragedy, understood. 'Come into the garden.'

The table laid for two suggested Holly had been awaiting her arrival and Julia felt a pang at the lackadaisical way she had wandered around the supermarket trying to focus.

'How's George coping?'

Julia wasn't deceived by the woman's casual tone. 'Too well.'

Holly looked troubled. 'What a bloody mess. I never met Francesca or Charlie, you know. We'd split by the time she came along. It's impossible to imagine. I am worried about George, though.'

'Everyone's asking after George.'

Holly carefully poured out the fizzing elderflower, holding the bottle with two hands. Julia knew better than to offer to help and instead picked up a napkin and mopped some of the liquid that had slopped over the glass.

'Don't take it personally,' said Holly. 'It's the reserved amongst us who take up most of our worry. George is one of those people. I'm not. You're not. We're copers.'

'Don't you get sick of coping, though?'

'Of course I do.' It was the harshest Julia had ever heard her. 'I'm sorry.'

'No. It's me who's sorry. How *are* you, actually?'

Julia drew a breath. 'I feel frozen. It's like a sheet of glass is separating me from the rest of the world. I'm trying to feel emotion but there's nothing there.'

Holly looked across her immaculately kept lawn. 'That's what shock does to you. Oh, I know you and George went through the trauma with your mother, but it wasn't like this. You never had a death, did you? The grief you feel about Elizabeth is being squeezed out of you like a grapefruit, drip by drip. This is tragedy on a different scale.'

'Did George ever talk to you about Mum?'

'Only the bare bones of what happened. I wasn't married to him long enough to get even slightly under that surface.'

Julia looked at Holly's calm face and couldn't bring herself to tell her about the police's suspicions. That they had been killed. That it wasn't a tragic accident. Was this to be her legacy? A dulling sense of shame.

'Police are still investigating the incident.'

Holly looked up sharply. 'Your father was a very careful man. The one time he came around our apartment, I had lit a candle in the windowsill. He stood next to it the whole time, anxiously watching it. I wanted to tell him to sit down. We didn't even have curtains. What could have happened?'

Julia rubbed her throbbing temples. 'He could never take it easy.'

'Take it easy? He was a bag of neuroses. I feel awful saying this now he's dead and I know you and George loved him. But he was adept at making George feel wretched. I sometimes think he enjoyed it.'

Julia took a gulp of her drink. 'Look, it's not the time—'

'Do you remember those letters? Did you ever get sent any? Long rambling instructions on how disappointed he was in something George had done. How he was unfit to take over the business.'

'I never had those.'

'We used to dread seeing the handwriting on the envelope on the mat. Thank God it was the days before email. Although, I suppose George was getting them too now.'

The last correspondence Julia had received from her father had been a question about her job. Not the concerned father query but a cold two-liner asking about her finances. Julia had responded that her money situation was no worse than usual, which was all she really needed to say. She'd never stopped to wonder if George was getting the same correspondence.

'Do you ever see him?' she asked Holly. 'George, I mean. Do you ever speak?'

It was a time for confidences, although Holly looked surprised. 'Of course not. Given how it ended, how could I?'

'The split seemed amicable enough at the time.'

'That's not what I mean, Julia, and you know it.' She spread a thin sliver of anchovies across one of the crackers. 'He's not allowed to come near me and, I'll give him this, he's left me alone this time. Found someone else to warm his bed for him and I don't care who.' Dark clouds began to gather overhead as Holly's face crumpled.

21

Jenny Moorhouse agreed to take the afternoon off school. An accommodating head, once she'd heard about what the inquiry was in connection with, had suggested covering her classes for a few hours. News of the tragedy had spread through the town and people were responding with shock and sympathy. Connie had been told from one of the officers at the house that a sea of flowers was forming around the tree at the front of the property.

An added benefit, not that she would have mentioned this to Matthews who was sitting in the passenger seat checking her phone, was that by interviewing the teacher away from her work environment she didn't run the risk of bumping into Oliver so soon after their night out. In the end it hadn't turned out too bad. They had managed to make conversation of sorts, which was no mean feat for her, considering she did very little else outside work. She was, however, pretty sure deep down he wasn't really for her.

Matthews put her phone back into her pocket. 'I've been checking the news sites. They've reported the fire but it's all fairly subdued. They're more interested in that actor who's taken out an injunction so they can't expose his night of infidelity.'

'I'm not surprised. The press are always more interested in stories that directly impact on them. I dated a journalist briefly. He said the same.'

'But a child has died. Doesn't anyone care?'

'Once they find out the mother's responsible, the press will perk up. That could be the start of our troubles. What were Francesca's parents like?'

'Not as I expected. Elegant, well-off, disengaged. I'm not sure what I anticipated but these two weren't it.'

'Grief produces strange reactions. They must be numb from the news. I bet they can't take it in.'

'They're numb, certainly, but I wouldn't be so sure about them not digesting the crime. They didn't seem very shocked about Francesca. I'd expected denials and disbelief and instead I got resigned acceptance.'

'Did Sadler think that too?'

Matthews turned to Connie. 'You don't trust my version of events? I'm telling you that although they were upset by the news we gave them, they weren't shocked or outraged. They're accepting our explanation without many questions. Do you want to check my opinion with Sadler?'

'Keep your hair on. I was just checking if the boss thought the same, that's all.' Connie pulled the car over and looked at the satnav. 'That's the problem with the maps around here. They want to send me down a dirt track. Let me just reset it.' She fiddled around with the settings until she found a better route. 'I don't think any parent could just sit there and accept the news that their daughter had just killed her husband and child. They're probably shocked beyond words.'

'I don't think so, Connie. There's something extremely off about the Marchesis' attitude towards Francesca.'

Connie sighed and turned the car around towards the main road. 'Let's see what the witness has to say. Parental relationships don't always give a good indication of a person's guilt or innocence.'

Matthews sat back in her seat. 'She really did keep herself to herself, you know. Door-to-doors have revealed very little about the family and, if anything, more about Peter than his wife. He was quite well known as a few neighbours had picked up antiques and furniture from his auction house over the years. Even Ruth knew of him.'

'Julia speaks well of her stepmother,' commented Connie. 'That must count for something given what she's accused of.'

'Not much put against everything else. Why didn't Francesca have many friends?'

'I don't have many.' *Any*, thought Connie.

Matthews shot her a sympathetic glance. 'This job is a nightmare when you're not in a stable relationship.'

'You do meet lots of solitary people in jobs like this. The ambitious and the driven. Like Palmer, for example. People who don't have any hobbies except their work.'

'Those happily married with kids, though? They're not usually the ones who are isolated. It's buggy city in Bampton some mornings. Mothers talking loudly about their children and breastfeeding over their lattes.'

Connie coughed with laughter. 'Oi! You're more right-on than that. Women are allowed to get their breasts out in public, you know.'

'That's what Ruth says. I'm just old-fashioned. Do you remember the mother who killed her kids because they were both disabled and she snapped because of the strain of looking after them? Do you think that could be it?'

Connie kept her eyes on the road. 'We've had the medical

records. Charlie broke his arm in a fall last year but the hospital didn't note it as suspicious. Other than that, all the doctor's surgery has reported are the usual vaccination appointments and check-ups for coughs, colds and rashes.'

'Then why did she do it?'

'If she did do it.'

Matthews jabbed Connie in the leg with her pen. 'Don't start that again. You'll wind up the boss and I can't help you once he's got a bee in his bonnet. You know full well what the evidence is pointing towards. We're going through the motions because we want to find out "why" not "if".'

'Are we going to mention to Jenny Moorhouse that her friend is prime suspect in the case?'

'Let's see if she asks. I'd prefer it if we limited questions to the suspicious fire and the relationship.'

'Fine by me.' Connie swung the car into the drive of the teacher's house and the front door opened immediately. She'd clearly been awaiting their arrival and, in the rush to talk to them, would have given them all the information she knew out on the front lawn. Matthews took charge of the nervous woman and steered her into the sitting room.

'It's just as well I'm not in school this afternoon. I've no idea how I'd cope with year eleven English.'

The living room was one of a bookish woman. Two walls were given over to shelves stacked high with paperbacks and magazines along with mementos from trips abroad. Sadler would have been itching to look at the shelves if he'd been here, thought Connie, and wished it was he who was alongside her rather than the kind Matthews. Sadler had the insight into people she needed. Connie was beginning to feel dislocated from the tragedy because nothing was making sense. She walked over to the shelves herself and looked at the row of orange D. H. Lawrence paperbacks.

'Did you know Francesca well?' she asked.

'I don't think anyone will have known Francesca intimately,' Jenny replied. 'She was a very private person. On the surface she was very charming and calm. Underneath, I couldn't tell you. Despite the fact she stayed in my house, I don't think I ever got to know her properly.'

'She came over as an exchange student, is that right?' asked Matthews, clearly keen to take the lead in the interview. Connie raised her eyebrows and sat down.

'That's right. I'm an English teacher and, as I'm single, the summer holidays can be a bit of a stretch for me, so I teach language classes in the college to foreign students. It's a bit of a laugh, actually. I only do adults so it makes a change from the high school grind.'

'You don't have any holidays at all?'

'Of course. I take two weeks, one after school has finished and one before it starts again. Then a month teaching in the middle.'

'So you met Francesca on one of these month courses.'

'It was an intensive class I was taking. Francesca's written English was better than her spoken. It's pretty common in students who have learnt the language abroad without any opportunity to practise speaking English.'

'How old was she when you met her?'

'About thirty, I think. She'd worked in a lawyer's office somewhere in her home town but she didn't really like it and wanted to perfect her English and travel a bit.'

'She didn't mention her plans then. Whether she intended to stay on in England?'

'I think she was looking for a job here almost straight away. After the class finished in August she went to work at Winson's auctioneers. She needed somewhere to stay so she rented a room here for a little while. Then, one day, she told me she was moving out and I automatically assumed that she'd found a place to rent. She never mentioned she was getting married. I heard about it from a friend. She went from here to the house in Cross Farm Lane and she married Peter Winson.'

'You heard? You didn't even get an invite to the wedding?' asked Connie. 'Didn't you think this was odd?'

'Of course I did. I tried to phone a couple of times but she didn't usually answer. The two occasions I did track her down she wasn't very forthcoming.'

'Oliver thought you'd met Charlie.'

'I never met the little boy properly but I did see them one day in Bampton. I think it was about a year ago. Charlie was having a bit of a tantrum and the man with her, he must have been her husband, looked furious. He was shouting "Be quiet" at the boy who was raging and, although I'm not a parent, I've taught enough kids to know bellowing at them makes them even worse.'

'How was Francesca when you saw her?'

'She had this curious look on her face. She ignored her husband and lifted the howling little boy up and put him into the car seat. I just put it down as a minor domestic drama. Kids aren't easy to control.'

'Did you get the impression that Francesca was in any way fearful of her husband?' asked Connie.

Matthews shot her a look. 'We're trying to make sense of the events leading up to the fire and one of the aspects we're investigating is the state of her marriage.'

'I can't tell you anything about that.' Jenny looked like she was making up her mind whether to speak. 'All I can say is Francesca was very, very, secretive and when someone is like that, my first question is, what have they got to hide?'

22

Julia tidied away the remains of their lunch and left Holly dozing under a tree, exhausted from their conversation. The sun
was beating down on her head as she closed the front door
and waited on the pavement outside the bungalow. She looked
down the cul-de-sac and saw with a start that you could see the
row of buildings where George's apartment was. She counted
along the rooftops. The estate agent, then the newly opened
cheese shop and the third building must be the apartment
block. She wondered if Holly could see it from the back garden
and, if so, how she felt about having her former home looming
over her sightline.

Pat arrived at Holly's house looking harassed and drove Julia
quickly to Cross Farm Lane. The road was still sealed off to
traffic but the restricted area had been reduced to her father's
home and the two houses either side. As they drew up to the
cordon, some people were huddled to one side, one of whom
was staring through a pair of binoculars.

'Press?'

'Would you believe they're tourists.' Pat's face was set. 'Don't
ask me. All I can say is they must enjoy very safe lives if they think
an ideal day out is to gawk at other people's tragedies. Me, I like to
watch *Call the Midwife* when I want to relax.'

Julia disregarded the people and instead focused her eyes on
the home where she'd spent her teenage years. It was a desperate

sight. Never a lovely house, it still had maintained a 1980s solidity with its straight lines and orange brickwork. Now one side of it was a ravaged wreck suitable only for demolition. The fire had not only obliterated the wooden windows but had burst through the side of the roof. The gaping hole was ringed with scorched soot that cascaded down the brick walls.

'We can't go inside the building, I'm afraid. The fire investigators and the forensic team are still working on the area. I don't even think any of the detective team have been inside yet.'

'Can I get out, though?'

'Of course you can, love.'

'There's no . . .'

'Your family's remains have been taken to the mortuary and the people working inside are very respectful of what's happened there.'

Julia stumbled out of the car and collapsed onto the wall of the house opposite. She watched as numerous people searched through the ruins dressed in overalls, their faces covered with masks.

'George should be seeing this too.'

'I did try, love. I leant on his bell for a good five minutes when he didn't answer his phone. I can't do much else than that. I left a message to say we were coming here today.'

'He often doesn't pick up his messages. In fact, he doesn't usually answer his phone. If I want to get hold of him, I have to hope I'll find him home.'

'That must make staying in touch difficult. Don't worry, it takes all sorts and I can still bring him over if he wants to come. He just needs to call.'

'I wouldn't bargain on him getting in touch.'

Pat shrugged and put on a pair of sunglasses. 'Not everyone would want to see this. He'll cope in his own way. Have you seen enough?'

They moved away from the house, the smell of charcoal still in their nostrils. 'When will you have more details for me? About what happened, I mean. We were told so little yesterday.'

'I don't know, and that's the honest truth. Inspector Sadler's not going to tell you anything until he's surer about what he's dealing with. It wouldn't be fair on you getting conflicting information.'

'They said the fire was of suspicious origin, though. Are they looking for someone else?'

Pat hesitated. 'Listen. Why don't I ask Sadler if he can give you an update today? I'm sure he'll be fine about it.'

Julia could feel the well of desperation bubble up inside her. 'Can you do that now?'

While Pat was making the call, Julia moved closer to the house. She was touched to see a cloak of flowers was spreading along the pavement from one of the large oak trees, forming a riot of yellow, pinks and greens. A film of tears covered her eyes as she watched a woman holding hands with two young children give a small bunch of freesias and a brown teddy bear to a uniformed officer. The policewoman took them over to the group and placed the items carefully on the ground.

Pat was at her side. 'Do you want to go and look at the flowers? I've spoken to Inspector Sadler and he'll see you tomorrow morning. Why don't you read some of the lovely messages people have left?'

Aware of Pat subtly propelling her towards the blooms, Julia wiped the smudge of tears along the bottom of her eyes with her thumbnail. Closer now, she could see that there were about thirty or so bouquets. Some tied up with cellophane, others looking like they'd been picked fresh from the garden.

The constable walked towards them and nodded at Pat. 'There's been a steady stream coming all day. Lots of people with kids. There's talk of Charlie's class coming down later if you'd like to stay for that.'

Julia shook her head. 'I don't think I could cope.'

The policewoman looked at her in sympathy. 'No, I'm sure not. They started early. I was here at six this morning and someone had already left a bouquet. Yellow roses. A huge bunch too.'

Yellow roses. Frightful flowers, and Julia's stomach gave a lurch. 'Who left them?'

'I didn't see. They just placed them at the cordon and I moved them to the tree. I thought there'd be bound to be more and here's a good place to leave them.'

'The yellow roses. Can I see them?'

The policewoman frowned. 'They're right at the back.'

'I'd still like to see them.' Julia's voice felt strained and she saw the constable shoot Pat a warning look.

'I'll just get them.'

The woman gingerly stepped between the blooms and rifled at the base of the tree trunk. She stepped back and came towards Julia holding a large bunch of flowers. Julia took them off her and looked down. They were shop bought, too uniform in their perfection to have come from someone's garden. Care had been taken, however, over the thick white ribbon that had been tied around the thorny stems. A card lay nestled in the leaves. Julia picked it up and read the short message.

23

Friday, 15 January 1982

'Another do-gooder has left more flowers.' George poured Rice Krispies into a bowl and added cream from the top of the milk.

Julia looked at the bouquet thrown onto the Formica table and frowned. 'We can't keep putting them in the bin. Can't I have them in my bedroom this time?'

George paused with his spoon halfway towards his mouth, milk spilling down his jumper.

'What do you want to do that for? Pretending you have a boyfriend?'

Julia felt her cheeks flame red and, in retaliation, shouted, 'What are you eating cereal at night for anyway? You're supposed to have it for breakfast.'

'Oh *are* you.' She flinched from his sarcasm. 'And who, exactly, is going to tell us any different? Dad? I don't see him here. So, if I want to have cereal for my dinner, that's what I'm going to eat.'

Julia picked up the flowers. 'There's a note here.' She opened the envelope and read it. 'Usual sort of message.'

'I thought they'd stopped coming. One of the neighbours is obviously having a sentimental moment. Chuck them in the bin.'

'I suppose.' She turned over the envelope and gaped. 'It's addressed to me.'

'What is?'

'The note. The flowers are for me.'

George snatched the envelope out of her hand and looked at the name on the front. 'So what. You, me, Dad. What does it matter who the note's for?'

'You mean there have been others just to me?'

'I don't know.' The fury erupted from within. He was shouting at her. 'I'm sick of these people sending us stuff. At least when they delivered food at the beginning it was useful. Now it's just flowers and cards.'

'But you said we hadn't had flowers for a while. So why is it starting again?'

'I don't know.' He threw his bowl into the sink, the cereal swimming in the milk. 'You've put me off my dinner.'

Julia touched one of the buttery yellow petals and looked again at the envelope. It was addressed only to her. Pocketing the card, she pulled one of the stems from the bunch and put the rest in the bin for her father to see when he returned home. She felt sure the act would meet with his approval. What would not would be the pressing of the stem between the pages of her school atlas. She sat on top of the book on her bed to squash the bud flat, all the time thinking of the card in her trouser pocket.

24

Superintendent Llewellyn was in a thoughtful mood as he walked back from the press conference. Sadler had rolled up his shirtsleeves underneath the jacket he had to wear in order to meet the journalists but still felt hot and sticky. He'd stupidly forgotten to turn off his phone and it had vibrated in his pocket throughout the session. Only the press officer had noticed and she'd hissed at him afterwards to make sure it was off in future. Llewellyn looked cool in full uniform.

'There was a stirring of interest when we said the blaze was suspicious but most of the journalists there were fairly laid-back. Do you think it was the heat?' asked Llewellyn.

'The local one, I think his name's Joe Murray, was attentive but he was more keen to know if there's a murderer on the loose. It's quite telling none of the neighbours have talked, although it's possible one of them saw the body through the window.'

Llewellyn nodded. 'It's quite an exclusive area, Cross Farm Lane. There was a spate of burglaries a couple of years ago. If I remember rightly the residents were very proactive. There was even talk of them clubbing together to get their own private security guard but in the end they all updated their house alarms.'

'It's only a matter of time until the story comes out. Someone will talk. I've got another briefing with the fire investigator later today but, first, I want to hear what Bill's autopsy reports say.'

Now Llewellyn smiled. 'You're not sending Connie to liaise

with Bill? I thought they were old friends.'

'Connie's gone to speak to a Lincolnshire colleague who was involved in the investigation into Elizabeth Winson's disappearance.'

'That'll keep her out of trouble.'

'I'm not so sure about that. She's showing more interest in the disappearance of Peter's first wife than I'd like.'

Llewellyn stopped in the corridor and leant back against the wall as three uniformed officers rushed past them. 'You think there's a connection? You know what I feel about old cases. They muddy the current investigations that we're working on.'

'The case was never solved but I share your concern.' Sadler kept his tone mild. 'I've suggested she speak to one of the officers who worked on the case. However, she's under strict instructions to ensure any questioning is related to our current investigation. We're going to need to look at the past even if it's to discount it. A woman doesn't just kill her family.'

'You're sure that's the sequence of events?'

'The fire investigator was pretty certain but I want to see what Bill has to say. Which is why I'd prefer it was me rather than Connie who saw him.'

'Are you saying she's not up to a multiple murder enquiry after the battering she took last year?'

'It's not that. She can't believe a woman would kill her family. She says it isn't the way these things usually occur. It's usually the male family member who is the perpetrator.'

'Well, she's got a point, hasn't she?'

'Which is why I want to speak to Bill.'

*

There were rumours that the large warren of Portakabins that made up the mortuary in Bampton hospital was soon to be upgraded to a building made of bricks and mortar. If so, Sadler could see no evidence of any changes since he'd last visited the place. Scott, Bill's long-haired assistant, was busy on the computer but looked up when Sadler entered.

'Connie not coming?'

'You're the second person to say that to me today. I'm beginning to feel not wanted.'

Scott nodded towards the next Portakabin. 'It's probably just as well. He's not finished yet. He came out about twenty minutes ago and said he thought he'd be another half an hour or so. Do you want to wait here? You could go inside, if you want.'

'Who's assisting him?'

'Mary. I did offer but she wanted to do it.'

'Is she new?'

Scott got up and switched on the kettle. '-ish. She's been here nearly a year. Proper keen she is. She's in medical school part-time. She wants to be a pathologist like Bill.'

'So they get on.'

Scott laughed. 'I wouldn't say that. I think she's a bit enthusiastic for Bill's liking. He prefers them a bit more sarky. Like your Connie.'

Sadler bit back the retort that she was hardly 'his'. But Scott was looking down at the computer. 'Is she all right? Connie, I mean.'

'She's fine.'

Scott picked at pieces of fluff between his keyboard keys. 'I meant to visit her in hospital but wasn't sure if she'd want visitors. Then I heard she'd been discharged so I sent her a text but she never replied.'

'You could try again. She's a bit thin on the ground for friends, especially now Palmer's transferring.'

Scott looked up. 'Palmer's leaving?'

'He's put in for a transfer.' Well, it was hardly a secret. He'd made sure the person who needed to know first had been informed. Connie, he suspected though, wasn't taking it very well. 'Why don't you give her another call?'

Bill came out in his scrubs, glanced briefly at Sadler and handed a folder to Scott.

'Connie not coming?'

Scott smirked into his computer screen as Sadler followed Bill into his office.

'Bring us both a brew through, Scott, would you?' Bill shouted his request at a volume, Sadler thought, capable of waking the dead. He noticed the pathologist looked a bit green.

'Are you okay?'

'Ever seen a burns victim, Sadler?'

'Yes, although never a child.' Sadler got up and took over from Scott, bringing an orange-coloured tea in for Bill and a paler one for himself.

'Just how I like it.' For a moment Sadler thought he saw tears in the pathologist's eyes. Bill coughed and picked up a report.

'Two of the victims died from severe blows to the head and body. It would be the head injuries that would have killed them. Severe skull fractures, multiple blunt injuries.'

'And the gender of these two victims?'

Bill looked up, his face grim. 'Male. One adult and one child. I've already had their dental records and they match those of Peter and Charlie Winson.'

'And the third victim?'

Bill sighed. 'The cause of death, from a medical perspective, is slightly harder to ascertain. I have one female, suffering from slight burns and some signs of smoke inhalation with marks around her neck consistent with the imprints left by a belt.'

'A belt? Why didn't that disintegrate in the blaze?'

'You'll have to ask the fire investigator that. The body had some burns but not as much as I'd expect. The fire can't have reached her.'

'Cause of death?'

'I can make a preliminary finding of strangulation due to the evidence of injury to the larynx but I've also sent off the bloods with an urgent request and I'll hopefully get them back later this week. They'll be able to confirm strangulation if the CO_2 levels are high.'

'There was no evidence of any defensive injuries?'

Bill looked up from the file. 'None I could see. One thing, though. She was around two and a half months pregnant. I'm guessing around ten weeks; a little soon for me to tell gender, although by the development I think it was a girl.'

'Ten weeks?'

'Around that. It's early stages but would most certainly have been indicated in a home pregnancy test.'

'Do you think it's significant?'

'Good God, Sadler. I don't know. That's your job, isn't it?'

'I suppose what I'm asking is if there's anything unusual in the pregnancy that might have influenced Francesca's state of mind.'

'Ah.' Bill leant back in his chair. 'I see what you mean. It looks like a perfectly normal early stage pregnancy to me.'

A knock on the door and a young woman walked in. 'Mary,

come in and meet Detective Inspector Sadler. It's rare that he turns up these days. We usually get to see the irrepressible Connie, who brightens up the day for both Scott and me, especially Scott.'

Bill winked at Sadler who stood up to shake the woman's hand. Mary had a raw, freckled face framed by dark blonde hair pulled back into a long thick plait that hung over her left shoulder. She took his hand. 'I've heard all about Connie.'

There was an archness in her tone that Sadler didn't like.

'What have you heard?' His tone was too tart and she recoiled.

'Nothing,' she replied and scuttled out. Bill looked after her in amusement. 'You scaring my personnel?'

'So,' Sadler said as he sat back down, 'the most likely scenario, pending confirmation of the blood tests, is the two male victims were first bludgeoned to death by the female who then died from asphyxiation due to strangulation, which also killed her unborn child.'

Bill continued to look steadily at Sadler. 'That would be the most likely scenario, but all the bloods will confirm, if it's the case, is that the victim died from asphyxiation. I won't be able to rule out murder given the state of the body.'

'But there were no defensive wounds?'

'As I said, none I could find.'

'So we're probably looking at a multiple murder. The fire investigator's initial conclusions back this up too. So, Connie will have been proved wrong.'

'Why, what does Connie say?'

'She says it doesn't make much sense.'

Finally, Bill dropped his gaze. 'Connie, as usual, is right.'

25

Connie's spirits soared as she left Bampton. She was a Derbyshire girl and loved all the seasons in the Peaks. But the influx of summer tourists clogged the roads and the huddles of walking groups made her feel guilty because, although she was stick thin, it was more down to genetics than an actual attempt to keep her body in shape. The news about Palmer's possible transfer had also given her more of a jolt than she'd let on. It was decent enough of Sadler to tell her before she heard from someone else. She very much doubted Palmer would have let her know. He'd given her a wide berth since the single night they'd slept together last year.

She took one of the pool cars and drove out of Bampton, the route taking her past the ruins of the Winson house. The road was still closed but she made a detour along a tiny side road, praying she wouldn't meet any tractors coming the other way. The drive to Lincolnshire took an age. Getting up and down England never caused any problem but, if you wanted to travel from west to east, it was a case of following in the slipstream of huge lorries or chugging farm vehicles. Only as she headed towards Lincoln was she finally on a dual carriageway and she put her foot down on the accelerator. The flatness of the county was evident once she headed towards the coast. She was following signs to Skegness, the famous turn-of-the-century poster the only thing she knew about the town. *Skegness is so bracing.*

The outskirts of the town were full of avenues of bungalows, most well kept but with a regimented feel to the layout. It reminded her of Blackpool and her regular jaunts to that seaside town when she was a child. She'd heard the centre would be even more rammed with tourists than the Peaks and she was anxious to avoid both the crowds and the aroma of frying chips and candyfloss sugar.

Detective Inspector David Stanhope had retired from Lincolnshire Constabulary seven years earlier at the age of fifty-five. He'd been a sergeant while working on the investigation into the disappearance of Elizabeth Winson and was the most senior detective Connie could track down.

David Stanhope was an example of why it was a damn shame that, after doing their thirty years' service, most police officers retired. He had the energy of a teenager and sprang around the small living room as if desperate to relieve himself of the built-up tension. She wondered why he had chosen to retire here, but perhaps the minibus emblazoned with St Luke's Boys' Brigade in the driveway gave up some clues. Stanhope would be a perfect leader of a pack of small children. He saw her looking out of the window.

'I used to try and help out a bit in our old church but now I've time on my hands I can do lots of things. Mainly the Boys' Brigade and I also mentor children the local authorities have identified as likely to, well, become acquainted with the law at a later date. There's a ten-year-old lad I'm supporting at the moment. Good, stable home. Hates everyone.'

Connie laughed. 'You think you can do anything about it by the time they're ten?'

He smiled but his eyes were serious. 'The point is you've got to try.'

'I suppose. Can I talk to you about Elizabeth Winson?'

He sighed and motioned for Connie to sit down. 'What a bloody awful case that was. We threw everything at it because, let's face it, we were looking for a missing mother of two small children.'

'There was nothing to indicate she was thinking of running away?'

'Nothing at all. No love affairs. She appeared to be the happily married mother of two young ones and had enough oomph to open a shop with an inheritance she'd received from her mother. We dug around all right but we came up with no explanation as to why she might have disappeared.'

'What about her husband?'

Stanhope relaxed into his chair. 'Well, he seemed to be on the level too. His reaction, when we were first searching for Elizabeth, was one of confusion that, in my opinion, was completely natural. There was something extremely odd about the case.'

'You mean the note?' asked Connie.

'Well, the note was such a strange thing. I mean when we say "two minutes" like "I'll call you in two minutes" we don't actually mean *two* minutes. It could be five or as much as, say, ten. But when we say "two minutes" we don't mean half an hour. So when Elizabeth wrote that note, she only expected to be away from her shop up to, I'd say, a maximum of ten minutes.'

'Like going to the post office or bank, you mean?'

'Exactly, although there was no evidence she had letters to post or cheques to pay in.'

Connie chewed at the tip of her pen. 'So Peter Winson was apparently bewildered at what might have happened at first. Did that change?'

'I don't think it ever did. We questioned him about his movements and he was in work all day. He was employed in Lincoln at the brewery as an accountant but also ran an antiques business on the side. Quite a go-getter like his wife.'

'So Elizabeth would have been left alone with the kids a lot.'

'Yes, but they weren't toddlers. Julia was around ten at the time of her mother's disappearance, George a bit older. They were self-sufficient kids. Even after their mother had gone, I remember Julia and George getting on with things.'

'They carried on going to school?'

'Well, no, not that term. They were coming up for the summer holidays so they just had an extended break. They went back in September, though. I remember checking and being astonished at their resilience.'

'Did you question them?'

'We did. The story was as we'd heard. They'd walk to school with their mother in the mornings and then, after lessons, go on to their mother's shop. There'd never been an instance where Elizabeth wasn't there so there were no precedents.'

'And Peter had a watertight alibi?'

'For the time of the disappearance, yes. Although . . .'

'Although, what?'

Stanhope hesitated. 'If truth be told I thought he was hiding something. I don't know what it was but I definitely got the impression there was something he wasn't telling us.'

'About Elizabeth?'

Stanhope shrugged.

'About himself maybe?' Connie could feel the urge for a cigarette build up inside her.

'We never got to the bottom of it. His alibi stood up and, if he got someone else to kidnap his wife, we never found a motive and possible suspect.'

'So what do you think happened to her? For starters, do you think her disappearance was involuntary?'

Stanhope grimaced. 'I'm sure of it. I'm not old-fashioned enough to think a mother would never leave behind her kids, it's just I can't get past the sheer ordinariness of Elizabeth Winson. She wasn't the type of person just to disappear.'

He hadn't asked the obvious question. Hadn't quizzed Connie on what she was doing here. He was a seasoned enough copper to let her lead the interview. 'When did you last see Peter Winson?' she asked now.

He rubbed his chin. 'Officially around the beginning of '82, I think. I accompanied the boss to say that, while investigations were still active, we were scaling down the search for Elizabeth. Pending new information and leads and all that. We'd run out of avenues to explore.'

'And unofficially?'

'I was driving past his house and I saw a removal van. It must have been around 1984. He said he'd waited until Julia was about to begin her lead into O levels and he wanted a new beginning. He'd got a job as the accountant for an auction house based in Derbyshire and he was moving there. Also good opportunities for the antiques trade. Fresh start and all that.'

'How did he seem?'

'Stressed. Have you ever moved house? Of course he seemed harassed. He also didn't want the kids to see me. I suppose he had enough on his plate that day. I asked if he'd leave details where he could be contacted and he seemed surprised I was asking. But he wrote me out an address easily enough and that was the last time I saw Mr Winson.'

'Did you think he did it? Murder his wife, I mean?'

David Stanhope didn't pause to think. 'Yes.'

26

Julia overslept for the first time in years, not from contentment but the exhaustion of a late night spent fruitlessly searching for the envelope that she had kept all these years. She'd gone first through the large pine chest that had taken three men to lift up the stairs. George had initially offered to help her move but some business deal had cropped up on the day. He'd come around later with a bottle of cold white wine and nothing else when she could have done with a sandwich and a cup of tea. The chest was where she kept all her mementos and the envelope should have been there. She'd pulled the chest apart but nothing had come to light. In the end she'd gone to bed, fretting.

Julia had already spotted the way things were in terms of hierarchy of the police and it was clear that Pat was only of limited help when it came to the investigation. At her father's house yesterday, she'd managed to find a plausible excuse to ask if she could take the bouquet home with her. Pat had been curious but sympathetic.

'Who's to mind? They were put down as an act of remembrance and it's your family, after all.'

Another possible hiding place for the missing envelope came to her as she woke. In her pyjamas, Julia went down the stairs to let Bosco out into the yard and opened one of her kitchen drawers. It was the 'spare' drawer, home for bits and bobs that accumulated over time. In it was a jumble of papers, straws, kitchen paraphernalia and stationery items. Julia found the envelope pushed to the back. As she was examining the handwriting, her eyes caught a flash of a head retreating over the top of her fence.

She marched into the garden and was joined by Bosco, growling, at her feet. 'What the hell are you doing?' she shouted into the space.

The disembodied voice of her new neighbour came from the other side of the partition. 'I was looking for my cat. I didn't mean to frighten you.'

Julia looked down at her dog. 'A cat won't come into my garden with Bosco here. Can you not do that again?'

There was silence the other side of the fence but she could detect a faint wheezing. She left the still growling Bosco in the yard and went back to the envelope.

When her mother had first disappeared, everyone had been kind. She could remember being given glasses of milk or fizzy green soda accompanied by plates of malted milk biscuits. But, after a few months, although the kindness was still there it had been augmented by something else. A sense of the un-explained. Not prurient but interested. Polite enquiries as to what might have happened that masked a firmer insistence as to Julia's thoughts about where her mother might have gone. There had been plenty of cards around that time and flowers but these, eventually, had dried to a trickle. Then, much later, had come flowers addressed not to her father, or the family, but to Julia herself. Twelve years old and her first flowers. They'd gone into the bin. Sentimentality didn't count for much in the Winson household.

The card, however, she'd kept and here it was now in her kitchen, creased with age inside a yellowing envelope. A memento of a never forgotten longing. She looked at the words now. *I'm so sorry*. No name and no indication who had penned these words.

Julia had clung onto the belief, battling with the ever-present fear her mother must be buried in some shallow grave, that those words had come from the missing Elizabeth. It was a stupid dream. Her mother hadn't been a yellow roses sort of person. Potted rubber trees and macramé-hung spider plants had been more her thing. Yellow roses were an object of delicate beauty. But nevertheless she had kept the card.

From the fresh bouquet, she retrieved the other, new message. Different card, same words and, she was pretty sure of it, identical handwriting. *I'm so sorry*. The past was calling out to her, telling her it hadn't finished with her and her family. The past must be connected to the present and the thought of it made Julia's head ache.

Her phone rang and she looked at the screen. Maureen. 'Bloody hell,' she shouted out loud but couldn't resist the lure of the ringing.

'Is everything all right?'

'I'm sorry about this but I've had that boy's father on the phone again this morning. He says his son had nightmares all through the night.'

'Which boy? Oh God, I remember.'

'He was insistent he wanted to talk to you so in the end I told him to bugger off. Said you'd had a family tragedy far worse than any of his son's nightmares could conjure up. It shut him up, for a bit anyway, but then he rang back and said he'd still like to talk to you. Are you okay with this?'

Julia took a deep breath. 'Maureen. I don't want to speak to him. There was nothing down those caves, just echoes and that little boy's imagination. Can you just tell him to stop calling?'

'Sorry, Julia. Sorry for ringing. I just thought—'

Julia hung up and turned her attention back to the original note, wondering if she could squeeze any new clues from it. The envelope was tattered with age. Written on the front was the old address in Horncastle in the days before postcodes were compulsory. Large swirls made up the 'H' in the town's name, a style that wasn't taught in schools any longer. She couldn't remember her mother's handwriting but she thought it was the same cursive script that graced both this older message and the new note.

She laid the messages side by side but the morning brought no new revelations. Either her mother had written the notes or she hadn't. Perhaps she had penned the first and not the second. Or the other way around. One thing for sure was the handwriting looked very similar. The problem was, given the catastrophe that had befallen her family, which was better? That her mother was alive or dead?

27

Mrs Stanhope delivered a tray with a teapot and proper cups and saucers, not the mugs Connie was used to drinking out of. On the side was a plate of custard creams, biscuits she hadn't eaten since she was a child. David didn't introduce his wife but reached out to touch her leg as she passed.

'When we looked into Elizabeth's medical records, there was nothing untoward except a doctor's note on the file from months earlier. Don't forget this was the early eighties. The issue of domestic violence wasn't given the same prominence and GPs, I suspect, weren't trained to identify the signs like they are now.'

'But there was something on the file?' Connie could feel her blood stirring.

'George Winson had been taken by his mother to the doctor with a severe ear infection. The examining GP, a young recently qualified man whose name I forget, looked at the child and as he leant over he glanced up and saw a red mark around Elizabeth Winson's neck. She'd made an effort to cover it up with a jumper but, as she was leaning forward to comfort her child, he saw this huge red weal.'

'What did he think it was?'

'Nothing, to be honest. His initial thought was it might have been a birthmark or an accident. It was her reaction to it that made an impression on him.'

'What did she do?'

'We interviewed the doctor after we spotted the note on the file. It simply said, "follow up bruising". He remembered asking after the mark and Elizabeth jumping up and pulling the collar tight around her neck. She didn't seem to know what to say and they were both distracted by George who, by all accounts, started to play up. The doctor thought it was because of the infection and he wasn't getting the requisite amount of attention. In any case, it distracted the GP, who left it at that but made a note in the file.'

'He thought it might have been a result of domestic violence? Like someone trying to strangle her, for example?'

'He wasn't sure but he was concerned enough to make a note of it.'

Connie reached out for a custard cream and dunked it into the pale orange tea that David had poured. In her mouth, the biscuit tasted divine and she mentally noted to buy herself a packet on the way home.

'And you think Peter was responsible for the weal on her neck?'

'I think it's a distinct possibility. When I questioned him about it, he denied all knowledge of the mark, which is odd because if it was visible to the GP, there's no way her husband could have missed it.'

'Unless they weren't sleeping together?'

David sighed. 'They shared the same bedroom. I remember having to confirm with the kids that this was the case. One of the less pleasant parts of the job. Both children said their parents shared a bedroom, although what went on behind closed doors was anyone's guess.' He looked shrewdly at Connie. 'You do have a point, though, and it's what my boss thought. He was convinced there was someone else in the background. A lover probably, who may have had a violent streak in him.'

'Which would account for Elizabeth's attempt to play down the mark.'

'I suppose. I also got to thinking, maybe George's reaction at the clinic wasn't right either. Maybe he had witnessed his father being violent towards his mother. These things happen.'

'But you couldn't prove it?'

'Unfortunately not and that was the end of that. So I've given you my part. Laid out what's happened, and now you tell me Peter's dead, by the hand of his second wife by all accounts. Poetic justice?'

Connie spread out her hands and looked at her ragged nails. 'It doesn't make much sense at the moment. Francesca appears to have been quiet and reserved, perhaps a bit like Elizabeth Winson. Men often have a type, don't they?'

'You think she was pushed to kill all her family? That's a bit extreme, isn't it? We've moved on with how we treat victims of domestic violence; there's help available for women in abusive relationships.'

Connie looked at David Stanhope's honest face. 'I agree, and that's what's worrying me. Don't you think acts have got to have a logic to them? More than forensics and timelines. Actions actually have to make sense.'

He shrugged. 'I never found a sense in 1980.'

28

The blond policeman listened to Julia's story, keeping his eyes on her all the time. She felt the scrutiny of his gaze; he was assessing her, and Julia wondered what it must be like to work under that kind of intensity. Only when she had finished did he pick up the card retrieved from the flowers left outside her father's house. He compared it to the other she had given him. He then carefully put them on his desk.

'What do you think happened to your mother, Julia?'

It wasn't the question she had been expecting. She thought he would make some comment about the handwriting or the presence of the card placed so early yesterday morning. Instead his eyes were on her again.

'I've no idea.' A thought came to her. 'You don't think I left those cards, do you?'

Next to her, Pat stirred and laid a hand on her. Calmed, Julia pondered the question Sadler had asked.

'When I was a teenager I was convinced she was dead. I mean it's the time a girl really thinks of her mother. During puberty and all the physical changes you undergo. We'd never had the conversation mothers have with their daughters. So I worked it out for myself and through chatting with friends. I remember a teacher, before I left junior school, telling me something too. Not to be upset if I started bleeding one day. I pieced together the story and it was all right but it felt like a patchwork. It was then I needed my mother and I convinced myself she must be dead because for her to have voluntarily decided not to be in my life was just too much to bear.'

'You never discussed this with your father?'

'It was a forbidden topic. He froze whenever we mentioned Mum and, in the end, it was easier not to. In my twenties and thirties I went through a few dud relationships and thought, well, life's not all it's cracked up to be and nothing is really black and white. It was then I considered the possibility that she might still be alive and had just walked out on us.'

And now? That's what she expected him to say but he wrong-footed her. Here was a man, she suspected, who would always be capable of surprises.

'What about immediately after your mother went missing? What did you think then?'

She thought back to those days of the summer of 1980 and the policewomen in their old-fashioned hats and nylon tights that sparked when they sat down on the sofa. 'Do you know what? Lots of people questioned me about my mum's movements. Where she might be and so on, but I don't remember anyone asking me what I actually thought. Whether she might be dead.'

'That's a lot to ask of a child,' said Sadler.

'I'd have liked to have been asked my opinion.' Her tone was more aggressive than she'd intended.

Keeping his voice even and his eyes still on her, he asked again. 'Have a think now. Don't dwell too long on it. What you've told me you felt as a teenager and as an adult are reflections of your experience. I want you to think back to when you were a child. Did you think she had intentionally left the shop and your family or had she been taken involuntarily?'

Julia leant back in her seat and, ignoring them both, looked up at the ceiling and asked her childhood self that question. Images crowded into her mind and she let them whirl around a little and then settle. She then thought of her mother. The dark curls that George had inherited set into a rigid style. The pale pink frosted lipstick and high-necked cardigans. Then she thought of absence.

She looked down from the ceiling and at her jeans. 'I don't know for sure but I don't think she was happy.'

'Why? Why don't you think she was happy?'

'The rational part of me thinks she can't have been content with Dad. He was so difficult. I think back to that time a lot but I've never really objectively thought about my mother.'

'Don't worry about being rational. I'd like your gut instinct in this instance and, from what you say, it's that your mother wasn't happy.'

'I think it's more to do with my parents' marriage, about what it must have been like, I mean. I think she was genuinely unhappy, trapped even. It doesn't really help, though, does it?'

'It does, actually. Unhappiness encourages us to make rash decisions sometimes but unhappy people also have things done to them.'

'So we're back at square one.'

'Julia.' His tone was gentle. 'I'm not going to be able to solve the mystery of your mother's disappearance. It's what happened to your father and the rest of your family that I'm trying to make sense of.'

'What do you think of the cards, though? The handwriting is similar, isn't it?'

Sadler picked them up, studied them once more and then handed them back to her. 'If anything comes up connected to the events of 1980 I'll look at these again. In the meantime you keep hold of them.'

His eyes checked to see her reaction and she nodded. 'Okay.'

'What I do need to talk to you and your brother about is the circumstances of the fire.'

Pat interrupted. 'I left a message for George about both our visit to the house yesterday and this meeting. I've had no response from him.'

Julia felt the need to defend her brother. 'We don't come as a pair. You might need to tell us anything you discover in future separately.'

'That's fair enough,' said Sadler. 'Briefing you both together saves time and ensures a consistent flow of information but I'm sure Pat will find a way of getting any news to your brother.'

'You think my family was murdered?'

'We're not looking for anyone else in connection with the deaths.'

'George thought this was the case. You mean, Dad.'

Sadler shook his head. 'The evidence, as it currently stands, is that Francesca may have murdered your father and Charlie and then killed herself.'

Julia looked between Sadler and Pat. 'Francesca? Are you mad? There's no way Francesca is responsible for this.'

'I'm sorry, but that's what it looks like. I'm sure it's hard to take in.'

'Take in? Francesca? No, you must be wrong.'

He didn't like that, thought Julia. He frowned and she felt him withdraw.

117

'Can you think of any instances where she indicated she was under pressure?' Sadler asked.

'Francesca? I don't think so. Not enough to warrant this.'

'Did you know she was pregnant?'

Julia felt herself go pale and a well of nausea build up behind her nose. 'No, I didn't. She certainly didn't mention it to me.'

'Would George have known?'

'George? If I didn't know there's no way he would have!'

'Did she mention she wanted another child?'

'She mentioned it once, that she'd like another child, but I wouldn't have dreamt of asking her for more details. We didn't have that kind of relationship.'

'What about your father?'

'Definitely not. We never spoke about that sort of thing.'

She watched the detective frown. He was around her age. His blond hair not yet thinning, which was unusual. Lines in the corners of his eyes belied his youthful appearance. Not from laughter. Worry. Julia felt the need to catch his attention. Press her case. She leant forward.

'I can't believe Francesca could be responsible for this. Are you absolutely positive?'

Sadler met her eye. 'Almost positive, yes.'

29

Tuesday, 5 August 2014

'Your father's not an easy man to live with.'

Julia started in surprise. Francesca was preparing lunch. Smoked salmon and pale pieces of melon with crusty bread. No wonder she was so thin if that's all she ate. Charlie had just learnt to ride his new tricycle and was whizzing around the kitchen with glee. Francesca bent down to stroke his head as he passed. Sun beat down through the window and, noticing her little brother's red face, Julia said, 'Why don't we eat in the garden?'

Francesca shook her head. 'Charlie's scared of wasps. It's easier to stay inside.'

A toddler scared of wasps? Surely children are fearless. She thought Francesca was being too protective but it was hardly her place to say so. Instead, she pulled out cutlery from the kitchen drawer.

'There's a big age difference. It can't be easy for either of you.'

The stiffening of Francesca's back suggested this reassurance wasn't what had been sought. '*I'm* the person in a strange country. It should be me who's finding it difficult. Your father's in the same house, doing what he did before we were married. What's hard for him?'

'He's retired.' Julia wondered at her need to defend a man she knew was difficult to live with. 'He's probably still adjusting to having a young child in the house.'

Francesca turned around, her face impassive. 'It's me who does all the work.'

'But he's here, isn't he? That's what's important for Charlie. To be near his father. Children need both parents.'

Francesca stared at Julia for a moment. 'Of course they do. Two parents are important. A proper mother and father.'

There was a catch in Francesca's voice that caused Julia to look up. 'He may mellow.' Julia wondered why she said this. Perhaps to appease Francesca. Her father wasn't going to change, was he?

Francesca had turned away again. 'It's not normal to be so angry all the time. What does he expect me to do? I came to England to start a new life, not be a punch bag.'

'He doesn't hit you, does he?'

Francesca dished the food into two shallow bowls. 'Hit me? Of course he doesn't hit me. He would be very, very sorry if he did.'

'That sounds like a threat.'

Francesca smiled into her long dark hair as she cut the loaf. 'I have a very long memory.'

30

'So, the DI in charge of Elizabeth Winson's disappearance reckoned her husband Peter had something to do with it.' Connie had driven at breakneck speed from Skegness and arrived in Bampton in just under three hours, making the team meeting by the skin of her teeth. She delivered her information to the assembled group and a short silence descended as they digested the information.

Matthews moved restlessly beside her. 'But from what you're saying, it doesn't sound like there was any evidence even that her disappearance was involuntary. Is it just a hunch of his?'

Connie made a face. 'I guess so but he didn't particularly seem the excitable type. Pretty straightforward guy. They never really got anywhere with the case, but he thinks, firstly, Elizabeth is dead and also her husband, Peter, was somehow complicit in her disappearance.'

Connie looked around the meeting for an ally. Sadler was at the front of the room, perched on a table, listening to the updates. By the window, she could see Palmer looking at the floor with his arms folded. He had already disengaged from the team, it seemed. She would find no help there. It turned Connie sulky.

'I'm just reporting what he told me. Peter Winson was a person of suspicion. This is what I'm trying to tell you.'

Sadler stood up. 'In the case of the fire that occurred two nights ago, evidence collected so far points to Peter being a victim. So, I think we're going to have to be careful when assessing the relevance of the disappearance of his first wife. I've had his daughter Julia in today and she's naturally upset about the case but is also asking questions about her mother. It's not our remit or jurisdiction to look into the disappearance of Elizabeth, however fascinating it might be. Not every tragedy is connected. What did Charlie's school say?'

Matthews rifled through her papers. 'He was in the reception class so it was his first year with them. It was a family who kept themselves to themselves but not in any weird way. Charlie was well behaved but not unusually so. I spoke first to his form teacher. Her only comment was that it was just the mother, Francesca, who attended the parents' evening last autumn and at the end of the spring term. Apparently it's more usual these days for both parents to come along.'

'Was any reason given for this?'

'Not really. The teacher thought, perhaps, the father worked away but there appears to be no evidence of this. I then spoke to the headmistress. Again it was Francesca she knew through the usual school administration. She'd never met Peter.'

'And what were their assessments of Francesca?' asked Sadler.

'They both thought her capable although perhaps remote. She didn't join in any after-school activities and wasn't seen at sports day two weeks earlier. Charlie did say his mother had been there but no one remembers her.'

'Does anyone have any comment on that?'

Palmer raised his head. 'In terms of the absence of Peter, my own father never came to any of my school events. Peter Winson was from that generation. Just because he had a child as an older man, it doesn't mean he was going to change. He'd probably be likely to repeat the patterns of his earlier fatherhood.'

'But . . .' Connie turned to face Palmer. 'He must have gone to school meetings because, after 1980, he brought up his elder two children by himself. So the norm, for him, would be to go to parents' evenings.'

'Maybe he'd had enough of them,' sniggered a voice at the back of the room. 'I'd happily never go to a school meeting again.'

'I'm not sure it's important.' Sadler looked around the room. 'It could take up to a week to get the fire report. Nigel Rooth gave us a pretty comprehensive account of what he considered to be the narrative of events of that night. It would help the forensic evidence, however, if we came up with a convincing explanation of Francesca's state of mind.'

'Do you think it's significant she was pregnant?' asked Palmer. 'I mean in terms of both her psychological state and whether it could have been a catalyst for something else.'

Jill Mayfield, a recent arrival at CID, put up her hand. 'We've had a preliminary look at medical records for the Winsons. There's nothing untoward in terms of the family. Peter was worried about palpitations and had been sent to a consultant and reassured that all was normal. There are a couple of other referrals we're also checking out. We're paying special attention to Francesca's records but she rarely went to the doctor's. She doesn't appear to have informed them she was expecting again.'

'Ten weeks? Wouldn't she have gone to the doctor by then?' asked Sadler.

'Not necessarily,' said Mayfield. 'With my second I waited until I was three months gone. They don't scan you until around eighteen weeks so there's no rush. You're a bit more laid-back after your first pregnancy.'

Matthews was doodling on a notepad in front of her. 'At ten weeks she would surely have guessed she was pregnant, though. You say Julia didn't know about it. I wonder if Peter did?'

'I'm not sure we're going to be able to find that out.' Sadler's eyes fell onto Connie. 'Francesca's pregnancy should be a line of enquiry. If we start with the assumption that Francesca knew she was pregnant, perhaps we might come up with some answers as to her state of mind. Connie, can you talk to Francesca's parents again about what she'd told them about the new pregnancy?'

'Me?' Connie was furious. 'What about Elizabeth Winson?'

Sadler shifted his attention away from her. 'Even if Peter murdered his first wife, and nothing you've told me except an ex-detective's hunch confirms this, it still doesn't alter the fact that he was a victim two nights ago.'

'He might have been an abusive husband. He may have driven Francesca to commit the act,' said Connie.

'What about her son and unborn child?' asked Matthews. 'She kills him too just because she's in a crap marriage? That sounds like she was mentally unstable, not downtrodden.'

'Maybe she discovered something about the past and—'

'I don't want you looking at the Elizabeth Winson case any longer.' Sadler was refusing to look at Connie. 'If domestic violence was a factor then we need to find evidence now, not from thirty-seven years ago.'

Connie was mad, as much with his dismissive tone as with what he was saying. In front of all the team members as well. She leant back in her chair and listened to him allocating tasks to other members of the team. Background checks on the family, speaking to neighbours, how Peter and Francesca had met.

'There's one thing.' Palmer was flipping through his notebook. 'Peter Winson had made an appointment to see his solicitors for the Wednesday after the fire. It was the earliest they could fit him in. He didn't tell them what it was about.'

'This is possibly significant,' said Sadler. 'He gave no indication whatsoever why he wanted to see them?'

'He didn't, and the partner who he sees does everything, house sales, wills, matrimonial. It could be anything.'

'Go and see them anyway, would you?' Sadler looked around the team. 'Anything else? Okay, let's reconvene tomorrow. Same time.'

The meeting dispersed. Only Connie remained seated.

'Fancy a coffee?' Matthews was leaning towards her with a sympathetic face.

Connie looked at her watch. 'Not much time to go out for one. Do you want to go to the canteen?'

Matthews grimaced. 'Let's nip out to Costa across the road. We can get a takeout and go our separate ways.'

Connie picked up her handbag and followed her colleague through the station. Outside, a blast of sunshine hit them and Connie pulled on her pink sunglasses.

'Nice shades.' Matthews offered her a cigarette and then a lighter. Connie lit both their cigarettes and inhaled deeply.

'Not very professional, are they? I might need to graduate to black frames if I go for my sergeant's exams.'

'Thinking about it?' Matthews put her cigarettes away and pulled out her purse. 'Coffee's on me.'

Connie fell into step beside her. 'Now Palmer's leaving there'll be a space in the team. It gives me a chance, if I pass my exams, to go for it.'

'Is that what you fancy? I rather thought that's what you liked to be, the outsider I mean.'

Hurt, Connie tried not to show it. 'I just voice my opinions. You think it's affecting my career?'

Matthews shrugged. 'Not as much as shagging Palmer did.'

The cigarette nearly fell out of Connie's mouth. 'Oh God. Does everyone know?'

'Pretty much, but given what happened, you ending up in hospital I mean, it sort of got swept up in other news. Anyway, Palmer's now playing the dutiful husband and father.'

'You think it's playing?'

Carole looked down at her. 'With Palmer it's all about show. I'm not sure you'd ever know what was really going on inside his head. You okay working with me?'

'Of course. If you're thinking—'

'I'm not thinking anything. I grew up on a farm over Castleton way. Load of peasants my family are and I don't have much to do with them to be honest, but you don't unlearn everything. Grievances, in my opinion, are best put out in the open and I want to check you've not got a problem with me.'

'Definitely not.'

'Right then, take a bit of advice from me. Don't get your knickers in a twist over Peter Winson.'

Connie opened her mouth but Matthews stopped her.

'I know you're upset at Sadler telling you to move on. I agree with you it's bloody weird, the disappearance of Elizabeth and all that. However, remember part of getting on in this world is toeing the line. The evidence almost conclusively points towards Francesca being the murderer. By all means keep an open mind if you wish, but don't argue against the facts, and do what Sadler tells you. Otherwise, the boss won't like it and it won't do your career any good.'

'I'm just voicing my doubt. Why would a woman want to murder all her family?'

Matthews stubbed out her cigarette on the top of a bin. 'That's what we're going to discover.'

31

Julia arrived at the gate of All Souls Church at ten to eight and a small group was already huddled under the canopy, laughing with the awkwardness of strangers about to embark on a shared experience. In the distance, she could see a couple of stragglers busy taking pictures of the medieval church and bemoaning the fact the door was locked. The darkening sky was red, an auspicious sign for the following day. This evening, however, there was a chill in the air and a couple of tourists were wearing walking jackets with their hoods pulled up.

'Okay, everyone. I'm expecting twelve but I can only see ten of you.'

On cue, a couple came running from behind the church. 'We were seeing if we could find a way in. Sometimes these places have a back door open or something.'

'The church is open tomorrow for those who are interested. Tonight's walk is outside only, I'm afraid.'

'It's a good name, though. Is that why we're meeting here?'

'It's an excellent name, I agree, from the religious feast day when we acknowledge the souls of those who have died.' Julia saw she had all their attention. 'Is this the first time for all of you? I mean, coming on a ghost walk.'

One woman at the back put up her hand. 'I've done other ones. One in London and one in York. Actually, the London one was a Jack the Ripper walk, so nothing to do with ghosts, really.'

Muted laughter.

'Okay, I just want to dispel a couple of things for you here. The first thing is that I'm not a ghost hunter. Those of you expecting discussions of ectoplasm and orbs are going to be disappointed. This is a tour of the places in Bampton where there have been reports of supernatural activity. That's why it's advertised as suitable for the sceptical as well as believers. The emphasis tonight will be on history and tragedy. You can choose to believe the sightings or not. Whichever, I hope you enjoy the tour.'

'Are we going to be outside the whole hour and a half?'

'Where we can enter a place, a pub for example, we'll go in. This is a regular tour and the landlords know us.'

'Time for a drink?'

Laughter and Julia nodded. 'At the end there will be, as I'm finishing in one of Bampton's oldest inns. Those of you who want to stay on are welcome to do so. Right, the existence of Bampton goes back to the second century and we're standing on what was part of the old Roman road. The Romans established Bampton as a centre for the lead mining trade and, in fact, where I work during the day, Anchor Cavern, is an old lead mine that's well worth a visit.'

Was it Julia's imagination or did a look of anger cross the face of the man at the back of the group? He was tall, dressed in a polo shirt despite the chill and standing apart from the rest of the group with his arms folded. She ploughed on. 'There are sightings of two centurions walking along this road but you can only see them from the knees upwards. This is because their feet are treading the original road, which is of course a foot or so below the current level of the road. Shall we move on?'

They set off down the hill and a woman fell into step behind her. 'I wasn't sure whether to come. I booked the tour when I paid the deposit on the cottage I'm renting for the week. Then I suffered a bereavement. A neighbour I was close to died and I'm not sure I'm in the mood for tales of horror.'

'That's not what you'll get. I love this place and I've worked in the tourist industry all my adult life. What you'll get is a history of Bampton based on ghostly sightings. I'm not out to scare anyone.'

'You don't believe in ghosts yourself?'

Julia stopped in front of her brother's building. He knew the days when she led this tour so she was pretty sure he arranged to be out when she stopped in front of his building. He'd refused to discuss her night-time job with her and yet, every week, she stopped under his window and recited her piece.

'I've just been asked if I believe in ghosts, which is a fair question. I do believe people have seen something but I don't consider them to be spirits, you know the sort that mediums contact. Instead I see them as echoes from the past, recordings as it were of what's gone before. For example, we're standing in front of a former workhouse, St Alkmund's, which was in use from 1796 until 1886 when it was declared unfit for human habitation. Given the fact it was a place that split up families who were already suffering from misery and starvation, you might think the sighting would be of someone in distress. In fact, two different people have spoken of seeing a small boy laughing in front of the building.'

'Laughing?' asked one of the group.

'Strange, I know. The first sighting was in the fifties and

recorded in a book of anecdotal Derbyshire sightings. The second was about twenty years ago when a milkman, doing his rounds, saw the child one early morning.'

For a moment, Julia faltered; an image of a giggling Charlie running across the garden flashed in front of her. She looked up and caught the man looking intently at her. He was out of place in the group. He was on his own, as was the woman who had walked down the hill with her. Although initially ill at ease, she was now writing notes on a pad. The remainder were couples, all in their sixties. She moved on, uncomfortably aware of his gaze.

She switched onto automatic pilot, allowing the familiar words to work their magic. She noticed the group begin to gel and trade ghost stories of their own, including those passed down by relatives. Only the man remained aloof, sometimes looking around him, sometimes looking at her. Never did he show any interest in the stories she was telling.

It was a relief when she arrived at their final destination. Although the façade of the building had a closed-off look to it, she knew the interior of the pub was cosy and atmospheric. She took them into the small lobby and began her final speech.

'So we're at The Peveril of the Peak, a historic name for a public house with a fascinating history. Do you all know what the Peveril was?'

Enthusiastic nods. 'A stagecoach from London to Manchester,' said one of the women.

'Exactly. The coach and horses would pass down what is now known as the A6 and passengers could stop here, in Bampton, for refreshments.'

'What was its name then?'

'Good question. For years it was called The Black Horse, but when the Peveril of the Peak was discontinued with the coming of the railways, it was decided to commemorate the stagecoach by changing the inn's name. There was even a ballot amongst regulars, apparently, to ensure everyone approved of the change.'

'So when was the pub built?' The woman with the notebook this time. The lone man was reading her words over her shoulder.

'It's about four hundred years old. There have been numerous changes and extensions to the building but maps show a farmhouse here in 1604. By 1700 it was a pub known as The Bull, which at some point changed its name to The Black Horse.'

'And the Black Horse was a ghost?' asked another, looking around as if he was expecting to see a large stallion galloping through the bar.

'There's been a fair amount of ghostly sightings over the years but not, I can safely say, of a horse. Legend has it that Dick Turpin stayed here, although, be warned, quite a lot of other pubs in the area claim this too. There haven't been specific sightings but there are stories of glasses inexplicably smashing, sounds of children crying and, more recently, a shadow on a photograph that may have been a figure of a man.'

'A highwayman?' asked a woman, hopefully.

Julia shook her head. 'Too difficult to tell.'

The man was leaning against the wall looking sceptical and had his arms folded. *Well he might*, thought Julia. For this was a job like anything else and nothing would convince her of the presence of ghosts in this building. People, however, had paid their money and deserved a fair crack. She did what she normally did with the unbelieving.

'I can see a few of you looking sceptical, so I'm going to share something with you. There are a lot of charlatans out there, people out to take your money and encourage you to believe that the creaks and groans of an old building are evidence of a supernatural presence. Well, I'm a natural sceptic but there is a very special feeling to this place and I think you'll come out of this evening feeling something and it's not just the alcohol.'

She left them to go to the bar. They had bonded over the hour and a half and two of the women were reserving a large table for them to sit around. Only the man remained.

'Can I have a word with you?'

'Yes, of course.'

He made towards the exit but she had no intention of following him out into the dark street. Her initial disquiet, wondering if he was the shadowy presence she had seen outside her front door, had been replaced by the certainty he was a journalist. Something about the confidence in his stance. She stayed put, keeping the distance between them, and he didn't move closer.

'Look,' he hissed. 'I don't mind you doing this sort of thing for a living if that's what you want to do, but you've got a bloody nerve involving kids in your shenanigans.'

'Kids?!' Her voice came out in a squeak. 'Everyone has to be over eighteen to come here. I don't allow kids on my walks.'

'I don't mean now,' he retorted. 'I mean scaring the life out of my son this week with your bloody ghost stories in the cave.'

She looked at him in shock. 'It was your son who said he heard whisperings in Anchor Cavern?'

'Encouraged by you, no doubt. I've heard you tonight.'

'For God's sake, you don't think I'd do that, do you? Look...' She pulled him away from the eyes of the group. 'I have two separate jobs. The first is doing tours at Anchor all year round and there I give the history of the caves and point out the geological features. I'm interested in Derbyshire's industrial past and I make it come alive to visitors. I don't need to make anything up or add any element of the supernatural. The truth is interesting enough.'

'And the ghost tours?'

'This is different. You've just done the tour with me. I base my walks on local history and legend. What people say they've seen and stories that have been written down. It's completely separate from my work at Anchor Cavern, and I meant what I said out there. I'm a sceptic. I love the idea of ghosts as an element of Derbyshire folklore. I don't actually believe or disbelieve what I see and hear.'

'So what did you tell them down in the cave?'

'I told them nothing. That's the point. I don't mix the two and certainly not where kids are concerned. It's a bloody dangerous thing to do and I'd never forgive myself if I gave anyone nightmares.'

'That's what Toby has. Nightmares. He said he could hear whispering in the cave.'

She shook her head. 'There was nothing there, I promise. There's a thing I do where I get them all to turn off their torches for thirty seconds and listen in silence. It's then your son thought he'd heard voices, whispers he called them in the cave.'

'You didn't say anything?'

'Of course not. I think I told him what he'd heard was the wind. That was probably it, anyway. I'm sorry he's now having nightmares. Maybe I'll stop getting them to stand in the dark. I like to do it because kids are so unused to silence these days and I want them to hear how it feels.'

The man had reluctantly relaxed. 'It's probably not you. I just got a bee in my bonnet about that Scout trip. It's the first time he's been away from home since my wife left and I thought it would do him good but he's come back a bag of nerves.'

'His mum left him?'

'Yes. She's met someone else. It's a long story but she basically can't see him at the moment. It's tearing Toby apart but there's nothing I can do. His mum doesn't want to see him until her domestic life has settled down.' He looked at her. 'You haven't said the obvious. What everyone else is saying, I mean. Asking how a mother could leave her child.'

Julia looked to the floor. 'She probably has her reasons.'

He stared at her for a moment then shrugged. 'Anyway, I'm in effect a single dad and probably a bit overprotective. I don't know what went wrong with the trip.'

'I guess it was just too much for him. As you say, he's probably feeling abandoned if his mother's gone.'

'That's an understatement. It's just he was all right until this trip.' He hesitated, looking her up and down. 'Listen, I know who you are. I put two and two together when the woman at the cave, Maureen, said you'd had a family bereavement. It puts everything into perspective, doesn't it, when something like that happens.'

'Does it?' She needed to get back to the group, who were expecting her to join them for a drink.

'Perhaps it doesn't. I'm sorry. I suppose something like that is impossible to fathom. Look, I shouldn't have come. Can I make it up to you sometime? Maybe we could go for a drink or something. I just wanted to have it out with you about what you'd said to Toby but it appears you didn't say anything anyway. I don't think I'll join the rest of the group, if you don't mind.'

He turned to go.

'A drink sometime would be nice,' she called after him. 'What's your name?'

He turned back to her. 'Ned. Ned Smith.' She watched as he scribbled his number on a piece of paper. 'Here. I'll buy them. It's the least I can do.'

She took the paper off him. 'Listen, Ned. What your son needs right now is a father. Forget about the mother bit. He can, and will, learn to cope with not having a mother. The important thing is he still has a father. Do you see?'

32

It was proving to be a long, draggy, summer week where Connie, unusually for her, wanted to be anywhere but in work. For the first time, she thought nostalgically back to the days following her last investigation when, after an attack, she had spent first three weeks in hospital and then ten weeks off work recovering. She'd enjoyed the cocoon of illness and there had been surprising insights into the people around her. Frank, her father who had remarried after the early death of her mother, had come down from his bungalow in Stirling and had stayed with her for the first week after she had returned from hospital. He'd been worse than useless as a nurse but had spoken about her mother for the first time in years. How they'd met at a dancehall in Matlock and the jobs he'd taken to support her while she had completed a pharmaceutical degree at Manchester University. Connie had gained an insight into her mother before the latter's alcohol addiction had afflicted their relationship.

She'd also had two visits in hospital from Sadler. Neither of them had felt comfortable. He'd refused to talk about any cases the team were working on and she'd not wanted to express how she'd felt about her enforced convalescence. She had, however, been touched by the fact he had cared enough to visit her, although he'd stayed away once she'd returned to her flat. Now he was back in full supervisor mode and not listening to her concerns.

A portrait of the family was emerging. Peter had a wide circle of acquaintances who had known him since the move to Derbyshire in the mid-eighties. The more reticent amongst them had referred to him as 'taciturn', the less so as a 'miserable bugger'. All those who met her, in contrast, described Francesca as friendly but no one was able to track down a friend or close acquaintance. She had been a reserved and private individual. Connie swung around in her chair.

'It's like trying to prise open an oyster,' she complained to no one in particular.

A head lifted. 'Talking of oysters, have you tried the new bar on the high street? Seafood and champagne is all it sells. It's gorgeous inside. Perfect for a date.'

'And talking of dates, have you got any lined up?' Matthews called over to Connie.

'Nope. The last one I had was interrupted by Sadler walking into the pub.'

'No!' Matthews looked around the office. 'Was he on his own?' she hissed.

'With a woman. I'm not sure she was his girlfriend, though. He looked a bit embarrassed.'

'Oh, never mind about him. All men look embarrassed when they're spotted outside work with a woman. What did *she* look like?'

'A bit cross. Red-faced and irritable.'

They sniggered together and then both looked towards Sadler's office in case he was around.

'I've no dates lined up, I'm afraid. I need to look further afield. Any ideas?'

Matthews smiled. 'No point asking me. I've been happily

settled for years. You're better off without him, though.'

'Who?' asked Connie, knowing full well who she meant.

Matthews raised her eyebrows and stayed silent. Connie turned back to her computer and thought of Oliver, the nearest she'd got to seeing someone in the last year. They hadn't communicated since the night in the pub. That was the problem with online dating. You go from intensive chat to arranging a meeting, and then a period of silence while you weigh up your options. This is where she was at now. What to do next. A second date suggested a certain amount of interest that she didn't feel, although he was nice enough. Too nice, in fact. She didn't go for the good guys. Sighing, she picked up her handbag and headed towards the back exit for a smoke.

It was bad timing as she spotted Palmer making his way down the corridor towards her. He clocked her a fraction of a second after she spotted him, casting his eyes downwards at the report he was holding in his hands. She stopped in front of him, forcing him to come to a halt too.

'Congratulations on the transfer. You must be pleased.'

He made an effort to look at her. 'Thanks. It came through quicker than expected so I haven't really had time to digest it. At least we're on the move now, though.'

'Sick of Derbyshire?' She sounded waspish and wished she hadn't forced him to speak.

'House prices are so expensive here in the Peaks. Bedfordshire's much cheaper if you know where to look. With Max growing every day, we'll run out of space soon.'

She frowned. 'He's only six months old.'

He moved away from her. 'You have no idea how much paraphernalia babies have. You all right?' He sounded like he didn't care, the night spent together last year forgotten. She didn't bother answering him and carried on down the corridor.

A uniformed constable came haring towards her. 'Have I missed Palmer?'

'He's heading towards his desk. Why?'

'Something just came up in the door-to-doors. I thought he might be interested.'

'Well, what?'

The constable looked unsure. 'You know the older brother, George. One of the neighbours on Cross Farm Lane, not one near the house but much further down, went to school with George.'

'Did he know the family?'

'Not the ones who died. It was the same story from him, to be honest. They kept themselves to themselves and all that. He only knew Peter Winson as the father of his school friend.'

'He said something about George, though?'

'He really didn't like him, you know. He didn't want to talk about it, initially. Just vague comments about he was a "nasty little shit".'

'That's not particularly vague.'

The constable grinned down at her. 'I suppose not. I eventually got him to tell me why he was so antagonistic towards George. Apparently they were quite close as teenagers and did a lot of the country larking about you get around here. You know, driving his father's Land Rover pissed in a field, shooting rabbits after dark. Anyway, George had a pet dog and Terry, this was the school friend, was pretty sure the animal was being abused. Its hair was all mangy and it looked constantly hungry. It was all skin and bones.'

'Abused by George?'

'That's what he said. It gets worse. One day, they were walking deep inside Witham Woods with their airguns. They were going to shoot some birds off the trees. That's another country teenager's pursuit.'

She rolled her eyes. 'Go on.'

'Well, instead of aiming at the trees, George turns around and shoots the dog instead. Right into its head. It died straight away. Terry said it was like an execution.'

'Jesus, that's horrible.'

'I know. Then, apparently, he kicked its body under a few leaves and carried on walking without saying a word. Terry said the friendship fell apart after that.'

'I'm not surprised. It makes George sound psychotic. Did he say anything else?'

'Not really. George was considered a bit odd in school but nothing specific. There were rumours the mother had left in mysterious circumstances but no one knew the exact details. Only the dog incident made an impression with the witness.'

'And this Terry believes George had been mistreating the dog leading up to this incident and then deliberately killed it for whatever reason.'

'Basically, yes.'

Connie leant back against the wall and allowed the PC to pass her. Not much, really, but an insight, perhaps, into the disturbed mind of George Winson. Hadn't she read something about psychopaths inflicting pain on animals before moving on to humans?

Moments later, the constable walked back looking downcast.

'What did Palmer say?'

'He wasn't interested. He doesn't think it's important and George is a grieving relative. So what if he was odd at school?'

'Palmer doesn't think it's relevant?' Connie glanced down the corridor. 'Look, if anything else comes up along those lines, can you let me know?'

'You don't want me to tell Palmer?'

Connie looked up towards the office where Palmer would be hunched over his desk, unaware of her existence. 'You can tell him if you want. I'm not sure if it makes any difference. He's already moved on.'

33

Julia was sitting outside in her little yard with the parasol open. She'd angled it so it blocked the view of her new neighbour's house. It was clearly to be a week for upsetting notes. On her knee she studied the scrap of paper that had just been pushed through her letterbox. Torn from an exercise book, the message was a model of brevity. *Your dog is ruining my life.* It must be from the man Jean had called Morell. It sounded like he had experienced his own share of tragedy, a brother lost underground and for ever missing, but that didn't give him the right to intrude on hers.

She looked over to Bosco. No one had ever complained about his barking before. What had made him so jittery? Aware of her scrutiny, he thumped his tail against the fencing panel. Julia picked up the note and went through her house and opened the front door, determined to have it out with her neighbour. A visitor was leaving his house. A man, who left quickly, walking away from her without looking back. Something about the set of his back or his walk was familiar and Julia, without her glasses, scrunched up her eyes to get a better view. It looked like the man who had come on the ghost walk yesterday evening. Ned. But why would he be at her neighbour's house? Julia rushed back inside to get her glasses but by the time she was on the street again, the man was gone.

With a sigh, she banged on her neighbour's door. He

opened it immediately and she thrust his note at him. 'What's the meaning of this? Sending me threatening notes.'

Morell took a step backwards, shutting the door slightly. 'Your dog barks all day when you're out. It's affecting my mental health.'

'Bosco? He hardly barks at all normally. Are you sure?'

'I can hear him through the living room. He's barking at the door. I can't stand it any longer. I'll complain to the council if it doesn't stop.'

Julia could feel the tears pricking behind her eyes. 'How can you be so cruel?' she shouted. 'He's all I've got.'

Morell shut the door in her face. She could see his outline behind the glass panel. Not moving but waiting. Julia stormed into her house and slammed the front door. Back out in her garden, she called Bosco over to her and he settled on her sandalled foot, a reassuring warmth.

Into her laptop she first searched the name 'Ned Smith'. He had an irritatingly common last name that meant dozens of potential matches came up. Feeling like a stalker, she clicked around a few of the sites but failed to find a match to the man she'd met last night. Then she typed in 'Morell' and 'Derbyshire caves'. Dozens of sites appeared with the story of the boy missing since 1965. She bookmarked the top few to read later.

Next she logged on to the *Missing You* forum and checked her post. Two hundred and thirty-six views. Nine comments, three of which were from mediums offering to help in her search. The others were expressions of support. Nothing of any importance.

Bosco shifted on her foot and Julia used the opportunity to flex her toes. She clicked on the statistics for her plea and studied the figures. Of the two hundred or so views, most users had read her post once or twice. Two of the mediums offering their services had clicked on her post five times and another two over ten times. There was one, named *NaturalScot*, who had read her post twenty-seven times. Julia clicked on the profile of the user but it gave away no information whatsoever. A blank where the photo should be. The location given as Scotland, not a revelation given the name they were using. Julia couldn't even tell if the person was male or female.

In frustration, she jerked her foot away and Bosco yelped at her. She patted him for reassurance and then did a search around the website. There was nothing that identified who *NaturalScot* was or their interest in being on a site dedicated to finding missing people. The only information she had was that, for whatever reason, they had viewed Julia's plea for information about her missing mother nearly thirty times.

34

After smoking two cigarettes in quick succession, Connie walked back to her desk and, ignoring Palmer, sat down. So George had abused his former pet. Was this significant? In ordinary circumstances she would have asked her colleagues, bounced some ideas around about the likelihood of a man who was cruel to animals extending this to his family. The problem was, she had no allies. Palmer wasn't interested in George's quirks and Sadler had warned her off focusing on any member of the Winson family other than Francesca. On impulse, she searched for George's name on the police database. It was with a sense of inevitability that she got a positive result.

Mayfield was typing rapidly into a computer and didn't look up as Connie came over to her.

'Do you know George Winson's ex-wife was granted a restraining order against him?'

Mayfield carried on typing, the tip of her tongue poking out of the corner of her mouth. 'Hmm.'

'There's not much detail on the file but things must have been bad if she went to court to get him to stay away from her.'

Mayfield stopped typing briefly. 'Is it important? He's got a good alibi for the night. I've just spoken to his girlfriend. A decent witness and, anyway, we're not looking at anyone else in relation to the fire.'

With a sigh, Connie picked up her handbag and stuffed in

the details of Holly Winson's address.

'Aren't you supposed to be talking to Francesca's parents?' Mayfield called to her as she left.

Holly Winson wasn't in. The bungalow had a bland façade, although Connie noticed the raised beds in the front garden were immaculately kept. Unusually for a cul-de-sac, no one was watching through the windows. She slipped a card through the letterbox that asked Holly to get in touch and she moved on to George's apartment.

Now she had more time, she stopped to look at the edifice of what had once been St Alkmund's workhouse. She knew of the existence of these former homes for the poor but they had always conjured up an image of huge out-of-town granite fortresses with a clock tower dominating the skyline. St Alkmund's was imposing, certainly, but it looked more like a Regency coach house. It fitted in snugly between the row of shops to the left and tall terraces on the right that sold for a fortune on the rare occasions they appeared on the market. Squinting closely, she could now make out the date carved above the door. 1796. She wondered what it must be like to live in a place with such a history of misery.

The wide front entrance opened and a well-dressed man left the building, holding the door for her, clearly not concerned about security. She took the stairs this time to get a good look at the building. The stone steps were modern, expensive replacements but the tall arched windows looked original with their plain thick glass obscuring the street below.

George was surprised to see her but willingly let her in.

'Do you want a coffee?'

She watched him walk into the kitchen and was annoyed to feel the small pinch of sexual desire. His blue shirt was slapped to his back and she could see the contours of his muscles through the material. The cappuccino he brought to her was divine. She tried not to show the satisfaction she felt as the caffeine ran through her body. He sat on the sofa, waiting for her to speak, and she watched him put three lumps of sugar into his cup. He exuded a sense of confidence mixed with insecurity and she guessed it must be a potent mix for some women. There was also, however, an essential coldness to him and she wondered how much of a misogynist he was to the females in his life.

'You have more news for us, about the deaths? Julia told me the gist of what Sadler told her and I've since spoken to Pat. You suspect Francesca.' His words had the studied carefulness of someone purposely moderating their tone.

'Does that surprise you?'

'Francesca came from nowhere. Well, nowhere we know. She appeared one day in the auction house, and shortly after she and my father started seeing each other. She could have been anybody so perhaps we shouldn't be surprised she turned out to be unstable.'

'Unstable? You knew she was dangerous?'

A flash of anger crossed his face. 'I never said that. I said I didn't know her.'

'Did you know she was pregnant again?'

'I did *not*.' His voice was indignant. 'The first I'd heard of it was when Sadler called me to update me.'

She let it go. 'What kind of man was your father?'

'What's that got to do with anything? He was murdered by her. Why can't he be left in peace?'

'We're still going to need some answers. It'll all come up in the inquest. People don't just murder their families. The coroner will be looking for a reason. Was he a violent man?'

'You've asked me this before.' He ran a hand through his long hair. 'Look. He was old-fashioned. Critical. Probably like a lot of parents of his generation. We could never do anything right. Everything we did was subject to scrutiny and ridicule.'

'Always? Even before your mother disappeared?'

George's lips settled into a thin line. 'For as long as I remember he was like that and, yes, even before Mum disappeared.'

'That must have been difficult.'

'Difficult?'

'To live with, I mean.'

George stared at her. 'Not particularly. He was the same with the colleagues I saw him with. Why say something nice when you could be disparaging?'

'And he was like that with your mother?'

'I told you he was the same with everyone.'

'No worse with your mother then.' Connie's mouth was dry despite the coffee. He was parrying her questions with a casualness that she was desperate to get beneath.

He flushed. 'What are you implying? We're not talking about her, are we? That's in the past.'

'I was just asking. It was never discovered why she disappeared.'

He downed his coffee in one angry gulp and slammed the cup back on his saucer.

'My father is the victim here, right?'

'It's one scenario.'

'What do you mean, one scenario? We've been told Francesca is believed responsible for all the deaths. Is that or is that not true?'

'We're doing some checking, that's all. Background and so on. Like your relationship with your ex-wife.'

He'd gone very still. The creeping prickle of fear began to ripple all over her body. She'd stupidly not told anyone she would be coming here. She could feel his anger directed at her, a fierce white rod of heat.

She stood up to go, trying to ignore her trembling legs. 'You appreciate I need to ask the questions. We're investigating all aspects of the case.'

'Well, let me tell you something.' He didn't get up. He didn't need to. She could feel his strength from where she was rooted to the spot. 'Firstly, my divorce was like a lot of marriage breakdowns. It was acrimonious and the break-up difficult.'

'She requested a restraining order.' Connie could barely get the words out.

'For a while, when I tried to see Holly she wouldn't let me in the house and when I tried too hard one evening she went to the police. If you've never been through a shitty relationship break-up, consider yourself lucky. Does that answer your question?'

Not really, thought Connie, desperate to get out of the flat.

'As for Francesca, she clearly was an evil little bitch. She just hid it well. As for my mother, she almost certainly buggered off because, like most women, she decided the grass was greener elsewhere. So I find, like many times before, once again it's just me and Julia left to pick up the pieces.'

Connie dug down into her reserves and asked the question that had been bothering her all day.

'Can I just ask what happens to your father's money?' She

had opened the door, ready to do a runner if necessary, but George's face had settled into the paleness of the very angry.

'I suggest,' he said through gritted teeth, 'that you speak to his solicitor about that.'

35

Sadler looked up as Margaret, Llewellyn's secretary, stood at the entrance to his office.

'Is everything okay?'

'The Super is out at a meeting in Glossop but I've just taken a call from a member of the public with a complaint.'

'Who?'

'His name's George Winson. The name rang a bell so I did a quick double-check on the system. He was interviewed in relation to the incident on Cross Farm Road.'

'He's one of the adult children of the family involved. What's the matter?'

'He said he'd been visited by Connie and she'd virtually accused him of being involved in the murder.'

'What? Are you sure?' Sadler stood up and looked behind her into the communal office. 'Where the hell is she, anyway?'

'I don't know. Can you deal with it, Sadler? Llewellyn is at a meeting about staffing. He'll be in a foul mood when he gets back.'

'Do you have George Winson's number?' Margaret silently handed over a slip of paper and left, closing the door behind her. Sadler looked at the number and dialled.

'Winson here.'

'It's DI Sadler. We met earlier this week.'

'I'm hardly likely to forget, am I? It's your boss I wanted.'

'He's out, I'm afraid, and likely to be for some time. Your message has been passed over to me. You say you had a meeting with a member of the team that you weren't happy with?'

'Meeting? It was a bloody interrogation. She virtually accused me of killing my family.'

'She actually said that?'

'Well, not in so many words but that was the tone. Asking me about my relationship with my ex-wife. What the hell has that got to do with the case?'

What indeed, thought Sadler, his mood darkening. 'I'll need to speak to the officer concerned.'

'Well, when you do, why don't you bloody well ask her what my father's relationship with my mother has to do with anything either? Is my mother's disappearance relevant at all?'

'She asked you about your mother?'

'She did. So, have you found a connection between my father's murder and my mother?'

'The investigation is in its early stages but I don't think—'

'So the answer is no. Then why turn up on my doorstep asking about the past which is very painful for me? Aren't you investigating Francesca?'

'Of course we are.'

'Your DC came at me like a tiger in a cage. If she'd been a bit less combative, I might have been able to tell her what I actually witnessed with Francesca.'

'Witnessed? You saw something?'

'Oh, it's nothing. It's probably not relevant to the case.'

Sadler sat down and pulled a notepad towards him. 'I'd like to hear it anyway.'

'Well, it was a little thing but I'm sure she was cruel to

Charlie. These things are so hard to prove. I once saw her slap him hard across the face when he was small. It was one of the things that made me stop going around there. He had a red weal on his face afterwards.'

'She hit him?'

'I saw it with my own eyes. It made me wince because I didn't think people smacked their children any more.'

'They don't.' Sadler thought of his sister Camilla and the 'naughty step' her children inhabited regularly during his visits.

'It's illegal, isn't it?'

'Parents are still able to discipline their children physically, but if the violence is severe enough to leave a mark, they could be prosecuted for assault.'

'Well, there you go then. Charlie's cheek was bright red. Francesca was a cauldron of violence, not all of it suppressed. Why don't you consider the implications of that instead of sending a member of your team to harass me?'

'I'll speak to the officer involved.'

'You do that. I don't want to see her again.'

*

Connie's phone went onto voicemail, but twenty minutes later she walked into the open-plan office and went over to Matthews's desk. Sadler strode over to the door of his office and yanked it open. 'In here.'

She walked towards him, half defiant. He waited until he had shut the door. 'You went to see George Winson.'

'I wanted to ask him about Francesca.'

'Did you? I don't recall asking you to do that. Why did you question him about his failed marriage and his missing mother?'

'It's background. Don't you see it's just so bloody odd. The forensic evidence says that it was Francesca who killed the family. You've asked us to look for a reason. I can't see any.'

'Did you ask him about Francesca? About the type of mother she was?'

'No, but—'

'If you had, he might have mentioned the strong disciplining of Charlie.'

'What do you mean?'

'George witnessed Francesca slapping Charlie. The act, it seems, was shocking in itself, as was the fact it left a mark on Charlie's cheek.'

'But what relevance—'

'You don't think it's relevant? We're looking at a mother who's killed her son. You don't think it's *relevant* how she treated him before? Have you done what I asked and spoken to her parents yet?'

'No, I was—'

'So you were just doing something you hadn't been asked to do.'

Connie's face was puce. 'The past has got to be connected to this case. A woman goes missing in a small town, it attracts media attention and then nearly forty years later there's another catastrophe involving one of the people involved. There's got to be a connection.'

'I told you. We don't have the resources to look into this and I'm not going to tell you again how Peter died. If he's the murderer of his first wife then he will be getting justice beyond us at the moment.'

'But what about justice here!' She was shouting at him. He willed himself to keep calm and held one arm with the other to stop his trembling.

'You are not to do any more investigating into Elizabeth Winson. Any liaison with the remaining Winson family members is to be done by Pat. It's what she's trained for. Is that clear?'

She refused to look him in the eye.

'Is that clear?' he shouted back at her, shocking them both. He saw a small tear appear in the corner of one eye.

'Perfectly clear,' she said and left the room.

36

Julia had gone inside to escape the warmth of the sun. After brooding in front of the laptop for over an hour she roused herself and rang Maureen at Anchor Cavern.

'Is it okay if I come in on Sunday? I can't stand sitting here any longer.'

'Of course you can come back. We've been managing with the seasonal staff but we've really missed you. Are you sure you'll be okay?'

'I've got to get out of here. I've now got neighbour problems in addition to everything else.'

Julia heard Maureen put her hand over the mouthpiece and a muffled conversation. 'Can you sit on reception while I take this call? It's a personnel issue.' A moment later, Maureen came back on the line. 'What's the matter? I thought you got on well with your neighbours.'

'This guy's moved in next to me and he's complaining about Bosco's barking. His name is Morell something or other.'

'Oh my God. Not Morell Thorn? The guy who lost his brother in the caves?'

'That's the one.'

'For God's sake, don't tell him where you work. He's been obsessed since his brother went missing.'

'I'd heard about him but never met him.'

'Don't get me wrong. Some of the stuff he's done is really

good. The legislation that regulates caving came about through his persistence. He's never got over his brother, though. I mean, it's unhinged him. He visits all the caves in the area as if trying to find out answers.'

'I've never seen him in Anchor Cavern th—'

'Oh, believe me, he's been here. Probably before your time. How long have you been here? Five years? Well, it must have been before then.'

'He's not dangerous, though, is he?'

'Look. Just don't tell him where you work, okay? I have to go. A group's just arrived. I'll see you on Sunday.'

As she was putting the phone down, George walked in through the front door, making her heart lurch with shock.

'Don't you bolt it when you're inside? Anyone could walk in.'

'Are you trying to give me a heart attack? I must have left it on the latch when I came back in. Jesus, I've been out in the garden as well.'

He shut the door carefully behind him and turned to her with a face of fury. 'That bitch has been around the flat. Asking questions about me and Holly and then she wanted to know all about Dad. What's she digging around for when it was Francesca who started the fire?'

'Started the fire?' She could feel the heat rising in her face. 'That's a funny way of putting it. You mean murdered everyone and started the fire.'

He grabbed her arm, the roughest she'd ever felt him touch her since they were children.

'I'm not likely to forget, am I? I'm trying to digest this the same as you. The point is, Francesca is the murderer, that's what the police have proved.'

'It's what they said to me too. What's the problem?'

'I've just spoken to Sadler and made a complaint about that woman detective, coming around my house and throwing accusations around.'

'Connie?'

'That's the one. Dad may have been a miserable old bastard but I'll be damned if I see him fitted up for something he didn't do. Either that or she's trying to pin the crime on me. Either way, I'm not standing for it.'

'How can she pin the crime on you? You were with your girlfriend that evening.'

'Well, Dad then. She's poking her nose into his and Mum's relationship. What's she asking me for? Relationships are a mystery to me, full stop.'

'It's quite a punishment, isn't it?'

'What do you mean?'

'Well, he and Francesca might not have had the marriage of the century but it's some punishment being bludgeoned to death in your own bed.'

He turned away from her. 'God knows what was going on in that woman's head. The point is they're not looking for anyone else in relation to the killings. Can I get a glass of water?' He went into her narrow kitchen and started to open her cupboards.

'So what did Sadler say? About Connie, I mean.'

'He seemed a bit resigned when I told him. She's obviously a bit of a trouble maker and he said he'd have a word with her.'

'They do still think—'

'Of course they do. You can't bludgeon yourself to death, can you? The police know Francesca's a murderer, we know it's true—'

'I don't.' The words slipped out and, for the moment, the mask of anger on his face dropped, to be replaced by one of surprise and something else. Julia carried on regardless. 'I don't believe it.'

He turned the tap on carefully and filled his glass. 'What do you mean, what don't you believe?'

'Francesca wasn't like that. She was secretive and, well, a bit chilly but not a cold-blooded murderer.'

'You think this was done in cold blood? With a hammer? It's the act of a furious woman. Still waters run deep, and that was the case with Francesca.'

'Angry with Dad *and* her child?'

'They're not looking for anyone else.'

Was it her imagination or had she detected a note of warning in his voice? She looked towards Bosco and was touched to see he had come to the kitchen door, standing watch and tensed as he kept a pair of wary eyes on George.

'Do you ever think of Mum?'

She had wrong-footed her brother and he shifted back a little.

'I never think of her.'

'That can't be true. You must think of her sometimes or, if not of Mum, those days after she went missing. That's what I keep thinking about now. How we felt those first few weeks when they were dredging the rivers and digging in the back garden.'

'You mean when they thought Dad had killed her. Do you

know what? I used to watch them and hope they'd find Mum's body.'

'For closure, you mean?' Julia asked.

'Don't be ridiculous. Of course I didn't want her to be dead. I wanted to feel something other than bewilderment. Pain, grief. Anything would have been better than not knowing.'

'Do you think Dad felt the same way?'

George slowly dried his glass with the tea towel. 'I couldn't have cared less what Dad thought. It was bad enough knowing we'd have to spend our teenage years putting up with the little digs, the put-downs and the constant pressure.'

'It turned out all right, though, didn't it? It could have been worse.'

George shrugged and looked at his watch. 'I have to go. I've got a date.'

'Do you think she's still alive?'

He didn't want to discuss it any longer. 'I've no idea.'

'Don't you ever wonder? Don't you care?'

He turned scarlet but held his emotions in check. 'Of course I wonder. Some days I think of nothing else, to answer your question. What good does thinking do, though? We're not going to find out now.'

Julia wondered whether to tell him about the forum and how she'd sat hunched over her computer for years trying to find an answer, however painful, to the mystery. It was only now, with the discovery of the note on the flowers, she could see she'd been buoyed by the first note received after their mother's disappearance. There was no way she could share this with George. The identity of the sender of the flowers was a minor part of a much more painful mystery. She tried one more time.

'Now. Take a moment now and tell me what you think happened.'

He folded his arms. 'I think she's dead.'

'Why? Why do you think she's dead?'

There was an expression on his face she didn't recognise and, for the first time, she felt frightened. Bosco felt it too and she could hear him growling from behind her.

He didn't answer her but fiddled with the laptop she'd left carelessly on the kitchen counter. *Don't look at it*, she willed. *Don't discover how desperate I am for answers.* He tried to open the screen but it was password locked.

He gave up and looked at the still growling Bosco. 'Some things are best left in the past.'

37

Tuesday, 9 September 1986

'Where's Horace?'

She'd noticed the silence in the house as soon as she arrived home from school. The little bandy-legged dog who would come trotting towards her was missed immediately. She found George in the outside shed, sanding down a chair he'd rescued from a skip the previous week. He stopped briefly to listen to her question then started again, not looking at her.

'I had to have him put down. Poor blighter.'

'What?' Julia could feel her bottom lip beginning to tremble.

George stopped and threw the sandpaper over onto the bench and wiped his hands on his trousers. 'He was sick. I told you, his fur was coming off in clumps, so I took him to the vet and he said there was nothing he could do.'

'He had the mange!' she shouted at him. She could feel the fat blobs of tears coursing down her cheeks. 'All we needed to do was shampoo him in the bath every other day and it would have disappeared.'

He shoved the chair out of the way and walked past her into the garden. 'The vet said there was nothing he could do.' He was bellowing at her across the lawn and, as expected, their father came out of the house looking at them over his glasses.

'What's the matter?'

She turned to her father. 'Did you know Horace was going to be put down?'

He was staring at George in silence, forcing an explanation from his son. 'He was sick. The vet said there was nothing to be done.'

'Which vet?' Her father had folded his arms.

'I took him to a cheap one up in Darley Dale. The Bampton ones are too expensive. This one did it for cash.'

'Which vet?' repeated her father. Julia didn't like the tone of his voice and moved away from them both. It allowed her a better view of how they were standing, like prize-fighters weighing up the opposition. It was her father who gave in first.

'It was George's dog,' he said to her, 'his responsibility.'

'But he only had bad skin. I'd have looked after him.' A thought occurred to her. 'Where's the body?'

'I buried it in the woods. You're too sentimental, you know. When it's over, it's time to go. He knows all about that.' He stuck a thumb towards the door and their father's retreating back.

'What do you mean?'

'Sentimentality is for losers. When it's over, it's over.'

38

Sadler went home and after stripping off his clothes and throwing them into his washing basket got straight into the shower. Connie had taken his reprimand badly. He had expected that. The question was, would she listen to him and keep away from the Winsons? George Winson had made it clear he wanted Sadler to formally discipline Connie. Well, there was no way he was going to do that. Yet. He had, however, spelt it out to her this time. Leave the grieving children of Peter Winson alone. Next time, he wouldn't be so polite.

As he turned off the shower he could hear, in the distance, his phone ringing. He'd never make it in time so he waited for the caller to give up. He dressed in the jeans his sister Camilla had bought for his birthday and then berated him that they remained unworn in his wardrobe. As he reached for a jumper the phone began to ring again; he rolled his eyes and went to see who was calling. It was a Sheffield number, the owner not programmed into his phone. He thought back to the glass of wine he'd had with Karen the other evening. At the end of the evening they'd made vague promises to keep in touch and had exchanged numbers. It must be her calling. Sadler felt a curious reluctance to pick up the phone, perhaps out of a long remembered loyalty to his friend Miles. Also, he thought to himself, as he went into his small kitchen, why would she call twice in the same few minutes?

By the time his sister had arrived with her two sons in tow, the smell of cooking wafted around his house. Sadler's nephews marched into the kitchen, trading jokes. 'Why was six afraid of seven?' demanded Ben. Sadler put his spoon down on the counter. 'I don't know. Why was six afraid of seven?'

'Because seven ate nine.' Samuel roared with laughter. Behind her sons, Camilla groaned. 'They've been non-stop in the car.'

Ben lifted the lid on the saucepan. 'Spag bol again?' he asked and was rewarded with a jab in the ribs by his anxious older brother.

'We like it,' he assured his uncle. Camilla fanned herself with a magazine pulled from her handbag.

'It's hot out there. I couldn't get the air conditioning to work in the car so I drove over here with the windows down. Remember? Like we used to do as kids.'

'Of course I remember. How's John?'

At the mention of her husband Camilla frowned. 'Working too hard as usual. He called to say he'll be back home around ten. I think he used the excuse to work late as he knew we were coming round here. He hates going home to an empty house. He'll get a takeaway at work.'

Sadler made a face. 'Ben is right, it *is* spaghetti bolognaise again.'

Camilla smirked. 'Can you make anything else?'

'Sausage and mash, but I think I did that last time.'

The phone rang again and Camilla looked towards it. 'Work?'

'It shouldn't be. They don't normally ring my mobile in the evenings because of the patchy reception.'

'Aren't you going to answer it?'

Sadler, with his back to her, stirred the thick sauce. 'It can wait until after.'

Camilla snorted with laughter. 'Not another married woman. Please tell me at least she's single this time.'

Sadler carried on stirring. 'Do you remember Miles?'

'Miles? Of course I do. I quite fancied him myself except he had that weird girlfriend around him. What was her name?'

'Karen.' Sadler didn't dare turn round.

'Oh my God, don't tell me it's her. Francis, seriously, please don't say you're seeing her?'

Now Sadler did turn. 'I'm not seeing her, no. But we did meet by chance the other evening and we went for a drink. She's rung a couple of times this evening, that's all.' He caught sight of his sister's face. 'What's the matter? You didn't like her?'

Camilla's face took on a mulish expression. 'Bunny boiler.'

*

Connie sat in the silent office and stared sightlessly at the computer screen. The admonishment from Sadler hurt more than she was prepared to admit. She was only doing what she usually did, pushing the boundaries further than was expected. Shaking the tree to see what fell out. The problem was, now George had complained she'd have to tread even more carefully. As far as Connie was concerned, he was a suspect whatever the forensic evidence might say.

His mother's disappearance must hold the key to what had happened up in Cross Farm Lane. Elizabeth was one of those genuine missing persons who are never found. Forces up and down the country had a couple of cases of them on their books. Men and women who just disappeared; sometimes voluntarily, sometimes not. The case appeared to have been periodically reassessed but no formal attempts had been made to put additional man-hours into the investigation. So, except for David Stanhope's belief that Peter Winson was responsible for his wife's disappearance, there was precious little to go on.

Connie clicked on the picture of the missing woman. Elizabeth had a large round face and a body prone to putting on weight. At thirty she'd been slightly plump, a roll of fat peeping over the waistband of her elasticated trousers. She had worn her blonde curly hair in the 'shampoo and set' style favoured by her own mother. It had meant weekly visits to the hairdresser and much fuss when it was raining. She looked slightly mumsy but that might have been the dated clothes. Tight brown terylene trousers and a striped polo neck that did nothing for Elizabeth's figure. What had Peter Winson looked like in the seventies? Connie did another search and held her breath when she saw him. At the time of his wife's disappearance, Peter had been startlingly handsome. He had jet-black hair, curled above his long sideburns. Wearing a pale grey suit, his smart attire seemed out of place in front of his wife's wool shop, the perplexing note still pinned to the door. She wondered if he'd dressed up especially for the cameras.

Connie clicked back onto the photo of Elizabeth and pasted it so it stood side by side with that of her husband's. Well, she'd come across some unusual couples in her time. That was for sure. Beautiful women married to ugly men, but only once had she seen it the other way around. In uniform, she'd been called to a house burglary and had been struck dumb by how handsome the man had been. His wife, like Elizabeth, had been dumpy and Connie, to her shame, had wondered how the two had stayed together. Was it a valid question?

*

'You remember how it was. I hadn't met John yet so I was around yours a fair bit.'

The children had been fed and were settled in front of Sadler's small TV, watching a programme. Ben, suffering from a summer cold, had his mouth open slightly. Both ignored the adults who were still sitting at the table. Camilla kept one eye on them as she spoke in a low voice.

'I remember. I don't recall Miles and Karen there that much, though.'

'They certainly were a couple of times. I liked them both, although Karen was fairly reserved. The problem was one evening I got a phone call. She sounded upset and said she needed to have it out with me.'

'About what?'

'She said something along the lines that she knew what I was up to and to remember Miles was her boyfriend.'

Sadler felt a spurt of anger. 'Why didn't you tell me?'

Camilla smiled and looked over to the children. 'I was a bit embarrassed, I suppose. I mean, Miles was attractive. Tall, ginger hair. Not a million miles from John when you think about it. I did fancy him, although I'd never have stolen him from another woman. It's just, well, I think Karen has antennae like a beetle. She could spot mutual attraction from a mile off.'

'But there was nothing between you and Miles.'

'Of course not, but that's not the point. We all feel jealousy, don't we? It's human nature and it partly shows we care. I remember dumping someone in my twenties because he fancied one of my friends and I couldn't have cared less because he wasn't for me. It's strong emotions that cause us the agonies of doubt.'

'She picked up the phone and called you?'

'Exactly. That's where she went beyond the point of protective girlfriend. How many people would actually *call* the person they're jealous of? That's not normal. How many times has she rung your mobile since you met?'

'Only this evening but she's called it three times.'

Camilla lifted up her glass and made a face. 'You do choose them, you know, Francis.'

39

Saturday morning dawned with clouds overhanging the Peak sky. It was a day of lie-ins for romantic couples, dozing teenagers and the hung-over. Anyone who had a life basically, which brought home to Julia the fact she didn't. Bosco was snuffling in his sleep, usually a reassuring sound but the thought of her little dog was failing to soothe her this morning. Something was niggling away at her subconscious. A little dog and the pain of loss. She turned over in bed and tried to ignore the thoughts jabbing at her.

She recalled George's anger last night. Her rational mind partly understood his fear. They were both uncomfortable not only with the detective's questions but also with the fact they were being forced to accept that their family's history was once more in the public domain. The press had made the connection, of course. Theirs was an unusual surname. The tone of the newspaper articles, however, had been doom-laden rather than salacious, along the lines of one tragedy begets another. Although she would never have admitted it, Julia had been hoping an enterprising journalist would take up their story and discover what had happened to their mother. No one was taking on the challenge and so her parents' marriage remained as much an enigma to her now as it had been then.

George's refusal to dig deeper into the tragedy that had befallen them was an extension of how he had treated their mother's disappearance. He just moved to the new reality and never again spoke of Elizabeth. His revelation to her that he thought of their mother often was just that. A revelation.

Her doorbell chimed and she frowned at the alarm clock in surprise. Eight in the morning; it couldn't be anything good this early. It surely wouldn't be her neighbour, for her dog hadn't barked once during the night. Bosco wasn't interested in the sound. The gentle chime of a doorbell was different to a loud knock and, as if to emphasise the point, he turned over onto his back and lay with his legs in the air. Some guard dog he was.

She stuffed her feet into her slippers and padded downstairs. Light streamed through the window in her hall and she opened the door a fraction until the chain holding it in place bucked at the tension. Outside was a man she recognised but couldn't place. He used his thumb to indicate where he'd come from.

'I live across the way at number 23.'

She recognised him now. He'd moved in with his girlfriend a couple of years earlier, although she'd spotted his partner moving out a few months later, conjugal bliss clearly not working out.

'Hold on.' She shut the door and undid the chain, opening the door to its full width. 'Is everything all right?'

'I hope you don't mind me knocking, love. It's just I saw someone hanging around outside your place last night. There isn't any problem, is there?'

'Hanging around outside? When?'

'It must have been about midnight. I'd been watching a film and I fell asleep. When I turned off the telly ready to go to bed, I saw someone standing outside your house looking up at it.'

'A man or woman?'

'I couldn't tell. He or she wasn't small. Tall and large, I'd say. They weren't trying to get in, they were just standing there, looking.'

'God.' Julia ran her fingers through her unkempt hair. 'I never noticed anything.'

'You got a possessive ex?'

'Me? Definitely not. I thought I saw someone the other night but I put it down to my overactive imagination.'

'Someone was definitely there. They went off when I opened the door to have a word with them.'

'You did that?'

'Why not? They might have been trying to break in for all I know. I was going to give them a piece of my mind but by the time I'd opened the door and stepped into the street they were gone. They can move quickly, I'll give them that. You sure you haven't got man trouble? I had an ex-girlfriend who used to do that sort of thing.'

'There's no one.' She thought of Ned, who'd seemed fine after their discussion on the ghost walk, but she could have sworn she had had seen him walking away from her neighbour's yesterday. Perhaps he'd come back again to look at her house. She remembered how she'd unthinkingly let Bosco out before she'd gone to bed. Whoever it was could have come down the alley through the back way and climbed over her fence. The thought made her dizzy.

'Are you all right? Look, I'll keep an eye on your place for you. I'm only across the road if you need help.'

When he'd gone, she saw Bosco had come down the stairs. He now looked up at her with a quizzical expression. She bent down to tap his head and his eyes narrowed in bliss. She picked up her phone and rang George and he answered, his voice thick with sleep.

'Did I wake you?'

'Of course you bloody well woke me. It's ten past eight.'

'That's the middle of the day for some people.'

'Is that what you've called me for? To abuse me?'

Julia sighed, hearing her voice hiss down the line. 'You weren't standing outside my house last night, were you?'

'Me? Why would I want to do that?'

'Just answer the question, would you?'

'Of course I wasn't.'

'Then never mind.' She cut the connection, feeling stupid. He'd said he had a date, which might have meant a late night and he may well still be in bed with the woman. She went to her coat pocket and dug around for the card she'd held onto.

Unlike George's sleepy tones, the voice at the other end was alert. 'Connie here.'

'I'm sorry for calling. I was going to call Pat but, well, you gave me your number too so I thought I'd try you first.'

'Julia? Is everything all right?'

'My neighbour saw someone hanging around my house last night and it's the second time it's happened. I'm not sure if I should report it.'

'Someone outside your house? What time?'

'Midnight-ish.'

'Do you think it might have been a journalist?'

Julia's body flooded with relief. The press, of course. 'I

hadn't thought of that, you might be right. One of them might be trying to get a story.'

'It's possible, I suppose. Look, I'm not really meant to be speaking to you. Your brother made a complaint about me and all contact needs to go through Pat. Why don't you ring and tell her?'

'But you think it might be just a journalist?'

'I'm sure that's it. Tell Pat what's happened.' There was a short pause. 'But I am here for you if there's a problem, I promise.'

It was only after she'd ended the call Julia thought to worry why a journalist would be looking up at her house at midnight and, perhaps more troubling, why George hadn't been more concerned for her welfare.

40

The Marchesis were packing their belongings when Connie showed up at their hotel room.

'We're going home tonight.' Stefano was folding neatly ironed shirts into a leather suitcase, taking his time.

'Does Sadler know?'

The man shrugged. 'I spoke to DS Matthews yesterday. She said as long as we had our interview with you before we left, it would be okay.' He looked up at her. 'We were expecting you before now.'

Connie sat down on the bed and looked over to his wife. She had an old-fashioned vanity case into which she was carefully placing a variety of bottles, each wrapped in tissue paper. She noticed Connie watching her and turned her back slightly away so that the task was out of sight.

His shirts all packed, Stefano appeared at a loss what to do next. 'You have more questions for us?'

'Yes, I'm afraid. We're trying to put together a picture of Francesca's state of mind. You knew she was having another baby?'

Stefano glanced at his wife. 'DS Matthews told us but we didn't know before.'

'She hadn't rung you with the news?'

'No.'

Once more Connie was assailed by the sense that nothing

was as it seemed. She took a deep breath. 'Knowing Francesca, can you tell me how she would have felt? Do you think she would have been happy?'

'Francesca never happy.' Maria Marchesi kept her back to Connie.

'Why? Why wasn't she happy?'

Stefano gave a long, deep sigh. 'She was glad to get away from us.'

Connie shifted on the bed in frustration. 'But why? Why was she glad to get away from you? Did you have a difficult relationship?'

Now Maria did turn. 'Francesca a bad person. Always. A bad person.'

Connie frowned. 'Why do you say that? Why was she bad?'

Maria stared at her for a moment and then resumed her packing. Connie gave it one final go. 'She killed her husband and child and the baby she was having because she was bad. Is that what you're saying?'

Maria stopped packing and stared out of the window in front of her. 'Yes.'

*

Matthews was spending her Saturday at her dining-room table with her notes spread out in front of her. Her partner Ruth owned an interior design shop in Bampton and summer meant longer opening hours at the weekends. Her love was 1970s design and the oval teak dining set was a triumphant find from an antiques market two years earlier. Ruth had departed with a coffee and kiss at seven that morning and Matthews, never a

177

morning person, had resisted the temptation to lie in. Now she spread her own notes around her and considered where they had got on the case.

She was as much disappointed in her career as those around her. Her failure to make inspector was not due to her competence, her qualifications or, as Ruth sometimes maintained, her sexuality. She'd simply been unlucky. But luck defies all attempts at analysis and Matthews continued to maintain the belief that only hard work would lift her from her career slump until an opportunity came up in Bampton or another Derbyshire division. She had toyed with moving forces. Appointments periodically came up in places where she would consider living. Devon, for instance. Ruth, however, had an elderly mother nearby and didn't want to move. Only in moments of abject disloyalty did Matthews consider applying anyway.

Francesca was a murderer. Connie would be moved from the case if she continued to assert her opinions to the contrary. Francesca had been a woman who kept herself to herself. A classic introvert and a keeper of secrets. It might not explain what had made her kill her family but she had the characteristics of a woman with much to hide. Her ringing mobile shook Matthews out of her reverie and she hurried to answer it. Connie's breathless voice came on the line.

'I'm back at the station typing up my notes. I've just been speaking to Francesca's parents. Her mother said Francesca was a bad person. Good God, I'm not close to my own father but I'd like to think he wouldn't say that about me. What kind of mother says that?'

'Did they say why she was bad?'

'Oh, something or other about always being bad. You know

it's not like that. She can't have been bad at, say, two months old.'

'Nature versus nurture.'

'I don't mean that. I mean the fact that her parents are willingly accepting a narrative of events that makes no sense. That it's usually the male head of a family who obliterates everyone, that acts such as these are usually preceded by issues of domestic violence.'

'George Winson states that he saw Francesca hit Charlie.'

'Oh that.'

'That? You don't think it's relevant?'

'My father gave me a slap a few times when I was growing up. It's probably nothing.'

'In this day and age? They don't smack children any more. I think, Connie, you're losing your sense of proportion over this case.'

'Me?'

'Yes— oh bloody hell. Can you hold on a minute?' Matthews could hear her home phone ringing.

Sadler was on the other end of it, his voice resigned. 'One of the papers has got wind of the course of events. The headline for tomorrow, according to the press office, is "Killer Mum". I'm calling a press conference for this afternoon.' He hesitated. 'Are you all right to come in? I know it's a Saturday.'

'Of course. I've got Connie on the other phone. Do you want me to tell her?'

Again the hesitation. 'Mention it to her but tell her she doesn't need to come in. She can enjoy her weekend in peace.'

*

Connie ended the call and marvelled at her ability to contain her fury. There was an important press conference and she wasn't even going to be there even though she was here in the station already. If it had been Palmer who was to attend over her, she would have been spitting blood. The fact it was the calm and capable Matthews made it worse, however. She was being sidelined and all because she had dared to challenge the perceived narrative of events. Francesca was going to be paraded throughout the media as a monster, a killer of children, her children, and a mass murderer, and no one seemed to have a problem that there was no evidence whatsoever of why she might have done so.

The Marchesis appeared to be a decent sort but there was something odd about their attitude towards their daughter. The couple were from a small town called Collodi and it didn't take long until she found the number of the local police station. The woman who answered the telephone spoke poor English but after Connie shouted Francesca's name into the phone, a man with a deep voice and a slight West Country accent came onto the line.

'I miss England, you know. The rain. I miss the rain.'

'I'll swap if you like.'

He laughed. 'I did an exchange with Avon police. It's where I improved my English. Do you know them?'

'I'm afraid not, they're the other end of the country.'

'Of course. Well, the English has come in useful. There's always a spate of thefts when the tourists come to Collodi, which is, of course, all year round.'

'I know the feeling, but it's not English tourists I've called about.'

'You're ringing about Francesca Marchesi.'

'Did you know her?'

She heard a long sigh down the telephone. 'We know everyone around here. It's a small town. Of course I knew Francesca. I knew her from when she was a child.'

'Sounds like around here. Everyone knows each other.'

'Exactly. You do something bad at thirteen, no one ever forgets.'

'That's true. Francesca's parents' response to the tragedy seems a little strange. I mean, they're acting a little odd.'

'Odd? They're probably in shock.'

'That's what I thought,' said Connie, crossing her fingers.

'So that's it then.'

'The thing is, her mother made a strange comment. She said Francesca had always been bad. I just wondered, what I mean is, you know your comment about something bad, did Francesca do something when *she* was thirteen?'

There was a pause and the sound of a door being shut. When he came back on the line, he sounded tired.

'I'm going to tell you a story, well, two actually. Then you can make your own conclusions about Signor and Signora Marchesi when they say that their daughter had always been bad.'

41

Just before the press conference, Sadler talked again with Nigel
Rooth on the telephone. He could hear young children scream-
ing in the background and, at one point, their conversation
was interrupted by a small voice asking their father to 'tell off
Archie'. To Sadler, Nigel was polite but firm.

'We've now conducted our interviews with the witnesses
and that, along with forensic evidence, supports our original
conclusion that Francesca was the perpetrator of the fire.'

'Go through this one more time, will you? The exact sequence of events.'

'Of course. Look, hold on, let me go up to my study and
shut the door. My wife can deal with the kids.'

The background noise quietened and Nigel sounded more
relaxed.

'Okay. So here, according to the fire forensic report, is what
we consider to be the course of events. The fire started in the
front bedroom in which the child was sleeping. We found remnants of what we believe to be the ignition, which was a piece
of child's clothing that had been set alight. Furthermore, evidence shows, and I'm getting technical here as you're asking,
when ignition occurred there was a low order explosion and we
have seen this through the dust patterns. There is also evidence
of a trail of accelerant that moved across the landing into the
back bedroom at which point it stops. There, we also found the

melted plastic of what we consider to be the receptacle containing the petrol.'

'There's no accelerant near the woman's body hanging in front of the landing window?' asked Sadler.

'There's petrol on the landing but it stops well clear of where the female was hanging.'

'It all seems pretty clear. Can I run past you some other possible scenarios? Play devil's advocate, as it were.'

'Please do. We've already done this ourselves.'

'Suppose the adult male, Peter Winson, killed his son, then hanged his wife and finally committed suicide, would that be possible with the fire evidence?' Sadler didn't add that it would also entail Peter battering himself to death.

Rooth had clearly thought through the possibility. 'It would be more likely he hanged his wife first. Then killed his child and then led the accelerant into his own bedroom. He would then have had to light the fire in Charlie's bedroom and run back quickly into his own room and kill himself before the fire engulfed his own bedroom. Which given how he died would be very unlikely.'

They were both silent.

'I'm sorry, I know my questions sound odd but I've got a press conference later and I need to be sure of my ground,' Sadler explained.

'Okay. Well, forensically it's possible but unlikely. Medically, I'm pretty sure it's impossible.'

'Another scenario. What about if an external element entered the family house? Killed, say, the adults first, the mother by hanging and the father through blunt force. Then the person killed Charlie before escaping. Is that a possibility?'

'If that were the case, then I'd see evidence of a break-in and possibly a hurried exit too. I didn't see any evidence of this, although if the external source had a key it would be possible to enter through a door and exit the same way, locking the escape route behind them. The only possible route, given the front and back doors were dead-bolted, would be the patio doors in the kitchen.'

'Do you think that likely?'

'I don't see any evidence of this at all and I'm not sure a lone individual would be able to overpower two fit adults. You would need more than one assailant and, again, I would expect to see some evidence of their presence in the house if that were the case.'

'So it's not cast iron, your scenario, is it?'

Nigel Rooth sighed down the line. 'It depends what you call cast iron. I can tell a lot from forensic evidence and I can often construct complete scenarios from just a scrap of material. If someone external had been in that fire, I should have seen something to suggest an alien presence. As it is, nothing is convincing me my initial assumptions are incorrect. What's bothering you, Francis?'

'What I thought was a conscience in my ear that's turning out to be an irritant.'

Next he called Bill Shields who was less sympathetic. 'Peter Winson didn't batter himself to death. I've had a few surprises in my career but this one would take the biscuit.'

'What about an external agency?'

A note of annoyance crept into Bill's voice. 'We had this out in my office. I don't see any of the usual things I would expect from a murder. No defensive wounds, no sign of a struggle. I can't conclusively say it's suicide but I can't find any evidence for murder. What are you going to say to the press?'

'That we're not looking for anyone else in connection with the case.'

'Well, there you are then.'

42

Connie sat outside Julia's empty house and wondered how much damage she might be doing to her career. All last night she'd fumed. The Italian policeman had been nice but inclined to prejudice towards wayward teenagers. All he'd revealed about Francesca was a spat with first her cousin and then her boyfriend. So, Francesca had seen turbulent teenage years. Join the club. A few adolescent quarrels hardly made Francesca a murderer. The problem was that so few people had known the mother of Charlie. This was what balanced policing was about – trying to get both sides of the story. A rounded view of what made somebody tick. Unfortunately, the one person who had clearly bonded with Francesca was supposed to be out of bounds. Leave the Winsons alone, Connie had been told. Easier said than done.

She spotted Julia coming back from a walk with her dog in tow. Her eyes met Connie's and she frowned.

'You want me?'

'Could we have a chat?'

Julia looked around. 'This is official? I thought you weren't supposed to be speaking to me.' She opened the front door and Bosco shot inside. 'I'm about to go to Anchor Cavern.'

'You're going back to work already?'

Connie's tone had made Julia defensive. 'I can't stay here

any longer. Have you any idea how hard it is to just sit and do nothing?'

'You think it'll take your mind off things?'

'That person hanging round the house gave me the creeps. The best way for me to forget how everything is disintegrating around me is to go to work. I'm sorry, I don't expect you to understand.'

Julia's skin looked grey and Connie took a step backwards. 'Look, it's nothing urgent.'

'But you've come round. There must be something you want to talk about.'

'Did you see the press conference?'

'It was always going to get out, wasn't it? It makes for a more interesting story than my father being the murderer.'

'You're happy with the official explanation then.'

'Happy? What have I got to be happy about? But if it's going to come out, now's as good a time as any.'

'Don't you think it's strange? First your mother's disappearance and then this. The world doesn't exist as a series of random acts. A disappearance occurs in 1980 and then a murder occurs now. Events interlock even if we can't work out how.'

Julia went still. 'I thought this was nothing to do with my mother.'

Connie's shoulders sagged. 'You think it's normal for two catastrophes to happen too?'

Julia looked at her watch and sighed. 'Look, come in for a minute.' Connie stepped inside the terraced house. A comforting smell of clean canine assailed her and, soon enough, a dog with a wagging tail presented itself to her, his jaws dripping with water.

'This is Bosco. He can bark for England, apparently, which is a new one on me, but he doesn't bite. Come into the front room.' Connie followed Julia into a messy but homely living room with stripped pine boards and bleached linen curtains. 'I really thought the police weren't interested at all. I mean, when I told Sadler about the note on the flowers, he wasn't in the slightest bit bothered.'

'What note? What flowers?'

Julia frowned. 'Didn't he tell you about it? Hold on.'

She left the room and returned with two envelopes. One was pitted with what looked like water marks, the other grey and foxed with age. She handed them to Connie.

'What are these?'

'The first I received around 1982, I can't remember exactly. It was with a bunch of flowers and I didn't think anything of it really. I kept the card first of all because it was the first bunch of flowers I'd ever received specifically addressed to me. Second, I thought maybe it might have come from Mum, although why she would be buying me flowers, I've no idea.'

Connie stared at the notes. 'What about the second one?'

'It was left with the flowers at Dad's house. It was attached to one of the first bunches to arrive. Don't you see it?'

'The handwriting looks the same.'

'I thought that too but Sadler didn't think so. He thought they were alike but not the same and just dismissed it. Didn't he tell you?'

He bloody well didn't, thought Connie. *This is a link between the past and present.* 'Julia?' she asked, her tone making the woman lift her head. 'Have you been back to Lincolnshire since you left?'

Julia shook her head. 'Of course not. We were encouraged to leave it all behind. Start afresh.'

'Do you definitely have to work today?'

It was madness, of course, asking her. Connie shouldn't even be here and yet she couldn't think of any other way.

Julia turned to her, her dark eyes revealing nothing. 'Why do you ask? I *should* be going to work. What are you suggesting?'

'If you went back, to Lincolnshire I mean, you might remember something.'

'What, now?'

'Perhaps not now. Well, actually, why not now?'

She watched as Julia thought for a moment. 'I'm supposed to be working.'

Connie turned away. 'It doesn't matter.'

'No. It does. This is madness but give me two minutes and I'll be ready.'

43

Horncastle had hardly changed in the intervening years. The town's bakery was still there, and unlike Bampton where the cakes had taken on a distinctly continental influence as the area had gentrified, Horncastle's confectionery was of the sugary, doughy type Julia's mother had favoured. The pharmacy was in the same place too and the doctor's surgery she and George had visited for their childhood ailments. Only the shop where Woolworths had once stood, where she'd gone with her pocket money to buy the vinyl singles of the bands she'd loved, was gone. It had been replaced by a store selling everything for a pound. For Julia it was a sense of time stood still. Everything, however, looked smaller and slightly more dusty.

'I can't imagine what I'd have been like if we'd never moved. Dad was only interested in antiques then, it wasn't a business. George and I are a product of our life in Derbyshire, not here. Him and his antiques, me and my local tours. What lives would we have led if we'd stayed?'

Connie looked around the town's square. 'It's not that different to Bampton, though, is it? Okay, Bampton is larger. A lot bigger by the look of it, but it's still got that old-fashioned feel to it, businesses that have been here for generations.'

Julia's eyes were glued to a small charity shop with a basket of cheap toys outside the door. 'Mum's shop was over there.'

Connie squinted in the sunlight. 'Cats Protection?'

'That's the one.'

Connie must have noticed the catch in her voice. She wheeled around to check on Julia. 'Are you okay? It must be strange being back here.'

'It was funny.' Julia bit her bottom lip. 'I spent years going to that shop and yet that's not what I remember. I look at it and what I'm thinking about is *after*. First waiting for Mum and then going back to school and then all the police and the questions. I had happy moments in the shop and they're not coming back to me at all.'

'It's only natural. That's what trauma does to you. Forces its way into the front of your consciousness.' Connie pressed the bridge of her nose as if to relieve the pressure behind her forehead. 'The note was on the door?'

'I'm pretty sure it's the same door, even. It's funny, though. When I came to the shop and I saw the "back in two minutes" note, it didn't look right.'

'Why? Why didn't it look normal?'

'Well, Mum wouldn't have put that on the door if she was popping out, especially with us due home any minute.'

'But Julia, the note had been on the door from around one. She wasn't expecting you to be coming then anyway.'

'But you don't understand. It was an odd thing for our mum to do anyway. She never went out when the shop was open. She used to close it between half one and two to have a lunch break. She would do any errands she had then or sometimes, when we arrived, we'd get to do any that she hadn't got around to. Don't forget, it can be exciting standing in a post office queue when you're ten. There would have been nothing to make her need to put up a note like that.'

'She might have needed urgent change or something, or cut herself and needed a plaster. These things happen.'

Julia shook her head stubbornly. 'It didn't make sense then and it doesn't now.'

'She might have seen someone she knew.'

'Then why shut the shop? She could have chatted inside.'

They walked in silence across the square to the shop. 'Are you okay to go in?' Connie asked Julia.

'Probably.'

Julia needn't have worried. If the exterior of Horncastle hadn't changed, the shops had at least tried to keep up with the times inside. The charity shop was all white plastic and red lettering.

'Isn't anything the same?'

'Nothing. Even the back office where we used to sit and wait for the shop to close isn't in the same place. It was over there.'

Connie followed her gaze. 'Don't worry about that. I wasn't expecting everything to be exactly the same.'

The trip had already proved useful. Julia had confirmed that the note was out of character for her mother. The note hadn't been pinned up and then something unusual had happened. The usual, the order of things, had been upset *before* the message had been written.

'Let's move on. Do you want to show me your house?'

*

Their old home in Brinnington Close had changed. What had once been an integral garage had been made into a living room. The front garden, once a drive alongside a small patch of lawn, was now all brick paving. The owners were forced to park in front of the new room so the occupants could look out onto a car. Not much of a living space but perhaps nobody looked out of the windows these days.

Connie stood beside Julia, smoking and watching her face. 'Are you okay?'

'It's the same as the shop. I don't remember much of being here with Mum. More afterwards, waiting for Dad to come home from work. George and I used to spend a lot of time by ourselves here.'

Connie took a long drag on her cigarette. 'It's only natural, but your memories of the time before do exist. You've just preferred to suppress them. I can talk them through with you. Did you always live here?'

'Mum and Dad bought the house after they were married. George and I shared an upstairs bedroom with bunk beds until I was about seven. Then he moved into the box room and I still slept in the bunks.'

'So your childhood was normal. Don't think about your mum, just think about you and George.'

Julia shut her eyes and tried to remember. 'What's normal? It was normal for us and it seemed like everyone else. Children's parties, being fed jelly and iced party rings. Out on the street in the evenings until dusk. It was a typical seventies childhood.'

Connie leant back on the wall. 'Not that typical. I'm younger than you but in the eighties my mum was one of the few mothers who worked. She had a shop like yours and it was unusual.'

'I suppose. Now I come to think of it, I don't think many of my friends' mums worked. It didn't really matter, though. As I said, it was our normal.'

'Did they need the money?'

'I'm not sure. I don't remember us being particularly aspirational but who was in the seventies? It was only after Mum left that Dad got this massive urge to become successful and make money. It seemed to fit in with the eighties ethos, I suppose. I never really questioned it.'

'So, if they weren't desperate for money, why was your mum working?'

'She must have been an independent spirit.'

'I suppose.'

Connie looked unconvinced and Julia felt compelled to explain. 'She might have wanted to get out of the house.'

Now Connie looked more gratified. 'Let's go back to the day she disappeared. As normal, she walked you to school. What about George?'

'He walked part of the way with us. My school was en route to his high school. It was still only his first year so he wasn't ashamed to walk with us.'

'You always walked?'

'Mum didn't drive so it had to be by foot. She'd drop me off about half eight, I guess, George would go on to his school and she would head off to open up the shop for nine-ish.'

'And in the afternoon, you'd walk back to the shop.'

'Exactly. George would meet me there and we'd do our homework in the back room, mess about, read a book. That sort of thing.'

'So we're going to go back to that day in 1980. Your mum is walking you to school. I'll leave the car here. Can we retrace the route you took?'

They trudged down the cul-de-sac with Julia feeling a

growing disquiet. At one point they passed down an alleyway with a 'no cycling' sign in the spot she remembered it. The high boards shielding neighbours' gardens had never been well lit and she had been glad of her mother's presence on the dark morning walks in winter.

Connie had her hands in her pockets next to her. 'Would your mum talk to you as you walked?'

'George was the chatterer. It was only after that he became more silent. He'd talk about school and stuff. I suppose I would too but not as much as George.'

'And your mum?'

'She didn't say much at all.'

'Was she a quiet person anyway?'

'Not particularly. I used to hear her with customers and she'd be having a laugh. I think, though, she used to use those morning walks to get her head together, if that makes sense.'

'She was a bit distracted then?'

Julia noticed, with amusement, that Connie was getting out of breath. 'Distracted possibly. Definitely bound up with herself.'

It took them ten minutes to reach the old school. It too had hardly changed. Once, on the far right of the building, there had been a small swimming pool where Julia had collected coloured badges relating to the distances she had covered: ten metres, fifty metres, a hundred. It was now demolished and the area grassed over.

Connie wrinkled her nose. 'It's like every primary school I've ever seen. Why do they all look the same?'

Julia kept her eyes on the school building. 'It's funny but I've recreated this journey in my head countless times.'

'What was your father like with your mum?'

'Dad didn't much like small children. He was better with us when we grew up a bit. I think babies and toddlers annoyed him. He would be out most of the week but at weekends we tended to tiptoe around him. Anything would set him off.'

'Were your parents happy?'

'They seemed content. There were no massive arguments and Mum didn't particularly bend over backwards to placate his irritable moods. She just got on with stuff.'

'And nothing changed in the weeks leading up to her disappearance?'

Julia stood still and allowed the memories to wash over her. 'It was summer when she went. In June and the school term was coming to an end. It was all about cut-grass smells and gingham dresses to school. The summer holidays were coming and it was going to be exciting.'

'What would you do over the summer?'

'We'd go to the shop all day with Mum. It wasn't as bad as it sounds. There was a back yard we could mess around in, and now we were older we could go and wander around the town by ourselves. No one minded.'

'So you were excited.'

'We were. That's what I can remember of those last days. Walking to school with an air of excitement. The only thing is—'

'What?'

'I'm thinking. Perhaps it wasn't just George and me who were excited. I think, maybe, Mum was too.'

44

Matthews made a rare trip out to the newsagent's and picked up two of the Sunday papers and read the headlines. Case closed. Francesca Winson had killed her husband and son. It was the recommendation that they would be making to the CPS and the investigation was, more or less, out of their hands. Ruth would be home around five and she'd offer to take her out for a Chinese to make up for being a grump the last few days. She'd clear away the papers from the dining-room table and spend the day outside cutting back the herb garden that looked like a jungle.

She wondered what Connie was up to and hoped she'd now leave things be. They'd done their jobs to the best of their ability and it was time to move on. Out of the corner of her eye, she could see a florist's with a tub of blue cornflowers bobbing in the wind. She pulled over and bought two bunches to surprise Ruth later.

*

Sadler needed to wind down with someone who was unconnected with the police. He nearly dropped in on his next-door neighbour Clive who was usually up for a chat, but his conscience got the better of him. Karen had continued to call all day Saturday and the rational part of him wondered what he was avoiding. He retrieved her number from his phone and, before he could change his mind, rang it. She answered quickly and readily agreed to meet, offering to come to him. He considered his options: there wasn't a huge amount to do in Sheffield on a Sunday that didn't involve the indoors and it would be a shame to waste such a summer's day. Asking her to drive to his house, however, was putting the obligation on her and so he suggested meeting on the edge of the Peaks towards Sheffield.

By the time he reached the car park outside the village hall, the weather had turned and dark clouds were gathering. Karen was already waiting for him and she'd accurately read the weather, clothed in boots and a windcheater. Sadler pulled up alongside her and got out. She was looking at his shoes.

'You're not planning on walking in those, are you?'

'I keep my boots permanently in the car.'

He sat on a stone bench and pulled on his walking boots, still muddy from their last outing.

'I heard you on the radio, driving over here. About that family in Bampton, I mean.'

Sadler inwardly groaned. He didn't want to talk about the case and think of the charred family still waiting to be released for burial.

'You sounded good. Authoritative.'

This is a mistake, he thought. *I should have gone walking by myself. All I want is a bit of peace and quiet.*

Unlike Connie or Camilla, Karen wasn't good at reading his moods. She continued a stream of chatter as they set off down the path, the increasing slope failing to stop her flow. He felt he should give an explanation for his taciturnity but she appeared unaware of it, updating him on the week she'd had in the pharmaceutical lab where she worked. Finally, she was quiet for a moment.

'Sorry, have I been wittering on?'

He looked down at her. Thin worry lines radiated from each eye.

'Not at all. I'm sorry, it's just my head is full of stuff.'

She appeared to accept his explanation and continued to walk in silence beside him. Sadler made an effort to be sociable.

'I found Miles's number last night in my address book. I wasn't sure if I still had a means to contact him but he sent me his number in Canada when he moved. I haven't thought of him in years. It's interesting how our lives move on.'

She said nothing, but he got the impression she was listening closely to what he said.

'Is it okay to talk about him? I can change the subject if you like. It's just since we met this week, I've been thinking a lot about our student days. Miles, you, me. Do you remember my girlfriend, Olivia?'

'How can I forget? She used to be all over you, draped like an octopus.' Karen's tone was sour.

'I think I liked it at the time.' He kept his tone light but could feel the hostility emanating from her now. 'I lost touch with Olivia. I guess she'll be married herself now, with a family.'

'She's in Winchester.'

He stopped, surprised. 'You kept in touch with her too? I didn't think you two got on.'

Karen carried on walking. 'She's on my Facebook page too. As you say, married, a couple of good-looking children, one of whom I think has just gone to university.'

So that would be the age of his children if he'd got married in his twenties. He'd been moved by the death of Charlie, not only as a human being but also because that would have been the age of his own son if he'd had a child with his last girlfriend, Christina. The thought he could be the father to nearly adult children made him wonder where the years had gone.

'What are you thinking?' She looked annoyed and, for a moment, Sadler was reminded of Palmer's wife, Joanne, who took offence at everything.

He sidestepped the question. 'You seem to have kept in touch with everyone.'

'Just looking at the life I could have had with Miles.'

'That was a long time ago, Karen.' Sadler kept his voice even. 'You were treated badly, we all knew that.'

'Did anyone say anything to him, though?'

'I remember telling Miles what he was doing was wrong. Pam was a friend of yours.'

'Some friend. I bet he couldn't have cared less either.'

Well, no, she was right on that one. For Miles had been in the grip of an infatuation with the Canadian, Pamela, that had blinded him to the niceties of how to behave when ending a relationship. The infatuation had been reciprocated but kept hidden, perhaps so as not to break the fragile bond that held the group together. Until one day they had been discovered in bed together by Karen who was supposed to be away at a conference. She had reacted with dignity and walked out on them, leaving Miles to collect his things and hotfoot it to Sadler's house. Miles had been ashamed but determined.

'It's coming to an end anyway. It's Pam I want. I'm just sorry it had to end this way.'

And that had been that. Miles was in Canada married to Pamela and Karen was walking next to him, still stinging from the hurt. Sadler just wanted to go back to his house and relax in his living room. Lost in his thoughts, he heard her ask him, 'Are you single?'

45

'There's someone following us.' Julia's voice had dropped to a whisper. 'I spotted him first when we were standing outside Mum's old shop and he's now over the road standing in that shop doorway.'

They were sitting in a café at the end of town that was perched on top of the river flowing below. Connie picked up her cup and angled her head so she could get a good look at their stalker. A short man was smoking a cigarette while talking into his mobile phone. He was ignoring them both.

She frowned. 'It looks innocent enough. You're sure he was outside in the square too?'

'Pretty sure. You don't think it's the man who's hanging about outside my house, do you?'

'You don't know it's a man,' said Connie. 'You didn't get a good look at them and neither did your neighbour.'

'I feel threatened. Isn't that enough? Does it matter whether it's a man or a woman?'

'Of course it matters. Can you hurry with that tea? We'll go back to where we parked the car and see if he follows us.'

Julia pushed away the cup. 'I don't want it anyway.'

They made a terrible pair of actors walking away from the shop. They were so determined not to look in his direction they nearly collided with each other on the pavement.

'Don't try to look at him in a shop window or anything. If

he's following us, he'll end up outside your old home anyway.'

It was torture not to turn around. If Julia had been on her own she wouldn't have been able to stop herself, but Connie was resolutely ploughing forward towards their destination. When they got to the car, Connie turned around. Julia followed suit and saw the man ambling up the street, holding his phone up towards them.

'Stay here.'

Julia looked after the detective in alarm. 'But . . .'

Connie was haring towards him and Julia followed her.

'Who are you?'

The man was unsurprised and unashamed. '*Daily Mail*.'

'Oh no.' Connie looked furious. 'Why the hell are you following us?'

'Can you give a reason why you're retracing the footsteps of Elizabeth Winson who disappeared in 1980?'

'Don't answer him,' Connie ordered, grabbing hold of Julia's arm and dragging her back towards the car.

'Is there a problem? I'm allowed to go back to where I'm from, aren't I? What's it got to do with him?'

'You are, I'm not. That's the problem.' Connie started the ignition and leant forward in her seat. 'If Sadler finds out I've brought you here, he's going to have my guts for garters.'

46

Sadler learnt about Connie's trip to Horncastle the following morning. The newspaper headline read, *What aren't the police telling us?* It took him an hour to decide what to do. He sought counsel from Llewellyn, who he trusted, and Palmer, who he didn't. Matthews kept her head down and looked like she didn't want to get involved. Both Llewellyn and Palmer were resigned in their own way.

'She'll never change. She always does exactly what she wants.' Palmer sounded distracted and was sorting through his desk.

Llewellyn said pretty much the same thing, only he was more tactful. 'If you told her not to pursue this area of enquiry and she's done so, you're going to need to discipline her. Send her home for a week or so. That'll give her a chance to cool her heels.'

Sadler was livid. He wondered whether he should get Human Resources to make the call but in the end he decided he owed her at least a conversation in person. She hadn't come into work yet; she must be deliberately avoiding the inevitable confrontation. As he shut the door of his office, he looked over to Connie's empty desk and saw Matthews looking through paperwork left to one side. She was seeing what needed doing, he assumed, picking up where Connie had left off. Helpful, but Sadler had to quell a spurt of irritation. *Efficiency mixed with opportunity*, he thought. With Connie temporarily absent and Palmer leaving, he would be relying on Matthews more than ever.

'Am I in trouble?' Connie answered on the first ring and her tone infuriated him. She was going to brazen it out.

'I specifically told you to leave the Winson family alone and all contact with them to go through Pat. What part of that didn't you understand?'

'It was the weekend—'

'All the more reason for you not to have been working.'

Connie was silent for a moment. 'Look, I just thought going back to Lincolnshire might help Julia remember something about her mother's disappearance. I was doing it in my spare time.'

Sadler's anger had turned to an icy hauteur. 'I don't want to hear any more. I've spoken to Llewellyn. We're both in agreement that you've lost your sense of proportion in this case.'

'Don't say that. I'm sorry but—'

'No, you're not sorry. I'd like you to take some time away from this case.'

'You're taking me off the investigation?'

'I don't want to formally suspend you, Connie, but I will if I have to. Take a week's holiday and think about the sort of detective you want to be.'

'I already know that.'

'You want to be someone I can't trust? Someone who constantly makes me wonder what havoc they're wreaking? Because that's where we are now.' He'd expected tears. The silence was more unnerving. 'Are you still there?'

'I think it's better if I just leave.'

'What do you mean leave?'

'You'll have my resignation in the post in the morning. If you can't trust me, what's the point?'

The line went dead. Sadler tried to call her back but Connie's mobile was switched off. He called Llewellyn who was out at a meeting, but his secretary, Margaret, sucked in her breath when he left the message that Connie was threatening to resign.

She won't do it, he thought. *She won't destroy her career over this. This isn't the end.*

PART TWO

The Right

47

Four weeks earlier

The figure crept down the stairs, pausing only to look at its shadow in the hallway mirror and gather strength for the second act. The house was pungent with the scent of slaughter, bitter and metallic. The opening of the kitchen door brought in freshness from the night air, a fragrance of pine needles and jasmine flowers.

The crunch of gravel underfoot had been expected and the figure moved away from the house and onto the grass, following a soft path to the outbuilding. The tall pine trees loomed into view but the full pale moon gave plenty of light for the task. The rusting door of the old Anderson shelter moaned gently as it opened despite the drops of oil applied earlier in the week. The figure stopped for a moment and looked around, anticipating danger, but the garden remained silent.

The petrol can was heavier than remembered, its weight causing the figure to stagger for a moment. Too much fuel? How much was too much? The blaze would need to be a fury and more was better than not enough. Now was no longer the time for doubts.

As the figure heaved the can towards the house, a sudden beam of light caused a heart-stopping falter. Was it over too soon? But the glimmer of light was from the house across the road, an upstairs bedroom illuminated behind closed curtains. The figure waited for a moment and then continued towards the kitchen door, a sense of fate in every step. The need to finish what had been begun all those years earlier.

48

If Julia had to say when she first began to worry for George's sanity, it was the evening he lashed out at the child outside his apartment building. Julia had gone around for dinner but, aware he wasn't capable of cooking anything remotely edible, she brought three types of cheese, crusty bread and some fruit from the new organic greengrocer's that had opened up in the town. George had agreed to prepare a salad but, in case he forgot or, more likely, could no longer be bothered, she had also brought some cherry tomatoes with her too. It would be enough and one thing George could be relied on to provide was the wine.

The buzzer to the apartment block wasn't working and the maintenance engineer had failed to turn up as promised. She telephoned George to say she was standing outside and, in a filthy temper, he came down to open the door. He was immaculately dressed and, for an instant, Julia thought of the phrase 'devil in disguise'. She shook the thought away.

'I'm not going to pay the building charges this month. I've been up and down these stairs constantly this week.'

She moved to enter the building.

'What the fuck are you doing?'

For a moment, she thought he was talking to her. His voice had gone from the smoothness of thick cream to repressed fury. She turned around and a small boy, aged around three or four, was peeing against the railings outside the building. His mother, who had been balancing him by the hips, looked up in shock.

'I'm sorry, he's nearly potty-trained but he suddenly needed to go.'

'And so you thought you'd let him piss against my house like a dog.'

The woman yanked up the boy's trousers with a snap and he howled in protest. She had turned puce.

'It's all right for the likes of you. There are no public toilets in the centre of town. What the hell am I supposed to do if my child is caught short?'

'That's not my business. I'm sick of this street being used as a toilet by the yobos and drunks of this town.'

'He's only a child.' Julia pushed her brother into the lobby while giving the mother an apologetic look. She needn't have bothered. She was strapping the child back into his pushchair and Julia could see tears in the woman's eyes. She thought of Francesca and of Charlie. It can't be easy bringing up children yet Francesca had appeared to do it effortlessly. A woman in a foreign country, married to a man much older than her with a short temper.

She rode up in the lift with George in silence. She could smell his aftershave and wondered if he was meeting someone that evening after they had eaten. She wanted to ask him, she could have once, but he had a closed-off air about him that forbade questions. Inside the flat, she was touched to see he had prepared a salad and made a decent stab of it too. She laid her purchases out on the table and he brought a carafe of water out onto the table. She looked in surprise at the bottle.

'You want wine?' he asked, his manner polite.

'Not particularly, I thought you might.'

'I have to drive later.' He gave her no more information and she sat in silence as he poured the water.

'How are things going with the shop?'

'It's summer. The place runs by itself. I don't particularly shift the big items but china, jewellery, that sort of thing, I have to stock up during the year to keep my shelves full.'

'So you're not there every day?'

He looked at her, his eyes cold. 'I'm there most days; why do you ask?'

She ignored the warning in his voice. 'You can be hard to track down sometimes.'

He shrugged and started attacking the mound of salad on his plate. 'It's all over, isn't it? I don't have to account for my movements any more, not even to you.'

She put down her fork. 'What do you mean account for your movements? Who asked you to do that?'

He kept his eyes on his plate. 'That bloody woman detective I told you about for a start. She made me feel I had to justify all of my actions.'

'Connie's been taken off the team.'

'I heard.' The satisfaction dripped from him.

'George! She was only doing her job.'

'Accusing me? Taking you to Horncastle? Francesca was bloody unstable. It was only a matter of time before she went potty and did something. It's just that none of us envisaged this.'

'It wasn't obvious Francesca was unstable, though, was it? She was a decent mother to Charlie on the surface. Whatever has happened is to do with something deeper than simply her surface personality.'

He pushed his plate away from him. 'Francesca manipulated everyone around her. She decided she needed an ally in the family so that was you. She also needed someone to hate. Someone to show to her own son how not to turn out. That was me.'

She had her mouth open now. 'It wasn't like that.'

'You know your problem. You try to make everything "nice" but not everything is. Some people just aren't "nice" and Francesca was one of them. She was,' he paused to take a gulp of water, 'a fucking murderer.'

49

Connie had bought her flat on a whim a few years earlier. The canal she so despised and feared, and which ran at the back of her tall warehouse building, should have made the flat off limits. Instead, noticing the *for sale* sign after investigating a burglary, she'd taken the chance to have a look around and had been seduced by the high ceilings and sense of solidity the thick walls gave her. In reality, her job meant she spent precious little time in her under-furnished home and it was only when recuperating from the injuries sustained in her last case that she'd finally got round to making the place feel like hers.

Now it felt like a prison and she had only herself to blame.

She had opened the latticed windows as far as they could go and a welcome wind was wafting around her sitting room. In the distance, from the Pennines to the north, she could hear the rumblings of approaching thunder. Finally, a spat of rain on the glass warned her the storm would soon be here.

Connie lay prostrate on her sofa, her limbs strangely heavy. She couldn't bring herself to do anything, even eat, and she could feel her skin tightening over her normally slim frame. No one had contacted her. Sadler would hardly bother, given the conversation they'd had at their last telephone call. Palmer must have left by now. Started afresh in a new police authority. And Matthews? She'd made it perfectly clear to Connie at the start of the case that she would always have her eye on her own career. Which, in this instance, would mean giving Connie a wide berth.

So there she lay, sulking, but convinced she was in the right. She'd briefly toyed with the idea of getting in touch with Julia. Telling her that she regretted nothing and how much uncertainty should a person have to live with? Nothing about the midsummer blaze made sense. Her instincts told her, however, that Julia was best left alone because if, as Connie believed, an outside agency was involved in the fire, then Julia could be as much a suspect as anyone else.

I can't sit here all day, every day, she thought. Her brain was a fog of indecision as she contemplated her receding career. It had been an act of control, handing in her notice. It had made her feel that she wasn't a passive player in her own destiny. The problem was she had willingly relinquished years of hard work and now had no means to fight the charges if her resignation was accepted.

Hands behind her head she stared at the ceiling. The sound of her buzzer made her jump. She jammed her feet into a pair of flip-flops and descended the stone steps. As she opened the heavy door, her mind was already laying bets on who it might be, but not once did she contemplate the man she found on her doorstep.

'Can I come in?'

Llewellyn's tall frame towered over her and she was surprised to see him out of his uniform. He was wearing fawn corduroy trousers with a jumper of an indeterminate sludge colour. On a man with a smaller personality it would have looked insignificant but Llewellyn had a presence even in civvies. Connie thought rapidly about the state of her flat but decided a few unwashed cups and cushions thrown onto the floor didn't constitute slum conditions.

'You're the last person I expected to see.'

He stepped inside and looked around the cavernous space of the entry lobby. 'What sort of warehouse was this?'

Connie shrugged. 'Salt apparently. Brought over from Cheshire and distributed around Derbyshire and beyond through the canal.'

Llewellyn smiled down at her. 'I like a touch too much salt myself. My wife complains I put it on my food without even tasting it. I blame my mother. She was the same. She even used to heap it up on the side of her plate and dip her food into it.'

Connie grimaced. 'I eat too many packets of crisps. Does that count?'

He looked at her more closely now. 'Are you eating properly? It doesn't look like it.'

'Not really.'

She saw a glint of amusement in his eyes. 'Can we have a chat?'

She led him up the stairs and she noticed he was a lot fitter than her.

'Has Sadler been here?'

She wheeled around in surprise. 'Sadler? No, never. Why?'

'He lives around the corner, I think.'

They'd reached the top and Connie was puffing slightly. 'I went around his once during a case. He's never been here, though, and I've not heard from him since I was told to stay at home.'

Try as she might she couldn't keep the hurt out of her voice. She got no sympathy from Llewellyn. 'He did the right thing, exactly as I'd have done. You were screwing up the investigation.'

She winced at his words and led him into the living room. 'Do you want a drink?'

He looked at his watch and sighed. 'It's a bit early for anything stronger than tea.'

By the time she'd brought out the cups he was sitting on the sofa looking uncomfortable. 'I got your resignation letter. I haven't decided whether to accept it yet.'

'Isn't it up to me rather than you?'

'Not necessarily. Who do you have in your life to give you advice, Connie?'

She opened her mouth and shut it again.

'I thought so. How are you passing your time?'

Connie thought over the last few weeks. The days after her confrontation with Sadler she had been distraught and had stayed in bed until two-ish every day, only dragging herself up to watch TV with the duvet wrapped around her. The second week she'd gone into some kind of cleaning frenzy and, despite the unwashed dishes, the flat still reaped the benefits of this very late spring clean. Then the last week she'd been in a kind of limbo. Wandering aimlessly around Bampton and lying on her sofa trying to decide what to do. To Llewellyn she said, 'Not much.'

Noting his surprise she felt the need to defend herself. 'Really, I've not done much.'

Llewellyn sighed and put his cup down on the table.

'I want you to tell me what conclusions you reached in your own *unofficial* investigations.'

50

George left the flat as Julia cleared up, still offering no clue as to where he was going that evening. With the exception of the salad, most of the food was untouched and Julia replaced the wrappers on the cheeses and put them back into her basket. She couldn't find a recycling container, he mustn't use the one given by the council, so she put her foot on the pedal bin and scraped the food into it. He clearly didn't use the paper recycling either. Various pieces of notepaper had been torn in half and thrown into the rubbish. She noticed how much his handwriting resembled their mother's. The large loops and swirls, a remnant of their country primary school that had still taught cursive writing. Whereas her script was small and restrained, George's mirrored their mother's romantic handwriting.

She picked up one of the torn sheets of notepaper and looked at it closely. Could it have been George who had left the flowers outside the house? The first time around, he would surely have been too young either to buy the flowers or to have arranged for them to be sent to her. Julia thought back to when she had received them and his dismissive attitude. If he had sent her the flowers then he surely would have been watching for her reaction. No, the first flowers had been from someone different. The second, though. Had he remembered her attachment to the roses?

Her head ached. The problem was she too had an assignation that night. Not a tour, thank God. Her frayed nerves wouldn't be able to cope with entertaining a group. No, instead she was to scout a new building that might suit as a stop on her regular walk. The contact had come via Jean when she'd arrived to feed Bosco.

'I don't know if there's anything in it, to be honest. He says he's lost a couple of tenants but can't prove anything. He says the building is atmospheric, though, so it might suit you. I got the impression he personally doesn't believe a word of it. He fancies it more as a moneymaking activity.'

Which was fine by Julia. She'd rather deal with a punter who was deeply sceptical than a loon who was into photographing ectoplasm and contacting the dead. There had been no more notes from her neighbour, no more sightings outside her house, and now that the fear had died down she wanted to know what Ned Smith had been doing in her street. She searched through her pockets and found the paper on which he'd scrawled his number.

He sounded sleepy when he answered. She took a breath. 'Sorry, did I wake you? It's Julia, from the caves.'

He stirred. More awake now. 'You? What time is it? I must have dropped off on the sofa. Monday night, so naturally there's nothing on the telly.'

'Is your son in bed?'

'Toby's at my wife's parents for the week. He stays with them during the school holidays.'

'How's he doing? I mean in relation to the nightmares.'

'Well, to be fair, they've stopped. I think he was just anxious about being away from home. I've checked with my in-laws and he had a bit of trouble settling in the first night there but he seems to be okay now.'

'So you're on your own then?'

A slight hesitation. 'I am. Why?'

Have you ever visited my weird neighbour? This is what she wanted to ask him but the words wouldn't form into a sentence. Perhaps it would be easier when she saw him. 'You mentioned a drink. How about if you do a favour for me, then I'll buy you one?'

'Okay. It does depend what it is, though.'

'You can say no but I've got a potential new venue for my ghost walks where I have to go to a deserted building by myself. I was wondering if you wanted to come. It would give you a chance to see how I work. Put your mind at rest about Toby.'

'I think you've already done that. Seriously, I believed you when you told me it was his imagination.'

'Oh, okay.' *This isn't going to work*, she thought.

'I'll still come, though, if you need the company.'

'Really?'

'Where do you want to meet? I could come to yours if you give me your address.'

Julia's courage failed her. Did he really not know where she lived? 'If you don't mind, meet me at the venue. I want to go and collect Bosco first.'

'Bosco?'

'He's my other minder. Or ice breaker, depending on what's needed.'

*

The building was very small, one storey, and compact like a miniature dolls' house. There was a downstairs living room off which two doors opened into a galley kitchen and bathroom. Wooden steps led up to a mezzanine floor where Julia could see a small double bed. You couldn't even call it a one-bedroom house. It was a compact studio no bigger than a caravan. The owner, John, showed them around with obvious pride.

'It's a former TSB bank. I remember using it when I was at school. I had a little book that I used to put my savings in from the paper-round I did.'

'And you bought it when it shut down?'

'Not to live in. You can see how tiny it is. I wanted to do it up as a rental place. Short-term lets. And on that level it's been perfect. It's virtually booked up all summer because it's right in the centre of town. You can walk to all the pubs and also use it as a base for sightseeing. Winter is slightly more difficult, though. It's comfortable but not luxurious, plus, as you know, Bampton empties in the cold season. So I was thinking of alternative uses.'

'You've heard about the ghost tour?'

'Well, exactly. The place is detached and in the centre so you're not going to disturb anyone if you get a bunch of people in here late in the evenings, however noisy they are.'

'I presume you've had supernatural activity. My clients don't just want to see inside an old bank.'

'That's why I thought of you. A couple of the guests have said they've heard the sound of counting money. I mean, when the first lot said it I thought they just had an overactive imagination. It's an old bank after all, that's how I sell it in the catalogues. Then another couple mentioned it to me and, last week, a woman who's been staying here by herself. She didn't seem particularly bothered. It'd have frightened the life out of me. She just said something along the lines of "I'll miss your resident ghost". So it got me thinking that if it's something that's benign, why not cash in, if you'll excuse the pun.'

'Did someone die here?'

'Not that I can find. Does that matter?'

Julia looked around her. 'These tours are part of the tourist trail. They're not scientific experiments. I need to tell them a story about the history of the place and who might have died here. It's easy with places like pubs, hospitals, hotels and the like. I mean, given the footfall, someone is going to have died, aren't they?'

'But people don't usually die in banks.'

'Well, no. Which isn't to say someone won't have. I need to do some digging around and get back to you. As you say, though, the venue's perfect.'

'I'll do it.' Ned made them both jump. 'The evenings are a bit long with Toby away. I'll dig around.'

'You're not the first person I contacted, you know.' John had his eyes on her. 'I thought first of all of maybe doing proper séances and so on. Getting people to try to communicate with the ghost.'

'I don't get involved in that sort of stuff,' she said quickly.

'Don't worry. I decided against it. The woman I spoke to about it was a complete nut job. She switched off when I said no one had died. I got the impression she was only interested in the gory stuff. She told me she was going nightly to Cross Farm Lane to that burnt-out house, you know, where the family died. She was trying to communicate with the spirits.'

Julia felt Ned stiffen beside her and he put his hand on her arm. 'Who is this woman?' she asked.

'Are you okay?' John looked alarmed. 'I told her I wasn't interested. She gave me the creeps. That poor family and there's that ghoul trying to contact them from beyond.'

Ned pulled her slightly. 'I think we should go.'

51

Llewellyn was sitting on Connie's sofa with his long legs stretched out in front of him and his large hands clasped behind his head. He stared into the distance as she talked.

'My problem is I never believed Francesca capable of the killings from the off. It didn't sound right based on previous cases.'

'You mean it's usually the man.'

'In that set-up, the annihilation of a family, it is usually perpetrated by the male. I did a fair amount of research on the subject.'

'So you'll know women kill their children too.'

'Yes, but differently. I mean, let's look at what we're saying happened. First the mother kills her husband and her son. Then she commits suicide. Let's forget about the fire for the moment. This rarely happens. Women who kill their children are often single mothers or estranged from their partners. They kill their children for four main reasons. First of all they are mentally ill. We looked at Francesca's medical records. She had no history of mental illness at all. Not even post-natal depression.'

'It might have been undiagnosed,' said Llewellyn. 'Not everyone goes haring off to a doctor these days. Go on, though.'

'Okay. Secondly there are retaliating women. Where they've split up with their partner, for example, and they want to punish him. Other than the fact they kept to themselves and Peter was clearly a critical sort of man, we've no cracks in their marriage. Even from those who did get close to them, such as Peter's daughter, Julia.'

'Third?'

'Then we have mercy killings. Women who want to alleviate the perceived suffering of their kids. You know, when they have a terminal illness.'

'I won't even bother asking about that in relation to Francesca. Charlie, I know, was in good health. The final reason?'

'Where there's been a history of abuse. So the children have been battered and the violence has spilled over to murder. There's no history of Charlie being taken to hospital with evidence of abuse. Schools and nurseries are trained to look out for these things now and nothing came to light at all except a broken arm, which appears to have been a one-off incident.'

'Sadler mentioned something about Francesca slapping Charlie.'

'Oh, that.' Connie stared at her undrunk tea. 'We've only got George's say-so for that.'

'What about financial difficulties? Don't you read about families where a parent thinks there's no way out and so they decide to take the family with them?'

'But that's usually associated with male violence. This is my point. In those cases, the father often commits suicide too. That's the other thing. Women who kill their children tend not to commit suicide afterwards. It's supported by research. The massacre at Cross Farm Lane mirrors more an act of male violence.'

Llewellyn rubbed his hand across his eyes. 'There's absolutely no way Peter Winson murdered his family.'

Connie moved across the room and sat down in the chair opposite Llewellyn. 'I know that. I think George Winson committed the murders.'

'Motive?' asked Llewellyn.

Connie could feel herself colour. 'I wasn't allowed to get that far.'

'Connie, you were suspended for mixing up two cases after you had been told to leave well alone. You have reservations about the case, okay, that's fair enough, but you allowed yourself to be sidetracked into another unsolved case. If you think George Winson is the murderer, what the hell were you doing looking into the disappearance of his mother?'

'I still think it holds the key to what happened on Cross Farm Lane.'

'You think *George* Winson might have been responsible for the disappearance of his mother?'

'He was twelve when Elizabeth went missing. Of course he could have been involved. He was a hefty lad and could easily have overpowered his mother. He wasn't even considered as a suspect.'

'I'm not sure. You know my feelings about police from that time. There were some bad practices but most of them weren't stupid.' Llewellyn reflected for a moment. 'Nevertheless, let's leave 1980 there for the moment. Even if he is responsible for that crime, what about now? What's his motive?'

'I don't know.'

Llewellyn shifted restlessly and looked at his watch. 'What you should have done was start with the motive and then follow correct procedure, under the supervision of your boss, of questioning him under caution if you, and we, thought there was a case to answer. Do you, in fact, have any motive at all?'

'There was once a complaint of harassment made against him.'

'It doesn't prove anything. You found a restraining order obtained by his former wife. Do you know how common this is? I've just submitted figures for cases of domestic violence in Derbyshire to a Home Office select committee. Do you know how many convictions we had here last year? No, don't bother guessing. I'll tell you. Over fifteen hundred. Ten per cent were recorded as high risk. None, thank God, ended up in murder. Those were people assaulted within their own homes.'

'This is the point. Domestic violence can lead to murder.'

'I'll grant you that, but you went around and, without any evidence against him in terms of this case, implied both he *and* his father were people of interest to the police. When in fact they were nothing of the sort.'

Connie looked at the floor. 'I have this strong sense of evil when I look at him.'

Llewellyn sighed. 'Connie. Do we have any evidence at all of a break-in at Cross Farm Lane?'

'No. If it was George, though, we wouldn't, would we? He might have a key to the house.'

'Is this seriously all you've got?'

'He was violent in his attitude towards Francesca when we mentioned her and cold towards the rest of his family. I saw no evidence of grief towards any of them that died.'

'Lots of people suppress their grief. Given George had lost his mother in 1980, I'm not surprised he had a strange attitude to loss. Why did you become so fixated on that case? Does it matter if Elizabeth is still alive or now dead? In relation to the murders here, I mean.'

Connie could feel all the careful arguments she had built up in her head begin to crumble. 'My initial view was that Peter killed Francesca and his son. When it became apparent he couldn't have been the killer in our case, I started to think about the other people involved in the Elizabeth Winson case. George was clearly affected by his mother's disappearance. School friends describe him as violent towards animals. Having little empathy towards other people. They're classic hallmarks of early psychotic behaviour.'

'Go on.'

'Well, research shows people who are violent often start small. On animals and so on. When his friend mentioned the animal cruelty he'd witnessed, I did wonder.'

'We still don't have a motive. He can't get much financial benefit from the killings. The house is a mess and any insurance claims will take years to sort out.'

'No, and, to be honest, it's Julia who seems to be the hard-up one.' She saw Llewellyn's face. 'Not that I'm blaming her.'

'So what were going to be your next steps?'

'I was going to try to trace George's movements that night. Okay, I can't find a motive but I do believe he killed his family. Do you agree with me?'

Llewellyn shook his head. 'No. Neither does Sadler. Nor Palmer nor Matthews. So, you find yourself in a bit of a pickle, don't you?'

'Why did you come around then? Did you think I had the magic solution that I hadn't told anyone?'

'I came around because you've been in the wars and I don't want to lose you from the team. I also agree something doesn't smell right about the murders. The problem is, reaching retirement though I may be, in fact probably because I'm coming to the end of the road, I'm not prepared to rock any boats.'

'You want me to drop it then.' Connie felt the crushing weight of disappointment.

He rubbed his face once more. 'If I rip up this resignation letter, how do you fancy a week or so more of suspension?'

'You mean . . .?'

He smiled at her. 'I will have that drink now if you don't mind. A small whisky. Do some digging and, Connie, for God's sake, don't bollocks it up this time.'

52

Julia left Ned at the bank without going for a drink. She didn't want him back at her house, as the doubts had resurfaced after seeing him again. It was definitely he who'd walked out of her neighbour's house. She was in no state to confront him and he accepted her goodbyes without comment. From her house, she rang Connie's mobile, which was switched off. Pat was another possibility but, for all the FLO's goodwill, Julia felt she wasn't inclined to take any concerns seriously. Instead, she waited for morning and then rang Bampton CID and asked to speak to a member of the team, hoping she wouldn't get Sadler, who'd made it clear to her that he considered the case to be closed. She got a Sergeant Matthews, who sounded distracted but resigned when she heard Julia's story.

'We have had a few ghouls around your parents' house. The place is sealed off but the layout of the plot makes it reasonably accessible to anyone who wants to get in, which it seems they have been doing.'

'Ghost hunters?'

Matthews sighed. 'It's been all sorts. Photographs of the burnt-out house have appeared on a couple of websites. They're definitely not police photographs, which means they've gained access somehow. One of the press officers spotted it.'

'They were taken at night?'

'Perhaps late evening. The light was fading in the photos.'

'What about at night?'

Matthews hesitated. 'One of the forensics team found a Ouija board in the back garden. I suspect it was kids but I can understand you being unhappy about it. I rather hoped it was a one-off.'

'One of the so-called psychics has apparently been going there regularly. Trying their parlour tricks with my family's spirits.'

There was a pause. 'I don't want to sound rude but I had heard you ran that sort of thing. The PC who found the board wondered if it might be yours.'

'Mine?' Julia's voice was hoarse. 'My talks are for tourists only. I don't try to commune with the dead. That's sick. My family only died a month ago, for God's sake.'

Julia could hear some papers shuffling. 'I'll talk to Inspector Sadler about it. We're not going to have the resources to station someone permanently overnight but we could send a patrol car past every couple of hours to check no one's around.'

'Would you do that? The thought of those people is making me sick.'

'I'll put in a request. I'm sure it'll be okay. You're not being pestered by anyone else? The press, for instance.'

'Not any more. Ever since you made it clear the murders were self-contained, it's yesterday's news.'

'That's good.' The sergeant's tone had a finality to it. She clearly wanted to put the phone down.

'How's Connie?'

The silence stretched out. 'I'm afraid I don't know. She's not currently working here.'

'It wasn't the fact she took me to Horncastle, was it? We

were just trying to recreate what happened to Mum. I never wanted to get her into trouble.'

'When I speak to her, I'll pass on your regards.'

Julia replaced the receiver and knew she wouldn't be able to help herself. She fired up her laptop and typed her father's address into Google. A website came up called *Under the Radar*. Clicking on the links revealed, not the outside shell she had seen that time after the fire, but an interior shot of the downstairs. Julia was shocked at how much was still recognisable despite the devastation and charred brown surfaces of everything. In the living room, the fireplace was intact and next to it a pot plant, its leaves brown spikes. The outline of the large sofa was there, where only six weeks ago Julia had played with Charlie and he'd screamed with delight.

The photographer had ignored the kitchen but had ventured up the ruined staircase into a bedroom. A double bed could be seen set off to one side and Julia squinted at it, trying to make sense of which room she was seeing. Through the window she could see a tall fir tree, which meant it must be facing onto the back of the house. It must be either the room her father and Francesca had slept in or the spare one. Julia enlarged the image and looked again for clues. She was sure her father's room had held a large wardrobe, a remnant from their Horncastle home she'd played in as a child, which stood next to the bed. In the photo there was only a space. Julia thought back to the house. The west side of the building was completely burnt out. There could be no access to a photographer to either her father's or Charlie's bedroom.

She was surely looking at the spare room at the back. The room for guests that was hardly ever used. Perhaps Francesca had thought her parents would come over more often to visit their grandchild because Julia could remember the room having been lovingly furnished. Julia clicked on another image. Same room but a different angle this time. You could now see the large bed with its floral duvet, which was covered by a layer of grime. The fire hadn't spread to this part of the house. To the left of the bed, away from the window, stood a chest of drawers. Damascus style with inlaid mother-of-pearl. Julia stopped. Where the hell had she got that description from? She knew a bit about antiques but not much. That sounded like a professional's description of the item. Something that might end up in a sales catalogue.

She tried to enlarge the piece of furniture. It was a dark wood three-drawer chest covered in an ornate pattern with swirls she would have just about recognised as mother-of-pearl. But Damascus style? Perhaps her father had used the term, or maybe George. She closed her eyes and let the phrase wash over her. It might have been her father but he had rarely talked antiques with her. George liked to show off, when he was in the mood. It must have been George.

53

As much as he hated to admit it, Sadler missed Connie. Palmer had found a new job: same rank, different police authority. One of the women in the despatch office had already organised a collection for him and an evening out later in the month was planned. Matthews was proving to be a competent replacement. She hadn't mentioned Connie to him, and Sadler wondered if they were in touch with each other. The case was concluded, the bodies released for burial and Sadler had stood in the graveyard, cold despite the August sun, or perhaps it had been the sight of the small white coffin that had sent a chill through his body. He had half-expected to see Connie there. Had looked forward to it even, but she had stayed away.

Sadler had been surprised at the lack of warmth in the eulogies for Francesca and Peter. The grief for Charlie had been heartfelt and expressed. Children from his class had prepared drawings for the coffin and the headmistress had spoken warmly of his life in the school. George had spoken about his father in formal terms and hadn't mentioned Francesca at all. Perhaps this shouldn't have been a surprise. She was a killer and was being treated as such in the local community. In the town's bookshop, Sadler had overheard a conversation where two women had tutted over the fact that a mother could kill her child.

Francesca's parents had chosen not to come for the

ceremony and he could hardly blame them and so she remained unmourned. George's eulogy for his father could have been for anyone. Hard-working, diligent and forthright were words of praise but Sadler rather hoped he would be given a little more than this when his time came. If he ever had children, which wasn't looking likely. Karen had contacted him once since that last walk and he had said they couldn't meet as he was swamped with work. She had put the phone down on him and Sadler had guiltily enjoyed the pang of relief.

The station was quiet. Too quiet. Sadler picked up his jacket and went down the corridor to speak to Llewellyn. Margaret wasn't at her desk and after a moment's hesitation he put his head around his boss's door. Llewellyn was hunched over the desk, frowning at a pile of papers. He looked up at Sadler with relief.

'Ah, Francis. Is everything okay?'

'I wanted to have a quick word about Connie.'

A closed look came into Llewellyn's face. Sadler wondered if the damage she'd done went deeper than he realised. He plunged ahead.

'I wonder if we could persuade her to revoke her notice. I'm sure it's just a reaction to her suspension. Is there any chance of bringing her back? She's probably cooled her heels by now and I could do with her back on the team.'

'Why? There's not been any new cases come up, have there?'

'Well, there's the tourist scam that's going on at the moment. A gang, possibly from Manchester...'

Llewellyn waved his hand at Sadler. 'You've got a perfectly

capable team. You don't need to get Connie back quite yet. I'll prevaricate about her resignation a while longer.'

Sadler's face must have spoken volumes. Llewellyn leant back in his seat. 'Feeling worried about her? Think you made the wrong decision?'

'Of course not.'

'Well then. She didn't do what she was told and nearly buggered up your investigation. Let her cool off for a little bit longer. We can reassess if something comes up in the meantime.'

Sadler opened his mouth to say something further and then closed it. Llewellyn was already hunched over his paperwork. Something in the way he was leaning over, for a brief moment, made Sadler think he was smiling.

*

Connie was fully aware how fleeting her reprieve was. Llewellyn had given her around a week to come up with a solid reason why she thought George Winson was guilty of murdering his family. She needed two things: motive and evidence. Motive she was inclined to leave to one side until she had done a bit more digging. George, she suspected, hated them all. His father for his cold eye and constant criticism. Francesca because she had insinuated herself into the family. Charlie? This Connie found harder to comprehend but George could show jealousy and they had, effectively, usurped him and Julia in the family. The only family member he was close to was Julia. She protected and defended him. No, it wouldn't be a good idea to approach Julia for the moment. What she needed to do was dig further around George without him noticing. First and foremost, Connie needed to crack his alibi because, if she couldn't get beyond this, nothing else she presented to Llewellyn would stack up.

George's girlfriend went by the name of Antonia Toynton. She had confirmed his alibi for the night and appeared to be a reliable witness. Connie needed to unpick this. Assuming that Antonia and George were still together, she couldn't just bowl up outside the woman's house and ask her why she was covering up for George. She was the mother of a fifteen-year-old daughter, however, and, as far as Connie could see, this daughter had never been interviewed. Connie was sitting outside Antonia's house waiting for her opportunity. She had already watched as the mother had rushed out of the door searching for something in her over-large handbag. Marianne was clearly following the habit of teenagers of using their school holidays to catch up with sleep. It was gone eleven o'clock and only now had Connie seen the curtains in the front bedroom part slightly.

She got out of the car to stretch her legs and heard water gushing down an outflow pipe. Marianne must be taking a shower, which might mean she was on the move. It was a good guess because twenty minutes later the girl also came rushing out of the house, combing her still wet hair as she hared off down the street.

Connie set off after her and they were both soon overtaken by the bus, which sped past the empty shelter a few metres ahead. Marianne halted and swore under her breath.

'Bastard. He could see we were rushing for the stop.'

'I can give you a lift.'

Marianne turned and narrowed her eyes, ready to give Connie a mouthful.

'I'm a journalist,' said Connie, 'scum of the earth, I know. But I'm in the shit with my boss because I've got nothing on that house fire. I'll give you a lift wherever you want to go if you'll talk to me. Off the record and all that; I need something.'

Connie had thought up the story that morning. It killed her to impersonate one of the bastards who had been responsible for her suspension. However, journalists were notorious for doorstepping people and generally making a nuisance of themselves. It was a good disguise for her to hide behind.

There were at least ten reasons why the girl shouldn't get in the car with her. It was the one she articulated that gave Connie hope. 'My mum will kill me if she finds out.'

'It's completely off the record, I promise. I need some background into the survivors, George and Julia Winson. I've got a chance to redeem myself with my editor. A story on those left behind. You know George, I think.'

'Me?' The girl looked surprised. 'He never pays any attention to me. It's my mum he's shagging.' The girl coloured at her crude phrasing and Connie suspected it cost her dear to use those words.

'They're still together then? Look, if you don't want to get into the car maybe I could take you for a coffee or something. I just want to hear about how George is taking it and what he was like after he first heard about the accident. Do you know what I mean?'

The girl looked with old eyes at Connie. 'You don't look like a child kidnapper. Which newspaper do you work for?'

'*The Mirror*. My job's at risk, though. This is why this story is important to me.'

Marianne didn't seem much interested in either Connie's

newspaper or her imaginary job prospects. She was looking at her watch.

'I'm supposed to be meeting the girls at twelve o'clock. In a car, it'll only take fifteen minutes. The bus goes around the houses. That gives us another ten minutes on top of the journey. Will that be enough?'

Connie nearly grabbed the girl to give her a hug but, instead, opened the car door for the girl, who slid inside.

'Your mum's divorced, is that right?'

'Right. Dad's in Saudi. He's an engineer. We lived out there for a bit but Mum didn't like it. She said she was bored rigid and unless you were prepared to teach, which she wasn't, there was no work that she could do.'

'She's a secretary?'

'PA.' Marianne suppressed a grin. 'She doesn't like it if you call her a secretary, even though that's what she is. She works at the solicitors and legal work is considered a cut above, if you see what I mean. She's also doing more qualifications, though, so she can become a paralegal in the office. More money.'

'She's ambitious. That's a good thing.'

Marianne shrugged. The insouciance of those who don't yet have to scrabble money together to get through each month. She eyed Connie. 'You want to ask me about George.'

'If that's all right.'

'There's not that much to say, to be honest. They started seeing each other after Christmas. They met at a party somewhere. By January she was humming around the house so I knew she'd met someone.'

'When did you meet him?'

'Not until around Easter. I'm not sure if it was because she was worried about me or the thought I might put him off. Either way, I didn't meet him until the clocks had changed. He picks her up in his car, you see. Takes her round to his flat. Anyway, when it was getting lighter in the evenings, she couldn't just slope out, could she? So, one day after I'd stuck my head out of my bedroom to get a good look at him, she shouted at me to come down so I could be introduced.'

'How was he?'

'Quite good-looking, I suppose. He's old, though. His curly hair must have been nice when it was black but now it's all grey.'

Connie thought of the grey silver she had spotted in her own dark hair recently. Marianne was still thinking of George. 'He has nice eyes, though. Dark brown.'

'How was he with you?'

'Polite, I suppose. He put out his hand so I could shake it, which was quite funny. Mum seemed quite keen to leave, which was a cheek since she was the one who had called me down.'

Connie ground the gears on her car, wishing she could look at the girl as she delved deeper into George's alibi. 'So let me get this right. Basically your mum normally goes to his flat. Does she stay the night?'

'Sometimes she does and sometimes she doesn't. If she doesn't, she has to get a taxi home as they both must have been drinking.'

'Your mum likes a drop, does she?' Connie tried to make her voice as natural as possible.

'They both do.' Marianne's voice was sour. Connie, the daughter of an alcoholic mother, could well imagine the distaste.

'On the night of the fire she stayed over, didn't she?'

'Definitely. I know 'cos she didn't go to work the next morning. She was puking so I had to call in sick for her.'

Connie frowned, trying to remember this information in the police notes. 'You sure about this?'

'Of course. I called in sick for my mum and then went to school. When I came home she was nearly hysterical. I asked her what the matter was and she said George's family had died. She'd only left him that morning and everything had been fine.'

'Did she say why she'd been so sick?'

'They'd been to a seafood bar, the new one opposite the hotel. Mum doesn't really like oysters anyway so I reckon she only went because he wanted to.'

'She doesn't like them or is allergic to them?'

They'd come to a stop outside the bus terminus. She saw Marianne glance at her watch. 'I don't think she's allergic to them. We had oysters once on holiday in France. I just don't think she liked them much. She must have had a bad one. I don't think she'll be eating them again.'

'Did she say if she'd been sick all night?'

Marianne looked at Connie properly for the first time. 'I thought you wanted to talk to me about George. What's Mum being sick got to do with anything?'

Connie thought fast. 'I want to do a piece on the personal angle. Did she say what George was like when he woke up? I mean, if she'd been sick all night, he might have been tired in the morning from helping her or something.'

'But she wasn't sick all night. It was as soon as she woke up, she felt nauseous and had to rush for the toilet. George was quite nice about it, I think. He brought her home and made sure she was safely inside. She was crap all morning but she perked up in the afternoon and was fine the next day.'

'So she ate a dodgy oyster, slept through the night and then was sick the next morning.'

'That's right,' said Marianne. 'Is that enough? I've only met him that one time in the street and then in the morning of the fire when he brought Mum home.'

'You saw him then?'

Marianne sighed. 'I told you, I had to call in sick for her, didn't I?'

'And how did he look?' Connie tried to adopt the air of a professional journalist.

Marianne thought for a moment. 'He looked like he was in a hurry.'

54

Friday, 8 November 2013

'Damascus style with inlaid mother-of-pearl.'

Julia wasn't listening. The quote for a new exhaust was making her sick with worry. It would eat into her meagre savings and would leave her nothing in case of a major emergency. She had considered approaching her father but wasn't sure how much money he now had on his retirement. There was also the possibility Francesca might not appreciate her encroaching on the joint finances, for surely she had very little money of her own. Which took her to George. She needed access to a car and her reliable but ageing Yaris had done the trick up until now. Julia had always known that, come an emergency, she'd struggle to find the funds to cover the costs. That day had arrived and here she was; even the backs of her knees were sweating at the thought of approaching her brother. For, with George, you had to gauge his mood, which was why she was in his shop making a stab at listening to the description of his newly acquired piece.

'Will it be difficult to sell?'

'Not at all. I already know who's having it. Someone with excellent taste.'

'It must be a woman, it's not the sort of thing a man would buy.'

'Don't you like it?'

His eyes were on her, as if he'd realised she wasn't paying attention. Julia started looking at the piece properly for the first time. 'It's quite ornate.'

'Decorative? Well, it won't suit everyone, of course, especially the lot who are collecting that horrendous seventies furniture that's suddenly back in fashion.'

'I quite like it.'

His eyes narrowed. 'Well, you can pick it up quite cheaply, which would suit your budget.'

It was the perfect opener. This was the point where she should jump in and say, talking of money . . . He was, however, clearly spoiling for a fight and she couldn't bring herself to ask. Unexpectedly, her eyes filled with tears and, so he wouldn't see them, she moved away from him.

'I'd better go. I'll see you again.' She clutched the keys of her hated car and left his shop and slid into the front seat, a film of tears in front of her eyes. She was about to start the car when she heard a knocking on the passenger window. Putting on her sunglasses, she pressed the electric buzzer.

'Are you all right?'

'Fine.' She didn't trust herself to say any more.

He opened the passenger door and climbed in, filling the space of the small car. 'You're not all right. What's the matter?'

'Don't you ever wonder what the point is sometimes?'

He didn't answer. 'Why are you asking this? What's wrong? Are you ill?'

She shook her head. 'I just wonder how I got to this. Tourism work that pays only a little more than the minimum wage. Scrimping around for money for the bare essentials. I couldn't even afford a holiday this year and when things go wrong it's a disaster.'

'You have a house, you pay a mortgage. That's more than some people.'

'But it's a struggle. Every month I spend more than I earn and I scrabble around to make ends meet.'

He turned towards her. 'You've always lived like that. You've told me before you don't like office work. What's changed?'

She let out a deep breath. 'I have hardly any money at all for emergencies. So when something happens, like this bloody car's exhaust which needs fixing, then I worry what will happen.'

'How much do you need?'

'About five hundred quid.'

'You could have asked me. I'll give you the money.' He opened his wallet and counted out five hundred pounds in fifty-pound notes. 'I don't want it back and, next time, talk to me if you're stuck.'

She wiped away a tear that was winding its way down her cheek. 'You can be bloody hard to talk to sometimes. It's not easy begging for money. I thought about going to Dad.'

'Don't ask him.'

'I wasn't. I mean, there's Francesca to think of.'

His mouth settled into a line. 'It's got bugger all to do with her.'

'She's his wife. She's got every right to object if I ask Dad for money.'

George looked out of the window, down the street.

'Francesca has no right to object to anything.'

55

Connie got out her smartphone and Googled 'food poisoning from oysters'. According to the first website she opened, the consequences of eating seafood containing the norovirus would start taking effect from between two to forty-eight hours. That was a wide enough margin for Antonia to have eaten the oysters, gone to sleep and then woken up to vomit. So her story was entirely believable. The only time Connie had ever been sick from food poisoning, after eating some chicken liver pâté that must have been standing in the restaurant kitchen for longer than was healthy, her body had rejected the food almost immediately. However, if a virus could incubate for up to forty-eight hours then it's entirely possible Antonia went to sleep and woke up feeling ill.

Connie's eyes skimmed over the rest of the article and stopped when she saw that the effects of the virus would be in the system for up to three days. According to Marianne, her mother started to feel better that afternoon. Would that be right? Sometimes vomiting cleared out your system, but more often than not didn't you feel rough for a few days afterwards? What kind of virus would leave you feeling perky by the afternoon?

Antonia Toynton was George's alibi and Connie's colleagues had spoken to her to confirm his version of events. If Antonia had been sick, then she would have clearly remembered the date and details, particularly as the evening in question had been followed by the discovery of the fire. She hadn't mentioned being ill in the night, though. Why had she kept quiet about this? Embarrassment? That was a possibility. Perhaps she hadn't thought it would make any difference. Whatever the reason, she had confirmed George's alibi for the whole night. If, however, she had slept through and then felt ill the following morning, surely it suggested something out of place with the course of events.

The drive to the mortuary took longer than normal. Two tourist cars were driving at around twenty miles an hour and the occupants were looking at the hills to the east, not at the road. When she walked into the office, Scott was at his desk pointing at the computer screen and a young woman was standing over him, laughing. As soon as he spotted her, Scott stood up, knocking a file to the floor. 'Connie!'

The woman bent over the mess of papers at his feet and gathered them up and Bill came out of his office. To her surprise, the tubby pathologist walked over to her and put his arms around her body. She could have wept into his chest but Connie contented herself by staying there for a moment, inhaling his smell.

'I hear you're currently one of us. A civvie, I mean.'

'I'm in so much trouble,' she mumbled into his jumper, forgetting for a second the errand that had sent her there.

Bill tightened his grip for a moment and then reached over to switch on the kettle. 'I have a cousin. My mother once said about her when she'd got into her umpteenth scrape and she was not yet twenty that she was the sort of person things happen to. I remember thinking that was a bloody unfair thing to say but she was right. Denise was a person who things happen to. As are you, my dear.'

'Is that supposed to make me feel better?'

'How about if I told you Denise is now nearing sixty and living on Naxos with a man in his thirties? Better now?'

Connie laughed.

'I'm going to take my lunch break, if that's okay.' The woman was standing up with the jumble of papers gathered to her chest.

'Ah, Mary. Meet Connie from CID.'

'She's not working there at the moment, is she?'

For a moment, Connie saw a flash of anger cross Bill's face. 'Yes, do take your break now. I'll see you later.'

Without a word, Mary dumped the pile of papers on a spare desk and walked out.

'I've got a fan there, I see. What's she heard about me?'

Connie risked a glance at Scott, who was looking embarrassed. 'I've not said anything.'

'Never mind about her.' Bill reached into a drawer and took some teabags out of a box. 'Tea for three?'

Connie went over to the spare desk and plonked herself down.

'What are you doing with your time? Keeping out of trouble, I hope,' asked Bill.

'Not really. Can I ask you a question, Bill, about drugs?'

He raised his eyes. 'You're not on the hard stuff now, are you?'

'Of course not. I'm talking about when you drug someone, perhaps by slipping something into a drink when they're not looking.'

'A Mickey Finn,' said Scott.

Bill turned around to him. 'This isn't a Raymond Chandler novel. I don't need to tell you about how lethal some of these drugs are now. Rohypnol, ketamine. They're nasty drugs that, when mixed with alcohol, render a person unconscious.'

'These are the ones that have been used on women in bars? So-called date-rape drugs?' asked Connie.

'Not just women. Men have been assaulted after being drugged too. Why do you ask? Is something going on in Bampton?'

'I'm spending my enforced idleness trying to make sense of something.'

Bill looked amused and wagged a finger at her. 'Remember. Someone who things happen to. Okay, miss. What do you want to know?'

'Well, first of all, say, a man takes a woman out for something to eat, for example champagne and oysters. At some point in the evening he gives her this drug. Then what happens?'

Bill picked up his tea. 'If we're talking Rohypnol, the effects will be felt quickly. Within about thirty minutes. You'll start to feel drowsy and have difficulty speaking and focusing. At some point you're also likely to experience loss of consciousness.'

'And how long does it last?'

'It depends on the amount given. Several hours. Perhaps up to four.'

'And how might you feel the next morning?'

'Most women don't remember anything, but the marks on their body suggest an assault . . .'

'I'm not suggesting an assault. I mean someone who might have been given it to render them unconscious.'

'Oh, I see.' He looked concerned. 'It's not you we're talking about, is it?'

'Me and champagne bars? Of course not. Go on.'

'If they've been asleep, they may wake up feeling unrefreshed and disoriented.'

'Sick?'

'It's possible. Nausea is a contra-indication of the drug. Of a lot of drugs, legal or not, in fact. If you have a reaction to medication, you're likely to vomit it up.'

'And presumably you're more likely to be sick if you've been given the drug with alcohol.'

'Almost certainly. The problem is these drugs are very difficult to study. They leave the body very quickly. Which is why women who suspect the use of a date-rape drug have to rely on other evidence, for example torn clothing or evidence of having sex but not remembering. It's difficult to prove the use of a drug afterwards, although Rohypnol can stay in the urine for up to seventy-two hours. GHB, which is often sold on the streets and is used for similar purposes, can leave the body within twelve hours.' He looked at Connie. ' I have a horrible feeling that the news I've given you isn't good.'

Connie shook her head. 'I never thought for a moment there was the possibility that the drug would still be detectable. It's just given me an alternative scenario where it might be possible for a crime to have been committed and for the person's partner to have been unaware of it.'

'What are you working on, Connie? You're suspended, aren't you?' asked Scott.

Connie looked over to Bill and winked. 'I'm a girl who things happen to.'

56

In Julia's eyes, there were two ways of dealing with trauma. Either you let it eat you alive or you got on with your life. The problem with the first option was that you were perpetually a victim, the second that you repressed the deep-seated damage that sudden shocks could cause. Both she and George had chosen the second route and they had ploughed that path alone. She loved George but she didn't really know him. He was a man who kept his secrets close and Julia, with her own deep-rooted fear of losing more of her loved ones, had let him be. Now she needed to speak to him. Have out what was niggling her subconscious.

'How well did you know Francesca?'

It had taken two hours of searching around his usual haunts until she found him in a place she'd once considered for one of her walks. The Trip to Jerusalem had been on the Crusade trail and parts of the original building dated back to the thirteenth century. There were rumours of the noise of spurs rattling late into the evening after drinkers had left the premises. The landlord, Justin, was a cheery and gregarious man who loved to see new faces. He'd have happily welcomed the extra visitors that a stop on her ghost tour would have provided. The problem was the inn was at the top of a steep incline and she would lose elderly tourists en route. She'd told George the story once and perhaps he'd remembered she never came here because this was where he'd sought refuge this evening over a glass of whisky. He was doing the crossword in one of the broadsheets. The pub was over half-full but no one was sitting near him. Justin gave her a nod as she entered.

'I'm sorry to hear about everything, love. Can I get you something? On the house, as it were.'

'Just an apple juice.'

'Nothing stronger?'

'I'd better not.'

Justin nodded over to George. 'Best not give him one for the road either.'

George wasn't drunk in the way that the average person would recognise it. His tolerance must be immense by now. Every January without fail he'd give up alcohol for the month and for a while Julia had hoped it might extend into the year. It never had. When he went out for a drink he stayed out all evening. That was his modus operandi. Some nights nothing. Others, out until the bitter end. Never moderation. He looked up as she asked her question and then back at the puzzle.

'What do you mean, how well did I know Francesca? As well as you, of course. She was our stepmother, so the answer is I knew her but not that well.'

'You knew her before, though, didn't you? Before Dad, I mean.'

'I knew her weeks before she met Dad. So what? She was working in the auction house and I briefly got to know her before she started seeing Dad.'

'What was she like? I mean, she got pregnant pretty quickly with Charlie, didn't she? I don't really remember her before she was part of our family.'

George looked bored. 'She was temperamental. She was basically a paid intern but she didn't like doing the menial tasks, photocopying, going out to buy the sandwiches and so on. I had to have it out with her.'

'What do you mean?'

'The point is, the reason we took on an intern is that we needed admin stuff doing. When she started sulking every time someone gave her an errand to run, she was basically complaining about what she was being employed to do. So I took her to one side and said I'd sack her if she didn't start behaving herself.'

'How did she react?'

George gave her a half-smile. 'I think she rather liked it.'

'And then she met Dad.'

George turned away from her. 'Then she met Dad and she could do what she liked.'

'Did she? Do what she wanted?'

'Not really. She wasn't experienced in the trade so she really could only do the menial stuff anyway. Then she was pregnant, Dad was retiring and we split the business so I could concentrate on the shop.'

'What will happen to the auction house?'

'We should inherit Dad's shares. Why? Are you thinking of getting involved?'

His tone was mild but he had turned to stare intently at her.

She coloured. 'I'm not interested, you know that. I just wondered, the antiques in Dad's house. It was all stuff he bought?'

'Yes, mainly after he got married.'

'Through you?'

'Me? He wouldn't have lowered himself to approve of my taste. He used other dealers around town.' George's tone was bitter. It must still sting. 'Why are you asking?'

Julia found the words wouldn't come out of her mouth. She wanted to ask if he had sold that chest of drawers but the words wouldn't form.

'I need to go to the bathroom.' George manoeuvred his bulk past her and disappeared off to the gents. She looked at the crossword he was completing. About half of the clues had been filled in. He had also doodled in the margin, a series of empty nooses, some made of rope, others with a buckle to one side. George reappeared and took the paper off her.

'You won't be able to do any of the clues so don't even try.'

'So you never sold Dad or Francesca anything?'

He looked like he was trying to restrain himself. 'I told you. Our father didn't come near my shop and, as I said, Francesca didn't know a bloody thing about antiques. So why are you asking?'

She needed to soothe him and decided on part of the truth. 'I looked at photos of the fire online. I saw burnt furniture. It was upsetting and spooky. It just made me think. I know there wasn't much from our childhood but I just wondered where he'd got the stuff they did have.'

George looked bored again. 'I've no idea. What were you looking at pictures of the house for anyway? You've seen for yourself what it's like. What do you want to go online for?'

She told him about the website and the other unwelcome guests Pat had mentioned. She saw him swear under his breath. She didn't dare mention the Ouija board in case that invited the same scorn he gave her night tours. Once more they had picked up their allotted roles. He the angry one, she the appeaser.

'What's the name of the site?' he demanded and she shrank from his words. There was no point lying.

'It's called *Under the Radar*. It's just some idiot who likes to photograph buildings.'

'He's trespassing on our land and making a bloody nuisance of himself. He should be easy to track down. You wait until I get my hands on him.'

'Not him. Her, it's a she.'

She watched her brother relax. 'Even better.'

57

Sunday, 19 February 2017

Julia stood at the window and watched as George started the car. His bad temper was obvious from the first loud rev of the engine.

'Another Sunday lunch ruined.' Julia's breath misted against the glass.

Francesca picked up Charlie and held him close to her. He twisted away from her, desperate to get back down to the toys strewn across the floor. 'He said he's not coming back again.'

'He always says that. Don't worry.'

'I'm not worried.' Francesca's tone was complacent. 'You can never completely let go of your family.' Francesca held Charlie closer, oblivious to the wriggling child.

'He's getting too heavy for you to hold onto him.'

'Time for another then.'

'Another? You mean another baby?'

'Well, why not.'

Julia was embarrassed to be discussing the subject with her stepmother. 'Is Dad okay with it?'

'I haven't talked to him yet.'

Julia exhaled. That'd be an interesting conversation. Would he be up for more disruption in his domestic life?

'Perhaps I'll tell him afterwards. Charlie needs a brother or sister.'

Julia wheeled around. 'Tell him afterwards? You mean, after you're pregnant? That's hardly fair.'

Francesca bent over Charlie. 'It's what I want. A family unit. It's important. Four of us together. It's what I'm dreaming of.'

58

The clean break he'd been hoping for had not materialised. Karen had called five times on his home phone this evening and had left two messages. The first one had been reasonable enough, asking him to return her call. The second one, she'd sounded angry, an unwelcome reminder of his ex-girlfriend who'd liked him to be easily contactable but had never answered her own mobile. He ignored the calls and tried to settle down. Tomorrow he'd need to travel into Manchester to speak to a colleague there about the gang of thieves who were buying a day return ticket out to Bampton, pickpocketing tourists and then returning to the city at the end of each day with their haul. One group had been caught at Chapel-en-le-Frith with a stash of wallets and items of jewellery. There would be others to take their place. Sadler had heard they were of eastern European origin, which made him groan. He'd already heard a comment about 'pikeys' from one of the uniformed constables.

After the phone had finished ringing for a sixth time, Sadler picked up the receiver and dialled a number retrieved from an old address book. Chances were the mobile was now out of date but it rang nevertheless and Sadler braced himself to make apologies for the wrong number.

Miles's voice, when it came through, sounded exactly the same as it had twenty years earlier. Sadler could hear the astonishment in his voice as he introduced himself.

'Good God, how are you, mate?'

'I'm fine.' Now he was through, Sadler felt foolish. 'I wasn't sure you'd still have the same number you sent me.'

'No reason to change it. Is everything all right? Camilla? Your mum?'

'They're well too,' said Sadler, touched. 'Am I disturbing you?'

'Well, I'm in work if that's what you mean but I have my own office these days. How the hell are you? You can't still be a constable.'

'Detective Inspector.'

'I'm not surprised. You were always hard at it, even when you were young. Are you sure you're all right? I mean, we've not really kept in touch.'

'I saw Karen the other day and she mentioned you.'

'Karen. Jeesh. There's someone I don't like to think about very often. Pam occasionally tries to bring her up but I tell her to leave her in the past. She made our lives a misery when we first got together.'

'I know she took it hard.'

'Well, we were technically still together. I'd tried to finish it a few times but every time I suggested parting, she'd threaten to kill herself. It's a form of emotional abuse, I can see that now. I just felt stuck and was seriously considering doing a runner. You know, packing up my stuff one day when Karen was at work and legging it.'

'Why didn't you?'

'Pam came along, basically. We've been together for years now so it's hard to remember everything but I did see that life would be so much easier with someone like Pam. Of course, we also fell in love.'

'Karen still talks about you.'

'Bloody hell. I'd heard she'd got married. Is she single again?'

'Divorced. I saw her a couple of times. Nothing romantic, just a drink, but she comes on quite strong.'

'Strong? That's got to be an understatement. Is this what you've called me about? If you want my advice, steer well clear of her.'

'She wasn't ever dangerous, though, was she?'

'Define dangerous. There wasn't ever anything specific in her threats but she made Pam and me feel uncomfortable. Pam was sure she spotted her hanging around our flat one time and there was some bother over scratched paintwork on our car. It's one of the reasons we decided to relocate to Canada. Once we were married we knew it'd be easier to bring up kids here and we felt life would be easier away from Karen.'

'She wouldn't let go.'

'Some people, Francis, find it impossible to let go. They might pretend they have but, in reality, something is festering away like a sore.'

As they switched onto more general chitchat about their respective families, Sadler couldn't rid himself of a suspicion that was trying to make itself felt. The voice in his head that was saying, *this is important.*

59

'Your dog's barking again.'

Morell Thorn caught Julia as she made her way down the street, laden with shopping bags. He stood in the doorway of his house awaiting her return from work. In the distance, she could hear Bosco howling in displeasure.

'God, I'm sorry. I don't know what's the matter with him.'

'He's been like this all day. He only stopped when that woman across the road came to feed him.'

'I'm sorry. I'll go and see what the matter is.'

'I don't care what the matter is,' Morell shouted and stepped out onto the pavement. 'I can't take the constant noise. I'm going to report you to the council. There are laws against this kind of thing.'

Hands shaking, Julia put her key into the lock and Bosco hurled himself past her and ran out onto the street. Julia dashed after him and dragged his panting body back into the house. A few seconds later, a knock came at the door and Jean stood there with a tea towel tucked into her waistband. 'I saw Morell talking to you. I tried to get to you before him but I've something on the stove. Bosco's been like this all day. I've never known him to bark like this. He wouldn't even settle when I went to let him out.'

'What's the matter? He just ran out of the front door. If a car had been coming he'd have been killed. I don't know what's got into him.'

'He's not been right since . . .'

'Since when?'

Jean looked embarrassed. 'Well, since the fire. I just wondered if he'd picked up on your anxieties.'

'Me? Of course I'm anxious. You think that might be it?'

'Look, I'm happy to have him all day for the moment until things settle down. I'll make sure he doesn't bark and it'll be company for us both.'

'God, Jean. I'd really appreciate that. Listen,' Julia dropped her voice to a whisper, 'is there something the matter in the head with Morell? He seriously gives me the creeps.'

Jean lowered her voice to match Julia's and leant into her. 'He's just a local oddity. I'm a bit older than him and I remember the tragedy like it was yesterday. There were four of them and it was the boiling hot summer of '65. They went into the caves to cool off and also have a bit of an explore. Anyway, during the larking about, Morell's brother, Troy, got lost. He was younger than the others, about six, I think, and to begin with they could hear him crying but they couldn't work out what direction the sound was coming from.'

'Oh God.'

'Yes, exactly. Then after half an hour or so the crying disappeared and the other three found themselves lost too. They had the foresight to stick together, though, and they discovered the exit and raised the alarm.'

'But Troy was never found.'

'Never. The theory is that when the crying stopped he'd probably fallen down a crevice and been killed. They never found the body. It affected all the lads but Morell most of all. He's been obsessed with cave safety ever since.'

'You don't think he's giving me hassle because I work in Anchor Cavern, do you?'

Jean frowned. 'Good lord, no. I doubt he even knows where you work. He's got a bee in his bonnet about Bosco, that's all, and we're going to sort that out, aren't we.' Jean patted Bosco on the head. 'By the way, who's the man friend?'

'What do you mean, man friend?'

'I thought I saw someone by your house the other evening. I assumed that you'd met someone?'

'Me? I don't have a boyfriend. What did he look like?'

'Large-ish. It was difficult to see as it was dusk. I could have sworn they were leaving your house.'

Julia's heart gave a lurch. 'I've no idea who you saw.'

60

Connie cursed her lack of official status. She had prised open a crack in George's alibi, which was a start but nowhere near enough. A motive wasn't calling out to her but that might come if she could discover *how* he had committed the murders. She must first start with the scenario that the murders were planned and he had left a drugged Antonia and driven to Cross Farm Lane. Okay, so where did that take her? That he had planned to murder his family for a reason unknown. In order to get away with it, he would need to pin the blame on Francesca. In order to do that, it must be crystal clear there had been no break-in.

George either must have had a key to the house or one of the members of the household had let him in. Either was possible. It was his childhood home and adult children didn't necessarily relinquish ownership of items when they grew up. Somewhere, knocking around her flat, was the key to her father's house although she hoped she'd never be asked to find it in a hurry. If George also still had his key, there would be no need to break into the building ,which would explain why there was no sign of forced entry. He would then have had to set about killing Peter and Francesca. The only way this could have happened would be for him to have stunned his father with a blow and then dragged Francesca to the landing to hang her from the beam. He could then have returned to his father to complete the killing. To have killed his father outright would have given

Francesca a chance to escape and there was no evidence of a struggle. After disposing of both adults, he could then have turned his attention to Charlie.

The other possibility was either Francesca or Peter had let in George after he had presented himself on their doorstep in the middle of the night with a ready-made excuse. It was a possibility but not that likely. Surely a roused household couldn't then be murdered upstairs? The important point, however, was that George had gained access to the house in order to murder his family. Then what?

Connie sat in her car and considered the building opposite her. Bampton had three petrol stations. Two of them attached to supermarkets had been scrutinised. They had the latest ANPR technology that automatically reads car number plates and compares them against database records. They were used to ensure anyone who drove off without paying for their petrol could be traced. Records showed that three members of the Winson family had used the pumps on a regular basis: Peter, Francesca and Julia.

The source of the accelerant hadn't been found, but what the fire investigators had been able to prove was that a receptacle full of petrol had sat in the outhouse until recently. This, for the investigator, had served to show that Francesca was the killer who had kept the means of starting the fire ready to hand. Although they had not been able to find proof of Francesca purchasing this fuel, the hypothesis was she had filled up her car plus the can and paid for it together.

The question was, Connie asked herself, if Francesca was always going to kill herself, why would she need to hide the fact she'd bought petrol?

No one had remarked that there was no record whatsoever of George using either petrol station. The two cheapest fuel outlets in Bampton, which competed with their pricing so the cost of petrol was always identical, and George had never visited either one of them. This had Connie's radar on high alert. He had a large Land Rover Discovery, which must cost a fortune to run. The petrol was being purchased somewhere and there was only one other option in Bampton.

Although Murkell Road petrol station was also attached to a supermarket, it was a tiny Co-operative store that you only used if you wanted a late-night pint of milk or the Sunday papers. The times that Connie had visited, the employees behind the tills were either frazzled or laughing amongst themselves. They had no ANPR camera, only an ancient CCTV camera that wasn't working, a regular occurrence according to the manager. If you wanted to fill a can of petrol out of sight, here was the place to do it.

Connie parked up in one of the side bays, waited for the sole customer to leave and then went inside. She approached the counter and flashed her ID.

'I'm just doing some enquiries about the fire in Cross Farm Lane. Do you remember the incident?' The two women stopped talking and gazed at her in fascination.

'It's still being investigated? It was the woman who did it, the mother. It's disgusting. If you want to kill yourself, fine, but why take the rest of the family with you?' The younger woman, around Connie's age, had decided to do the talking for the pair.

It was a common refrain that Connie had heard a few times in the case. 'I don't know,' she said. 'My colleagues have spoken to your manager but we're still trying to discover the source of the petrol used in the attack.'

'If they've spoken to Dave, our boss, there's nothing else we can add. There's a few of us on a rota and he sent us all an email to ask us if we'd noticed anything unusual. I don't think anyone had, though.'

'Did you know the family?'

'Only by sight. Peter Winson was a bit of a name here in Bampton. It wasn't just the auctioneer's. He sat on the Rotary committee and then there was his shop. Everyone knew who he was.'

'He'd come in for his petrol?'

'Not very often. No one's loyal to one garage. They'll go where the petrol's cheapest or there's the least queue.' She turned and served a customer who wanted cigarettes.

The older of the two women looked her up and down and finally spoke. 'I've known George and Julia since they were teenagers. Julia was in the Girl Guides when I helped out there. There's a pair of siblings who are chalk and cheese, I can tell you.'

'How so?'

'Well, Julia drives this clapped-out red car. It looks like it's going to die any minute. And she buys her petrol here some-times. She always asks about Jessy, my daughter, which is more than can be said for her brother.'

'What's he like?'

'He doesn't give me the time of day. He's here more often and he stands there with his feet tapping while I'm putting the card through the machine. I'm not brilliant with it since it's been changed and all the other customers are fine when I tell them. Him, though. He was so angry one time, when I messed it up, kept looking at his watch. The next time he paid with cash, just to have a go at me.'

'Surely some people pay with cash, though.' Connie felt the prickle of interest.

'If it's twenty quid or something, then yes they do, but he's got a massive car. A tank is about a hundred quid and that time he came in and paid with cash just after I'd cocked up the machine. I was mortified. He did it just to make a point.'

'He paid a hundred pounds in cash?'

'Nearer a hundred and thirty it was. He must have filled it to the brim because I don't know many cars that take that much petrol.'

'And he always pays in cash now?'

'No! It was just that once. As I told you, although he didn't say anything, I'm sure he was making the point that it's quicker if he doesn't have to wait for me with the machine.'

Connie kept her tone nonchalant. 'When was this?'

'Oh, ages ago. I can't remember.'

'Before the fire?'

'Oh, definitely before that horrible thing. I remember being really annoyed with him and I've made a real effort with him since. Not that it makes any difference to him, of course.'

'You sure about this?'

'Positive. I feel sorry for what happened to the family but one thing's for sure, George Winson is a nasty piece of work.'

61

'There's been someone around asking after you.'

'Me?' Julia felt the blood rise in her face. She'd been looking forward to relaxing in her lunch hour, safe in the knowledge that Bosco was ensconced with Jean and she wouldn't be facing her angry neighbour for a second time this week. She kept herself apart from her colleagues who were largely seasonal workers, university students who sat in the staff room together discussing destinations that they would travel to once they had graduated. Julia had stopped going into the room. Her grieving made them uncomfortable and the weather was kind so she'd taken to eating her sandwiches outside, often accompanied by Maureen. She was sitting here next to Julia now, her long floral skirt billowing out around her thick legs.

'Who's been asking after me?'

'Well, that's the problem. I don't know. One of the kids who looks after reception when I'm on my lunch said a lady had come in and asked if you were working that day. It was your day off so he said you'd be back in tomorrow.'

'This was yesterday?'

'Apparently so. I asked if he'd seen the woman before but he didn't think so.'

'A woman? What did she look like?' Julia could feel her heart thudding in her chest as she thought of the yellow flowers.

Maureen looked concerned. 'Michael said she was elderly. I'm sure he described her as tall and thin.'

Julia could feel her enthusiasm deflate. Not her mother. No interval of nearly forty years could change her mother into someone who was tall and thin. Disappointment flooded her. Whoever wanted to speak to her, it wasn't her mother. In the background, she could hear Maureen continuing to speculate on the visitor.

'She didn't look like the normal type of visitor we have, apparently. I mean, we get the elderly, of course, but not on their own.'

'She went down into the cave then?'

'No. That's the point. She went away when she heard you weren't in. She must have been a visitor, though, as Michael says she had a Scottish accent.'

'Scottish? Are you sure?'

Maureen looked doubtful. 'That's what Michael said. Does that sound more like someone you know?'

Julia thought about her online watcher and the name that user had chosen. *NaturalScot.* Could this woman know what had happened to her mother?

'She's not been back today, has she?'

Maureen bristled. 'No, she hasn't. It's why I'm taking my break out here. I can keep an eye on the front door. If she comes back, I'll see her.'

*

For the rest of the day, Julia was on tenterhooks. Every time a group tour finished, she looked up the iron steps hoping to see Maureen hovering there with news of her visitor. Each time, Maureen's face conveyed that she was as disappointed as Julia was that the woman had failed to materialise. Only as she glided along in the barge bringing the last visitors of the day back to the front of the cave did she see on the monitor on the dock that Maureen wasn't at her desk. Desperate as she was to get to the surface, she had to stay at the back of the group climbing the stairs, ensuring the stragglers reached the top safely. When she got to the surface, Maureen was there waiting but behind her was a person she hadn't been expecting to see. Connie.

'I've cleared the students out of the staff room. Go and use that,' said Maureen.

Connie didn't look well. She'd been slim when Julia had last seen her but as she turned around to enter the little room, the saggy bottom of her black jeans hinted of sudden weight loss. She looked unhealthily thin, a suspicion confirmed when Julia spotted the jutting shoulder blades rising above her T-shirt.

'Why are you here? I heard you'd been suspended.'

Connie grimaced. 'I have. In fact, I've resigned. I thought I might as well go before they sacked me.'

'Was it because we went to Horncastle?'

Connie sat down on the sofa. 'It was the straw that broke the camel's back, that's all. I was showing an excessive interest in your mother's disappearance.'

'You also accused George of having something to do with the murders. He was furious.'

Connie smiled but said nothing.

'Why are you here?'

Connie leant forward. 'Because I need your help. You *do*

272

want to know what happened to your mother, don't you?'

'You know I do.'

'Okay, so I'm going to ask you. Is there anyone we can contact who knew your mother around that time? Anyone at all.'

Julia slowly shook her head. 'She didn't really have that many friends. She knew loads of people through the shop but that's not the same thing, is it?'

'She didn't have any girlfriends, women she would see in the evening?'

'She would be in the shop all day. Evenings were for cooking meals, watching television and so on. I don't remember any female friends.'

'What about customers? You spent lots of time in the shop with your mother. You told me this. Can you remember any customers who used to come in?'

'Hardly! They'll all be dead now. This was the seventies. Anyone who was a customer of my mother's was usually over the age of forty. They'll be long dead.'

'If they were forty in 1980, they'll be seventy-seven now. Why shouldn't they be alive?'

Julia shifted in her seat, interest segueing into irritation. What was the point of all this? 'I was being generous when I said forty. In fact, most of her customers were over fifty.'

'Don't you care?'

'Of course I care!' She surprised them both by raising her voice. 'The problem is that customers were interviewed by the police at the time and nothing came of it. You're not suddenly going to find a witness who happened to be twenty-five and who my mother confided in. She wasn't that type of person for a start.'

'She must have had some friends to talk to.'

'*I* don't have any. Do you?'

The detective coloured and Julia felt ashamed. She sat down beside Connie and resisted the temptation to put her arm around her.

'This is my obsession. Don't let it be yours.'

Connie frowned, her wan face accumulating more shadows. 'How does someone just disappear? In these days we have CCTV, of course, but even then it was difficult to go completely undetected.'

'I remember the police saying that to us. How strange it was. It's why my father always felt he was a suspect. He thought the police couldn't possibly have believed she could travel anywhere and not be spotted. Therefore, her body must still be in Horncastle.'

'There was that one sighting in Aberdeen. It was the most credible of them all. You didn't have any family there, did you?'

'Aberdeen in Scotland?'

For the first time, a look of genuine amusement came into Connie's face. 'I don't think there's another one.' She stopped smiling when she saw Julia's expression. 'What? Why are you so interested in Scotland?'

62

Matthews followed Sadler into his office. 'Can I have a word with you, sir?'

He motioned her to sit and then caught sight of her worried face. 'Is everything all right? We've not had any more trouble from that Manchester gang overnight, have we?'

'There are reports of a disturbance at a campsite near Taddington but the owner scared them off. They're all on high alert at the moment because it's been all over the news. My guess is the gang will move up into the Dark Peak soon enough.'

'About time too, although that moves them on to Glossop's patch.'

'They're just recovering from the mass pile-up on Snake Pass. I feel guilty about not catching the gang and saving our northern colleagues some legwork. We did our best.'

He caught a note of defensiveness in her tone. 'It wasn't a criticism. Is that what you wanted to see me about?'

She sighed, a long deep exhalation. 'We've passed the files over to the CPS on the Cross Farm Lane fire but we're still getting evidence in relating to the case, naturally. Something's come up that I want you to see before we forward it on.'

She handed over a letter written on good quality white paper. An embossed logo of a snake wrapped around a staff was in the top right-hand corner, the universal medical symbol. He scanned the letter briefly. It was from the Westmoor private hospital in Leeds. In response to a query letter from Peter Winson's GP, they were able to confirm they had seen Mr Winson as a patient but, without a court order, could not release any further information about the test results.

'What's this about?'

'We did the usual of obtaining the medical records of the deceased. Going through the entries, we spotted some referrals for Charlie and Mr Winson to other hospitals so we wrote to them requesting further details. They're starting to trickle in now. Charlie Winson went to the paediatric department for a severe ear infection one Christmas, for example. The Westmoor was on the list but, as it's a private hospital, we weren't sure what it was about.'

'Well, we're not now, are we? This letter doesn't tell us anything.'

'I've gone back to the GP file and it was in response to Peter Winson asking for a referral to a fertility clinic in 2012.'

Sadler frowned at the paper, trying to make sense of it. 'Peter Winson wanted to visit a fertility clinic?'

'Apparently. The team noted it but weren't especially bothered because, well, he was a guy in his sixties when he met Francesca and if he wanted more children then it's no surprise that he needed to go to the clinic.'

'So why are you showing it to me?'

'We need to make a decision about whether to get a court order to see the records so I gave the hospital a call. They're much more lax, you know, than the NHS. I've worked on tons of cases dealing with the public health system and they tell you nothing. Too many data protection training seminars, I fear.'

Sadler closed his eyes. 'You're beginning to sound a bit like Connie.'

'Anyway, I gave them a call. The receptionist put me through to the reproductive health reception and from there I got to speak to a doctor.'

'Just like that?'

'Well, no, he rang me back. He didn't tell me everything, of course, but he did tell me plenty, not least that Peter Winson had visited the clinic twice. The first time in 2012 and the second this year. The second time, he came back as a private patient so it's not on the NHS records.'

'Any reason why he might do that?'

Matthews shrugged. 'I guess it's quite common. You want to go to a hospital so you get your GP to refer you. Then, if you like it and the fees are reasonable enough, you go back as a private patient to somewhere you feel comfortable.'

Sadler leant back in his chair. 'So, Peter visited the clinic twice, around the dates that Francesca became pregnant. The most likely scenario is that, for the first visit, he was about to marry Francesca and he wanted to check whether he was still fertile.'

'Agreed. And for the second visit, they had decided to have another child after a period of five years; he was now in his late sixties and wanted to check nothing had changed. Or, possibly they had been trying and nothing was happening so he decided to get checked out.'

'That all sounds probable. So . . .'

'I put that scenario to the doctor I spoke to and he went, well, all funny on me. He said something in a strangled voice along the lines of, "That's one possible sequence of events".'

'You think he was trying to direct you towards an alternative scenario?'

'Trying? I think he was desperately trying to communicate something. He was basically telling me in the tone of his voice, without actually saying it, that's not what happened. Do you want me to call him again?'

'No, I do not. If this is significant towards providing an explanation as to what happened, we need the records. Can you prepare an application to the court and I'll telephone Llewellyn to let him know when to expect it on his desk?'

'What do you think is going on?'

'I'm not sure. It's probably nothing.'

Matthews looked like she wanted to say something else but, instead, quietly left the office.

*

Llewellyn heard out his inspector and then replaced the receiver. He shouted through the open door. 'Margaret, when a court application comes in from CID, can you bring it straight through?'

His secretary, who'd told him in a recent 360-degree appraisal that she loved her job but one minor criticism would be that she preferred not to be bellowed at from a disembodied voice when he had a telephone on his desk, appeared in the doorway.

'Of course. Is everything all right?'

Llewellyn leant back in his chair and rocked slightly. 'I think it's time to retire when you root for the wrong instead of the right, don't you?'

She stared at him in confusion. 'I don't know what you're talking about.'

'I'm talking about the difference between wrong and right, Margaret. That's why we do this job.'

'Sometimes I can't tell the difference,' she murmured.

He nodded in assent. 'Right answer.'

63

For the first time since the killings, Julia made an effort to cook something decent. Of course, according to the stories she read in women's magazines, what should have happened when Elizabeth disappeared was that Julia became a competent cook, whipping up meals for her father and brother to keep the family going. No chance. It had been neighbours first supplying hot dishes, then the fish and chip shop and then sausage and mash or lamb chops when their father could be bothered to cook. Things had improved in the mid-eighties when varieties of pasta sauce and flavoured rice had appeared on supermarket shelves. Her father had begun to make more of an effort too after their move to Bampton, with Sunday roasts and the occasional rice pudding.

Julia's cooking remained erratic but she downloaded a chicken recipe onto her laptop and set to work. As she waited for the dish to cook, the aroma of coq au vin filled her kitchen and even Bosco was sniffing the air. Glancing at her front door, she saw a large shadow fill the space. The light evening gave her courage and she bolted to the door and flung it open. Ned looked at her in shock. 'Christ, what are you doing here?'

'What am *I* doing here? What the hell are *you* doing here standing outside the front door, scaring me half to death?'

Ned drew back in consternation. 'I had no idea where you lived. You never gave me that information.'

'So what the hell are you doing here?'

Out of the corner of her eye, Julia saw Morell shut his front door. 'You've been visiting that weirdo. Are you two in cahoots?'

'Morell isn't weird.'

'He is with me.'

'Have you heard his story? He's never got over losing his brother. You should know something about what it is to grieve.'

'Right.' Julia made to slam the door, aware that Bosco was howling behind her and that her relaxing evening was going pear-shaped.

'Julia, please. I didn't mean it to sound so blunt. Let me explain. Can I come in?'

She looked at him again, noting his dishevelled appearance, and opened the door. He followed her into the kitchen as she opened the oven to check on her food.

'Go on then. Tell me what you're doing at Morell's.'

'I had a call from my in-laws last night. Toby's been having these nightmares again. I know Morell slightly and I went to see him before when Toby was so scared after his visit to Anchor Cavern. He's an expert on caves. I just wanted to be sure that nothing might have happened down there.'

'I told you—'

'I know, but I wanted to check. And now the nightmares have started again, I wanted to see Morell to chat about them. I had absolutely no idea you lived here.'

'Does Morell know about my job?'

'He never mentioned it and he had plenty of opportunity to tell me.'

'Was he helpful? About Toby, I mean.'

'A bit. You really should talk to him, you know. He's an

expert on caves and he told me about the wind that echoes.'

'That's what I told you!'

'I know.' Ned looked over to the oven. 'I think your dog likes what you're cooking.'

Bosco had his head pressed against the oven door. 'Right, that's it. I'm throwing him out into the garden.'

Bosco took his punishment with equanimity and trotted towards a spot at the far end of the yard.

'I really didn't know where you lived.'

'Okay, okay.' Julia took a deep breath to calm down. 'Look, it's the first effort I've made with food for ages. Would you like some?'

'Seriously? I'd love to. It smells delicious. Are you sure there's enough for two?'

'I've jointed a whole chicken. I had visions of eating it all week.'

Ned looked around the kitchen. 'Shall I go out and get some wine?'

'I have it. You can open the bottle, though.'

She took out a red from a case that George had given her for Christmas. He took it from her and, as he pushed in the corkscrew, looked out into the garden. 'Do you feed your dog outside?'

'No, in here. Why?'

'It looks like he's eating something, that's all.'

'It's probably squirrel poo. Hold on.' She rushed outside to retrieve Bosco from whatever foul thing he'd decided was edible. She pulled him away and squinted down at the brown mush. It looked like ordinary dog food. She yanked at his collar again. It wasn't the stuff she normally fed him, favouring the dry biscuits that wouldn't go off in the summer heat. This looked like food out of a tin, wobbling and glutinous.

Bosco began to be sick, his small body shaking as he retched. Ned joined them in the garden and looked anxiously at the dog. 'Is he all right?'

'I don't know. It's not unusual for him to eat something he finds in the garden nor, to be honest, for him to then be sick afterwards. The problem is that stuff looks like dog food, and not the stuff I buy either.'

She crouched down and put her arms around the shivering Bosco who was still heaving. She could smell a chemical tang on his breath. Ned was poking the remains of the food with a stick. 'It looks normal enough. It's tinned dog food that's been emptied onto the path. Do you know anyone who'd feed him like that?'

'Of course not. The only person with a key is Jean and she knows to feed him his biscuits too. Oh my God!'

Bosco was on his back and his eyes had rolled to the back of his head. Ned swept the dog up in his arms. 'We need to get him to a vet as soon as possible.'

In Ned's car, she rang the number of her vet and was directed to an out of hours service in Macclesfield. It would take at least half an hour to get there but there was no other option. As they sped down Cross Farm Lane, she passed the ruin of her father's house but was too preoccupied to look to see whether a nocturnal intruder was paying another unauthorised visit. As they drove up the hill towards The Cat and Fiddle pub perched on top of the moorland, Bosco began to whimper and she forced water from a bottle down his throat, praying all the while, *Don't let me lose Bosco too.*

On the way back, both she and Ned were subdued. Of the three of them, Bosco was the most alert, looking out of the window and whining occasionally. The vet had been competent and experienced.

'You did right not to make him vomit any more. With poisons, it can aggravate as much coming back up as going down in the first place. I'm giving him some activated charcoal to neutralise whatever he's ingested.'

'What was the poison?'

The vet wrinkled his nose. 'Judging by the smell on his breath, probably paint thinners or turpentine.'

They'd watched in astonishment as Bosco, over the course of the two hours in the surgery, gradually perked up.

'Do they normally recover so fast?'

'Most dogs do, if you get them here quickly enough. The food was in the garden, you say? Then you need to make it more secure, otherwise it will happen again.'

She could feel Ned's eyes on hers but she shook her head slightly. She knew what he was thinking. The garden *was* enclosed and the back gate padlocked.

Now, in the car, he asked quietly, 'Who has a key to your house?'

'Jean over the road and Dad had one.'

'Anyone else?'

'There's only my brother George and I've never given him one. He gave me the keys to his flat ages ago as a spare set but I never gave him mine. George is impossible to track down. I'd have no idea where he'd be if I lost my key. Dad was more reliable.'

'Anyone else? A cleaner, for example?'

'I can't afford a cleaner. I have three sets apart from mine. One hanging inside a cupboard, Jean has one set and Dad had the other.'

When they reached her house, they went straight to the cupboard under the stairs. The keys were still dangling on the hook.

'You don't think it was Morell who put down the food, do you?' Julia asked.

'Morell? Listen, Julia. I know him. He was telling me about a neighbour's dog barking but he was stressed rather than angry. He wouldn't hurt a fly, I promise you. Anyway, how would he get into the yard? That food wasn't chucked over the fence. It was placed in a heap.'

'Who would want to kill Bosco? Everyone loves him except Morell.'

'It must be someone who's got hold of the keys from your father's house. There's no other explanation.' He turned to her with a look of concern. 'Do you want me to stay here tonight? I can sleep in your spare room.'

'It's a mess. You can't even get to the bed it's so full of junk.'

'Then I'll sleep on the sofa. I don't want you staying here alone.'

'Look, I can go to my sister-in-law's, Holly. I'll get some clothes and lock up here.'

She rang Holly, who sounded concerned. As she was putting some things in a bag, she heard Ned checking each room.

'Everything looks okay but call me anytime if you're worried. Toby's not back until the weekend, so I can come over whenever you want.'

She put her overnight things into the boot of Ned's car and they packed themselves in once more, Bosco happy to curl up on the back seat. As Ned turned the car around, she looked over her shoulder and saw a figure pull back into the shadows. She reached over and pushed down the lock.

'Are you okay?'

'I'm fine. I'm just feeling a bit security-conscious.'

'Are you sure? We should be calling the police, you know.'

'I don't want to call them at the moment. I need to think about a few things.'

He drove slowly away from her house and she didn't turn her head again. She refused to think of her missing mother or her dead father. Or of the lovely little boy or of the cool, composed Francesca. She particularly refused to think of the shadow standing watching the house and the brief glimpse of the outline that she'd had. How the height and curly hair thrown by the meagre moonlight had revealed itself as the shadow of her brother George.

64

Connie pulled into an Eight Till Late and bought herself a can of deodorant, which she sprayed liberally under each arm. Fumes of 'spring cotton' filled the car and she wound down a window to let in the evening air. Refreshed, she leant back in the car seat and pondered her next move. Julia's news about a possible Scottish link was interesting but was hardly going to crack the case. Grudgingly, Connie acknowledged Sadler was right about that one. It was the present day that would hold the answers. The problem was she was stymied by her unofficial status. Everything at the moment was conjecture.

If she'd been part of an investigation into George as suspect, they might have examined the interior of his car for traces of petrol. There was the issue of the accelerant they'd found in the garden shed. It suggested that George had left it there in readiness for the killings, but, given he had not been to the house for months, he must have done it without the family noticing.

The night was falling fast and she didn't fancy doing her final task after dark. It was the last hurrah for the tourist season. Children were due back to school in a few weeks and the town had quietened down in readiness for a more sedate autumn. There would be one infant school with a pupil less this term, which would need to be managed by the teaching staff. She shook away the thought of the empty desk and started the car.

When she arrived at the gaping wound in the otherwise

salubrious suburb she slowed down and took a good look at the remains of the former Winson home. It reminded her of a set from a horror movie, the thin arched window still visible. Bampton's own Amityville horror. The road was deserted. The house opposite where the young mother had first spotted the fire and called the police had all its curtains drawn. The adjoining houses were hidden behind trees in full leaf.

If George had driven here the evening of the killings, he would have had to leave his car somewhere out of sight. He couldn't have walked the journey from his apartment and it wouldn't have been conducive to a quick getaway. He must, therefore, have driven. They'd appealed for witnesses but no one could remember seeing a car parked up outside or near the house. There were no obvious spots to conceal a vehicle on the way out of Bampton so she needed to keep going beyond the house and towards the rolling countryside. A car, obviously irritated at her slow speed, overtook her although the second was more obliging and followed behind her.

After a minute she noticed a short gravel track that led not to a house but towards a large field that opened up towards the hills beyond. You wouldn't be able to park on it for long; the farmer would need access to his land and a vehicle might be spotted by any walker coming down the path. Not, however, late at night. In darkness, you could leave a vehicle near the trees and it would remain hidden.

Connie got out and pulled the powerful LED torch from the back of the car. She'd heard rumours of unwelcome visitors at Cross Farm Lane and, if she came across any of them, she wanted to be prepared. As she was reaching the road, she saw a police car approaching the house slowly. *Shit*. She leant back into the hedge and crouched down, aware how explaining her presence in the area might scupper everything she'd achieved so far. The car passed on and Connie wondered if it was idle curiosity or a more tangible reason they were monitoring the house.

She kept the torch in her pocket and walked up to the entrance. The large gate was secured by a padlock but it was easy enough to squeeze herself through the hedge, even if it felt her body was being assaulted by sharp spikes. On the other side, a lawn spread up to the house. Glancing around, she could see the headlights of passing cars through the hedge but she couldn't be seen from the road. She didn't dare use her torch in case the patrol passed by again. Instead she crept towards the house and one of the downstairs windows with the shattered glass. She peered inside but the gloom only illuminated the devastation that the fire had wrought. There was nothing to actually *see* so why was she here?

She made her way around the back of the house to the brick outbuilding. The door was still open and now she did switch on her light and swept the inside with an arc. The presence of the forensic team was evident, the floor covered with white powder and imprinted with scuff marks from booted feet. She followed the path George might have taken, from the outbuilding to the back door. The back door that led onto a narrow passage had been locked and bolted from the inside. There was another rear entrance, a set of double doors that led from the kitchen and onto a small patio. Perhaps this was the way George had entered the house, although that, too, had been locked. Had anyone asked George Winson if he had a key to his father's house?

Connie's head ached. However George had entered the house, he must have then come downstairs for the petrol *after* the killings. You couldn't break into a house with a full can of petrol without anybody noticing. To test her theory, she needed to get inside the house. The problem was she'd had enough of hospitals to last her a lifetime and she wasn't going to put herself in the path of injury now. She'd need to look at the inside of the house from the official photos, which meant a call to Llewellyn.

With a sigh she turned off her torch and made her way back to the hedge and the main road. Connie felt a prickling on the back of her neck and she stopped in the darkness, breathing heavily. The scent of recent rain had combined with the remnants of smoke and something else, wild garlic. The Winsons must have had the plants growing in the garden and it was a pungent, putrid aroma. The smell of death. The feeling of being observed was still there and her sense of survival kicked in. She put down her head and barrelled through the hedge, ignoring the spikes and protruding stems. Her speed nearly sent her into the path of a car that had to swerve. She must have given the driver a heart attack but they drove on after sounding their horn.

She jogged back to her car and slid inside, breathing a sigh of relief. As soon as she put the key in the ignition she knew something was wrong. The steering wheel bucked and although she put her foot down hard on the accelerator, she couldn't get the car to move. What the hell was wrong? She slid down her window and shone the torch on her front tyre. It was flat. She must have run over something on the way down the path.

She opened the door and went to retrieve the spare tyre when she noticed the rear one was also flat. With a finger she traced the path of the knife blade that had made the slash. Grabbing her handbag from the passenger seat, Connie fled towards the house opposite and the welcome glow of the front porch.

65

Despite her disability, or perhaps because of it, Holly was a reassuring presence in the face of adversity. The previous evening she'd listened to Julia's story and sent her straight to bed with a hot-water bottle and a large cushion for Bosco. She'd not asked any questions about Ned and had given him a cup of tea before he went on his way. Even though the bedroom was on the ground floor, Julia had slept a long, deep sleep. When she awoke, for a short moment she'd revelled in the luxury of the bedroom before remembering where she was, and what had brought her here.

She looked down beside her and Bosco was nowhere to be seen. She grabbed a jumper to put over her nightdress and went into the kitchen.

'Where's Bosco?'

Holly nodded over to the garden where Julia could now see him chasing after a frog.

'I'll have to stop him. If he eats that, he'll be sick again.'

Holly wheeled her chair forward and took two slices of bread from the freezer. 'Let him be. He's eaten a whole bowl of doggie biscuits this morning. He's fine. It's you I'm worried about.'

Julia flopped into the kitchen chair. 'Is there any coffee?'

'I'm brewing it now. Look, I didn't want to question you last night as you'd obviously had a shock, but what's going on? And, now I think of it, how long have you been seeing this Ned?'

'I'm not seeing him. He's a single dad and he thought I was trying to frighten his son down the caves. Never mind about that. It's a long story. I have to say he was brilliant last night, though.'

'You think it was deliberate? That dog eats anything, you know.'

'It was proper dog food, Holly, mixed in with paint stripper.'

'Jesus. What sick person would do that?' Rather than lay the table, Holly brought over a tray, perfectly arranged with a linen handkerchief and shining cutlery. A pot of home-made marmalade lay ready to be spread over the toast. Julia stared at it, her mouth dry. 'I have a neighbour who doesn't like dogs. It might be him.'

'Well, there you go then. Call the police and report him. You don't want to be living next to a neighbour with a vendetta.'

'There's something else.'

'What? Has it happened before?'

'Not that. Can I ask you something?'

'What is it?' With shaking hands, Holly placed the tray on the table.

'You know when you and George split up, I remember there was some difficulty.'

'That's putting it mildly. He wouldn't leave me alone. I had to get a court order out to make sure he stayed away.'

'I never really understood it. I always thought the initial split was amicable.'

Holly reversed up and retrieved her cup of coffee from the counter. 'Did you?' Her tone was flat. 'We never really talked about it, did we? I was so desperate to keep hold of your friendship, I was never going to interfere with your relationship with George.'

'Can you tell me now? What it was like.'

'Julia, I took out a restraining order on him. He didn't want me but wouldn't let me go. I didn't want him inside this bungalow. This is my space, nothing to do with him. So he used to come outside and try to speak to me.'

'If it was amicable, why didn't you talk to him?'

'Amicable? It wasn't friendly at all. What on earth made you think that?'

'You seemed so grown up. My relationships have all ended with tears and recriminations. I thought you two had reached an agreement.'

Holly was grim. 'The agreement was that I would go from the flat and he would leave me alone.'

'He couldn't cope with you being sick.'

Holly froze and put down her cup. 'Julia. I know you've been through a lot and I value your friendship more than I can ever say. So I'm going to give you the option of you not hearing what I'm about to tell you. In your eyes, it can be that we did have an amicable split, George did have some issues about letting me go but now everything is fine.' She looked at Julia with her large, dark eyes. 'Is that what you want me to tell you?'

Julia looked down at her uneaten tray of food. 'No. I want the truth.'

'Well. The truth is that George was a cold husband who left me feeling inadequate for the three years that I was married to him. He was distant, critical and unloving.'

'But that sounds like my father.'

'Possibly. I only saw your dad a few times. I can, however, tell you my experience with George. Then I was diagnosed with Parkinson's. Research into the disease is still patchy. I may have had the degenerative elements in my body already but there's strong evidence extreme stress can trigger the symptoms. I didn't just get the disease and then George and I split up, I consider our toxic relationship to have directly caused the illness to progress.'

'Toxic? The pair of you always seemed so composed.'

'I can assure you what went on behind locked doors was something completely different. There are some things a woman doesn't need to know about her brother and I've no intention of telling you. What I can say, since you ask, is the split was not amicable.'

Holly's hand was shaking and her coffee slopped over the sides. To stop the liquid scalding Holly's thin body, Julia reached over and took the cup from her hands.

'I'm so sorry.'

Holly turned her face to her, ravaged with illness and stress. 'Julia, your brother is a very dangerous man.'

66

Connie had called the RAC from the safety of a kind family who were recovering from the alarm of a stranger banging on their door late at night. She couldn't pretend she had a flat tyre as one look at the vehicle would have told the recovery man what had happened. So, she was upfront with the family. She was visiting friends down the road but they weren't in. In the short time she had left her car in the layby, someone had slashed the tyres. The woman of the household gave her a cup of tea.

'We're thinking of moving. I can't stand it any more. I know cul-de-sacs are unfashionable these days but give me one over a main road anytime. Did you see what happened four doors down?'

'I heard about it on the news.'

'I bet you did. A woman killed her whole family. We've also had two serious car accidents on this bend in the last two years. One of them ran straight into our lawn. A young lad. He was shaking like a leaf when we found him.'

The driver of the recovery vehicle took one look at Connie's car and shook his head.

'Kids. They're bloody hoodlums sometimes. Do you want driving home or to a garage?'

'Home, I think. I can't deal with this now. Can you drop me off home and take the car on to be repaired?'

As soon as she'd arrived in her flat, she'd taken off her

clothes and climbed naked into her bed. Twelve hours of deep sleep later, she'd woken refreshed, picked up her car from the garage, and returned home to run herself a bath. Only now, lying in the bubbles, did she allow herself to reflect on what she had discovered. She'd found a hole in George's alibi, a means by which he could have bought the accelerant and how he might have approached the house unseen. What she needed was a motive.

Why do people kill? Money for one thing. Both George and Julia stood to inherit from their father's will, although Connie had heard this would be complicated. Francesca's family, under the Forfeiture Rule, would not benefit from her husband's estate even though she was last to die, because as killer she was excluded from the inheritance. Money, therefore, would be coming to both George and Julia through their father's estate but it would take time to sort out. What next? Sex? Revenge? George had made plain his dislike of Francesca but could that be a mask? For, if George was a killer, he had definitely set Francesca up as the scapegoat. This suggested something that went well beyond malice. It suggested revenge.

Holly Winson had been scared enough of her husband to make a complaint about him but there was nothing to suggest this was ongoing. He was now in a relationship with Antonia Toynton, and her daughter hadn't hinted that her mother was unhappy. Connie sank further into the bath and thought. Could there have been something between Francesca and George and how would that make him erupt in a frenzy of violence?

Connie dunked her head under the bubbles. She was getting closer to George and the problem was that possibly he knew it.

For who else would have slashed her tyres, trying to scare the wits out of her and partially succeeding? If he knew she was on to him, she would need to proceed with caution. Julia was a possible ally but, when it came to the crunch, where would her loyalties lie?

*

'Is Connie all right?'

Sadler frowned at the phone. Camilla had called and, as usual, launched into her speech without introducing herself. It was a habit that discomfited the unwary but Sadler was well used to it.

'I haven't seen her recently. Why do you ask?'

'You know what the Bampton grapevine is like. A friend of mine has just come back from Pickard's Garage and her car is in there after having its tyres slashed.'

'Is she okay?'

'How would I know? That's why I'm calling you. Jack Pickard was adamant they'd been set upon with a knife. Two of them on the driver's side. He showed my friend Andrea the slashes. Aren't you in touch with her at all?'

'I'm the one who disciplined her. I can hardly go around and ask after her health.'

'Why the hell not? You're still a human being, aren't you?'

'Camilla,' Sadler warned. 'This is work. Don't interfere.'

She breathed huffily down the phone at him. 'I don't recognise you sometimes, Francis. She's still your colleague. How about a bit of compassion?'

The phone went dead. She'd cut him off. Sadler scrolled

down his contacts list until he came to 'P'.

'Pickard's Garage.'

'It's Francis Sadler.'

'Francis! I've just had one of your lot in to pick up her car.'

'She's all right then?'

'Right as rain. The car came in late last night and I had to give her two new tyres. She winced at the price but I did them at cost for her. I don't want her to suffer because of the work of some lunatic.'

'She saw who did it?'

Jack Pickard hesitated. 'She didn't say. It's probably some vendetta. You must get that in your job.'

'Why do you say vendetta? It's probably some random hooligan with a knife. Those amnesty bins we've put in the centre haven't yielded much.'

'Ah. Well, I didn't tell her about what they'd scratched on her boot door. She must have missed it in the dark. It was one word and not very nice.'

'Well, what was it?'

A short silence. 'Slut,' Jack mumbled.

'Is it still there?'

'Nope. I got a dab of repair paint and sorted it out myself. She'll never know the difference. I don't want to bother her. She looks like she's got the world on her shoulders, that one. I thought I'd do her a good turn.'

'It had been done with a knife? Not a key?'

'Looks like it. Probably the same weapon they used for the tyres. You need to keep an eye on her. It didn't look particularly random to me. How would an indiscriminate vandal know the car belonged to a woman?'

67

Julia called forward the ghost tour by two hours. Even when it was raining, eight o'clock was usually a perfect start time in the summer season, still warm before the chill dropped and with enough light to ensure she could keep track of the group. The threat of near darkness also added that element of fear everyone needed to enjoy an evening of supernatural tales. Everyone that is, except Julia. For the axis of her world had shifted and she was now doubting assumptions she had made and the people she relied on. Perhaps, in her efforts to overcome tragedy, she had turned, twice, to the wrong person.

She'd contacted all nine participants by telephone about the new start time and two had dropped out after Julia refused to budge on the timings. She wanted to be back home in her house, barricaded in, before night fell. She also changed the meeting point. All Souls Church with its gloomy edifice and foreboding churchyard was also too much for her that evening. She would soon have to stop running the tours at this rate. A leader chronicling the hauntings of Bampton past who was scared of her own shadow would not be much of a draw for the punters. The fact it wasn't just her own fears that she was afraid of was another reason why she needed to get home fast.

Bampton's old gaol wasn't a former prison at all. It was a building that had been attached to the police station obliterated by a bomb from a German plane, heading towards the munitions dump at Harpur Hill. Fortunately, the hapless bicycle thief sitting in the cell at the time was spared death and recounted the story for the rest of his life. The duty constable, however, a local farmer who had taken on the law-enforcing role for the duration of the war, was killed and it was his ghost who was supposed to guard what was left of the building at night. Her punters always liked this story. The war still had a resonance and they were charmed by the thought of a diligent volunteer unwilling to relinquish his post even in death.

Julia told the group to meet her outside Bampton gaol at six and she arrived ten minutes early after locking Bosco in her bedroom. There was only one key to the room and she had it in her purse. As a precaution, she had also pinned a thin bit of cotton across the threshold of her front and back doors. If anyone entered her house while she was out, they would snap the cotton without being aware of it.

A woman on her own was the first to arrive. She was elderly, probably around eighty, tall with white hair pinned up into a bun.

'I'm in the right place for the tour, aren't I?'

The soft Scottish lilt was out of place in the cool Derbyshire evening. 'You're the first to arrive. Are you on holiday here?'

'Not a holiday as such.' The woman turned away from Julia to look at the old building. Julia waited for more but the woman was content to stand there. *It must be her*, she thought. *The woman who's been asking about me at the cavern. She even matches the description.* 'I think here are some more coming now.'

A group of six friends walked towards them, laughing. In their twenties, they were gripping their phones ready for photographs. One of the men was fiddling around with a voice recorder. 'I thought I'd bring it along just in case we hear anything.' He looked up at her. 'You don't mind, do you?'

'Not a problem but it's really not that kind of tour. You're going to hear the history of supernatural Bampton.'

'Don't rain on his parade,' said one of the girls. 'He's been looking forward to this all day.'

Julia made an effort to lighten up. 'You don't have a thermometer too, do you?'

The man delved in his bag and solemnly produced one, prompting laughter from all except the elderly woman. Julia turned to explain. 'We do occasionally get more serious ghost hunters on the tours with bits of equipment.'

The woman zipped up her coat to her neck. 'I don't mind what people believe as long as I don't see anything.'

Then what are you doing on a ghost walk? thought Julia. *Following me? Don't I have enough to worry about?*

She began with the history of the former police cell. Pictures were taken and the temperature measured. The voice recorder was useless in the face of the squawks of laughter in the quiet Bampton evening. Only the woman stayed apart and Julia felt an unexpected comfort from her presence. Before moving on, she studied the woman briefly. She would be around the age of Elizabeth if she were still alive. A different body shape, of course, and a confidence in her stance that Julia never associated with her mother. Still, this was the age her mother would be.

She moved the group on towards the site of the former cottage hospital and the location of a woman once seen in full Edwardian nursing costume. The route took them past the old TSB bank and Julia couldn't resist a look inside but the darkened windows held their secrets. She guided the group through the park and stopped by the large pond with clear blue water where fat goldfish swam. 'I bet you weren't expecting to stop here. Any guesses as to what haunts this place?'

'A fish,' suggested one of the young people.

'Close,' said Julia.

'A frog?'

'Nice but not quite. Apparently, a duck can be seen gliding across this pond early in the mornings before the others arrive, but as it heads towards the bridge, it disappears. It's the most common sighting we have in Bampton. I know about five people who tell me they've seen the ghostly duck.'

'Turn on your voice recorder,' suggested a girl. 'We might hear some supernatural quacking.'

The young man looked mock-offended. 'It's not quite what I was hoping to catch,' he said, winking at Julia.

The park was across the road from George's apartment and the building loomed in the distance. While she waited for more interminable photos to be taken, her eyes drifted up the façade to George's window. She could see him there in the kitchen, his broad outline unmistakable, watching the group, watching her.

I'm being stupid, she thought. *Why shouldn't he watch me? He knows who I am and why I'm here.* She tore her eyes away and met the concerned ones of the elderly woman.

'Is everything all right?'

Julia shook herself. 'I think someone just walked over my grave.'

The woman didn't smile but looked to where Julia had been

staring. Julia forced herself to look again and the shadow had gone.

'Shall we move on?' She led them further into the park towards the tree where it was said the devil himself liked to sit on a branch. It felt like a place of safety tonight.

68

Matthews finished updating Sadler and stood waiting on the doorstep. He'd invited her in but she was en route to Buxton Opera House and her partner would be furious if she missed the first half of a play again.

'Does it change anything?'

'I'm not sure.' Sadler leant against the doorpost. 'I need to have a think about it.'

'You don't mind me dropping by? The consultant caught me just as I was leaving the office. The court order arrived at the clinic at lunchtime and it was the first chance he got to call. The system had double-booked him an hour of patients, apparently. He wasn't very happy about it.'

'No, you did the right thing.' Matthews turned to leave. 'Do you remember Palmer saying before he left that Peter Winson had an appointment with his solicitor the following week? Did he follow it up? Interview them as I asked?'

'He definitely visited them. He was none the wiser. All the solicitor could tell him was that Peter Winson had called him up and said he'd like to discuss a matter with him.'

'Was the solicitor experienced in probate?'

'He's one of the partners and therefore does a bit of everything. He tends to foist off house sales to more junior staff but even those he'll do for his old clients. Peter Winson could really have been going to see him about anything.'

'He gave no hint at all?'

Matthews hesitated. 'The solicitor thought he sounded a bit upset but, when pushed, backtracked. I don't think either of them are men who show their emotions easily so Palmer discounted it.'

Sadler watched as Matthews ran to her car. He was rooted to the spot, unable to make a decision whether to go out or try to settle for the evening. He believed there was an order to the world. He wasn't a religious man but he had faith in stability and normality. Occasionally there was a rupture in this order. The death of his father, the brief life of his premature-born niece, and the night last year when he thought he had lost a member of his team, Connie. This evening, there was a shuffling of his order that he couldn't fathom.

In the end, he made himself a plate of pasta and ate it with a glass of red wine. Neither the soothing food nor the silky wine could mask the uneasiness still eating away at him. He considered ringing Camilla to check she and the kids were fine but it was too late to call unless it was an emergency. He sent a text instead and was informed that she was relaxing in front of the TV and their mother was staying the night. His family were safe.

Connie was probably in her own flat just along the canal thinking she had been the victim of a disgruntled teenager and unaware of the profanity imprinted on her car paintwork. Would she be watching television too? Connie who had brought all this trouble on herself and fastened onto a doubt that neither he nor his team had been willing to acknowledge. The improbability of a woman killing her family in this way.

He'd pushed her away and ultimately removed her from the team.

In a rare moment of self-realisation, Sadler saw that it was no different to how he had treated other women in his life. Christina whom he ignored when her needs didn't suit his. More recently, Karen, who had briefly attracted him but, when she had reverted to the insecurities that had plagued her past, had also stirred irritation and resentment inside him. He had wanted rid of her and that need not to see her, not to have to listen to her any longer, had caused him to act in a way he didn't recognise.

Connie had been trying to tell him something about George but her certainty alongside lack of any evidence had irritated and repelled him. Perhaps here was the source of his discomfort. He had acted unfairly. Now, sitting in the twilight, unwilling to turn on the lamps, he tried to review his contribution to the case dispassionately. He could say that he had been right to doubt Connie's version of events. There was no evidence to connect George to the fire. However, unbidden, his thoughts turned to Karen and the obsession she had, not only with Miles but also with the relationships of others of their contemporaries. There was a spark of the same obsession in George. His attitude to Francesca contained a savagery beyond stepson jealousy. It had a sexual element that Connie had instinctively recognised and he had not.

Sadler felt alone in his dreary house. Through the open window, across the airless night, he could hear the canal lapping against the towpath. Head in his hands, he thought about the past and the future, and made a decision.

69

'You work in Anchor Cavern?'

Morell caught Julia as she was putting her key in the lock. She refused to look at him. 'Now's not a brilliant time.'

'If you ever want any advice or help, I'm happy to oblige.'

Astonished, Julia turned to her neighbour. He was dressed in his usual uniform of dingy grey jumper and charcoal cord trousers. His hair was as dishevelled as ever and a line of pink rimmed his eyes.

'How did you know where I work?'

'Your friend Ned called me this morning. I think we started off on the wrong foot. Your dog was scaring my cat and the barking was bad. It's much better now your friend over the road is having him.'

He doesn't miss much, thought Julia. 'You haven't seen anyone hanging about my house, have you?'

The pink-tinged eyes met hers. 'I've not seen anyone but I have the sense of someone near. Often late at night.'

Julia looked at the floor. 'I'm sorry about your brother. It must be awful to be still grieving after all these years.'

Morell moved away from her. 'As I said, if you ever need to know anything about the caves, come to me.'

Without going into her house, Julia shut her front door and went across to Jean's. Bosco ran towards her and she patted him briefly on the head.

'Can you have him for a bit longer? There's somewhere I want to go this evening. I might be late back.'

'Take as long as you like. He'll be fine with me.'

At these words of comfort, Julia left them. She arrived outside George's flat and waited. Looking up at the windows, she saw it was dark although a light burnt outside the front door of the building. She looked at her watch. Ten o'clock. She wouldn't have long if he was in The Trip to Jerusalem. Last orders were ten to eleven and George often stayed to the bitter end when he was drinking by himself. If he was on a date that might prove more tricky but she had her story sorted. She'd spotted an intruder outside her house and she was worried. She'd used her keys to his flat to come and take refuge until she felt safe.

She let herself into the building, her fingers fumbling at the unfamiliar lock, and then took the lift up to the third floor. Inside the flat, she turned on the bathroom light. It couldn't be seen from outside but would shed enough light for her hunt around. She went straight to his bedroom, which she had only ever glimpsed from the living room. It was immaculate like the rest of the flat. She rifled through his bedside drawers but they contained nothing but medicine and travel detritus. In the wardrobe, a row of trousers and jackets hung from expensive-looking hangers. She swept her hands over the top shelves but they revealed nothing more than carefully folded scarves and jumpers. Next she moved to the living room and his desk. It was locked. If there was anything important, that's where it would be. She tugged fruitlessly at the drawer and then left it. She hardly had the wherewithal to pick his locks undetected. She then made a quick sweep of the rest of the flat but the place was refusing to yield up its secrets. In desperation, she let herself out.

She slipped down the stairs and leant over the banister at the bottom to see if the lobby was empty. The only sound was the ticking of a large station clock. Her eyes fell on the row of post boxes, one allocated to each occupant. She studied the keyring that George had given her. Nestled in between the larger keys was a small brass one. She tested it in the lock of the door printed with 'G Winson' in gold letters. It swung open, revealing at least a week's worth of post. She flicked through the envelopes while keeping an eye on the door. She might be able to defend her presence in the building but would have a harder time explaining why she was going through his post. There were a couple of bills and formal-looking letters. Nothing of a personal nature. She was about to put them back when, on impulse, she shoved one of the official-looking letters into her coat pocket.

Hurrying back into her car, she slammed the door shut, clicked on the central locking and opened the letter. When she'd finished reading the three short lines, she started up the car and headed down to the canal and towards the answers.

70

It had been a wasted day for Connie. Reflection wasn't really her forte. She preferred action and, although she had her car back, it wasn't much cause for celebration because she didn't know where to go. She was slipping back into the old lethargy and the knowledge that her suspicion may for ever remain just that. Images of the past crowded into the present, which had the odd effect of inducing hunger pangs for the first time since her suspension. She'd devoured a large pizza from the local takeaway and was on her second glass of wine. She stood on the small balcony overlooking the canal puffing on a cigarette, her towelling dressing gown wrapped around her small frame. Her neighbour came out onto the balcony below hers and shouted up at her.

'I've just let someone into the building the same time as me. She looked innocent enough. Said her name was Julia and she was coming to see you.'

Connie lobbed her cigarette into the canal below and went to her heavy front door and slid back the bolts. Julia was looking harried, her hair sticking up at angles and a thin cardigan hanging off one shoulder. 'I look a bloody mess. I know.'

Connie pulled back the door to let her in. 'No need to apologise to me. Do I look like Victoria Beckham?'

'You're young. It's when you're middle aged and haggard like me you end up looking like a bag lady.'

Connie thought longingly of the rest of the bottle of wine and took Julia into the living room. Her second guest in a week. More than she'd had in the past year.

'Can I get you a coffee? Or do you want to join me for a glass?'

Julia looked at the red wine. 'I wouldn't mind.'

'Coming right up.' She sloshed the wine into a glass and held it out to Julia. 'Sure you're all right?'

'I'm fine. Well, now you mention it, actually I'm not.' Julia gulped at her drink and then nursed the glass against her stomach. She appeared unwilling to say anything further.

'Are you still feeling threatened?' *I'm not playing ten guesses*, thought Connie.

'Yes, but not from my neighbour any more. Or maybe a bit, but that's not the problem. Can I ask you a question?'

'Go on.'

'When you took me back to Horncastle, you weren't just being nice, were you? You were trying to work something out. The same yesterday when you came to the cave.'

Connie hesitated. 'It might be best if I don't involve you, Julia. I need to do this by myself.'

Julia took another gulp of the wine. 'But I am involved. I have been right from the beginning. Although what was the beginning, I've no idea.'

Connie picked up her own glass and swirled the wine around, thinking.

'I think your mother's disappearance was the start of things.'

'You've always thought that, haven't you?'

'I've never thought it was Francesca who was responsible for the killings. I know what the official police line is, and I know what's likely to be the conclusion of the inquest. It's just I'm having trouble believing the narrative.'

Julia was pale. 'If you don't think Francesca did it, who do you think is responsible?'

Connie struggled to form the suitable sentence.

'Me?'

'Of course not!' Connie coloured. 'Of course I don't think it's you.'

'George then.'

Connie could feel her face a flame of red and cursed her pale skin; there was the tang of fear in her nostrils. Julia was leaning forward. 'Connie, please, tell me. Do you suspect my brother?'

'I do.' It was out in the open and Connie felt awash with relief. Julia was staring at her and trying to articulate her own words.

'It's why I've come here, to talk about some things. I don't know who else to go to. If I go to the police, I'm going to start down the road of . . .'

'What?'

Julia looked at the floor. 'Well, the possibility of George being a threat.'

'You think that's the case?'

'I don't know. I think I'm going mad sometimes. That my mind is playing tricks on me and I'm imagining everything. Then I try to look at what's happening dispassionately. There's still a presence outside my house. I've felt it, caught glimpses of a shadow and my neighbour has also spotted someone. I just pushed it to the back of my mind until the other night I saw the outline of who was standing there.'

'You think it's your brother? That it's him who wishes you harm?'

'I caught a glimpse of an outline. It was difficult to make out but it was his silhouette.'

Connie took the chair opposite Julia. 'So you think George is watching your house. Why would he do that?'

'I don't know.'

Connie wanted to scream. She took a deep breath. 'Is that it? I'm not being difficult but I am playing devil's advocate. Why else are you scared of George?'

'My dog was poisoned yesterday. The person who put down the food must have access to the house. I'm not losing Bosco so I went to George's flat when he was out.'

Connie looked at Julia, astonished. She remembered interviewing George at his flat and the spark of fear she'd felt when his anger had erupted. Yet, his sister had willingly gone to the home of someone she thought was trying to harm her. Perhaps here was the Julia that she hadn't noticed before. The capable woman prepared to confront a tragedy direct.

'What did you find?'

'Nothing in the flat. There's a desk but it's locked. I looked in his letterbox, though, and found this.' She held out a letter.

Connie took it and read the few lines.

Thank you for your letter dated the 10th July. The acknowledgement of funds that will come into your account in due course once probate has been settled goes in some way to assuage our concerns. We look forward to hearing more from you shortly.

The letter was headed Tower Asset Management.

Connie looked up. 'George is in debt. That didn't come up in the investigation.'

'He's always cash rich. His wallet bulges with money so I've assumed he didn't have any financial problems.'

'How did he buy your father's shop off him?'

Julia shook her head. 'I don't know.'

Connie stared at the letter again. 'Do you think this is enough? That George would kill his family to save his shop? People go bankrupt all the time. My mother was in the same business. It's perhaps shameful but not uncommon. You get over it.' In the back of her mind she remembered about the research into killers and how financial difficulties could be a trigger for the obliteration of families.

Julia looked pale but determined. 'Something is not right. Although he denies it, I'm pretty sure he was friendlier with Francesca than he's making out.'

'How do you mean?'

'He sold or gave her a piece of furniture. It's a tiny thing so why lie about it? It doesn't make sense.'

'That's not much to go on, is it?'

'He also hates children. Hates them. And animals too. Someone put poisoned dog food down for Bosco. I think it's him. He despises everyone and I'm beginning to think that includes me. He won't get near me while Bosco's around but I'm scared for us both.'

Connie put her glass down on the table with a bang. 'There's someone I need to call.'

71

Sadler shut the front door quietly behind him and, switching on his torch, walked the canal path towards Connie's flat. Each step in the moonlight felt like a penance. As he reached her building, he saw the front door had been propped open with a fire hydrant. The hall and stairway were in darkness and, after fruitlessly searching for the switch, he made his way up the stairs using his flashlight. As he neared the top, he could see a shaft of light illuminating the way. Connie's door must be open too. Suddenly fearful for her safety he sprang the rest of the steps three at a time and entered the room. A tableau of three figures stood there to greet him. Connie in her dressing gown, Julia washed-out but composed and Llewellyn who was taking off his jacket.

The group shifted in response to his presence. Julia retreated towards the back of the room and Connie looked away. It was Llewellyn who took the initiative.

'Come in, Sadler, and close the door.'

Sadler blinked and then did as instructed. Connie took the opportunity of his turned back to leave the room and returned a moment later wearing a pair of jeans and a jumper. Llewellyn went towards the dining-room table and pulled out a chair. 'You're owed an explanation, Francis, and you'll get one. First of all we're going to listen to Connie.'

'Why are you all here?'

'Let's hear what Connie has to say first. My guess, by the fact you're also here in the middle of the night, is that you're worrying over something and it's more than the thought of that poor child.'

Sadler took the proffered chair. 'You allowed her to continue the investigation?'

'I did not. You did exactly the right thing in removing her from the case. I came to see her to check she was okay and, when I heard what she'd said, suggested she might use her free time in a particular way.'

Sadler closed his eyes.

'Come on, man. You're as willing as I am to think outside the box. Why are we all here, in various states of night-time dress, dancing around each other? Because all of us, for one reason or another, are unhappy with the forthcoming verdict for the fire in Cross Farm Lane. So let's not pretend we're going about our daily lives with a clear conscience.'

Sadler's eyes strayed to Julia who met his gaze.

'There's been a man hanging around outside my house, well, I think it's a man, at the dead of night. I caught a glimpse of him yesterday evening. I'm pretty sure it was George.'

'You found it threatening?'

'I was worried. I thought I'd seen the shadow a few times, and once a neighbour told me he'd seen something similar. I was worried but I had Bosco.'

'Your dog?' asked Sadler.

Julia nodded. 'But Bosco was sick and it was obvious he'd been poisoned. I've heard of people putting stuff down for the foxes but this was in my back garden.'

'You think it was George?'

'I'm pretty sure the shadow I saw was my brother.'

Sadler risked a glance at Connie who was showing none of her usual triumph. She looked subdued. Llewellyn was listening, his posture relaxed.

'Have you found out anything that would connect him to the fire?' Sadler asked Connie.

'I've found a way he could have committed the murder. I think his girlfriend Antonia, who supported his account of his whereabouts, may have been drugged. It's going to be difficult to prove but, in court, it would rise to reasonable doubt. Antonia would need to be re-interviewed.'

'Anything else?'

'I think George knew Francesca more than he let on. There was always something odd about his attitude towards her and even now she's dead, he's angry towards her. Why would he behave like that?'

'You think they were having an affair?'

The group were silent. 'Again, it's going to be really difficult to prove,' said Connie. 'Julia's found a chest of drawers she thinks George gave as a gift to Francesca but that's hardly going to stand up in court. She also found a letter where he's clearly in need of access to funds. I've been doing my own digging and I found out that George filled up his car with petrol in the weeks leading up to the fire and the amount that was filled up is more than a tank would hold. He probably used a large container.'

'But he could easily say that was for spare in case of emergencies.'

'It would have been quite a lot of extra petrol but, again, I can't prove it on my own.'

'Anything else?'

Connie looked to Julia. 'I think there's a connection to the disappearance of Elizabeth Winson. It's nothing I can prove but I consider George to be a possible suspect in that murder.'

Julia was shaking her head. 'I can't believe that. George was twelve when Mum went. He was a big lad but still a boy at heart. I can't believe he would have had anything to do with Mum's disappearance. He worshipped her and was devastated when she left. He's frightening me now but I can't believe he could be involved in Mum's disappearance.'

'There was the neck burn incident that the doctor reported in relation to Elizabeth Winson. Inspector Stanhope took it as evidence that her husband had been violent. It may, in fact, have been her son.'

Llewellyn stirred. 'Perhaps I was wrong to put 1980 in the past. Connie was right that it does shed light on this case, not least to show the personality of George.'

'The problem is,' said Connie, 'it's going to be virtually impossible to prove without a full investigative team. The case will need to be reopened. We do, however, have the chance of putting right this case. Proving he was involved in killing this family.'

Llewellyn rubbed his face. 'We have a motive of sorts. George Winson, despite appearances of relative affluence, is clearly in need of an injection of cash if the letter Julia appropriated from his apartment is anything to go by. Is that enough, though? It's not threatening, it merely suggests George's financial situation is being eased by the likelihood of money coming towards him. Is this heinous crime simply down to money?'

Sadler felt the weight that had crushed him like Atlas suddenly lift from his shoulders. 'I think I might be able to help you with a motive.'

72

The following morning, Matthews accompanied Sadler to George's apartment. Sadler would have liked to have brought Connie but she was with Llewellyn, who was making arrangements for her return to work. No mention had been made of her resignation letter and Sadler was happy to leave the pair of them to the admin. What he wanted to do was confront the man he suspected was guilty of what Connie had been arguing since the start of the case, the murder of his family.

Peter Winson visited the Westmoor Hospital in 2012 to discover how, given his vasectomy in the 1970s, he had managed to father a child with his wife-to-be Francesca. The clinic had been cagey. The test had shown a certain amount of live sperm in his semen, a not unusual outcome of vasectomies according to the clinic, as one in a hundred operations didn't reduce the sperm enough to prevent pregnancy. Peter had been willing to accept it as one of those things, a miracle that nature occasionally surprises you with.

Peter was a man from a generation who wouldn't have discussed the specifics of birth control. Francesca might have been a little more cunning in relation to her second child if she'd realised the improbability of him getting her pregnant again. She had, however, told him she was expecting again and Peter had revisited the clinic. This time, he'd been informed by the doctor of the odds of pregnancy happening twice.

George wouldn't let them into his flat. 'If you've got any-thing to say to me, you can say it now.'

His face was a visage of astonishment as they made the ar-rest. A man along the corridor came out of his flat, hands in pockets and whistling tunelessly. As they led his cuffed neigh-bour past him, out of the corner of his eye Sadler saw him reach for his mobile.

In the bare interview room at Bampton station, George was willing to admit to the paternity of Charlie but nothing else.

'So you guessed? You've no idea how hard this has been for me, knowing part of the solution to the puzzle but not being able to tell you. Francesca and I made a pact that no one would ever know and I felt bound to honour this, even after everything that had happened. Francesca may have been a mur-derer but I couldn't see how breaking our promise would help the investigation.'

Matthews sighed heavily beside Sadler. He'd updated her over the phone in the middle of the night while they were or-ganising the arrest warrant. Her silence had spoken volumes. She must have been resentful at the fact she wasn't present dur-ing the overnight confab where they had assessed and weighed the evidence against George Winson. Matthews, however, knew when discretion was the better part of valour, or ambi-tion, and kept her views to herself.

'When did your father discover Charlie was your son?'

George looked at them both in astonishment. 'Dad? He never found out. Good God, you don't think that was the rea-son behind the murders? Dad never knew.'

Behind the fake surprise was a wariness in his eyes that sickened Sadler. 'I don't think your father was a stupid man. He had made an appointment with his solicitor. He may not have been intending to have it out with you but he was going to take action. I don't think your father was a man to stand around and allow himself to be made a fool of.'

'He didn't know anything about the paternity of Charlie.' George would not budge on this.

Matthews handed him the letter from the asset management company and George's tone turned sour.

'I was made to pay full whack for my father's shop. A high street bank wouldn't lend me the money so I went to a loan company. It was all legit but it's been hard to make repayments. The pressure was on but it was all very civilised. I simply wrote to them to inform them of my changed circumstances after my father's death.'

After a day of questioning, Sadler had George moved to the custody suite and went to update his team. In his office, he tried to call Julia a few times but her mobile was switched off and her home phone rang out unanswered. He spotted Connie at her desk, concentrating on following the still active trail of the Manchester gang. She'd done what she'd set out to and Llewellyn wanted her away from the ongoing investigation. She was there now, her head hunched over some papers, and he hesitated for a moment.

'We need to have a talk, Connie, at some point, about everything that happened. Not now but we do need to have that chat.'

'You mean about not believing a word I said.'

'Connie.' He could feel the anger coursing through him and willed himself to be calm. 'We *do* need to chat.'

He walked away and wondered if he would be able to work

with her again. In his experience, she wasn't one to hold grudges, but emanating from her this time was coldness and disappointment. The problem was, given the opportunity of doing it all again, he'd pursue exactly the same course of action. Resisting the urge to slam the door of his office, he picked up the phone and called Pat.

'Julia's doing okay, considering,' she told him. 'She's taken the dog with her and is staying with a friend outside Bampton. George's ex-wife offered her a room but she rang a male friend called, hold on, Ned Smith. She's staying with him for the moment and they've gone away to pick his son up from family. It'll do her good, take her mind off things and so on. I don't envy what she's been through.'

'How is she? I mean, it must have taken a lot of courage to come to us and tell us about her brother.'

Pat snorted. 'Courage with a large dollop of fear. She was scared of him and rightly so. Don't worry about Julia. She's got her head screwed on. She won't be going anywhere near her brother for a while.'

PART THREE

The Wrong

73

Six weeks earlier

The figure crept through the downstairs rooms, checking the locks on each of the windows. Securing the house and any means of escape, although there would be no one left to seek flight this night. Memories of other times jostled within the deathly silence. First, in the vaulted living room where a laughing child had demanded another game of hide and seek. Next, in the gloomy dining room, the scene of routine and interminable meals. Then in the kitchen, furnished with every appliance that no one ever needed. The large patio doors next to the fridge were secured by a three-bolt lock. The shadow checked everything was in place. Moved away, and then went back and checked again.

Then the slow climb up the stairs towards the tall arched window, a perfect frame for what was to come next. The shadow entered the bathroom to wash away the spatter and the gore. The crimson T-shirt and trousers were dropped into a black refuse sack and tied with a neat bow. The fire would do the rest. The meagre light from the overhead mirror lamp illuminated the water in the sink turning from clear to pink to deep red. Beads of sweat fell from the shadow into the basin, mimicking tears.

Now, finally, time for the moment of the last act.

74

Julia had stupidly thought that, just because you were on remand, you'd be kept in a facility that would in some way be different from an ordinary prison. She was wrong. George, until his trial came around, was being held in Category B HMP Leicester, a prison straight out of the Victorian age. Its castellated walls and imposing turrets could have been from a medieval castle but the place was a modern-day repository of the convicted and those awaiting trial.

Over the past week, Ned's former in-laws had been kind but she'd felt stifled in their thirties semi with the woodchip wallpaper and supper on a tray. She was also uncomfortably aware that she was taking up precious space in their home. Ned slept in one spare room with his son and she was in a small box room furnished with a single bed and little else. She also missed Bosco, who must now feel at home in Jean's comfortable terrace.

George had not admitted to the murders but the police had built a case against him. They could prove petrol had stood in his boot and George had admitted he was the father of Charlie, giving them, in their eyes, a motive for the killings. Antonia wasn't retracting her statement but there was enough reasonable doubt, given her illness the following morning, for the prosecution to put forward a convincing sequence of events. What the detectives hadn't managed to do was discover if, or why, George had been shadowing Julia. He claimed he wasn't outside her house, nor had he tried to poison her dog. She didn't believe him and she doubted she would get answers if she waited for the police.

She'd rung the prison anyway and arranged a visit. They had made it clear that he would have to approve her as a visitor. *His last control over me*, she thought. *You can only come if I say so.* He had, however, agreed. The previous night, unable to sleep in the stuffy unfamiliar room, she'd logged onto the internet and searched for the prison's history. It had both fascinated and repelled her. There was a wing, according to the government website, set aside for vulnerable offenders: police, judges, child molesters. A disparate bunch joined only by the fact that to place them with other prisoners would be catastrophic. There was also, bewildering for her, an 'enhanced' prisoners' unit for those who had accrued privileges during their stay. Her eyes skimmed over the information that interested the history buff in her. Leicester prison had also had its share of hangings in the inner courtyard, the last one in 1955. Hangings. Julia stopped over the word, a niggle at the back of her memory.

Sitting across from George, she wondered how he was coping in the confined space. Surprisingly well, if his face was anything to go by. His features were as coldly handsome as ever and he looked like he'd lost a little of the bulk that had been a constant sore to him. He also looked supremely unconcerned.

'You look well,' she said, aware of the note of accusation in her voice.

'It's because I've nothing and everything to lose. I'm going to use the trial to put everything out in the open. I've spoken to my solicitor and he'll instruct the barrister accordingly. All our dirty linen will be aired. There've been too many secrets.'

She stared at him and wondered why she'd been so scared of him these last weeks. He now sounded like a boastful school-boy.

'It's nothing to be proud of. Why did you kill them? Dad and Francesca. And, why little Charlie? What did he ever do to you?'

Now she looked a little closer, she could see his eyes were bloodshot. Not the boiled red that any normal person's would turn under the circumstances but the white part infused with lines of crimson.

'I didn't kill them.' He was outraged. 'I'd never kill my own son.'

She noted his refusal to address the other victims. 'I don't believe you.' Her voice had raised slightly and one of the guards looked over to where she was sitting. 'George,' she whispered. 'You've done nothing but lie to me. How long had you been seeing Francesca?'

He looked down at his hands. 'We got together before she and Dad became an item. I turned up one day at the auction-eer's and she was there. I clocked her at once and went to talk to her. She'd only just started work and didn't know the ropes. You know how incestuous the business is. So, I gave her a pot-ted guide to the antiques business.'

'If she was so out of place, what the hell was she doing work-ing in an auction house?'

He shrugged, uninterested. 'I think she just needed the money. It was a day when Dad was out valuing something so he wasn't in. I took her out for lunch and we ended up back in my flat.'

Julia was shocked. 'That was quick. I thought Francesca was more, well . . .'

'Reserved? Oh, she was reserved all right but she always went for what she wanted. Ambition is a very powerful aphrodisiac.'

'She wanted you.'

'Initially, yes, but we were going to keep it quiet. I wasn't sure if Dad would approve of me seeing one of his staff. It then sort of fizzled out and it was only after that I realised she'd let us slide because she had her sights set on greater things. Namely our father.'

'George, that must have hurt.'

He refused to look at her. 'I've been through worse.'

'I never understood the two of them together. Francesca seemed all right but Dad was one of life's misanthropes.'

'I told you, Francesca was ambitious. She didn't like Italy and she wanted to stay in England. Dad offered her financial security and a chance of a new life.'

'I thought you were financially secure too.' A part of Julia ached for the humiliation George must have felt when Francesca chose their father over him.

'I was then. As I said, she had bigger fish to fry. It was only later I had money troubles. It was a knock-on effect. Dad marries Francesca, Dad sells the shop to me, I'm short of dosh. I was getting back on my feet. The police are mad if they think that's enough for me to kill everyone because things had got a bit tight.'

'It's not just that, though, is it? It's also about you and Francesca. Did you carry on seeing each other after she and Dad got married?'

He looked shocked. 'Of course not. We stopped seeing each other as soon as she took up with Dad. I may not have had much of a relationship with Dad in the end but I respected him enough to know the boundaries.'

'When did you find out Charlie was your son? Did you know all the time?'

George's face closed once more upon itself. 'Of course not. I'd never have let her marry our father if I'd known Charlie was mine. It crossed my mind when I heard she was pregnant. I asked her and she said not.'

'So when did you find out?' Julia was aware she was speaking to her brother in a tone she'd never adopted before. He'd noticed it too and his eyes narrowed.

'When she turned up on my doorstep one day and told me she was trying to get pregnant again.'

75

Thursday, 20 April 2017

George felt Francesca's hot breath on his face as she rocked against him. She'd turned up at his shop and demanded he close it for the rest of the afternoon and go back to his flat. He'd acquiesced for reasons he couldn't even begin to understand. How utterly humiliating. He was being used as nothing but a stud and he would be giving part of himself to his father again. Had nothing changed?

Francesca's eyes were closed. What was she thinking? It had always been like this, even when they were together. She was as unfathomable now as she had always been but still utterly desirable. He wanted to hurt her, to punish her. He thrust deeper and, for a moment, she opened her eyes.

'Hurry up,' she said.

He couldn't tell if the command came from irritation or desire. He grabbed the curls at the back of her head and pulled her to him as he finished. She twisted away from him and pulled her skirt back down, locating her discarded underwear and stuffing it in her handbag.

'I need to sit down. I need the stuff to stay inside me.'

'Jesus, I really am nothing but a sperm donor, am I? Like I was for Charlie.'

At the mention of their son's name, Francesca's features

softened. Her senses, however, were on full alert.

'You're not going to tell, are you? It won't do you any favours.' It was a threat and a surprise to hear a woman speak to him like this. George felt the hot searing of anger reverberate around his head.

'Don't mess with me, Francesca. You've got what you wanted but don't push it any further. I'm warning you.'

She stood up, all concerns for his seed forgotten, and smiled over him. 'You really don't want to be threatening me, George. You really don't.'

76

Although she wouldn't have admitted it to anyone, Connie was enjoying the attention in the CID room. At first, she'd been petrified the press would get hold of the story of her leave of absence. An old flame, a journalist she'd had a fling with during a previous investigation, gave her a call out of the blue. She managed to fob him off, which he took in good humour, and then, to her surprise, asked her down to London for dinner. Connie, shuddering at the thought of a trip to London, said she'd think about it.

A bunch of flowers had been waiting on the desk when she first arrived. She half-hoped it was Sadler's doing, feared they might be from Palmer, but was touched to see Matthews's name on the card. *Welcome back, love Carole and Ruth.*

Sadler was desperate to speak to her but she was giving him a wide berth. Part of her, deep down, thought he'd done the right thing in suspending her. The sense of unearthing the truth away from the scrutiny of her superiors had been satisfying, if risky. Now she was investigating the Manchester gang and the grind of routine CID work beckoned.

It was the end of wakes week in Bampton, the time the town had historically taken its holiday in the seaside towns to the north. The days of vacationing en masse had long gone but the town adhered to the old tradition of celebrating the wakes period. There was to be a party down by a canal lock organised by British Waterways and Connie was going. After a long deliberation, she'd picked up the phone and called Scott, Bill's assistant. It was answered by a female voice. 'Scott's extension.'

'Is he there?'

'Who's calling?' The voice radiated suspicion.

Connie plastered on her brightest smile. 'Is that Mary? Can I have a quick word with Scott? Something's come up I need to talk to him about.'

She could hear the receiver being placed on the table followed by a long silence. For a moment, Connie wondered if she'd be left hanging there but shortly came the sound of approaching footsteps.

'Is everything all right?'

'What have I done to upset your new girl?' Connie demanded.

'She's after me.' His voice dripped satisfaction. 'And she thinks you are too.'

'No chance.'

'Oh, thanks very much.' He was laughing and he whispered, 'Can you play along a bit?'

'I was actually calling to see if you fancied coming to a barbecue by the canal tonight. Mates only and all that, but feel free to tell her if it makes you feel happy.'

'You're on.'

Later, as Connie threaded gold hoops through her ears, she wondered why some women were so antagonistic towards her.

Scott was waiting for her at the lock and the party was already under way. Tinny music squeaked out of speakers connected to an iPod and a barbecue was belching dark smoke across the water.

'I'd stay away from the burgers,' he said, handing her a plastic cup of white wine. 'They looked like they went on the barbecue frozen.'

Connie made a face, sipped her drink, then grimaced again. 'We don't have to stay here if you don't want. We can go to a pub if this is rubbish.'

'You might not want to stay anyway. Look who's here.' Scott nodded across the lock to the other side of the water. There stood Sadler with his arms folded across his chest, listening to the woman she'd spotted him with in the pub in those days when they were still on speaking terms. She watched them both. Sadler appeared to have fallen out with the woman too. She was gesticulating at him while he stood stock still.

'Lovers' tiff?' asked Scott.

'Looks like it.' Connie couldn't take her eyes off the pair. Sadler turned away, putting his back to the still gesticulating woman. He spotted her and, with one hand dismissing the woman, made his way towards them.

'He's coming over.' Scott raised his glass to his mouth. 'This should be fun. We're clearly a safer bet than his girlfriend.'

Connie couldn't help the thrill of satisfaction as she watched Sadler walk over the narrow lock gate and approach them. She looked over at his companion who was staring at Connie. Not Scott, just her. Connie turned her back to the woman and smiled at Sadler. 'Coming to join us for a glass?'

Sadler smiled down at her. 'You won't believe how pleased I am to see you both.'

*

When the revelries had died down, both Scott and Sadler offered to walk her back to her flat. Given it was only two minutes down the towpath, she hesitated. It was Scott who made his excuses, saying, 'You might want to talk about work.' He finished his glass of lager and made his way back towards town on slightly unsteady legs.

Sadler and Connie walked towards her flat, leaving behind the sounds of clearing up. Connie had sunk at least four glasses of wine and was feeling the effects. She dug into her handbag for a smoke and lit up.

'That's better.'

For a change, he didn't make a comment but kept his eyes on a group of teenagers from which was wafting the unmistakable smell of cannabis. They stopped talking as Sadler and Connie passed and then continued their laughter.

'I think I've just remembered why I don't take this path at night.' Sadler turned back to look at the group. 'I'd feel better if you didn't either, Connie.'

The former salt warehouse came into view and Connie, in the darkening evening light, looked at her car parked in the bay. 'What the . . .' She ran over to her red Fiat and there, scratched into the bonnet, was the word *slut*. On her passenger door, BITCH, this time in capital letters. She stared at the insults, unable to comprehend what she was seeing.

'I don't believe this. George Winson is locked up. I thought it was him who slashed my tyres. Who the hell is this?' An idea came into her head at the same time as she heard Sadler swear.

'I told her to leave me alone and now she's targeting you. This,' he said through gritted teeth, 'is the final straw.'

77

'He says he's innocent.'

Julia and Ned were sitting in the gardens of Haddon Hall, an Elizabethan manor house, watching Toby and Bosco play a game of tug of war with a rubber ring. Ned was lying on the grass, looking at his son while pulling green blades through his fingers.

'To coin a phrase, he would say that, wouldn't he. I've never met George but, from what you tell me, he isn't the type to shoulder his responsibility.'

'He says it wasn't him outside my house but it must have been. It started the night of the fire, or at least that's when I first noticed it. It's too much of a coincidence for it to be anyone else.'

'Look.' Ned sat up. 'You're all he has left. He's facing a life sentence in prison and he's going to have to come to terms with that. It's the unthinkable so he's going to do two things. First, he'll protest his innocence to everyone who's prepared to listen, and second, he's going to make sure he doesn't alienate you. Who else is going to visit him in prison? Holly? What about that woman he drugged? Is she going to visit him?'

Julia rubbed her eyes, late season hayfever making them itch. 'Some things still don't make sense, though. What about the flowers? He didn't send them in 1980, he was a child then, so who laid flowers at the murder scene?'

'Maybe the flowers are nothing to do with it. Maybe they are from your mother. George's arrest has gone no way towards solving what happened to her.'

'Connie wondered whether George might have had something to do with her disappearance. They're talking about reopening the investigation with George as a potential suspect.'

'He was only a child.'

'Twelve, and a well-built boy at that. They're saying there's a possibility he might have killed my mother, and my father helped him dispose of the body.'

'Do you think that's likely?'

'What do I know? Look at me. My brother had a host of secrets that I never knew of. Now I've lost everyone.'

Ned pulled up a clump of grass and let the blades slide through his fingers. 'You can stop with us, you know. I know staying with my in-laws wasn't ideal but we're back now. Stay with us until you feel safe enough to go back to your own home. Toby likes you, especially now he doesn't call you the scary lady from the caves.'

Julia laughed. 'I'll think about it. I'm hoping I feel a lot safer now George is in prison and my neighbour isn't as odd as I first thought.'

'Morell? I told you he wasn't. He's just another person feeling loss across the years. He'll be fine with you.' He rolled onto his front. 'At least let me cook dinner tonight?'

'It's a deal.' Julia lay back on the long grass and stared at the blue sky. 'Do you really think my mother could have left those flowers? Then why not come forward? There's been enough water under the bridge for all of us. If she's alive, she needs to show herself and then we can at least absolve George of that crime. I never got to speak to that Scottish lady either.'

'You know George is capable of murder so why don't you think he's responsible for your mother's disappearance?'

Julia covered her eyes. 'I remember that time as if it were yesterday. I was traumatised and so was George. That's what I remember. He was stricken.'

78

Saturday, 14 July 1984

The furniture was packed and Julia was left in her empty bedroom. She put her lips to the wall and felt the cold vinyl wallpaper meet her warm skin. She kissed the place above where her bed had stood.

'Goodbye. I'll miss you.'

She put her ear to the wall to listen to its response but the house was keeping its secrets. She turned around and saw George watching her from the doorway. 'What are you doing spying on me? I'm saying goodbye to the bedroom.'

'Do you think she'll know where to find us? If she comes back, I mean.' George looked over to the window and stared out of it, his hands bunched into fists. 'Suppose she finds us gone and thinks we've forgotten her?'

'She can go to the police, can't she? They'll track us down.'

'Will they? I thought that's why we were moving, to start afresh. What's the point if the police can still find us?'

'We're not running from the police. We don't have anything to hide. We're starting a new life. Everyone knows us here. That's what Dad says. We're starting again and going to a place where no one knows what happened.'

'So they can still find us?'

Julia moved over to her brother. 'I promise, if the police still want to find us they will.'

A shadow crossed George's face. She couldn't decide if it was relief or fear. She decided it was the former.

79

It was a warm August evening and Connie's shirt was sticking to her. She pulled at it in frustration and bent over the task that was refusing to hold her attention, the Manchester gang who were proving resilient to Derbyshire Constabulary's best efforts. One bright spark had suggested, instead of using the train every day, they might now be holed up in a B & B or, more likely, a house of multiple occupation. Connie was supposed to be looking for potential properties, a thankless task. The list of addresses she had identified as possible locations for the gang were dotted around Bampton's less salubrious parts. If you were a visitor here, you'd never notice there was anything except Victorian splendour and modern-day tourists. Up the backstreets and, in particular, on one former local authority estate were houses that told a different story. She looked at the words swimming around the page and then put down the paper with a sigh.

After the drama of yesterday evening, all she wanted to do was go home and crawl into bed. The office was deserted; everyone else either had a family to go to or plans for the evening. Sadler was nowhere to be seen. This morning he'd given her the money for her car to be resprayed and she hadn't asked for explanations. He'd been discreet about her love life in the past and she was happy to repay the favour. She had, however, taken the cash. But sleep had refused to come last night and not, as she had expected, because of her damaged car outside. Instead, at the moment when she should have been exulting in her return to active duty, voices in her head were once again whispering doubts.

She'd been warned about this when she'd been discharged from hospital the previous year. She'd been told to expect occasions of blurred vision, possibly moments of disorientation. Nothing, however, had materialised and, in any case, these voices were not from an external source but coming from her conscience.

She logged into her computer and retrieved a number that she had used weeks earlier. She considered making the call now and her hand hesitated over the handset of the telephone. In the end, she wrote the number on a piece of paper and stuffed it into her handbag. There was still time to change her mind, leave things be.

Back in her flat, she stood on her balcony and watched the scene below. One man was walking three dogs while talking on a mobile phone. A woman jogger sped past, her long legs measuring out the strides. Connie pulled her cardigan tighter around her and looked at her watch. It was quarter past six. She either made the call now or waited until the next morning. She was probably too late to catch the person she wanted to speak to anyway.

She was wrong. The Italian police station sounded like it was still in full swing from the noise in the background. There was either a major operation on or, perhaps, they kept later hours there. Connie hoped it was the latter, otherwise she wouldn't get to speak to the man she needed. Tinny music blasted through the handset, broken, finally, by the deep voice with its West Country burr.

She took a deep breath. 'I'm sorry about this. I know I'm going to sound totally stupid, but would you mind going over again what you told me about Francesca when she was a child?'

80

Julia returned to Ned's house and, while he was cooking dinner, she regaled Toby with ghostly tales from Bampton, a watered down version of her talk. Once she had explained to Toby that the noises he had heard in the caves were just wind echoing around the limestone caves and his imagination, he relaxed enough to ask her why his dad called her *juju Julia*. Ned looked embarrassed and Julia, half-annoyed at being lumped in with long-forgotten witchcraft practices, explained about her night-time activities.

Toby rested his head on Julia's shoulder, as Charlie had once done. 'I'm seeing Mum at Halloween. She's going to arrange a party for me. All scary stuff and ghosts. Whooo!'

'Brilliant! The scarier the better,' said Julia, noting that the party was over two months away. Another mother in no rush to see her child. When they had finished eating, Toby trotted upstairs, satisfied with his fill of the macabre.

'You can always stay over if you want? Toby won't mind and we can open another bottle of wine.' Ned kept his voice casual.

'Not tonight, I'm sorry. I want to settle Bosco back into my house. Next time, though.'

It was that easy; being offered something and turning it down with a promise for the future.

'Will you be all right walking back? I can't leave Toby on his own but I could call you a cab.'

Julia looked out of the window. Twilight was falling slowly and it was a gorgeous evening with just a hint of red thrown from the setting sun.

'I'll walk, I think. It won't take me long and I have the dog. I'd better leave now before I'm tempted by that bottle of wine.'

The alcohol she'd drunk made the walk at first enjoyable and then a chore. After twenty minutes, her mouth was dry as parchment. Taking the shortcut through the backstreets meant she passed no shops and the dull thud of her head suggested she'd regret the wine in the morning. She recited a poem in her head to make the time pass quicker. *I leant upon a coppice gate when Frost was spectre-grey.* The rhythm helped her relax and the noise of her own voice inside her head at first blinded her to the footsteps that were matching her own a short distance behind her.

She remembered the time in Horncastle. Don't look around, Connie had warned, but there had been two of them then. Now it was just her, slightly tipsy in a darkening evening wearing strappy sandals on feet that were unused to any footwear other than trainers and boots, and Bosco who was trotting happily beside her.

She quickened her steps and listened in horror as the person behind her hurried too. George was in prison so who else could wish her harm? She was passing a row of terraced houses, some of which had their lights on. *I'm going to bang on a door*, she thought, clocking one ahead full of blazing lights and a child pressing his face against the window. She ran towards it and, as she neared the astonished child, she heard a voice behind her.

'Julia. It's me.'

Julia stopped dead and a wave of nausea washed over her. She spun around and came face to face with a woman with a pale face imprinted with a web of fine lines. Her hair was unruly like George's, the curls loosened over the years.

'You! I just don't believe—'

'Don't believe it's me? It *is* me. I'm so sorry, Julia.'

'Sorry?' Julia was fighting for breath, her body chilled from the shock. Now her eyes had cleared, Julia took in the features of the woman she had last seen thirty-seven years earlier. 'You've changed, I mean, you look the same and so different.'

'I'm sure I've changed. It's been such a long time.'

'A long time? I'd have hardly known you.'

'You recognised my voice before you turned around, though, didn't you?'

Had she? It was more the sense of the inevitable that had stopped Julia in her tracks. The feeling that everything that had happened in the last few weeks had led her to this point.

'You've come back?'

'I couldn't stay away. I needed to . . .'

'Needed to what?'

'To see you again. See you both.'

Julia put her hands over her eyes. 'You needed to see us *now*?'

'And before, of course.' Was that shame that Julia could hear in her mother's voice?

Thirty-seven years of anguish erupted from Julia. 'We thought you were dead.'

Elizabeth Winson shook her head. 'I'm not so sure, Julia. Did you really think I was dead?'

'Of course I did. I heard nothing from you.'

347

'But you never stopped looking, did you? What about the websites you posted on?'

'You know about those?'

Elizabeth leant against the wall and put out a hand to steady herself. 'I did look for myself occasionally. Like other people do. I put my name into the internet and searched for it.'

'You'd have found yourself, wouldn't you? Seen all the press coverage of your disappearance.'

'Of course I saw those. Apart from those articles, though, I found you looking for me in forums, leaving messages.'

'And you never, ever, thought of replying. Even once?'

'This is just so painful.'

'Painful? You want to try having to write them, time and time again.' Julia was shouting and the mother of the window-licking child was looking out at them with suspicion.

Elizabeth said nothing. She was looking defeated but not, thought Julia, sorry. Just tired and determined.

'So why now? Actually, not why now. Why not before? Why didn't you try to contact me before?'

'Your father was still alive. I assumed that you'd made a new life for yourselves. I was declared dead, I saw that in the paper. I assumed you'd all made lives for yourselves beyond me.'

'We made a life for ourselves all right. I'll give you that. And look where we ended up.'

81

'The issue is, the CPS are questioning the evidence of George buying the petrol. There's no ANPR for a start.'

Llewellyn was looking furious and Sadler could feel his own temper rising.

'Of course there isn't. Why would George go to a garage with up-to-date plate recognition technology to buy the means to commit a crime? The woman behind the counter at Murkell Road remembers him making a cash purchase for petrol that was much larger than a full tank. That must count for something.'

'Of course it does, as does the fact there's evidence in the boot of George's car that he rested a can of petrol on the floor. The problem is he has a perfectly good story of why the petrol ended up there.'

'He's still sticking to the story that Francesca asked him to obtain it for her?' Sadler asked.

'According to George, Francesca said the sit-on lawn mower was out of petrol. Peter had been in a foul mood all day and was refusing either to go out in the car or to keep an eye on Charlie while she did. So she telephoned George and asked him to bring some over that evening when his father was out visiting an auction. Which is what he says he did.'

'So we can prove the petrol was taken by George from the garage and delivered to the house but not who requested it.

This isn't new, is it? We often have alternative explanations to evidence. We presented all this to the CPS and they agreed we had enough to charge him. It's up to the CPS to get a jury to believe that George delivered the petrol ready to use it later that evening.'

'They don't like it, apparently. We're awaiting the DNA evidence to confirm Charlie's paternity but it's irrelevant because George has come clean about it. He also says Francesca had approached him about fathering a second child and that Peter Winson knew nothing about George's involvement and was pleased about the pregnancy.'

'So pleased that he went back to the fertility clinic he'd first visited after the conception of Charlie to confirm it was unlikely he was also the father of a second child. If Peter was about to discover the true father of his son then that gives George a very strong motive.' Sadler kept the tremor out of his voice. He felt he'd already lost too much on this case and it seemed they weren't done.

'It's also a motive for Francesca. Don't you see? They're worried about how this is going to play out.'

'What do you want me to do?'

Llewellyn ran a hand across his thinning hair. 'I don't think there's anything else we can do, is there?'

Sadler strode back to his office in a foul temper. He needed a drink. The first time he had ever felt like this while he was working, but then there were first times for everything, weren't there? Like him getting things wrong. Or right. Or perhaps he was going mad and this job was finally getting on top of him. He looked at his watch; he couldn't stay here any longer. He walked back through the office and

Connie's empty desk enraged him even more.

He drove back to his house and dug out his muddy walking boots. He ran them under a tap to soften the mud and then used some kitchen tissue to pull off some of the clags. The act of walking made him think of Karen and he nearly abandoned the idea. His warning to her had been clear. Stay away from him and, more importantly, stay away from Connie, otherwise she would be getting a visit from one of his colleagues. He remembered Miles's throwaway comment about scratches on his car when he'd left Karen. When Jack Pickard had first told Sadler about the word *slut* scratched into Connie's car, he should have made the connection. Instead it had taken a second act of vandalism and Karen on the scene to have revealed what should have been obvious. *Epic fail*, as his nephews would have put it.

He needed to clear his head and to stay indoors was intolerable. He set off down the towpath and followed, for the first part, the route he'd taken when he'd come across Karen last month. He was climbing the path steadily when a feeling of being watched came over him. In a temper, he wheeled around. There was no one immediately behind him but, squinting his eyes, he could see a small figure standing outside his front door.

In a fury, he turned his back on his intended destination and only the fear that if he fell he could do interminable damage made him pick his way carefully back down the path. As he got closer, he composed the words he intended to say, how she needed help, that she needed to leave him alone and she must stay away from his house in future. As he neared the figure, he saw, with a shock, that it wasn't Karen and the words emptied from his brain.

Connie was standing outside his door with her head leaning against it.

'Are you okay?'

She turned to him. 'Oh Francis.' Then she burst into tears.

82

They were back at Julia's house. Once a place of safety, it had been assailed by threats not only from the present but also the past. She took her mother into the living room; Elizabeth sank into the sofa with a relief she made an effort to mask.

'This is a lovely room. I wondered what it was like inside your home. What sort of life you'd made for yourself.'

Julia looked around the living room, trying to see it from a stranger's eyes. 'It's nothing special.'

'It's nice. Simply furnished but a home. It's just I've only seen it from the outside.'

'But . . . you knew where I lived?'

'I've, well, I've been shadowing you for a few weeks. I've stood outside this house a few times.'

'You? Outside?'

'I thought you saw me one time when you turned on all the lights and looked out. I had to run down the passageway.'

'You? Are you sure? I'm certain it was George I saw standing outside the house when my dog was ill.'

'George? Why George? It was me. I've stood outside his house too. I've been out in all weathers recently.'

'But why? Why have you been standing outside our homes?'

Julia tried to sit next to her mother but it felt too intimate so she contented herself with perching on the side of the sofa. Elizabeth slipped off her shoes and massaged her feet.

'It's so hard to explain and I'm going to make a terrible hash of it, which is nothing new. I had this feeling that something wasn't right.'

'Not right?'

'Oh, I know. It sounds ridiculous. I'd seen your messages in the forums but, I don't know, they didn't seem desperate in any way. Just curious. I could ignore them.'

'Thanks very much.' Bosco had settled at Elizabeth's feet. *Traitor*, thought Julia. Elizabeth patted him absent-mindedly.

'I had this growing sense something wasn't right. You weren't posting much at the time, you'd gone quiet. So I kept thinking it couldn't be you that was making me worry. So I looked up George and found that he had a shop. Then one day, I picked up the phone.'

'You called him? Just like that?'

'I know. I don't know how I managed to pluck up the courage. I pretended I was a customer. I asked him if he had a tea set with a willow pattern.'

'We had one like that.'

'Do you remember? It was the first thing that came into my head but it was a stupid thing to say. He was silent just for a moment then said something along the lines that he didn't sell china.'

'You think he guessed it was you?'

'Not that. No. He sensed something was off, though.'

'Then what?'

'Well, the phone call didn't tell me anything, did it? So I came down to see if you were both all right. I didn't dare show myself, but watching him, he reminded me so much of Peter, all fuss and no heart.'

'What about me?'

'You were harder to find, but after hanging around George's flat for a few days, I saw you visit him.'

'You recognised me?'

'I'd have recognised you anywhere, Julia.' Tears welled up in Elizabeth's eyes. 'So then I started watching you as well as George.'

Julia massaged her temples, the headache that had threatened earlier now hammering in her head. 'I can't believe it was you outside my house.'

'It was quite comforting. It's impossible to explain but some of the missing years fell away during those nightly vigils.'

'But, if it was you, then I was never under any threat from George.'

Her mother looked grim. 'No one has been under threat from George. It's one of the reasons I'm here. He's not a danger to anyone, you or your father, and I can prove it.'

83

Sadler had given Connie a brandy that she was trying to drink, making a face with each sip. The familiar irritation returned and he took the glass from her.

'We're all allowed to be wrong, you know.'

'But how many times?' Connie wailed.

Sadler, deathly tired, suppressed a smile. 'I don't know. Maybe there isn't a limit. Maybe you're always allowed to be wrong.'

He sat down opposite and took a sip of the drink. Its warmth coursed down his throat. Connie was looking smaller than he'd ever seen her. The weight she'd lost during her enforced absence hadn't returned. She could be mistaken for a teenager if it wasn't for the worry lines that forked above her eyes and the tremor as she lit a cigarette. Sadler resisted the temptation to open a window and waft out the tobacco smoke.

'Start from the telephone call. You made a call to Italy this evening.'

Connie stared at him, her eyes dark pools. 'It's not new what he told me. I had a conversation with him just after Francesca's parents left. He told me about two incidents when Francesca was younger. Twice when she came to police attention.'

Sadler frowned. 'I don't remember any of this on file.'

'It was towards the end. Just before I was suspended, I mean. There was nothing to say, really.'

'You mean it didn't fit in with your theory.'

'That's right.'

Sadler wondered how much this admission cost her. 'Why don't you tell me now?'

'Ever since I came back to work, maybe before then, but certainly since I've come back to work there's been something that's been gnawing away at me. The scratches on my car, for instance.'

Sadler felt himself go hot.

'What I mean is, you said that this woman, Karen, has always been jealous. Which I understand. If you're a jealous person that's never really going to go away, is it? Just like being manipulative. Getting everyone to dance around you. I've just been thinking about what Francesca's parents said and then the police captain so, in the end, I called him again and asked for specifics.'

'The nature of the crimes Francesca had actually committed.'

'He did try to tell me in detail last time but I, well . . .'

'Tell me now.'

'So, the first incident took place when Francesca was thirteen. There was a cousin, Mia, who she took a dislike to. They went for a bike ride around the local village and Mia was found with head injuries. Francesca cycled to a local shop with a story that her cousin had fallen off her bike and was injured. While the owner was calling an ambulance, Francesca bought herself an ice-cream and proceeded to eat it. The girl, when she recovered, had no memory of the incident whatsoever.'

'But the police thought Francesca may have been responsible?'

'She was acting so strangely, the police were suspicious. It also caused a rift in the family.'

'It's possible it was an accident. Children do react oddly to accidents. We've seen it before.'

'That's what I thought.'

'And the second incident?'

'This is harder to explain away. Francesca had a boyfriend when she was nineteen called Marco. It was serious and her family thought she might get married. What they didn't know was that she had also begun a relationship with Marco's father.'

'Like Peter and George Winson.'

'Well, yes, but the other way around. It was the relationship with the father that was secret.'

'And it was eventually discovered.'

'It was Marco who found out about it and he half-throttled Francesca when he caught her with his father.'

'It only proves that Francesca liked complicated relationships.'

'I'm not so sure. According to the captain, enquiries revealed Marco had informed Francesca he would be visiting his father that evening in the family home. She didn't pass the message on to his father and police think it could well have been a set-up, Francesca playing son off against father.'

'So she enjoyed setting up one man against another? Where does that take us?'

Connie rubbed a spot on her trousers. 'She may have dropped hints to Peter about the parentage of Charlie and the unborn child. Overplayed her card. It's possible, isn't it?'

'So you think, when Peter Winson did contact his solicitor, it wasn't to disinherit George but to start divorce proceedings against Francesca.'

'I don't know, Sadler. I just don't know any more. Have I got it all completely wrong?'

84

A loud rap on the front door caused Julia and Bosco to jump. Only Elizabeth looked unsurprised. 'That'll be Suzan.'

'Who's Suzan?'

Julia opened her door and a thin, grey-haired woman stood on the threshold of her house.

Elizabeth appeared behind Julia. 'This is my friend. I asked her to give me an hour or so with you and then check up on me.'

'I know you.' Julia pointed at the woman. 'You came on one of my walks this week, didn't you?'

'I enjoyed the tour if not the deception. I'm glad to meet you properly now.'

'Are you *NaturalScot*? Have you been looking at my posts?'

Elizabeth stepped forward. 'It's my fault, Julia. I asked Suzan to keep an eye on you.'

'Online? How's that keeping an eye on me?'

Elizabeth sighed. 'There's so much to explain, I hardly know where to start. First, I need to go to the police and tell them George couldn't have committed the crimes. This has gone on long enough.'

'But why didn't you go straight away? After George was arrested?'

'I wanted you to hear it from me, not them, that I was alive. I owed you at least that.'

It had started to rain but still Suzan stood on the doorstep. 'If everything's all right, I think I'll go back to the B & B. Are you sure you don't want me to come to the police with you, Lizzie?'

'It's something I need to do myself. I'll call you when I've finished.'

Julia turned to her mother. 'Let me come instead.'

'I can't, Julia. I just can't.'

'But why not?'

'I have to talk to the police. Explain about George. We can talk afterwards.'

'If you say George is innocent then I want to hear it.'

Elizabeth was looking at the retreating back of Suzan. 'This is difficult, Julia. You need to let me go. Do you know who's in charge of the case?'

'Inspector Sadler. It's evening, though. He won't be working now.'

Elizabeth's mouth set in a firm line. 'I'm not explaining myself to a duty officer. Do you know where he lives?'

'Of course I don't. Connie, his assistant, will know.'

'Can you call her?'

Julia hesitated. 'I don't know her number,' she lied. 'I can take you there, though.'

They drove to Connie's apartment building in silence. Elizabeth looked out of the car window at the spatting rain. 'Have you ever spied on someone? Of course you haven't. You watch them go about their business and you feel like the child at the cake shop, desperate to go in.'

'But you *frightened* me. Can't you see that?'

Her mother turned a puzzled face to her. 'Frighten you?

How could I frighten you?'

They had arrived at Connie's building and Julia looked at her mother and shook her head. She made her way towards the door buzzer and pushed it hard. And then again. And again.

'She's not here.'

Her mother was beside her, her voice calm. 'Are you sure you don't have Connie's number?'

'Let me check.' Julia made a pretence of searching through her contacts list, avoiding the recent calls. 'Oh, I do have it. What shall I say?'

Elizabeth swayed slightly. 'I'm not sure. Can't you just ask her where her boss is?'

'Connie will want to know why.' But the call was answered not by Connie but Sadler. 'It's Julia. Actually, it was you I wanted. Can we speak?'

'Is everything all right? Connie and I are talking together. Do you need us?'

'I have someone who needs to talk to you urgently.'

She'd expected him to ask more questions. Worried that she might be forced to reveal that she had her mother standing by her side.

'Where are you?'

'Outside Connie's flat.'

She heard him sigh. 'Stay where you are. I'll come to get you.'

'We can come to you. Aren't you nearby?'

He hesitated. 'Go down to the canal and turn left. I'm ten minutes along the towpath. I'm setting off now too. The path is dead straight so you'll see me as soon as you reach the canal.'

Although it was still light, the lone, tall figure walking

towards them was a reassuring outline. Her mother was finding the walk an effort, her breath laboured. It was what had been niggling away at Julia since they had met. The shortness of breath, a hoarseness as she spoke.

'Is everything all right?'

Her mother frowned. 'What do you mean?'

'With you. You sound out of breath.'

'Don't worry. I have bad asthma, that's all. Old age.'

They reached Sadler. He looked between the two, his eyes giving away that he'd guessed who Elizabeth was. 'Can we wait for explanations until we get to my house? I think Connie will want to hear this.'

Connie was waiting for them under the wooden, inverted 'V' that served as a front porch. Julia had always been struck by the detective's force. Her small frame that belied her strong personality. She appeared diminished this evening. As she approached, Julia could see Connie's eyes were ringed in red. She looked beyond Julia to Elizabeth but kept silent.

'I suggest we go inside.'

Sadler's living room was small and served as a place both to sit and to eat. The oak dining table was strewn with paperwork and he pulled out a dining chair to add to the three armchairs. Connie took the least comfortable option and sat bolt upright as the others settled around her.

Elizabeth wheezed and emitted a cough that lasted a few minutes. Sadler went out for a moment and returned with a glass of water. Elizabeth took a long gulp.

'I'm sorry. My throat gets so parched.'

'Do you know how much police resources have gone into looking for you?' asked Connie.

'I can guess.'

'You don't seem that bothered.'

Julia wondered why Connie was so angry. Elizabeth accepted the anger as if it were her due.

'I know a lot of people have been looking for me. I can explain but not tonight.'

'What do you mean not tonight?' Connie's face was reddening.

Sadler intervened. 'I think we should let Elizabeth speak first. You've been in Bampton a while?'

'Since before the murders.'

'You were here the night of the fire?' asked Connie.

'All night and nowhere near my ex-husband's house.'

'Where were you then?' Julia could see Connie recovering her equilibrium.

'I was standing outside George's flat the night of the killings before I moved on to Julia's. All night until dawn broke. Long after the blaze started.'

'And you saw what?' Connie stood up, her hands on her hips. 'What did you see?'

'I didn't *see* anything. That's what I've come here to tell you.'

'You didn't see George leave the building?' asked Sadler.

'Nothing.'

'But there's no back entrance.' Connie was staring at Sadler. Trying to communicate something to him. 'If he started the fire, he must have gone out of the front entrance.'

Elizabeth was shaking her head. 'I can tell you he never left the building.'

'Which is why you're here,' said Sadler.

'I wasn't sure whether to come forward at first. You've no

idea how much my anonymity means to me. But when I heard you'd charged him, I had no other choice.'

'You're sure?' Sadler was looking unsurprised at the news. 'You're positive your son, George, never left through the front door.'

'Positive.' Elizabeth looked at the assembled company. 'George is definitely innocent. I stood outside his apartment all night when the fire occurred. Then, when dawn broke, I went on to Julia's to check she was okay too. No one came out of the apartment block while I waited. I saw him come in with his girlfriend around eleven the night before and he never left.'

85

Connie hadn't slept. What was the point? George would be released from prison today, his alibi confirmed not only by his girlfriend but now by his mother. All her work had been in vain. She wanted to crawl onto her sofa and stay there for the next few months. Instead, she was sitting in the bare interview room listening to the formal statement made by Elizabeth Winson. Sadler also looked unrefreshed after his night's sleep. Dark smudges coloured the skin beneath his eyes, although she could barely look at him after she'd embarrassed herself by weeping on him the previous evening.

Elizabeth was barely recognisable from the woman she'd been in 1980. She'd looked bowed and defeated last night. This morning she was magnificent. In the days of her marriage, she'd been dowdy and homely, a response, it seemed, to how her husband Peter liked her to dress. Throughout the original investigation, no one had ever taken seriously the possibility she might have run off with a lover. Plain, reliable Elizabeth with her tight curls and frumpy smock dresses had represented suburban motherhood. Although Peter had been a handsome man, no one had guessed that behind the smocks and the thicklensed glasses was a good-looking woman. David Stanhope had been right to dismiss the possibility that Elizabeth might have gone off with a man. It wasn't a man but a woman who had offered Elizabeth the escape she desperately needed.

Elizabeth and Suzan sat side by side, holding hands. Suzan was the older of the two. Her lined face was make-up free and covered with freckles, still beautiful; she had the figure of an ageing ballerina. Elizabeth was a large woman, where early plumpness had given way to a regal magnificence. It was no surprise that Julia had mistaken her outline for George. In both hair and stature they were identical.

She and Suzan made a striking couple. They had never undergone a civil partnership or marriage, presumably because that involved paperwork. It meant birth certificates and passports and Elizabeth couldn't take a chance with anything that revealed her true identity. So they had lived, in limbo, in a small community that asked no questions, for nearly forty years.

Connie was struck by the serenity of the women and tried to swallow the natural outrage she felt towards someone who would voluntarily give up her children, leaving them bewildered just when they needed her most. She also felt angry on behalf of David Stanhope for the wasted man-hours and fruitless searches. Sadler appeared to share none of her anger, taking charge of the questions calmly.

'You're living now where you first disappeared to in 1980?'

Elizabeth Winson looked at her hands. 'I went to Shetland in the summer of 1980 and I never left. It was completely unpremeditated. I was in the shop as usual and I thought, "This is it. I'm going to leave for a few days and sort out my life." So I put a note on the door, just to show I'd popped out. I didn't realise so much would be made of the "two minutes". If I'd known that, I'd have never written anything so stupid. It was just something to give me a chance to get away.'

'How did you leave Horncastle?'

'I went to the call box over the road and rang Fred.'

Connie looked up in surprise. 'Who was Fred?'

'He was a guy who did odd jobs around the town. I'd had him into the shop a couple of times to fix shelves and so on. I called him and said I needed help and to come fast.'

'And then what?'

'Fred parked in the alley behind the shop. I had some money hidden in a drawer in the counter. My savings were separate from the family finances. I took it and asked him to take me to Lincoln station. It was as simple as that.'

Sadler looked to Connie. 'Was Fred ever interviewed as part of the investigation?'

'Not that I know of.'

Elizabeth smiled. 'Fred was a keeper of secrets. I told him I wanted to get away for a while and asked if he would help me. My head was all in a flurry and I had no idea what to do. I just wanted to get away and go north. I'd always dreamt of the Scottish Highlands and I wanted to clear my head for a few days.'

'You travelled by train from Lincolnshire?' prompted Sadler.

'Yes. All the way to Aberdeen. I paid for my tickets with the cash I had and I wore one of the headscarves that the shop sold. No one gave me a second glance.'

'There was that sighting in Aberdeen,' said Connie. 'What happened when you reached Scotland?'

Elizabeth looked at her hands. 'I had this contact through the wool shop. A women's collective produced Shetland wool in undyed colours. It's all the rage now, of course, but in the seventies, the era of baby pink and pale lemon acrylics, it was wonderful to get some real stuff. I remember it on my fingers.

Hard and solid. It was a joy to knit with.'

Connie, uninterested in wool, folded her arms.

'Anyway, in the winter of 1979, Suzan came down from the farm to meet some of her English clients. I remember looking forward to the visit. The thought of meeting a person who was pushing the boundaries of craft. When we met, there was an instant connection. We talked all day in the shop, and then when the children arrived after school she had to leave.'

'I was supposed to move on that evening. I had a few visits scheduled for Norfolk but I postponed them and stayed another day,' said Suzan.

'She came back into the shop the next day and I couldn't believe it. I think my face must have told her how I felt about her. I remember my stomach leaping over.'

Suzan looked at Sadler, challenging him to mock. 'Then I really did have to leave. It was hard for both of us.'

'You kept in touch?' he asked.

'Not at all. It's not like now where you can use social media or emails. It was letters or the telephone. I couldn't call. I wasn't sure how she felt about me. So I wrote a letter that was full of inconsequential chat. She replied, sending the letter just the once to the shop, but it was enough to give me hope.'

'It was bad at home?'

'I was so miserable. I was sick of Peter and the notes he'd leave about the house. Little bites of criticism. Meeting Suzan gave me a glance of a life I could have and I don't mean just to be with her. It was the opportunity to be something other than a dumpy provincial housewife with a dreary future.'

'So you decided to escape.'

'Peter never guessed there was someone else. That, funnily

enough, was one of the hardest things to bear. That he thought I was so unattractive that I couldn't possibly meet anyone else.'

'So you just left them?'

'It was only going to be for a while. The children were all right and were already moving away from me. They could be left by themselves no problem and Peter was the same as ever. The school holidays were coming up and I kept thinking, before they start maybe I'll just go away by myself for a few days. I won't tell anyone, I'll just take myself off and see where Suzan lives.'

'You left the note on the door?'

'I wasn't thinking properly. I thought that if I left a note, it would be clear that I'd gone away intentionally. I hadn't been kidnapped or anything. So I wrote the note and rang Fred as I told you.'

'You knew he wouldn't tell anyone what he'd done?'

'Fred had a record of a few minor offences. I mean minor. He'd never pay his bills on time; he was caught driving without insurance once. He hated the police so there was no way he'd have voluntarily gone to them; but he must have been confused because in the car to the station, I told him that I was going away for a few days. That I needed to clear my head and see someone.'

'But the children?' Connie couldn't hide the disapproval in her voice. 'You never thought about getting in touch with either of your children again?'

Elizabeth disengaged her hand from Suzan's. 'I don't expect you to understand, but parents can cause more damage if they stay.'

86

Monday, 21 April 1980

'Mum!' George put his school bag onto the floor and walked into the kitchen. The taunt from that bully Patrick Farthing had been too much. It wasn't his fault his trousers were too tight. They'd been okay when his mother had bought them at the beginning of the school year but he was growing quickly and she'd told him there would be no new ones until the following term. The sneer of 'fatty' was still ringing in his ears and he hadn't even made it to the first lesson. He's simply picked up his bag after the form teacher had taken the register and walked out.

His mother's shop was shut. He'd pulled fruitlessly on the door but it was locked and the lights were off. Instead he'd walked back to the house and used his key to let himself in, which was supposedly only for emergencies. He'd felt the thrill of the illicit as he'd slotted the key into the lock. But it appeared his mother wasn't here either, the house was still and empty. He pushed open the doors to the other downstairs rooms but no one was there.

He stomped upstairs. He wasn't sure how long it would be before he was missed at school and he needed to get his story straight. Perhaps he should strip off his hated uniform, climb into bed and pretend he was sick. As he reached the landing, his eyes widened as he looked into his parents' bedroom. His mother was standing on a chair with a belt around her neck, her fingers at the noose. Their eyes met and, for a moment, locked. Then he watched as his mother undid the belt and climbed back down from the chair. She picked it up and returned it to the corner of the bedroom and came out to him.

'Are you feeling poorly? Why don't you go downstairs and I'll get you a blanket.'

George nodded and followed her to the top of the stairs. He turned for a last glance, to reassure himself that he hadn't hallucinated the image that danced in front of his eyes. The bedroom looked as it always did, although the long black leather belt was lying coiled at the foot of the bed. George put his hands to his throat.

'I really don't feel well.'

87

Julia waited outside the prison. Ned had wanted to come with her but this was something she needed to do herself. She too had believed in George's guilt, and now their mother had appeared when he perhaps needed her the most, to prove his innocence. She'd come out of the shadows, from where she had been hiding, to say, 'I saw my son that night and he wasn't anywhere near Cross Farm Lane.' Julia left her car in the huge car park opposite the prison, intended to service a large DIY store but also used by visitors to this institution. A door swung open and her brother emerged. He looked calm, shook hands with the officer and left.

'I didn't realise they'd let you out straight away.'

He came down the steps towards her. 'My mother has confirmed that she saw me inside my apartment on the night of the fire. My solicitor asked that they release me and they have.'

'Our mother. She's my mother too, you know.'

He didn't reply and they walked to the car in silence. Once inside, Julia put the key in the ignition. 'Where to?'

'Can you take me back to my flat? I stink of inside.'

'They're interviewing Mum and her partner now. Did you know?'

He turned and looked out of the window. 'Funny how freedom looks. What's she said about running off with that dyke?'

Julia coloured. 'For God's sake. Can you blame her? She met

someone she fell in love with. It's more than she would have got from our father. I don't blame her.'

'You were always such a liar, Julia.' He kept his head turned away from her. 'She could have come back any time in our lives and she chooses now. Has she said why?'

'I don't think she's well. She hasn't said anything but she looks ill. Do you think that might be the reason?'

George screwed up his face. 'I don't care.'

'Don't care?' She stared at him. 'It's a good thing she did come back anyway, otherwise you'd have found yourself longer inside that prison. If she hadn't been standing outside your flat, what other defence would you have had?'

'The fact that I bloody well didn't do it for a start.' He spotted a woman staring at them, suspicious of a couple sitting in a stationary car, and lowered his voice. 'Francesca was a bloody nightmare. She was convinced Dad had found out about us. She came around to the flat. I told her I didn't want to see her again after . . . well, after the last time. But around she comes, saying Peter had guessed about us. I told her it was nonsense. Dad would have had it out with me, not written to his solicitor to disinherit me.'

'They think it was actually about divorcing Francesca. The legal side.'

'Dad never knew about us. Francesca might have thought he did but I never told him and neither did she.'

'You're sure about that? He suspected he wasn't the father of Charlie and the new baby. How many other men were in Francesca's life?'

He looked down at her and said nothing. She looked at the top of his head, with his greying curls so like their mother's.

'I thought it was you hanging about outside my flat. I also thought you'd poisoned Bosco.'

'Why would I do that?'

'Do you remember Horace? The dog we had as teenagers. I thought you'd killed him too.'

George continued to stare out of the window. 'Horace was sick, which is why he was put down. It's dangerous to become too attached to anything or anyone.'

'But attachments can last a lifetime. Look at Mum. We thought she'd gone for good and when we needed her she was here, watching you and me. We've both got a lot to be thankful for.'

'Have we? What exactly do we have left, Julia?'

88

Elizabeth looked stricken. 'It's my fault things have turned out how they have. When things were bad, I mean really bad, I tried to kill myself. I originally had this idea of leaving the car engine running in the garage but Peter never walked anywhere. There was no chance of me having the car to myself. So I fixed a hook up on a beam in our bedroom and used one of Peter's belts to try to hang myself. I made a complete botch up of it because I'm useless at knots and I couldn't work out how to secure the leather. I just kept fiddling away and the more I tried, the less courage I had. That wasn't the worst of it, though. The most terrible thing was that George walked in and saw me. He'd just started high school and was struggling to settle in so he'd walked out of the gates and come to the shop to find me. It was shut and so he came home. Another few minutes and it would have been him who discovered me hanging there. The thought is unbearable.'

'Did he tell his father?'

'Yes. I don't blame him. It's too much hurt for a child to carry. Why shouldn't he have told Peter?'

So Peter knew of his wife's unhappiness although not of her love affair. She had run and Peter had assumed that she was dead because of her attempted suicide. What was less clear was why he hadn't told the police about what George had witnessed. It would surely have directed suspicion away from him as Elizabeth's potential murderer. Perhaps it had been a pact between father and son never to speak of the incident.

What was interesting to Sadler was that Peter had remained the same person throughout. Cold, critical and detached. The problem was that with his second marriage he had wed himself to a woman with demons far greater than his own who had also created a new life and was determined to defend it at all costs. No, Peter had been a bully but no more prejudiced than many men of his generation. Francesca had been a monster.

'What did your husband say?'

'It was the coldness that was too much. He said I was a disgrace and an unfit mother. He was right.' Elizabeth closed her eyes. 'It seemed the best way. Leave and clear my head. It was never going to be permanent. I needed to decide what I wanted in life. I fully intended to see my children again and while they were still young, not wait until they were adults.'

'So what changed your mind?'

Elizabeth looked across to Suzan. 'On a trip to the newsagent's, I caught sight of a paper and I was on the front page. I couldn't believe it. I'd cut off my hair so I wasn't recognisable in Shetland but I was mortified that all these people were looking for me. It was then I had to make a choice and so I did. I decided to sever my ties for ever.'

'Was it you who sent the flowers to Julia?'

'When I realised this was it, I'd never be going back, I wanted to get in touch with Julia and say something along the lines of "I'm still thinking of you". So I sent the flowers. Suzan wrote a cheque, which she posted to the florist along with the card I'd written. The shop probably assumed it was from a relative. I wrote what I felt, which was that I was sorry.'

'And after that?' asked Connie.

'Of course I thought about them but as the years went by they receded further and further into the distance until . . .'

'Until what?'

'A couple of months ago, I was beset by this sense of unease. Its cause is twofold. First, I'm sick. For reasons I don't need to go into, I'm not prepared to undergo extensive treatment and my time is coming to an end. I wanted to see my children before I die. However, learning about my illness didn't ease the sense of something being off-kilter with the world. People talk about the maternal instinct and I would have said mine was dead to me. I couldn't settle and it's hard to explain but I had this sense of feeling something was wrong outside of my illness.'

'So you decided to see them again. Were they difficult to find?'

'Unbelievably easy. They all had online profiles. Peter and George with their antiques and Julia with her ghost walks.'

'You'd never looked for them while they were teenagers?'

'Are you asking me these questions because I'm a mother? What about all the divorced fathers who've left their families behind? Do you use the same tone with them?'

'I'm just simply asking the question. Did you never search for your children before they were adults?'

'I didn't.' She looked at them without defiance. 'I don't intend to justify myself to you. I found them when I needed to; I travelled down from Shetland to check they were all right. First by myself and, after the fire, Suzan joined me. They needed me and I came. George never left that apartment because I stood there all night. He needed me and now I know what for.'

89

Julia stopped on the road outside George's flat and put on the hazard lights, keeping an eye out for one of the numerous wardens who would be patrolling the streets.

'I never realised you saw Mum's suicide attempt. Dad was always adamant she'd "walked into the river", which never made sense as the water's not even fast flowing in Horncastle. I double-checked when I went back with Connie. It's shallow. If you drowned there, you'd be found quickly.'

'Lincolnshire's full of waterways. He didn't just mean the river running through our town. Trust you to take it literally, though.' George's voice, harsh, betrayed the stress he had been under.

'But I never believed him. When I was young, I thought it was wishful thinking on his part, that Mum was dead and he could get on with his life: you, me and him. Now, though, I think he was trying to tell us to forget about her. She was unhappy and wanted to die and so she was better gone. The drowning in the river story was just to embellish the point. She was dead to us.' Julia paused and kept her voice even, careful not to insert a note of accusation. 'All along you knew something I didn't.'

'I didn't know she was alive now. I thought she might have killed herself too, eventually I mean. I remember reading if you throw yourself into the River Severn, you might never be found. The strong current means your body sinks into the depths for ever. That's what I thought. I did know, wherever she was, that she was better off away than being with us.'

'After what you saw?'

'It's impossible to describe. I came in from school and I saw her standing on that chair they used to keep in their bedroom. For a moment, our eyes met and I thought she was going to jump.'

'She didn't, though.'

'She just climbed down and put the chair back where it normally sat but she forgot about the belt. I've never been able to stand them since. I never wear them. Francesca bought one for me once, the only Christmas we spent together as a family. Do you remember?'

'I remember the Christmas but not the present.'

'We were in the kitchen and I opened the parcel in front of Francesca and Dad. You were probably in the living room playing with Charlie.'

'Francesca wouldn't have known the significance, would she?'

'At the time I thought not. Dad turned away. He knew I didn't wear belts and he had probably guessed why. I thought Francesca had made a simple mistake from ignorance. Now I think about it, though, I'm not so sure. There was an expression on her face as if she was waiting to see how I responded. She and Dad were married, after all. He may well have told her about Mum's suicide attempt.'

'Do you think that's why she chose to hang herself too? To hurt you.'

'She wanted me to take the blame for everything. She never thought that the police would initially believe she'd committed the murders. She got me to buy the petrol, she called for me to come over and made it known about the split between me and Dad.'

'She must have hated you. She must have hated everyone to do what she did.'

'It nearly worked, though, didn't it? Even you, in the end, thought I'd done it.'

You couldn't wipe away nearly forty years of secrets and silence in an afternoon and Julia didn't even try. She said nothing and, watching George, he appeared to accept that. For he too had kept his secrets.

'I'm thinking of getting in touch with Holly and asking about giving it another go.'

'Holly?' Julia couldn't keep the astonishment out of her voice. 'Do you think she'll be okay with that?'

His dark eyes were on her. 'I'm not taking anything for granted but I'm going to ask her. It's up to her. I've never forced myself on any woman.'

You have a problem letting them go, though, she thought. 'What about the woman you were seeing before, Antonia, wasn't it?'

George shook his head. 'Holly is the only one that's ever really mattered. The problem was that once she became ill, we wrapped it up too quickly. We were married and then it was over. She tried to see me in prison, did you know?'

'No, I didn't know.'

'Before even you. As soon as I was arrested, she tried to visit me. I said no.'

'Why?'

'I turned down the request because I thought she, like everyone else, like you, thought I was guilty.'

'You saw me, though.'

'Blood is thicker than water.' The tone of his voice chilled her. 'Anyway, the point is, she tried. I'm going to ask her to give it another go.'

I need to wish him luck, she thought. Should she talk to Holly? The problem was that she had a relationship with Holly independent from that of her brother. Would she be able to articulate the tumult of emotions she felt at the news?

George was watching her closely. 'What about you?'

Julia thought about Ned and his kindness and Toby with his fragile, familiar lack of self-confidence. 'I'm going to see how things go.'

She didn't tell him how, the previous evening, Toby had put his mouth to her face, his breath smelling of the fruit gums he's been eating earlier. 'Are you going to marry Dad?' he'd whispered.

Either he'd forgotten Ned was still married to his mother or it was wishful thinking, perhaps both. George took her reserve for a negative. 'There are worse things than being by yourself, and anyway, you have Bosco.'

Well, yes, she did have Bosco, although only a man would think to say 'oh you have a dog' and expect that to be recompense for a fulfilling relationship. 'We have Mum too.'

George's eyes darkened and Julia understood that to have been frightened of him was not her own imagination. He opened the car door and heaved himself out. 'There's no reason for us to see her again.'

Us? It was a rhetorical question, which was just as well as Julia was in no mood for arguments today. *No reason*, she agreed, silently. *But do you need a reason to see your mother?*

90

Llewellyn was subdued but not as downcast as might have been expected. Sadler reflected perhaps that's why his boss had done so well not only in his career, but in life too. The ability to shrug off life's vicissitudes was an underrated talent and resilience was a characteristic Llewellyn had in spades. Sadler wondered, not for the first time, if Llewellyn ever woke in the early hours, or whether dark nights of the soul were for lesser mortals like himself. As if guessing Sadler's thoughts, Llewellyn took off his glasses and rubbed his face.

'It's not been easy, has it? Don't beat yourself up about what happened. You know as well as I that investigations take their own twists and turns. You never lost sight of the victims, did you? Whatever decisions we made, it was done on the evidence that was presented at the time. Not to mention the fact that you were right all along. Francesca had a psychotic illness and you were spot-on to take the evidence for what it was. Proof of her guilt.'

'I allowed myself to get distracted. I was right, then I was wrong and, finally, right again. I don't know whether to feel guilty about Connie or resentful. If we'd left well alone, it would have been the right answer anyway.'

'I'm as much to blame for that. I encouraged Connie to carry on with her investigations. It's not exactly doing things by the book, is it?'

'In the early hours I do wake up thinking about our late-night meeting in Connie's flat.'

Llewellyn laughed and leant back in his chair. 'Would it have made you any happier if you'd been in the station? Don't worry about the location of what happened. It's my fault we were there. How many coppers does it take to make a mess of things?'

Sadler thought of his nephews. 'I know two little boys who could tell a joke like that.'

'Well, for God's sake don't ever ask them. You might not like the answer. Look, Connie was right to raise the objections she did. It didn't make sense in light of the events of 1980 and, by sticking her oar in, we got more answers, didn't we? Elizabeth came forward to explain what happened to her. In doing so, she was not only able to exonerate George from killing her thirty-seven years ago, she was also able to give him an alibi for the night in question.'

'I may have been right, but I still can't shake off the feeling of being in the wrong.'

Llewellyn looked at him from underneath his ginger brows. 'Sounds like you need a break. Take yourself off somewhere. Things are quiet here for the moment, thank God. We've had a decent summer here, weather-wise, why don't you go and top up your tan somewhere hot?'

Sadler made a face. 'There's nowhere I fancy going.'

Llewellyn stood up, went over to his office door and shut it. He returned to his desk but pushed away the papers in front of him.

'You can't go on like this.'

'What do you mean?' Sadler felt his stomach flip.

'What have you got outside this station? I know you're close to your sister but what else? Who else do you have to talk about things to?'

'Well, no one.'

'Don't you think it's about time you did have someone to go home to in the evenings?'

'There are plenty of single police officers in this job.' Sadler could see the way this conversation was going. His light-hearted tone didn't sound right to his ears.

'How many are happy, though? Don't let this work get in the way of what you want to do with your life. Don't you want to get married, have children?'

Sadler looked at his boss's honest face and thought he deserved the truth. 'I've never seen myself with children. I enjoy being with my nephews but it's never something I've thought about myself.'

'But why not? It's not an unreasonable thought to have. Men of your age have usually at least considered the possibility of a family life.'

'I've never met anyone I wanted to settle down with.'

Llewellyn sighed and pulled the paperwork on his desk back towards him. 'Everything does feel more complicated, in terms of dating and so on. I got married straight out of university and I'm not sure how I'd cope in the game now. You're younger than me, though. Don't sit in your house watching the world go by. Connie, for all her defects, is out there fighting, finding her place. You seem to have given up.'

'That's a bit harsh.'

'Don't take it like that. I'm telling you because I care. Don't atrophy in this job. I'd rather see some honest mistakes than

rigid certainty. Let down your defences and get out there.'
Llewellyn put his glasses back on. 'It's up to you, of course.'

Sadler left the station and walked down to the canal. It was
wider here than the section that ran past his house but less well
maintained. Tourists rarely came to this part of town and the
overhanging weeping willows gave the water a dank hue. Sadler
watched as a boat approached from the far distance. It was
immaculately painted and, as it neared, he saw it was named
Odyssey. A vanity project, he thought, judging by the look of
the man steering it through the black water. He was dressed
in cream chinos and a blue shirt. Probably a professional from
Sheffield. It was a common enough occurrence. Monday to Friday spent slaving at a desk and flattering clients that they feared
or despised. The weekends haunting the canals of England, in
a barge less like a boat and more a mini house with expensive
fittings and a fridge stocked full of booze. Sadler watched as
the boat passed, ready to shout a greeting but the man ignored
him. The *Odyssey* floated past him and, turning the bend, disappeared from view.

Sadler, thinking of what Llewellyn said, reached into his
jacket and pulled out his mobile. He looked at it for a minute,
thought of making a call, and then returned it to his pocket.

91

Summer might creep slowly into autumn in the Derbyshire Peaks but on the Isle of Shetland autumn gusts across the heathered hills to announce its arrival. Elizabeth kept her eyes on the gravel road stretching out in front of her, glad that her journey was nearly at an end. They'd passed most of the trip north in a silence nurtured by years of companionship. Helping Suzan cope with her seasickness completely occupied Elizabeth on the ferry from Aberdeen back to Shetland. Through the rough seas, she held onto her partner's hand, squeezing it when the fingers tensed on hers. Only as they were reaching the safety of their cottage did she ask for the reassurance to conclude, not only this journey, but also the far longer one that had started in 1980.

'Was I right to go back?'

Suzan, confidence restored back on dry land and behind the wheel of the car, reached out and placed a hand on Elizabeth's knee. 'You'd needed to make that journey for a long time. It was an overdue trip.'

'I just wonder if it helped. They were living their lives. Will they be any better knowing that I'm alive, even if it's for a moment?'

'You listened to yourself and you went. It's not just about your illness, is it? You're not the first parent to have felt their child was in danger. You heard the appeal and you returned. Perhaps sickness makes us more receptive to these thoughts.

I don't know.'

'Yes, but what further damage have I caused? I'll be gone again soon and this time for good. They're going to have to face losing me again.'

Suzan stared grimly ahead. 'It was certainly worth it for George. His lawyer would have a harder time proving his innocence without your evidence. Lucky for him you were there outside his flat.'

'I saw him go in with his girlfriend and I stayed outside all night. He didn't emerge before I left as dawn was breaking and went on to Julia's house. The murders had been committed well before then. There's no back entrance to that apartment block; George didn't leave the building.'

Perhaps it was the tone of her voice that made Suzan take her eyes off the road for a moment.

'Are you sure about that, Elizabeth?'

'I gave the police my statement. I didn't see my son leave that building.'

Elizabeth focused on the dot on the horizon that was growing in size and ignored the spear of conscience that had suddenly jabbed her. *You're supposed to tell the truth.* She had made her decision and was now headed to hearth and home and her refuge for nearly forty years. Some rights are paid for through many wrongs. Deserting your family, wasting valuable police resources.

One day, very soon, she would talk to Suzan about her Sunday school classes and ask her whether she had ever spoken about atonement. The expiation of past sins through an act of penance. Some wrongs can never be righted but everyone deserves a second chance. George would have his.

'What's the matter?' Ned came over to Julia and put his arm briefly around her shoulders. 'Are you reading your mother's letter again?'

It had been Elizabeth's parting gift. She wanted to return to Scotland as she had a scheduled hospital appointment and intended to make it. She had offered Julia no other information but had promised to keep in touch. There had, however, been no invitation to stay. Instead, she had given Julia a letter.

'It's all down there. It's my letter of confession, if you like.'

As Julia had read it, the past unfurled for her. It started in 1964, the day Elizabeth had met Peter Winson. It ended the day she had followed Julia from Ned's house.

'It must be hard to take in.' He left his hand on her shoulder and she reached out to touch it.

'Impossible. I need to go over and over it again.'

'That's natural. Don't beat yourself up about it.'

'There's so much I can't take in. Look at this, for example.'

Ned pulled out a chair and sat next to her. 'She says she was outside my house on the early morning of the fire.'

'We know this.'

'She then says she came back to check I was okay after I'd learnt about the killings. My neighbour spotted her and she had to leave.'

'You knew this too.'

Julia looked at Ned with his open, kind face. 'She doesn't mention the time when you drove me away and I thought I saw George standing there.'

'But you've said the silhouette was the same. You mistook her for George.'

'She doesn't mention it here, though.' Julia jabbed at the paper. 'She apologises for scaring me the night of the fire and then when she followed me from yours. She also says she was outside my house that one more time. What about the night of Bosco's poisoning?'

Ned shrugged. 'Maybe she forgot. It's a long letter as it is.'

Julia thought back to the moment when George had come through her front door and she had cursed herself for leaving it on the latch. She could have sworn that she had never done so. She was always careful about shutting the door behind her. The problem was, how else could George have entered her house that day unless he had a key?

'But Ned,' Julia put the letter down on the table, 'who poisoned Bosco?'

*

Holly listened in her kitchen as the front door shook as George pulled on the handle. His voice was quiet, alert to the sound of his words carrying to the neighbouring properties. Holly, however, could hear every pleading and cajoling expression and still she did not answer the door. It had been a mistake to contact him in prison. She had been after explanations not a rapprochement and she was now reaping what she had sown. The glass front door had seemed like a good idea when she had chosen it. She would be able to see any visitor and the reassurance of plain view and the panic button around her neck, in theory for medical emergencies, should have been enough. The glass now only served to show George's bulky outline and the black shadow made the acid in her throat burn into her gullet.

She reached for the phone and stared at it for a moment. The numbers were already punched in from before: Julia and the police. Which should she ring? With a sigh, she put the phone back into its cradle and wheeled her chair forward towards the dark figure.

92

92

Two months earlier

Francesca staggered to the back bedroom where the man she had married was lying. She shook three huge gushes over him, the last one missing the messy pulp on the bed and kicking back onto her face. She recoiled at her temporary blindness and backed out of the room, dribbling a precarious trail of petrol.

'Where's the key to Charlie's room?' she shouted. 'I want to unlock it and get him outside now the petrol's down.'

She started towards her child's bedroom when the shadow emerged from the bathroom. Through filmy eyes, she saw George smile at her as he took the petrol can out of her hands and put it on the floor. She looked to the open door of her son's bedroom and opened her mouth to howl.

Charlie dying was never part of the plan. He was to come with them. He *had* to come with them as he was an essential part of the plan they'd concocted to fashion the shape of their new family. A proper unit with her child and the one yet un-born reunited with their father. *This* was the family that she had always wanted. A father, a true father, reunited with his children.

Pacts with the devil, however, are made with very short odds. Before she could struggle, George hooked the first belt he'd worn for nearly forty years around her neck and with one gloved hand looped it around the hook in the rafters, screwed in the day he had brought around the petrol. She felt his solid arms lift her up and wondered how it had come to this. As he kicked away the stool, she saw the light on in the house opposite and remembered that her neighbour had recently had a baby. Her last thought was that, in the end, it had all been for nothing.

The devil's work is never done, the saying goes, but even he can recognise a good ending. George fingered the key to Julia's house he'd taken from his father's drawer, the keyring helpfully labelled with a large 'J'. Then he checked he had the key to the double doors in the kitchen. The one he needed to make his exit. Finally, he picked up the plastic container and carefully continued the trail of petrol to the child's bedroom. Pulling out a box of matches, he lit the hem of Charlie's duvet and dropped the match into the spreading blaze. As he hurried down the stairs, he paused briefly to look behind him at the swinging figure. Sometimes in life, he reflected, things really do come full circle.

Acknowledgements

Thanks to my editor at Faber & Faber, Louisa Joyner, for her enthusiasm and perceptive comments on this book, and also to Mitzi Angel, Sophie Portas, Samantha Matthews, Lauren Nicoll, Daisy Radevsky and Richard Fortey.

Thanks to my agent Kirsty McLachlan at David Godwin Associates for her hard work on my behalf. Alison Baillie is the first reader of my books and gives me a much needed critical commentary. Tony Butler casts his eye over the book further down the process and finds errors that only an excellent crossword solver would spot. Thanks too to Nigel Adams for talking through the logistics of how fire spreads. Thanks as always to Peter Wetlake for the police help. Any inaccuracies in this book are mine.

I wrote a good chunk of *A Patient Fury* while in Skagaströnd, Iceland, writing in a flat generously lent to me by Quentin and Gudrún Bates. Thanks to my other Icelandic friends, Lilja Sigurdardottir, Markus Mar Efraim and Yrsa Sigurdardottir. I'm also grateful for the continuing support of the Iceland Noir regulars: Ewa, Jacqui, Mike, Tana, Suzan and Jim, and Karen Sullivan.

Thanks to my fellow Petrona judges Barry Forshaw, Kat Hall and Karen Meek and to the many bloggers and reviewers who have given their time to support my books, including Leah Moyse, Craig Sisterton, Moira Redmond and Anne Cater. Also thanks to librarians Aniliese Gilbert-Wright, Avril Luke, Lena Smith and Marie Davis for their enthusiasm for my writing, and to Peter and Sylvia Dixon, Neil Smith, Judith Butler, Chris Saccali, Carol Angelopoulou and Jill Yakas for their continued support.

Love and thanks to Dad, my brothers Adrian and Ed to whom this book is dedicated, and to Katie, Luke, Jacob, Amelie and Wendy. And, of course, to Andy Lawrence for the love and support and for introducing me to Sonny and Tubbs.